MARCUS

BY
GRIFFIN GARNETT

PublishAmerica
Baltimore

First printing

All characters in this work are fictitious. Any resemblance to real persons, living or dead, is purely coincidental.

ISBN: 1-4241-1932-4
PUBLISHED BY PUBLISHAMERICA, LLLP
www.publishamerica.com
Baltimore

Printed in the United States of America

Dedication

To my beloved wife, Harriet, my severest critic and staunchest supporter. And, to "Bobbie" Graves, my secretary for more years than I can remember, computer specialist and formatter.

Acknowledgment

For their many valuable contributions I wish to thank my reading committee: Marion E. MacLean, Robert M. Cockrill, Marc E. Bettius, M. Patton Echols, William G. Dukas, H. Paul Mount, Daniel and Virginia Weitzenfeld, Tricia Ann O'Hara, Bartley A. Fugler and Charo Angustia.

PROLOGUE

12 June 1949

When you have read Marcus *you will know why the narrator of the book invited me to write this prologue. And why I was delighted to comply.*

Marcus A. Bosconovich reported for duty on board the U.S.S. Landing Ship Medium (L.S.M.) 460.5, in late June 1944. The vessel, a 203-foot oceangoing, amphibious assault ship was tied up for major repairs at one of the docks of the Norfolk Shipbuilding Company, in Norfolk, Virginia. I was then an ensign and her executive officer, later her commanding officer.

One cloudless morning during those dockside repairs, while I was working with Yeoman Troy Bell, the ship's clerk, arranging studies for seamen who were striking (studying) for an advance in grade, Marcus was escorted to the yeoman's office area by Eric Henekin, Chief Gunner's Mate. I merely glanced at our new crew member, but I could tell he was a well-built blond, cocky, self-assured with mischievous, sparkling, hazel eyes. "Good morning, Sir," he greeted me, and dropped his personnel folder on the yeoman's desk and left. Troy Bell looked at the folder then showed it to me. Marcus A. Bosconovich, twenty-six years old, had been trained at the Bainbridge, Maryland, Naval Training Center Cooking School. His personnel jacket, under "previous occupation," read "Professional Gambler—House Dealer."

"Do you believe that?" asked Bell.

I replied, "Who knows, it takes all kinds to make a crew."

Several days later, while shipyard workers were tearing the guts out of the engine room, I roamed our seagoing mistress checking on various matters. I noticed many of the crew were sullen as hell. Just before 1100 hours, I returned to the ward room and was sitting alone at the table preparing reports when there was a knock on the ward room door. "Enter," I said. Marcus Bosconovich slid gracefully down the ladder handrail. He came over to me, smiled, then said, "Sir, after I came aboard and gave the yeoman my personnel jacket, word got to the crew that the new smartass cook had faked his occupation on his personnel record. I didn't mind the kidding, but when they began inferring I was a liar I decided to call their bluff. I know, as does every other member of the crew, that gambling and cards for money are against Navy regs. But, what are a bunch of guys going to do on this bucket with time on their hands and no women? So I kinda' inveigled five of the supposedly best card players, backed by crew money, into a little poker game. They now believe what my file says. I made a record of every dollar I took from each player." He lowered his voice to almost a whisper, "Here's the take, four thousand three hundred and sixty-nine dollars," he said, handing me a galley cookie jar jammed full with bills.

I was surprised. I had no idea there was so much loose money aboard ship. The total crew complement at that time was fifty-one members not including the five officers.

Marcus continued, "Please show the players this list." He handed me a sheet of paper with an amount beside each name. "And give each named player his share of the lost loot. As house dealer playing against the five novices, I didn't deal a fair hand all night. What's more, not even the best of the players suspected I was crapping all over them."

Now I knew why many of the ship's company were so sullen.

Just before Marcus left the ward room, he added, "Sir, I'll never skin them again, not the crew. I assure you. In addition, I'll keep my eyes peeled to see that games are kept under control." The new cook interested me.

I called in the various players, chewed them out, showed them the list and returned the money. They were dumbfounded. By the end of the day the mood of the losers and their cohorts had changed one hundred eighty degrees. Marcus was held in high esteem by the crew. "He is one hell of a guy," was the universal theme. Following that episode, he was known by one and all on the 460.5 as "Cooky B."

When the ship headed for the southwest Pacific, one of my duties as the executive officer was to read and censor outgoing mail. For almost sixteen months, the correspondence by Cooky B to a girl in New York City named Mariana Lucas fascinated me because each letter to her was accompanied by a poem in his flowing handwriting. The poems, whether in rhyme, blank or free verse, were damned good—and many were romantic—sexy. I wondered from what work he was copying them but never asked.

Marcus turned out to be a good cook, serving acceptable meals. There was a minimum of griping. However, always there was somebody who would bitch. Marcus never lost his composure.

At some time each day, when off-duty, he went through a rigorous exercise routine, including pushups, rope skipping and various muscle stretching activities. From the ship's bridge, I frequently watched him in the late afternoon as he worked out near the fantail. Months later, after we journeyed to the southwest Pacific, I learned he had erected a small punching bag in one of the dry goods storage rooms.

Though Cooky B frequently played pennyante poker with crew members and would delightfully dazzle them with sleight-of-hand card tricks, he never again took advantage of "his guys." Despite the fact that he was accepted as one of the boys, he wasn't, and most of the crew, including the officers, sensed Cooky B was someone different. That difference popped out at the damnedest times, in the most surprising ways. I often wondered if he ever realized how different he was from the rest of the ship's company. I doubt that he did.

One of three "unfit for sea duty" men put aboard the ship at Balboa, Panama, by the base personnel command was Jerry Vacinto, who turned out to be a problem, a dangerous drug addict. Shortly after the 460.5 left Panama and headed seaward, various members of the crew were unable to find their wallets, watches and a number of personal articles previously stowed in their bunkside sea bags. On the third morning out of Balboa, Eugene Foyle, the pharmacist's mate discovered that his secure medicine cabinet, holding pain suppressing drugs, had been broken into. Most of those drugs were gone. He was furious. Mutual distrust was spreading through the crew. Later that same day, Bos'n Mates Hatch and Maynard caught the bowery scum, Vascinto, in the act of stealing. He was high on drugs. They cornered him but were leery of approaching the street-smart, out-of-control addict. He was wielding a rapierlike switchblade while threatening to disembowel both of them. That evening, at a wardroom meeting concerning the incident, Hatch reported to me, "As if by magic, Cooky B arrived on the scene and quietly said, 'Stand aside. I can handle that little burned out bastard.'"

Hatch continued, "I never saw a man move more swiftly. He was like a mongoose snaring a cobra. One quick dart by him, the knife flew from Vascinto's hand and the out-of-control, little prick was screaming in agony as Cooky all but tore the druggy's arm from its socket." The crimes were solved and the lost items recovered. Vacinto was placed in a holding cell, constructed by crew members, until he was put ashore in Hollandia, New Guinea.

In July of 1945, before the war in the Pacific ended, Cooky B was granted a seven-day recreational leave by the Seventh Fleet Command. Though Bell, the yeoman, and I knew Cooky had applied for some kind of recreational break, neither of us knew why. A week after Cooky left on his leave, our ship was swinging at stern anchor in the Leyte Harbor, Philippines. I was standing by the ship's boarding ladder when a small boat pulled alongside. Cooky B scrambled up the ladder and came aboard with just a hint of a swagger. He had a mouse over his right eye, under his left arm he carried a large blue velvet bag. When I inquired about it, he untied the draw strings and pulled out a boxing trophy, with a jabbing male silver figurine on top of a square mahogany base. On one side of the base was a small silver plate inscribed "Marcus A. Bosconovich, Finalist, Middleweight Division, U.S. Navy, 7th Fleet, 27 July 1945." I was amazed. His comment was, "I had a hell of a good time. The guy that beat me had a right cross with the power of a mule kick."

Later that day, I talked with gunner's mate Henekin, and much to my surprise learned he had been a light heavyweight club fighter. He had worked out with Cooky B in the dry goods storage room that had the punching bag. He commented, "Cooky is one classy boxer. He learned to fight while at some school named Cornell and he won the Ivy League middleweight championship, whatever the hell the Ivy League is, won it at the Princeton Center, wherever in hell that is." He spoke of how his boxing shipmate could have won the fleet championship if he had more training and ring time. "Now," said

Henekin, "I am too old to be of much help. I can't take the punchin'."

From Henekin's remarks, I surmised that Cooky B was a graduate of Cornell University. I never inquired of Cooky about his background and he never offered. For whatever reasons, he apparently didn't want his past known.

In November 1945, while the ship was anchored in the outer harbor of Inchon, Korea, I transferred command of the 460.5 to Norman Chesleski, my exec, and headed for home—Arlington, Virginia. Just before I boarded the Milwaukee Road Special in Seattle, Washington bound for Chicago, I purchased three small paperbacks to while away time as the train traveled east. After breakfast on the third day of my trip homeward, I returned to my Pullman seat and opened one of the three little paperback volumes. It was entitled *Poems by Three Pacific War Poets*. On the random page I had turned to was a poem, "The Mistress of Hell." When I finished the first couple of lines, I knew I had read that poem before. For a few seconds I was bewildered then remembered I had read it, enclosed with a letter from Cooky B to Mariana, whoever she is. I thumbed to the table of contents and there, Part 2, *The Poems of Marcus Arent Bosconovich*. I flipped the pages. The poems were preceded by a biographical sketch of the poet—before he entered the service. I read the brief bio with ever-increasing interest. For the first time, I was truly introduced to my former shipmate. The vignette was written by Mariana Finley Lucas.

Marcus had been born in Chicago, Illinois. His father was of Russian descent, his mother was Italian. He had graduated from a Chicago high school with honors and won a scholarship to Cornell University. While there, he became a star member of the varsity boxing team. He graduated from Cornell with a double major; math and English. He remained at the university for an additional year to obtain his masters degree in math. His masters thesis had been a writing entitled, *How to Gamble Right*. After college, he had been employed as a card dealer in a Reno casino. During his dealing days he became interested in poetry and started to seriously study the art.

Just prior to the United States entering World War II, Mariana Lucas, on vacation in Reno, met Marcus while he was working as a dealer at the casino. She was the young owner/publisher of The Purple Canary Press, a small, independent publishing house on 63rd

Street off Lexington Avenue in New York City. She had encouraged the poetic efforts of Bosconovich and had included many of his poems in the volume published before the end of the war.

I gleaned from the vignette that Mariana and Marcus had become more than just friends. However, in early 1944, there appeared to have been a serious disagreement between the couple. Shortly thereafter, Bosconovich entered the U.S. Navy. Mariana professed not to know where in the Pacific the young poet was serving his country. Even after their apparent spat, the couple continued to correspond and he had sent her his poems. She entered several in poetry contests. One of them had won a prestigious award. As evidenced by Mariana's writing, she had experienced a change of heart about Marcus. She was eagerly awaiting his return. Furthermore, she expressed the belief that he could have a successful career ahead of him as a poet and creative writer. I agreed with her, particularly after I had reread his poems. Most flowed with imagery, feeling, color and frequently with a hint of different interpretations. As I have said before, they were damned good.

When I finished reading Marcus' bio and poetry, my thoughts centered on my former shipmate. To me he was an enigma, seemingly content as a lowly ship's cook, yet he had more charisma, concealed physical and mental power and agility, more hidden controlled drive than any man I have ever known. In addition and under his surface appearance, he was endowed with an astounding gentleness, sensitivity, at that time revealed only through his poetry. Just how Marcus could and would put all of these characteristics to work for his benefit in civilian life, piqued my curiosity.

I resolved to keep in contact with him after he left the Navy. That resolution was easier made than kept.

Never in my wildest dreams did I imagine what follows these snippets of Cooky B's service career—the true life story of my most unusual friend, Marcus A. Bosconovich, from the day he left LSM 460.5 through the date of this prologue.

Gregory T. Morgan
Former Senior Lieutenant, U.S. Naval Reserve
and former Commanding Officer, U.S.S. L.S.M. 460.5

CHAPTER 1

The auburn-haired, big-bosomed, cherubic-faced, experienced, self-anointed Queen of the Evening was seated on her throne, one of the blue, plush velvet seats of booth number six. From there, she comfortably sipped her watered-down bourbon highball, and watched the entrance of The Shanghai Lounge and Seafood Grill. The famous mixing bowl was located just off VanNess Avenue in San Francisco. Across from her sat the aging, half-potted "john" she had earlier chosen to share her evening's performance. Cherrie saw several of her *mades*-in-waiting quietly head out the grill door, each with her respective catch of the evening. She wasn't overjoyed with hers. So, she gazed at the entranceway with its loose-swinging brown door, and let her mind wander.

Cherrie's mental wanderings ended with a jolt when the grill's door swung open. Even from where she sat, she felt a gust of the December chill as it ushered in an unusually attractive potential "john" about five-foot-eleven, in seaman's blues. She eyed him with interest: Though it was cold as a witch's tit outside, the sailor's winter pea jacket was open and she could tell he was an attractive solidly built blond. Maybe he was thirty. His white seaman's cap was worn at a jaunty angle. She saw that angle as a symbol of a blithe spirit. She knew she was a good judge of spirits, for she had been Queen of the Evening far longer than most who struggled to attain her status. She observed that the guy moved with the grace and ease of a dark blue panther. His hazel eyes sparkled, and his squarely set jaw matched the angle of his shoulders. He took off his cap and ran a hand through his wavy blond hair. "Even that movement is exciting," she thought. Cherrie watched as the sailor's gaze studied the alcohol guzzlers seated at the bar. To her those eyes were absolutely fascinating, inviting all kinds of happenings. "Why didn't I wait a little longer before making my choice for the evening?" Her musing was interrupted by her evening's catch reaching across the table, taking her free hand, raising it to his lips and slobberly kissing her palm. In a slurred, whiskey voice, he rasped, "Cherrie, the time is now."

"Shit, what a wasted evening this will be," she thought as she arose with her *john*, and headed for the brown door. Out of the corner of her eye, she saw the sailor swing onto one of the low-backed bar stools. As he did, the stool to his immediate right was vacated. "My timing has been stinking since the war ended," Cherrie whispered to herself, then wrapping the fake mink jacket around her fulsome upper body, she cast one wistful glance over her shoulder, and left for her evening's performance.

Marcus A. Bosconovich dropped his pea jacket over the low back of the bar stool, then sat. He was excited, elated to be back on U.S. soil. He had left LSM 460.5 in Honolulu, Hawaii, in early December, 1945. The journey stateside on the troop ship had been most fruitful, five thousand dollars fruitful, all because he knew how to play his game. Today, 27 December 1945, he had arrived in San Francisco. The first thing he did was to hightail it off the ship, go to a branch of the Bank of America, and wire four thousand of that coming-home money to his bank account at the Chicago Bank and Trust Company. Next, he went to a public phone and called his parents in Chicago. They were delighted that he was on home soil, safe and sound. He tried to telephone Mariana at her office in New York, only to learn that she was in Philadelphia, at a convention of small presses. He left a message for her that he expected to be staying at the Huntington Hotel in Frisco until he could get transportation home. Following a visit to his family in Chicago, he would be in New York as soon as possible. His telephone calls completed, he took a taxi and headed for the hotel on Nob Hill. He had stayed at that quiet, upscale hostelry before the war. Marcus convinced the front desk clerk that he had funds, registered, and took his gear to the room. He luxuriated in the hot shower of the modern bathroom. "Almost heaven," he sighed as he stepped from the tub shower. "No more four-hole latrines and slippery steel showers," he thought as he toweled down. He shaved and put on fresh winter blues. He was horny. On the trip to the U.S. his sexual desires had soared, even carried over into his sleep. After a few moments of self-debate, he said to no one, "It's been eighteen months since I've seen Mariana, who knows what might have happened?" then slipped a three pack of condoms into his pea jacket inner pocket. He was ready for action, most any kind of action. On his way out, he dropped by the little room behind the front desk area and deposited his excess cash in a hotel safe deposit box.

A couple of buddies on the troop ship had told him about the Shanghai Lounge and Seafood Grill. They said it was located at the edge of Chinatown, where that area melds into upscale Nob Hill. They told him there was a certain ambiance about the place that was exhilarating, a blending of attitudes and life styles. When Cooky B pushed open the brown swinging door of the grill, he saw the highlighted wall mural of lounging, smirking, nude femme fatales of every color, shape and size imagined by the artist. A diaphanous, serpentine-like film wove across the entire melange, murkying the centers of attraction. The mural was above the mirror behind the bar, and covered the entire wall behind the bar. He sensed what his buddies had told him was true. This was his kind of joint, a place of reality mixed with illusions.

Marcus settled onto the bar stool, looked at the fat, bald-headed bartender across from him, and said, "Joe, I'll take a Scotch on the rocks." To Marcus, all bartenders were "Joe" until they otherwise identified themselves. He was salivating as he watched his first U.S. shore drink in eighteen months being slid across the gleaming mahogany surface to him. As he started to raise the cold glass for his first sip, he could tell someone had sat on the barstool to his right. He closed his eyes. To him this was truly an anticipating time, rejoicing time, poet's time. The drink had barely touched his lips when he felt a light tug on his right arm, and almost dropped the glass, recovered, then looked down into the blackest, most unrevealing eyes he had ever seen. Those smoky lenses, set in the delicate facial features of a petite brunette, hid all feeling behind those eyes and her smooth white marble textured, unlined face. She was smartly poured into a pair of black velvet overalls, whose shoulder straps covered a blazing red blouse. To him, an aura of shock and deep hidden anger seemed to enfold her, almost strangling her. On the surface she appeared so feminine, so demure. Before he could further study the trim young lady, his observations were brought to a screeching halt. "Buy me a drink," she said calmly, without a hint of a smile. "Then, after the drink, let's find a place to fornicate for an agreed price."

Marcus was momentarily nonplussed, sat his drink on the bar and studied his newest acquaintance. He knew a dozen verbs longer or shorter that more clearly defined what she was suggesting, but fornicate?—that's a legal word or a preaching word, he didn't know which way she was using it. What gives? As worldly as he considered himself to be, he had never experienced such an approach.

"Come again?" he asked.

"That's what I want you to do." Her eyes never left his.

"Holy, just-passed Christmas, lady, we haven't even been intro—"

"My name is Samantha, not lady. My friends call me Sam." She stuck out her right hand. He was delightfully confused, amused and met the firm grasp. "Don't ever again mention the word 'Christmas' to me," she said.

Marcus noticed that she shivered as if someone had just walked over her grave. He wanted to ask her why not, but thought better of it, and said, "My name is Marcus. My enemies, as well as my friends, call me Cooky B."

"Why?" asked Sam.

"Because I was a cook in the Navy."

"Oh," said Sam. "I see, or rather, I hear."

Marcus was fascinated by the demeanor of the young lady and with her bizarre opening dialogue. For the moment, he couldn't help but think "Those guys on the troop ship were so right. The ambiance of this joint is something else." He continued to stare at Sam, his Scotch on the rocks, for the moment, almost forgotten. "Let's get back to your greeting. What do you want to drink?" he asked, looking at her with an impish grin.

Sam's look never wavered. "A chocolate milkshake with plenty of vanilla ice cream."

"A what?" Inwardly, Marcus was howling with laughter, but he appeared to be quietly smiling.

"You heard me, a chocolate milkshake with plenty of vanilla ice cream."

"Holy smoke, why that?"

"I'm hungry and thirsty." Sam's eyes never left his face. She was searching. Searching for what? To avoid her staring gaze, he began to scan the occupants at the bar, then throughout the grill.

"You looking for somebody?" she asked.

"Your pimp," he answered and grinned. "I've heard all kinds of come-ons, until now never one like yours. He needs to change your approach."

"Don't you dare denigrate me, Marcus, whatever your last name is, I've got no pimp. I've got nobody but me." Her cheeks flushed with anger.

"I can't believe I'm having this conversation. How old are you?"

"I'm a damned sight older than I appear to be and you think I am. I'm over twenty-one, how much is none of your business."

Marcus was increasingly intrigued: God only knows where this conversation will wind up, but I just have to find out. "Okay, I'll order your milkshake. I guess they know how to make one. Tell me, why do you want to find a place to, as you say, fornicate, after you finish your shake?"

"Because I really need the money."

"How much?"

"Seventy-five bucks."

"Hell, Sam, for seventy-five bucks, I could get a real classy wh—."

"Don't you dare say that word. I'm not one."

"You're not one, but want seventy-five bucks to fornicate. Why do you need that much money, for drugs?"

"No, you degenerate, so I can get my clothes out of hock." Sam's eyes shot hot sparks of frustration at Marcus. He saw and wondered, "Just what in the world could this gal be up to? She is one of the most quirky characters I have ever met. I can't begin to fathom her. Does she really want to screw?"

"Why do you need your clothes tonight?" he asked.

"Because I have a new job starting Monday morning and I can't show up in this outfit. They'd fire me on the spot. These are the togs I wore to my farewell office party yesterday afternoon. When I went back to the boarding house, my landlady, Mrs. Waple, took my house key before I could get to my bedroom and, wouldn't you know, the old she-devil made me leave."

"What kind of new job?"

"An engineer draftsman at the Slogle and Reingold architectural firm in this city. I was released three weeks ago by Consolidated Shipyard. Now that the war is over, they've already started personnel cutbacks, and the first to go have been women in my kind of employment."

"Didn't you save any money on your old job?"

"Yes, but in the last month, it had to be spent."

"How?"

"Marcus, it's none of your business how. And, I don't like the nickname Cooky B."

Marcus ignored the slur. "Don't you have family you can call in a pinch?"

"No. And it's none of your business why not."

Marcus detected that some of Sam's calmness and cockiness was wearing a little thin. She fidgeted with her milkshake, her hands trembling ever so slightly. She began to drink the large, brown frothed brew. He took a long swig of his scotch, sighed, and gazed at the ceiling. Her approach was so odd. He turned to look into her two dark unreflective orbs. "I tell you what, I'll go with you to get your clothes. If their retrieval costs no more than seventy-five bucks, I'll pay for them. But," and he stopped and watched Sam, she really is going after that milkshake. Maybe she is thirsty and hungry. Sam continued drinking, and nodded for Marcus to continue. "But," he said, "Only with the understanding that you will spend the night with me." He watched her intently, wondering what her response would be. "If she's a pro, she is going to say no. This isn't the first time I have been approached in a bar, however it is the most direct and weird one I have ever experienced. Maybe she is in some kind of shock, or maybe she is just a nut, yet a very attractive one."

Sam lowered the large glass, licked her upper lip with her tongue to remove the chocolate mustache. "That's fair enough," she said then heaved a gentle sigh, not at Marcus' suggestion, but at the satisfying feeling from her shake.

Marcus was surprised and a little uncertain: Did he really want to be involved with this odd, disturbing gal? What would Mariana say if he did and she found out about it, whatever it would be? This was starting to evolve like no other chance meeting he had ever encountered. There was, for him, a subtle challenge as to where it would lead; kinda like it wasn't really happening, nevertheless it was. He could sense she was seeking something far more than just her clothes or sex. What was it? Why he wanted to be involved bothered him.

Sam finished, wiped her mouth with the back of her hand, studied him with those unfathomable black eyes, and said, "My friend, Alice-Lee, returns from her vacation tomorrow. I can stay with her until I find a new place to live, also she'll lend me a few bucks until my first payday. In addition to what little cash I have in my purse, I've got twenty dollars stashed away in one of my suit jackets. That'll help. Let's get going before old lady Waple retires for the night. She wouldn't answer the front door for the Lord Almighty himself, after she goes up to bed. Besides, as I've told you, she's got my house key."

Marcus paid the bar bill, helped Samantha with her coat, grabbed his pea jacket, and the twosome headed for the grill's door.

"You'll have to pay for the cab. The distance to the boarding house is too far for me to walk tonight. All this because I couldn't pay in advance for this month's room and board," said Sam.

"How long have you been on the streets?"

"Only since yesterday. I spent last night in Lafayette Park, most of it in the ladies room. The park attendant forgot to lock it before he left."

"You're lucky you weren't raped or mugged."

"I kept out of sight until I came to the grill."

"Didn't you tell Mrs. Waple you had a new job and would pay her soon?"

"Sure did, but she didn't believe me. She said I had given her that line for the last week."

"Had you?"

"Yep, but now I really do have a new job. She says she has rented the room, however I can have my clothes if I pay the seventy-five dollars. I've just got to get them."

Marcus hailed a cab. Once in, Sam leaned over the back of the front seat and gave the cabby her street address. The driver nodded understandingly.

"When we get there, wait for us. We won't be long," said Marcus.

Again, the cab driver nodded.

The cab stopped in front of an aging, red brick, three-story townhouse. Marcus stepped from the auto and looked down the street. To him, the street grade looked like the first down slope on a monster roller coaster that disappeared into a dimly lit abyss. The couple climbed up the front steps to the stoop. He looked at the houses up and down the block, and wondered how they kept from sliding down hill. Sam rang the door bell. No answer. She rang again. No answer. As he rapped on the glass of the front door, he thought, "just what am I getting into?"

"Hold your horses. I'm coming," shrilled a rasping voice.

"That's her," said Sam.

Someone inside unbolted the door and it opened inward until the inside latch chain kept the door from opening further. A sharp-featured, elderly woman peeked through the opening, saw Sam and asked, "What do you want, you no good hussy?"

"My clothes," replied a seething Sam.

"Only if you got seventy-five dollars cash."

"I've got it," said Marcus, and he knew better than to try to negotiate with the old hag. She meant business.

"I'll take the money now," said Mrs. Waple.

"I'll give you the cash when Samantha has her clothes."

"Let me see the color of your folding money, boy. I don't trust Sam or anybody she's with, 'specially no sailor."

Marcus's eyes narrowed slightly as he looked at the thin-lipped landlady: How many odd women can a guy meet in one night? He took out his billfold and extracted the bills. "See," he said, as he waved them before Mrs. Waple's eyes. "When Sam has her clothes, I'll give you the moola."

Mrs. Waple was surprised, pleasantly so. "Okay, but you can't come in. It's late and besides, this is a respectable boarding house for young ladies only."

Marcus grinned and nodded. Sam entered the house, turned to him and said, "I'll just be a little while." She left the front door open.

"You won't be that long," responded Mrs. Waple sharply. "I put your stuff, all of it, in your two suitcases and brought them downstairs. They are here in the front hall closet. I'll get them. You can check them in the hall. You can't take the cases out 'til your boyfriend gives me the money."

Mrs. Waple turned to go to the closet. Sam's eyes were now expressive, spitting fury. If looks could kill, Mrs. Waple would have been dead on the spot. Marcus almost laughed out loud as Sam mouthed silently, "You mean old bitch."

Mrs. Waple returned to the door dragging a big suitcase over the floor. Sam immediately opened it and began to examine the contents. Mrs. Waple soon came back with the other, smaller one. Sam checked that one carefully.

"Where's my makeup kit?" she asked.

"I've kept that for interest," sneered Sam's former landlady.

Marcus sensed a hen-fight brewing. "Come on, Sam, don't argue. You can get plenty of makeup at the hotel gift shop."

"I don't need any help from you."

"Don't be too sure of that," he said, dangling the seventy-five dollars in front of her.

"Oh, okay." Sam calmed down.

Marcus gave Mrs. Waple the money. Sam took the little suitcase as he took the big one. When they reached the cab, the driver put the suitcases in the trunk. Just before Sam entered the cab, she turned to the watching Mrs. Waple and in a clear, ringing voice, sang out into the night, "Goodbye you witch. I hope your sad soul burns in hell." The front door slammed shut.

Marcus guffawed. "Take us to the Huntington Hotel," he told the cab driver.

"That's kinda' upscale for a sailor. Are you going to get a room there?" asked Sam.

"I'm already registered there."

"So," said Sam and she looked at her deliverer. There was a hint of real indecision in her black eyes. But, on the back seat of the cab, Marcus couldn't see the hint.

☐

The cab pulled up to the hotel entrance. A doorman opened the passenger door, then helped with the luggage. Marcus paid and tipped the cabby. He noticed he had only three bucks left to tip the bellhop who escorted them to his room. Marcus opened his room door on the fourth floor, told the bellhop to place the suitcases on the luggage rack at the foot of each bed, gave him the last three bucks, put the Do Not Disturb sign on the outside door knob, closed and bolted the door, then turned up the lamp on the table between the beds.

Sam looked around the room. She was confused and surprised. The room was tastefully appointed, including the lovely Audubon prints on the walls, and had two double beds.

"Why do you have two beds?" was all she could immediately think to ask.

"Because all the single rooms were taken when I arrived. So, they let me have this one for the price of a single."

"How long have you been here?"

"I checked in late this afternoon. Time enough to clean up before I went to the lounge."

"Have you had any supper? Aren't you hungry?"

Marcus was a little surprised. For the first time Sam had shown concern for someone other than herself. Or, was her question a delaying tactic? He wasn't sure. "I had a big lunch today. I don't need supper. Besides, it isn't good for one to take on strenuous exercise immediately after eating a big meal," he said and grinned.

Sam looked at him. The evening wasn't turning out as she had so carefully planned.

"Are you hungry?" he asked.

"No, the shake was all I needed." Sam knew she wasn't hungry. Before she met Marcus, she was in absolute shock, had been for the past week. Now she was scared pea green inside. She hadn't expected the situation to turn out the way it was headed. She thought that she would be escorted to some flea bag hotel. And, she had planned on first getting the money from the jerk, then raising hell, threatening to call the police if her alleged benefactor wouldn't let her go, claiming she was being forced against her will to be with him. She just knew the hot bed dump wouldn't want trouble, neither would the guy she had inveigled to pick her up. Yet, here she is in a lovely hotel room on Nob Hill with a cocksure attractive blond who had been every inch a gentleman, at least until now. What could she do? She couldn't scream or threaten him, her luggage was in the room and she had only fifteen dollars in her purse. Though she had done her level best not to let him know, and despite the turmoil within her, she glanced slyly at him: Marcus really is attractive in a kinda' open, spellbinding way. His conversation and the tone of his voice are calm, courteous, even if those flashing hazel eyes are devilish and beguiling. "Cooky B," that isn't the right name for him, Marcus is better, but Marcus what? Certainly not Marcus Aurelius. This guy is no stoic. St. Marcus? No, that didn't fit either. There isn't much saintliness in his attitude. But there is an air of blithe romanticism that is a part of him. So he was to her, Marcus, no last name, until she found out. Somehow she imagined it would fit.

Marcus knew he was now committed, but to what? He was increasingly curious as to the outcome. This gal is no streetwalker. He could sense she was desperate for help, but what kind? For some strange reason, he had to find out.

"You better get the clothes you're going to wear on Monday and hang them in the closet or they will be so wrinkled your new boss will wonder if you slept in them all weekend," he said.

Sam brushed the hair from her forehead with one hand and glanced at him. "He is really much nicer than I expected," she mused.

"You're right. I hadn't given that a thought."

Sam opened one of her suitcases and began to fumble for the business suit she would wear on the first day of her new job. As she took the garments out of the suitcase and started to place them on a hanger, she caught a glimpse of Marcus out of the corner of her eye. Bang! The hanger and suit hit the floor. She was all but paralyzed. He had stripped to his boxer shorts, heading for the bathroom. Never before had she been in a hotel room with any man stripped to his shorts. She pretended not to have seen him, reached down and nervously picked up the hanger and suit. Her hands trembled, little beads of perspiration broke out on her upper lip. "Oh, my God, what have I gotten into? I never intended to be in such a pickle," she whispered. Her fingers trembled as she straightened her jacket on the hanger and she thought, "Who knows what he might do. Why did I go to the grill?" She had never been to such a joint before in her life. She only knew of the lounge from snide references she overheard, made by guys at the office. And Marcus, the stranger she watched as she stood in a corner of the grill, Marcus, whom she chose to sit by at the bar, figuring he was the easiest of the seated strangers she could dupe with her plan—for her a desperate plan, set in motion by the recent events she could not control, and had, until recently, never imagined would happen. Marcus was nothing like she first thought he would be. He was no uncouth seagoing rowdy. He had been honest, open from the very beginning. He had parried her planned approach from the start. He questioned her in ways she hadn't envisioned. For all his apparent devilishness, he listened to her problem, offered a solution she hadn't expected, stuck by his agreement with resolute calmness, and handled Mrs. Waple far better than she could have. "What can I do but try to meet my share of the bargain." she thought. Now, on top of her other problems, Sam felt dirty, worried for more reasons than one about the whole episode, past and what was to come. She was chagrined at herself, for him and yet she was so desperate and so lost. She decided when the time came, she would, at least, tell him what he should immediately know and then she would take her chances with whatever might happen. She now was upset at her initial approach to him. "This was my first attempt and in retrospect I must have sounded like an idiot. Maybe I am one," she thought.

Marcus came out of the bathroom, went to the wall-mirrored double sink adjoining the bathroom, brushed his teeth, then smiled at Sam. "Your turn," he said with natural calmness, as if they were a married couple. She took a set of blue PJs from her bag, went into the bathroom and closed the door. Never had she undressed in front of any man—not even in view of her father when she was young: Never in front of that bastard. As she changed into her PJs, she shivered slightly and realized it wasn't just from fright. "There is something intriguing about Marcus, just what I don't know, but he is exciting as well as disturbing." When she finished changing, she brought the clothes she had been wearing to the closet, hanged them, went to the sink, brushed her teeth and turned to the bed area. Marcus had pulled the bed covers above his waist. His naked, muscular, upper torso was propped up by a couple of pillows. He was watching her with a slightly puzzled expression. When she faced him, he said, "Sam, you truly are an attractive young lady."

Sam gazed at him, was completely befuddled. "So are you," she said.

"I'm no young lady," said Marcus, his hazel eyes danced with merriment and anticipation.

"Oh, you know what I mean," Sam said with nervous apprehension as she approached the bed.

"Do I?"

"You better had," was all Sam could think to say as she crawled in beside him.

Marcus switched off the bedside lamp. There was a small beam of light that shown through the partially open bathroom door. He rose on one elbow, reached over, unbuttoned her pajama jacket, put a hand on one of her breasts and pressed gently. Sam gasped audibly. Then he leaned over and kissed her on her lips. Sam was frightened, yet sexually aroused, and she was still in shock. She knew her reaction to the kiss was not what Marcus had anticipated. He sensed her genuine uneasiness and drew back. "Sam, are you sure you want to do this?" he asked.

Her black eyes beseeched understanding, were almost screaming for help. "Oh, my God, how much should I tell him?" Her true feelings were being exposed. "Marcus," she said and her lips quivered, "Please be gentle. Though I'm over twenty-one, I've never done this before, I'm a virgin. You've lived up to your bargain and I'll live up to mine."

"Oh, man," muttered a confused and perturbed Marcus.

Sam's words continued to pour out as if she never heard the utterance. "All that talk at the bar was from franticsville, even if I didn't show it. I have been, and I guess I still am, almost out of my mind with what has happened in the last three weeks, particularly the past week. Things I still can't talk about. In the bar, I couldn't show how I really felt. I never intended the evening would turn out like this." She stopped, tears of release streamed down her cheeks, but beneath the release, she was excited.

Marcus now believed she was telling the truth, and the tears were real. He wondered more than ever what in the world was Sam hiding? "She's only told me the smallest part of her terror. Except for that first odd approach at the bar, she is so like my kid sister, Irma, sensitive, decent, but hides her feelings to the point of being panic stricken. Though I have been at sea for eighteen months, and am horny as hell, no way am I going to be so selfish, even on my first night ashore, that I am the cause of an unwanted lost virginity by a disturbed, emotionally upset, but attractive young lady. Besides, there is something about her, beyond the apparent shock and deep simmering anger, almost a screaming need for trust -trust about what? I truly am attracted to her in a way I cannot describe. If things work out, this might result in a real relationship, a different kind of relationship from any I initially anticipated."

"Thanks for being honest with me, Sam. Just what recent torment you have been through, I don't know. Someday maybe you'll tell me. I promise not to dig. And someday maybe you'll feel differently toward me and I will toward you. You just relax, get some sleep. You've offered to carry out your end of the bargain. That's what counts. I would rather have you as a friend than as a regretful woman—who may hate my guts forever for not listening," Marcus said, and felt relieved.

Sam looked at Marcus, her troubled eyes revealed to him an unexpected absolute trust he had never anticipated. "Please put your arms around me gently, hold me and let me cry. I need to cry so badly," she responded.

Marcus, for some strange reason, felt more sympathy for Sam than he had ever felt for any woman, even Mariana, as he held Sam in his arms. She wept unashamedly, and was wracked by violent spasms of sobbing. Her sobs gradually diminished as she finally relaxed, exhausted. Even though her whole body was one big pain, she drifted into a much needed deep merciful sleep.

Marcus, now more bewildered than ever, straightened the pillows, laid her gently on the bed, pulled the covers over her, and kissed her on her forehead. He went to the bathroom, peeled off the unused sheath, dropped it into the toilet, and flushed the tank. An impish smile lit his face as he looked down. "My friend, my sensitive, very good friend, I know this has been a vexing night for you. Just be patient. I promise there will be more exciting, more climactic times in the near future. Even if I have to lead you by hand." He tucked his friend into his boxer shorts and returned to the empty bed. He sat on the far side, looked at, then spoke softly to sleeping Sam, "My God, how trusting you are, and what a lovely feminine armful to hold.

How in the hell did I, a horny bastard, ever get mixed up in such a screwy nonscrewing deal on my first night ashore? I never imagined I could act so much the gentleman." He continued looking at Sam and he sensed a different kind of feeling for her than he had ever experienced in his romantic life. He just couldn't define it. When push came to shove, she had, without the slightest hesitation, put absolute trust in him as if his being her knight-in-shining-armor was the only way he could act. She had treated him as if he was her dearest friend, not an aroused stranger who, during the last eighteen months, had fantasized sexual relations almost beyond imagination. Did she have any idea the control it took for him not to let his animal instincts take over, particularly after he had held her alluring body in his arms? And she had a most delicate, natural body aroma.

Marcus continued gazing at Sam. He was deeply disturbed, perplexed. "Never in my life have I met anyone like you. Are your emotions an act? Are you as sincere as you seem to be? If so, why? When and if you awaken during the night, will you leave while I sleep, now that you have your clothes?" The words were barely audible.

Marcus knew he was a sound sleeper, had been one all his life, not by training, but by genes he surmised. One part of him argued that Sam's demeanor revealed an almost naively honest, trusting, inexperienced, and a very perturbed young woman. But the other part reminded him that some of the best crooked card players he had ever met first appeared to be honest, convincingly so. Time would tell. "What the hell, I have only known her for about three hours. If I am wrong, so be it, but I hope I'm not. There is an essence of Sam that appears so genuine, so appealing. I'll wait to see what tomorrow brings," he said softly, then dropped onto the empty bed.

Marcus reached into his seabag by the side of his bed, pulled out a notebook with a pen stuck through the ring binders. He turned on a lamp on the far side of his bed away from the sleeping Sam. For a half hour he made notes, brief and seemingly staccato notes, of various events, among them the events of the evening, his emotions, sensations, and ended, "With so much unknown." He reflected that sometime in the future when he was quieter within and there was solitude, he would from those notes place the events, the emotions, the sensations he had experienced, in a written form he needed to share with someone, anyone who had stumbled through an experience similar to his of this evening.

After replacing his notebook in his seabag, he turned out the light, and again glanced over at Sam. "Whether you are for real or but a fantasy, I'll know by tomorrow morning. For now, good night, you odd goddess of spirituality, at least for me. I must be growing up or old or something," he whispered, then stretched out in the bed and, after his libido and curiosity had subsided, he slept, but restlessly.

CHAPTER 2

Marcus awakened slowly. He squinted at the sunlight straining through the filmy white window curtains, then his eyes followed those dancing beams of light across the room. They were centered on the comely figure of Sam. "I'll be damned," he mused, "she is for real. She's still here. Why?" Sam, completely unaware that Marcus had awakened, was standing, a la naturale, facing the mirrored double sink and toweling after her shower. Now he was wide awake, sat up quietly and was fascinated as he watched. She, with a part of a large bath towel draped around her neck, over her right shoulder and breast, was busy with the remainder of the towel in her left hand, wiping her face and drying her hair. He gazed unabashed and uttered softly, "My God, she is lovelier in the daylight than in the nightlight. She is an exciting, beautifully proportioned young woman. I held her in my arms last night. Except for her delicate aroma, I hadn't truly concentrated on her body, though I knew it was alluring. Last night I was genuinely worried and bothered by the emotional pain she apparently was suffering, maybe physical pain too. How could I not have succumbed to my desires?" Marcus was sexually aroused by what he was seeing. He continued his troubled stare as she looked in the mirror at her reflected image, and heard her calmly say, "Samantha, most of your camouflage is still in place. How long will it hide the enemy within?"

"What the hell does that mean?" murmured Marcus.

"Aphrodite without her nightie, god almighty, what a sighty. Good morning. That's no camouflage, but a beautiful body, almost the loveliest I've ever seen," he said spritely.

Sam, for a second, stood as if frozen. Then she cast a glance over her shoulder at a grinning Marcus. "Oh, I didn't know you were awake. I'm so sorry," she replied, then smiled in return, grabbed her underthings off of the sink, stepped into the bathroom, and shut the door.

Sam's act of putting on her bra and panties was almost movie slow-motion. She was filled with emotion, her mind whirled. "Yesterday evening I thought I was looking for an easy seventy-five bucks to get my clothes from Mrs. Waple. That's not what I really have been trying to find. The years of sublimation of my instincts and desires, have festered within me. The yearning to be understood, accepted and loved for what I am, the giving and receiving of affection, before it is too late for me, that's what I have truly been searching for. And, by dumb luck, I have stumbled onto a guy, a more attractive guy than I ever imagined I would meet, one who more nearly fills my concept of agape Christian love, even as preached by my ubiquitous father. Despite Marcus' apparent blithe surface manner, he has shown himself to be the one person I never thought I would encounter, before it is too late for me. He doesn't seem to recognize his attributes, just accepts them as a part of his being. I only hope that part of his being doesn't lead to his ultimate downfall. With the understanding, compassion, and gentleness he exhibited last night, I care for him, even now, more than I ever have or will care for any other man. He is no stranger to me. He is my life-long dream come true. How do I tell him? How do I prove it to him?" She finished slipping on her bra.

The image of Sam was still there for Marcus. "She is like a delicate white marble nymph sculpture, glistening in the morning sun as the dew leaves her figure. Even with that aura of shock and simmering, hidden anger, she is so desirable. What the shit should I do?" he murmured. Before he could ponder further on a solution of his desires, the bathroom door opened and Sam, in a pink bra and panties, came into the bedroom. Much to his amazement, she calmly walked over to his bed and sat, turning toward him. He inhaled her delicate aroma. That scent and the sight of her were raising, among other things, his blood pressure.

"Marcus Arent Bosconovich," she said calmly, her eyes caressing his upper body. "I awakened during the night and saw you sleeping so peacefully. I saw your wallet on the table by your bed. I just had to know your identity, your full name. So I looked into that calf-hide pouch of revelations. Do you realize you haven't a cent of money in there? You spent it all on me last night. And you, a graduate of Cornell University, in the Navy as a cook? I saw your alumni card."

Marcus replied, "I've got plenty of funds in one of the hotel lock boxes. I didn't want to take a chance on getting rolled last night and losing a bundle. Yes, I am a graduate of Cornell and was a Navy cook. What's wrong with that?"

"I don't know. It just doesn't fit. That you have other funds is a relief to me, particularly after my actions of yesterday evening. While you were sleeping, I wasn't looking for money, I was looking for identification. Something to tell me who you really are. The wallet didn't help much, except for your full name. I like it. Then, as I again looked at you, I realized you had truly identified yourself to me during the past evening and night in a way I had never before experienced from any person, no one."

Marcus was puzzled as he gazed at her beguiling figure and pondered. "Just what in the hell is she driving at?"

"I'm not quite the blithering idiot I seemed to be yesterday evening and last night." She reached down with one hand and pushed his wavy hair from his forehead. "I am also a college graduate, but from a small Christian fundamentalist college in Iowa. My dad is a professor and chaplain there."

Marcus was becoming increasingly confused.

"I can tell you've known other women. I don't fault you for that. I envy them."

Marcus could stand the torture no longer. "What in the hell are you trying to say?" he asked sharply. He observed that she was now more relaxed than he had ever seen her, more desirable. He could barely restrain himself.

To his surprise, she took one of his hands in both of hers and spoke softly, "You are a far stronger man than I am a woman. Last night, when I asked you to be gentle and told you I was a virgin, I told the truth, but not all."

"For Christ's sake, get to the point," responded Marcus. Now it wasn't her lovely body he was focusing on, but those black eyes that no longer were dull, but gleaming like black diamonds.

"If we had engaged in sexual intercourse last night, I don't know what might have happened. And, suddenly, I wanted you more than you will ever know. The results could have been ghastly, grim for both of us."

"Why? What in the world are you talking about?"

"I didn't tell you then because, God forbid, I was selfish, I wanted you to be the first man in my life, damn the consequences. I should have told you then. I have to tell you now. You remember yesterday evening when I said I hated the word 'Christmas?' I do, I loathe it. The sound of that word makes me sick, violently ill."

"Such a lovely season, why?"

"My loathing has nothing to do with the season. The sound of that word makes me shiver. I have Christmas disease." She dropped his hand.

"What in the world is Christmas disease, some kind of emotional reaction against the holiday?"

"My God, I wish that was the true definition. The disease is a rather odd form of hemophilia. I am a rarity, a female bleeder, a serious bleeder. In addition, I am a carrier of that genetic flaw. Odds are any male child I might bear will inherit the illness and there is a chance, an outside chance, like me, that a female child I bear could inherit the illness also. That's why I am a virgin. I'm no kinky religious nut like the rest of my fundamentalist family. Sure, I'm innocent, but not an ignoramus. I know the human body, have studied physiology at college, and read much more on sex than *Lady Chatterley's Lover*. I have suffered through an almost isolated childhood, teenage years, to womanhood. Now, there are times, normal times for most women, when I literally flirt with death." She stopped to draw breath and smiled with tenderness at Marcus. He was really perturbed. She continued, "Yesterday evening was my first, and I can assure you, my last attempt at so called solicitation.

doorman opened the front door and helped with the luggage, then hailed a cab. Sam turned to Marcus. "I've got the cab fare, and I still have the twenty dollars you wouldn't let me spend." Just before she entered the cab, she tiptoed, gently kissed him on his lips, and said, "Goodbye, my maker of dreams that came true."

Sam shut the door and the cab drove off into the deepening night fog. Marcus watched until the red tail lights disappeared into the dark mist. Then, he looked across the street at the silent, mist-shrouded, towering cathedral. He felt as if he had just returned from a strange fantastic journey with so much to write about. He looked down, saw the street gutter in front of the hotel and he knew that most of what had recently happened was real, not a dream, not fantasy. Just before he turned to reenter the hotel, he said softly into the foggy night, "Marcus Bosconovich, you do meet the most unusual, memorable people." Entering the doors, he experienced a strange comforting sensation, accompanied by a feeling of guilt and unaccounted for sadness. "Besides being one lucky bastard, who am I? What am I?" he asked aloud, as he walked through the empty lobby. There was no answer.

CHAPTER 3

Like some wounded prehistoric yellow-and-black-spotted carnivore, the Checker Cab moved cautiously, panting through the swirling fog, one night eye beaming brighter than the other. It struggled onto the lighted driveway and up to the porticoed entrance of the Sealcrest Apartments then stopped. Sam got out, paid and tipped the furrowed-faced, elderly, Asiatic driver. He went to the cab trunk, took out her suitcases, placed them by the heavy, glass-paneled, double entrance doors, turned to her and asked, "Missy, do you live here? Can you get in?"

"No," answered Sam, "I'm going to call my friend on the intercom. She'll press the button in her apartment to unlock the front door."

"I'll wait until you're inside. It's late for you to be standing out here alone on a night like this."

"Thanks so much," responded Sam, as she walked to the panel on the covered alcove wall, and saw the nameplate of her friend, Alice-Lee Taliaferro. "How in the world did they ever get the pronunciation "Toliver" from that name?" she wondered, then stabbed at the code numbers, the intercom button and waited. Shortly, a sleepy, southern drawl, female voice inquired through the intercom, "Who in the world wants to see me at this time of night?"

"I do—me—Sam."

"My God, Samantha, what are you doing out at this hour? Are you alone?"

"I surely am. I need a place to spend the night. Can I sleep on your living room sofa? Would you mind?"

"Wait a sec. I'll let you in. Then I'll come on down and meet you." The front door lock buzzed. Sam opened one of the heavy doors, shoved her luggage into the swank lobby area, turned toward the cabbie, who was watching from his driver's seat. She waved a thank you. He nodded and drove away. The apartment entrance door closed swiftly behind her and locked with a solid "thunk."

Sam slid her luggage across the marble-floored foyer to the elevator area. As she was straightening up after moving her big suitcase, one of the two elevators stopped at the lobby floor. The elevator doors opened slowly like stage draw curtains in a big theater. There, on the diminutive stage with lights beaming down on her from the four-ceiling corners of the elevator, stood society reporter, Alice-Lee Taliaferro, like a lone center stage performer, garish in appearance; tall, slim, in a dark green dressing gown, sloppy gray bootie slippers, her blonde hair in curlers, the curlers covered by a yellow curler net and her sharp-featured, patrician face smeared with white night cream. When she stepped from the elevator, Sam smiled and said, "Gee, you look awful."

"You're not the freshest-looking, black-eyed Susan I've ever seen either," replied Alice-Lee, and her blue-gray eyes beamed affection for her diminutive friend. "What brings you here at this ungodly hour? Have you been on some wild pawty and gotten the heave-ho?"

"Not exactly," said Sam. "I knew you were supposed to be returning today from your trip home for the holidays. I just took a chance. I had to. Is Joe still with you?"

"No, the cheap, dull leech left before Christmas so he wouldn't have to give me a present. I told the bum if he returned I would call the police."

Sam looked aghast at her friend, opened her mouth to say something, something sympathetic. Alice-Lee laughed at Sam's apparent shock. "I'm kidding," said Alice-Lee, "He left yesterday on a three-month assignment for *The Chronicle*. He's gone to Europe to cover the aftermath of the war. I hated to see him go but before he left he did all right by me." Alice-Lee raised her left hand. A lovely diamond ring in a Tiffany setting glistened from her third finger. Sam squealed with delight, hugged her friend and much of the night cream from Alice-Lee's right cheek was in Sam's hair.

Alice-Lee beckoned to the open elevator. As they entered the lift, she said, "You look like you are really bushed. What's the matter?"

"Well, you know I lost my job about three weeks ago. Mrs. Waple, my landlady, threw me out three days ago because I couldn't pay my monthly rent in advance. Since then, I've had the most unusual experience of my life. Now, I am so tired, dead tired."

"I can tell," responded her perturbed friend. The elevator stopped on the fifth floor, the top floor. Alice-Lee helped Sam with her gear. "What in the world have you got in this suitcase? Rocks?" she asked, as she struggled to take the big case down the plush carpeted hall to her apartment.

Sam was carrying the lighter one. "No, just most of my clothes," she replied.

Alice-Lee opened the door to her large designer-decorated, two-bedroom, two-bath apartment. The balcony looked out over the bay. Sam walked in. "My, it's good to see this place again," she said, then looked across the room at the glowing embers in the fireplace, walked over to a new fireplace-facing sofa, and melted onto its comfortable seating cushions. "Are the Jeffries still renting the second bedroom?"

"No, he was transferred to Butte, Montana, just before Christmas so they've gone for good. I'm alone. You can sleep in what was their room. You'll have to make up the bed. I didn't get a chance to do so before I left for the holidays. Since my return, I've been too busy until tonight. When I returned from meeting the deadline for my column, I said to heck with it. I didn't know you would be here."

Sam leaned against the soft backrest pillows. "Gee, this is a lovely, comfy, new sofa. I don't think I can move from here to get to the bedroom," she said.

"Well, sooner or later you will have to. I just bought that baby for six hundred bucks. You can sit, but not sleep on it. I'll help you make the bed in the spare bedroom when the time comes. God knows what might happen to the sofa if you've finally been out on your first screw. Have you? You look like you have."

46

Sam cast a stern look at Alice-Lee, hunched her shoulders, stuck her hands into her topcoat pockets and was silent. Alice-Lee watched. She saw Sam stiffen, quickly turn her face to the right and down, as if someone had slapped her hard. Sam's eyes widened in bewilderment as she pulled from a topcoat pocket the three hundred dollars in fifty dollar bills Marcus had placed in there during their last embrace. She gazed at them in amazement, then counted the money. The bills fluttered from her hand to the sofa.

"You really have been on some pawty," smirked Alice-Lee, and the Tidewater, Virginia, accent broad a of party seemed to have been exhaled as if she had excess gas on her stomach.

Sam sat stunned, tears began to flow and she was nearly hysterical. Alice-Lee recognized that her normally cool, aloof, younger friend was suffering from something or some things far more devastating than her chronic Christmas disease. Alice-Lee got out of her chair, came over to the sofa, sat and put her arms around Sam. "Honey, calm down," she said. What in the hell did he do to you?"

Sam bawled.

"The bastard," said Alice-Lee, "We'll call the police if you say so."

"How did you know it was a man?"

"At this time of night what else could it be?"

Sam turned her tear-streaked face to her friend. "It's not what he did to me. It's what I did to myself and what I did to him."

"You didn't kill him for a measly three hundred. Did you?" Alice-Lee released her hold on Sam and looked at her with mock seriousness. Those gray-blue eyes of hers were dancing in anticipation of Sam's answer.

"No, no, no. Nothing like that," and Sam wiped her tearful eyes with a sleeve of her coat.

Alice-Lee was pleasantly puzzled. "What are you trying to tell me?"

Sam smiled that lovely whimsical smile of hers and replied, "I'll never live through another experience like the one I've just had. I don't want to. Nothing could surpass it. Right now, I'm so tired. I can't talk about what happened. I really can't talk any more about anything. I'm exhausted, almost numb." She picked up the bills from the sofa. Her tears flowed again. She pressed the fistful of dollars to her breast, then put them in her purse.

Alice-Lee saw that Sam was almost faint with fatigue. "Come on, Hon. I'll help you make the bed. Then you crawl in. We'll talk tomorrow. I'll be off work for the next few days. Pat Kranfield is ghosting my column through New Year's Eve. Sleep as late as you want to."

When the twosome had finished changing the sheets and making up the king-sized bed, Sam stripped down to her bra and panties. Too tired to change to her PJs, she just dropped onto the bed. Alice-Lee pulled up the covers. Sam was out like a light.

Alice-Lee turned off the bedside table lamp. Aided by the glow from the hall light, she looked at her friend and wondered, "Just what kind of an episode have you experienced that caused you to be so emotional, so absolutely wiped out?" She knew of Sam's chronic problem. Her friend handled it well, concealed it with such dignity, almost stoicism. Yes, she knew Sam had lost her job, but she also knew Sam had found a new one, a damned good one, just before she, Alice-Lee left for her holiday. And she knew that Sam wasn't destitute, at least not when she, Alice-Lee, went home. Something wild must have happened. She could tell Sam had changed in such subtle, but definite ways, at the moment undecipherable. She would try and find out tomorrow after her friend had a good night's sleep.

As Alice-Lee in her slippers padded to her bedroom, she remembered her first meeting with Samantha. Alice-Lee had been invited by Theodore Ridgeway, the CEO of Consolidated Shipyard to witness the launching at the company's Frisco yard, of a new naval troop carrier, an APA. It was the largest ship Consolidated had ever built. After the launching, she had two invitations, one for her, the other for Joe, her fiancee and co-employee, to attend the party at "The Ridge," the Ridgeway palatial home on swank Nob Hill overlooking San Francisco Bay. There she would mingle with the Frisco financial, military, political and social leaders and their wives. She knew they expected to be mentioned in her column the day following the event.

When Alice-Lee took her assigned seat in the temporary bleachers constructed for the launching, she noticed that on her right sat a petite brunette with sparkling black eyes. Those eyes were intently focused, almost in a spellbound gaze, at the towering already Navy gray ship awaiting christening.

The 1943 fall day was brisk. The diminutive bundle of energy sitting next to her had on an attractive parka with the hood thrown back. The christening party ascended the steps to the raised dais at the bow of the ship. It was quite apparent that a blonde, well-known movie actress was to do the honors by breaking a bottle of bubbly on the bow as the ship was christened. When, at the appropriate time, the actress arose to perform her task, the brunette sitting beside Alice-Lee turned to Alice-Lee and with her bright eyes twinkling, asked, "Isn't she beautiful?"

Alice-Lee remembered looking at the attractive bundle of energy to her right and replying, "She's quite an attractive young lady but her hairdo is atrocious."

The girl giggled and replied, "Not the babe, the ship. I helped make her possible.

Alice-Lee had laughed, responded, "Who are you, Rosie the Riveter?"

The brunette with the sparkling eyes smiled, then replied, "No, I'm Dottie the Designer." She stuck out her hand. "My name is Samantha Kingsbury, but you can call me Sam. I'm an engineering draftsman with Consolidated. I helped to design certain small sections of the APA, my first ship."

Alice-Lee was delighted with her new acquaintance. "My name is Alice-Lee T-a-l-i-a-f-e-r-o, only its pronounced Toliver. I am a reporter for the *San Francisco Chronicle*," she had said.

Sam's immediate response was, "Neat, I've never met a reporter before. What do you report, ships?"

"No," replied Alice-Lee, "society."

Sam looked around, smiled and said, "What a society! Most all I see are ship fitters, welders, yardmen and dock handlers from Consolidated."

Alice-Lee was amused, enthralled by her new acquaintance. "You're right," she had responded, "I had to come here and witness the event so I could talk sensibly about it when I go to the after-launching cocktail party at The Ridge. All the local power players and their wives will be there. I had to have a little advantage."

Sam's eyes were bouncing between the ship and her lanky new friend. Suddenly, she pointed toward the ship and said, "Look, quick, they've knocked out the two keys."

Alice-Lee looked at the ship, saw two large blocking timbers roll back from the front skids. The ship started to slide in its cradle toward the water.

"What a thrilling sight," Samantha exclaimed. Alice-Lee was pleased her new acquaintance had directed her attention to a truly interesting happening she had never witnessed before. She too was awed as the enormous troop carrier slid into the waters of the bay. Immediately, two tugs could be seen hurrying toward the partially completed vessel. Soon all was secure and the launching a success.

Alice-Lee remembered looking at Sam, was silent for a few seconds, then asked, "Sam, how would you like to go with me to the after-launching cocktail and buffet at The Ridge? Joe, my boyfriend can't make it."

"Oh, I would love to see The Ridge. I've driven by it many times but I'm afraid I would be a liability for you."

"Why?" asked Alice-Lee as she carefully appraised Sam. "You're dressed just right for the affair. You are my cousin from…where?"

"Iowa," Sam had spritely replied, then added, "I have one little problem you should be aware of. There's a reason I can't drink liquor."

"That's okay, that's more for me. There will be plenty of other kinds of bellywash—tea, cokes, ginger ale, carbonated water and whatever. You can eat, can't you?" queried Alice-Lee.

"You better believe I can and I'm starving right now."

"Lets go," Alice-Lee urged.

As she entered her bedroom, she said softly, "The loveliest little friend I've ever known in my life."

□

"Good morning," said Sam as she, in nothing more than she had slept in, walked into the kitchen where Alice-Lee, fully dressed, was sipping a mug of steaming black coffee.

"And, the top of the morning to you, Miss Bright Eyes. You look a heck of a sight better. But, you'll freeze your butt off with no more clothes on than you're wearing."

"It's toasty in here," responded Sam. "I feel better. I really needed the rest."

"Sam, maybe it's none of my business, but you know me. I'm a snoop. That's why I am where I am today on *The Chronicle*. What went on while I was away?"

Sam looked at her friend, "just how much should I tell her?" Sam then went to the stove, poured a cup of black coffee, came back and sat across the table from Alice-Lee. She then told her lanky friend the essence of what had occurred during the last three days, but omitting most of the intimacy, the name of her new best friend, where it had happened and not mentioning the results of the physical tests she had undergone just prior to her being evicted. When she finished, Alice-Lee said, "I wish I could have found a guy like that. I would have never let him escape. He sounds even better than my Joe, except Joe has such lovely uncontrollable hormones. Bless him. And you say the guy you were with was a cook in the Navy?"

"That's what he said," replied Sam. "Just before we parted there was an inkling by him that the cooking deal may have been a cover for his real background. I did find out he was a graduate from Cornell University."

"What's his name?" asked Alice-Lee.

"What difference does it make? I'll never see him again. He is from Chicago."

The snoop in Alice-Lee was sniffing harder. "So, what's his name if you'll never see him again? No reason for not telling me."

"His name is…is Marcus A. Bosconovich but he calls himself Cooky B," said Sam.

"Marcus A. Bosconovich—Bosconovich," repeated Alice-Lee as if she was trying to identify a name she had heard of or read before.

"Don't tell me you know him. I think he is younger than you are," said Sam.

"So is half the world, and I'm only thirty-one," responded Alice-Lee. "Oddly enough, I know I've heard or read that name before. When or why, I can't recollect."

While Sam had been telling her story, Alice-Lee observed her closely. Gone was the stoicness, the hidden reserve. Sam seemed much more comfortable with herself even her emotions showed quite normally. Something had been released within her. She really is a more attractive gal than ever before. However, Alice-Lee sensed an air of anger, a resignation about her friend, resignation about what, she mused.

"Sam is that all of your story about what happened while I was away?"

Sam looked at her discerning friend. "All that's important," responded Sam. Then she diverted Alice-Lee by asking, "You say Joe will be gone for three months?"

"That's right."

"When he comes back, are you going to marry him?"

"If I have to hogtie him and haul him feet first to the altar," responded Alice-Lee and she grinned.

Sam giggled at the thought, because she could actually see Alice-Lee carrying out her threat. "Can we make some definite arrangements for me to live here for the next three months at least until Joe returns?" asked Sam.

"I can't think of a better deal for me," replied Alice-Lee. The two women sat at the table and worked out an agreed financial arrangement. When they finished, Alice-Lee said, "Even if you're a month late in your rent, I won't kick you out. But, if you're two months late, I'll start bitching."

"You'll never have to," Sam paused, then continued, "I'm getting a little chilly. I better get dressed and unpack my clothes. When I finish, let's go out for brunch. I can afford so much more than I ever expected to." Inwardly she ached to call and thank Marcus. But, she just couldn't because she would melt when he asked where are you?

"Good idea," responded Alice-Lee.

Sam left the kitchen, her heart singing, as much as it could sing under the circumstances, went to her room, put on the garments she had worn the day before, then started to unpack. Under her undies she discovered the paperback, *Poems by Three Pacific War Poets*. Where in the world did that come from? She never had bought such a book. She opened it, turned to the table of contents, read them and then, feeling exhilarated, faint, she sat hard on the bed. She turned to Part 2: *The Poems of Marcus Arent Bosconovich*, read the vignette of the only man in her life, and started to read the first poem. Suddenly, her feelings surged to the surface, all but engulfed her, "My God, I was right, for one of the few times in my life, it wasn't a dream or fantasy. I have met a most unusual guy—sensitive, decent, caring, but oh so creative. He has already given me true emotional release from the secret yearnings I have concealed for so long. I sorely miss him, his body, his dancing hazel eyes, his upbeat approach to life, his gentle passion and his understanding. If only I could call him, thank him. I dare not because I love him more than life itself. And I know his life is ahead of him, not behind him, like mine," she said softly, then started to sob.

Alice-Lee heard the sobs and walked rapidly to Sam's room. As she entered, she saw Sam holding the little paperback to her bosom as she rocked back and forth and wept. "What in heaven's name has happened to you this time?" asked Alice-Lee.

Sam smiled. Sure she was crying but the tears were of sheer joy. Alice-Lee saw the sparkle in Sam's eyes not even dimmed by the tears.

"Look," said Sam and she handed Alice-Lee the paperback. "He put it in my suitcase while we were packing. I didn't know the book was there until a moment ago."

Alice-Lee, looking in the book, saw "Part 2: *The Poems of Marcus Arent Bosconovich*." She skimmed through the vignette, looked at Sam. "I knew I had heard or seen that name before. About two months ago, in the Sunday book section of our paper, I read a review of that volume of poetry. I remembered the name, Bosconovich, unusual for an American poet. So he was the cook, the guy you fell for? You have taste, my dear, real taste. I've always known that. But, why did you chase him away?"

Sam smiled. She was in control of her emotions. "There is a reason," said Sam, "But, I just cannot and will not talk about it presently."

"I hope it isn't because of your Christmas disease."

"No. He knows about that. He was most considerate. Some day in the near future we'll talk and I'll tell you."

Alice-Lee was not easily dissuaded. "How did you get here last night?"

"On gossamer wings that I left behind the bushes in the driveway?" responded Sam, then she grinned impishly.

Alice-Lee tried another tack. "Where was your rendezvous, your love nest?"

"In a little inn called Almost Heaven," said Sam and she added, "Please no more questions. I know you would love a scoop and an interview with him. But, if you did, he would learn where I am. For me, that would be disastrous." Sam's eyes were begging her friend to close the questioning.

Alice-Lee sensed the same finality in Sam's tone and look that

Marcus had experienced the day before. She knew that if she endeavored to get behind that finality, she might wreck a friendship. She really didn't want to do that. "I have my priorities and secrets. I guess Sam is entitled to hers at least for the time being," she mused.

"Okay, Sam, let's go to the Top of the Mark. It has the best brunch in town."

"I'll be ready in a few minutes. Can I use a little of your makeup, until I stop by the cosmetic shop in The Mark Hopkins? My former landlady kept my makeup kit," said Sam.

"Sure," replied Alice-Lee and she realized that Sam was indeed pale, much more so than usual.

CHAPTER 4

After Sam's cab had been swallowed by the night fog, Marcus reentered the hotel, went to his room and closed the door. He hadn't noticed as he helped Sam pack, now he did: the beds were freshly made, clean drinking glasses in tissue paper wrappers sat on the basin ledge, fresh towels were stowed on the racks by the mirror, and a thin strip of paper draped across the toilet seat evidenced sanitizing. "How empty and sterile," he said softly. Even Sam's delicate aroma had vanished, replaced by some foul-smelling antiseptic air spray. For him, the room would never be the same. It lacked her aura and the vibrancy of the trust he had so recently experienced. Why the trust? He really couldn't fathom the reason because his desires initially were anything but noble. Maybe his actions were so-called decent, however that was due to Sam's absolute trust after her whimsically strange introduction. How abruptly the relationship had apparently ended. He was awash with disturbing, tangled memories.

Marcus sat on what had been her bed and wondered, "Why do I sense that she walked constantly in the presence of pending death from something other than her Christmas disease, shielded death? Why couldn't she share her deep anguish with me? Why should she die alone, if that's what is happening? I am her friend, I hope her very good friend, and I have an affection for her in an entirely different way than my love for vital, earthy, robust Mariana. To me the two feelings are not competitors. They are complimentary. Sam has really introduced me to trust, a trust beyond my imagination."

Marcus crawled into the bed he had slept in the night before and looked over to where Sam had slept. He could see her image so clearly. "You are still my goddess of spirituality. Tucked away in a small, hidden, quiet part of my heart is the ever warm gift you gave me. Will I ever experience it again? Should I? Maybe once is enough. Can I ever grow to the level that I can give that gift of trust to someone as you gave it to me? Sam, I've got a long way to grow," he said quietly.

Marcus awakened a couple times during the night. Each time he could almost swear she was standing over him with her enticing smile and saying, as she disrobed, "I'll tell you what." But then she wasn't. And, he knew she would never again be there.

□

Marcus was awakened by the bedside phone ringing stridently. He roused, fumbled for the receiver, said "Ullo," and looked at the radio clock on the bedside table by the phone. The clock read 7:00 a.m.

"Come on, lad, get your arse out of bed. Time to get about the civilian world." He could just see those blue Irish eyes dancing.

Now his first view of Mariana Finley Lucas was sparkling clear in his mind: It was midday, he was off duty and lounging in a deck chair near the outdoor Olympic-sized swimming pool of the Reno hotel whose owners ran the casino. The sky was blue and spotless. Suddenly, in bold relief against that cloudless background, a beautifully-proportioned young lady, about five feet six inches tall, walked onto the pool springboard. Her lithe body was snugly fit into a white one-piece tank suit. She wore a color-matching swim cap. She was lightly tanned, with eyes that reflected the sky. She gracefully approached to within six feet of the end of the board, stopped and her eyes were focused ahead in concentration. She placed her hands at her sides. Her posture was erect but relaxed. Then she took two steps, jumped, landed just short of the end of the board, sprang out and up, like an upsoaring white and tan eagle with wings outspread. She arched her back, threw her head back, and, as she passed the zenith of her dive, gracefully drew her arms beside her head and locked her thumbs. With hands outstrechted and fingers together, she sped downward and split the water head first, like a vertical spear. Only the barest circular ripple noted the point of her entry. "What a beautifully executed layout, half-gainer dive," he thought at that time.

Marcus watched intently, saw the sea siren perform a series of dives, as if she was training for a meet. When she came to surface from her last dive, the diver waved to a couple of girl friends sitting on the edge of the shallow end of the pool. With a thrust of her legs, she was on the surface. A six-beat crawl propelled her smoothly and rapidly to join them. Many eyes watched from the pool side. She was, to him, not just an eye-catching young lady, but one hell of an aquatic athlete. "What is her name? Why is she here? Just who is she," he wondered?

He would be ever thankful that he met her that night. There was mutual instant attraction. They became not only comfortable, new friends, but there was something about the components of their such different personalities that seemed destined to intertwine and meld to a warm, strong union. He had a hard time believing she was only six months younger than him. A couple of nights before Mariana's vacation was over and she was to return to the Purple Canary Press, a small publishing company owned and operated by her in New York City, Mariana's and Marcus' hearts rose together like a pair of soaring eagles looking down at the world far beneath them. Their very different components were beginning to intertwine and to meld. He and Mariana were in love, he hoped forever.

"Hey Marcus, wake up."

"My God, Mariana, it's only seven a.m. out here."

"That's late enough m'love, unless you were out late last night chasing babes. And, you better hadn't be. Have you bought your train ticket to come home to Chicago?"

"No. I didn't reach Frisco until just before I called your office. Since then, I haven't had time to do much of anything except get rid of my sea legs and sleep."

"With whom?"

"With whom, what?"

"With whom have you been sleeping?" asked a prodding Mariana.

"Shouldn't that word have been who, in the accusative case?" asked a kidding Marcus.

"I'm only asking, not accusing," responded an equally swift Mariana.

"I've been sleeping with nobody," answered Marcus. He felt he was partly right, but even saying what he did made him uncomfortable. Trust be damned. He could never really explain what had happened in the last thirty-six hours. Sam had been right, Mariana would never accept his explanation.

"Doesn't sound like the Marcus I know," Mariana's voice was lilting, teasing. "Remember, I've got a single brother, Sean, your age, and he has just returned home from north Africa after being released from the Army. He couldn't wait to snuggle on a bed with something live, even if it was one-eyed Freddie, our family cat. And Sean's nowhere near the man you are, I know."

For the first time since his return stateside, Marcus let out a belly laugh, long and satisfying. "There'll never be another like you," he was finally able to say.

"And don't you forget it my poetic jock." Mariana loved hearing the uninhibited joy emanate from Marcus. That's the guy, good, bad or indifferent, she knew and loved. She vowed to herself that from now on she would not appear to Marcus to be so positive and controlling in her demeanor, except there had to be the present exception.

"Marcus," and Mariana was serious, "I realize there is difficulty, right now, for service men to get cross-country transportation. Sometimes it takes days or even weeks to get cross-country rail tickets on travel orders."

"I know," he replied. "I checked out on travel time as soon as I arrived stateside. I took travel time rather than transportation. I've got twelve days to report to the release center at home. Just how I will get there I have no idea at the moment but I will start to work on it today."

"I do." Mariana continued, "I pulled a few strings through Dad. There's a lower berth ticket waiting for you at the main ticket office of the Union Pacific in Frisco. It's for the *City of San Francisco* leaving tomorrow for Chicago. But you've got to pick up the ticket before five p.m. your time, today."

"How do you know I want to come home so soon?" he queried jokingly.

Mariana was not amused. "Suit yourself. But I'll be damned if I'm going to the trouble of getting you another one. You just go to the station and find out how long it will take you to get a cross-country ticket on your travel orders. You better take the ticket waiting for you if you want to see me in Chicago."

"What in the world are you doing in Chicago?"

"Staying with your family."

"Staying with my family? I thought you were in Philly at a book dealers convention."

"I was until I got the message from my office saying you had arrived stateside and would be staying at the Huntington. I called the hotel to make sure you were registered, got your ticket, had it wired to Frisco then took the next flight to Chicago. You crap out on this deal and it will be a long time, lover, before you see me, if ever."

Marcus thought, "She is still positive Mariana."

"Your mom is seated on the sofa across from me nodding her head in agreement. She says, 'Bambino, get your fanny home now.'"

Marcus grinned. "I'll be there, hon. I was just asking. How I've missed you, you can't imagine."

"And, because I'm a woman who cares, I've missed you in ways no man can understand, not even you." Marcus heard hand clapping in the phone background, then his mother's warm strident voice, "Mariana, you say it better than I ever could."

Mariana continued, "I'll be waiting at the station for your return. Please see that the train is on time. It's freezing cold here, and I hate chilled feet from standing around." Her voice lowered and there was the disarming, thrilling gentleness of tone that had truly grabbed him during their first serious conversation at the casino, "I've prayed daily for your safe return. Even through our last set-to I loved you. I've tried not to. But for me it is just meant to be. Please hurry home. I need you so." Marcus heard her soft sob.

"My beloved Boston Babe, I'm on my way. Though at times we have fought like two Irish terriers, snapping over nothing more important than a rag doll. In the end mutual respect has been our referee, holding up a hand of each of us declaring a draw. As a result, we understand each other better and love each other with ever-increasing honesty. I ache to be with you."

"Gee, you're mouthy, but I love it." Then Mariana's voice dropped back to the gentleness, "And, I know you mean it. You've already proven that. See you soon, my adorable Cooky B."

The phone went dead.

Marcus arose from the bed, stretched, then looked down at the silent phone and thought, "Could any other woman ever mean as much to me? It was her drive, her insistence that I should, I could, write really good poetry. And this at a time when I was struggling as to whether or not to give up the effort and solely seek a business career using my mathematical knowledge. She in no way demeaned my capability with figures, but insisted that the math knowledge, even if it was the basis of a business career, could aid in the structure, the pacing, yes, even the tone of my poetry."

"Math is the science and poetry is the expression of the best of good dreamers," she said one evening as they sat at a corner table in the casino lounge. "You are a dreamer, a lovely creative dreamer. Your master's thesis, "How to Gamble Right," and your poems attest to that. Once you lose the desire or deny your God-given ability to dream and express those dreams, you will no longer be Marcus Bosconovich but a dull plodder like ninety percent of all humanity. Me included. I can't dream and express those dreams as you can, I would be a far better woman if I could."

Right then and there, Marcus knew he loved this vital savvy young lady who sat across the table from him. And one whose perception of him seemed to reach his soul.

"Why does she have to be so positive about what's best for me and almost always be right? That's what caused the trouble the last time." He sighed, for he realized that behind the positiveness was the caring, nurturing, her desire to be by his side through thick or thin. Even before their last spat, prior to his entering the Navy, she had told him with those blue eyes sparkling, "You better think twice about marrying me. If you do there's going to be a passel of kids. I love children, even more than I love the publishing business. If I have to make a choice, there's no question as to what it will be—kids."

God, she is so vital, so real, and so feminine for all her positiveness. Now Marcus was energized.

By 10:00 a.m. he had his ticket, a lower berth, number 17A in the Laredo car. The train, he found out, not only had a dining car but a club car, the Embarcadero, the last car of the train. His ticket included use of the club car. Mariana had thought of every detail. He was restless, excited. He was going home to his family, to Mariana and she was with his family. She must have become a friend of his family while he was overseas. However, until her phone conversation, he didn't know that. And she must be quite close to his mom because his mom's background voice on the phone was that of a woman sharing joint knowledge about him. He felt comfortable with their sharing for his mother, Marla, who was much like Mariana, only his mother's knowledge was mostly empirical from her family in Bergamo, Italy. Mariana's came from her Irish family in Wollaston, Massachusetts, her formal education at Radcliffe College, then from her business career in New York made possible by her arrogant but doting father Brian O'Flanagan Lucas. He had the money to spoil all three of his kids—Sean, the older son, then Tully the rebel, sullen and devious and Mariana, the true love of her dad's life. Marcus knew from Mariana that Brian Lucas never thought he would have a daughter, for the Lucases, Marcus guessed by genetics, bred five-to-one male over female heirs.

After leaving the ticket office, Marcus strolled over to Fisherman's Wharf for a late lunch at Joe's Place. Before he entered the famed seafood restaurant, he watched a street mime perform. The actor was made up like a French clown. Damn, he's good, should be on the stage and have an agent. He was one of the best mimes Marcus had ever seen, particularly when the clown reminded him how hungry he was. Now, Marcus looked forward to a steaming platter of Alaskan king crab legs.

CHAPTER 5

Marcus, lugging his seabag, took an afternoon ferry from Frisco to Oakland. As the ferry neared the terminal, fog began to roll in and a light rain filtered through the haze. Not the brightest day to start a trip home, he thought. He walked the short distance from the ferry landing to the Union Pacific Station, went to the reservation window, had his ticket cleared and headed for the door that led to the platform where the train was waiting to take him home. He left the station building, sauntered onto the covered platform along the tracks, read the overhead sign at the platform entrance, "City of San Francisco— Ride with Pride—The Best in the West." He tingled slightly, "Damn, it is really beginning to happen, I am going home."

The fog slithered in underneath the covered platform and Marcus for the first time, saw the streamliner. As he approached, the train appeared to him to be a sleek, long, silver-tinted, glass-scaled, loose-jointed reptile, the head of which was shrouded in fog. The ghostly quiet mist seemed to trap the exuding scent of the serpent, diesel. Now Marcus' excitement was joined by mild apprehension as he continued gazing at the streamlined train, "Kinda' like riding in the mythical beast whose frightened young sought refuge by entering through side apertures in her belly. Damn sight more confining than the 460.5," he thought, as he walked the platform alongside the last car. It almost backed up against the line end bumper guard. Marcus saw the car name under the middle windows in bold black and gold letters, "Embarcadero" and glanced through one of the windows. The interior was softly lighted. Gosh, it's swanky, he mused, as he almost stumbled over a conductor lounging against one of the roof uprights. "Excuse me," said Marcus, "But could you tell me where my seat is located?" He held out his ticket.

"The Laredo, two cars down," replied the conductor, then he pointed.

Marcus approached the car entrance, his seabag slung over this shoulder. "Señor, I'll take it," said a short, stocky, Mexican porter, who reached out from the car platform and took the canvas carrier as Marcus lifted it to him. When Marcus was on the platform, the porter said, "Señor, por favor, may I see your ticket for your seat number?" Marcus showed his ticket. The porter said, "Follow," and Marcus did. Halfway through the Pullman car, the porter stopped, pointed to his left. "Your seat is 17A, lower. There is room to stow your bag on your seat. The diner is dos cars there." He pointed to the front of the car. "The club car is dos cars there," and he pointed to the rear of the car. "Your ticket says you to use the club car. Here is the call button if you need me," and he pointed to the call button on the walnut seat side panel nearest the aisle.

Marcus, noting the black printing on the aide's shining brass breast pocket nameplate, said, "Thanks, Jose. Here's a buck for your trouble."

The porter smiled, "Gracias, Señor," he replied and left.

Marcus took off his white cap, pea jacket and hung both on the clothes hook on the inside of the walnut aisle shielding seat panel. He stowed his seabag beside him on the seat then ran a hand over the maroon plush velvet bench that, at night, would become a part of his bed. He wondered how much this lower berth had cost Mariana? It surely seemed comfortable.

Settling in, he looked at the vacant double seat across from him. He wondered, "Who will sit opposite me to be my riding companion or companions?" He didn't have long to wait. Jose, the porter, came ambling up the aisle followed by a squat woman of undeterminable age. She was swarthy complected, wore no makeup, and her black hair was short-cropped, almost a bob. She wore dangly, gold, hooped pierced earrings. Her dingy, brown blouse was tucked into black culottes. She, with her long artificial eyelashes, overhanging two enormous brown eyes, looked like a sullen, bloated, ill-kept, cow. She was chewing a wad of gum, all of which added to her bovine-like appearance. Behind her straggled her miniature, a daughter about eight years old. He observed that the girl was, unfortunately, destined to grow into adulthood even more unattractive than her mother. It had to be her mother, no other two humans could bear such close and gross resemblance. When the mother reached the backward-riding Pullman seat opposite Marcus, she plopped down. Marcus was sure he heard the seat give a gentle sigh of resignation as she did so. The daughter squirmed firmly onto the seat portion nearest the window and whined, "I'm hungry. I didn't get no lunch like you promised me."

"Hush, Verbena. We'll get something to eat in a little while."

The porter looked at Marcus with sorrowful contemplation. His expressive, black eyes were speaking loudly, "Man, I'm glad I'm not you." Then he said, "Señora, here is your overnight bag. The rest of your luggage is stowed forward. Here are your claim tickets."

Marcus watched as the woman reached out a grubby, chubby hand with flaming red fingernails of varying jagged lengths. She said, "Okay." Jose delivered the claim checks, waited a moment, winked at Marcus and left emptyhanded.

The woman carefully scrutinized the compartment, looked out beyond the seat aisle partition toward the front of the car. The daughter was balefully studying Marcus.

"I hate to ride backward," the mother said in a wheezy, guttural voice, to no one in particular, but the remark was obviously aimed at Marcus. "It makes me nauseated, makes me constantly feel like I want to throw up." Then her eyes steadied on Marcus. As large as they were, they appeared mean. Marcus sensed their malevolence. Without any introduction, she asked, "Mister Sailor, how did you manage to get a lower berth?"

"What a hell of a salutation," thought Marcus. He smiled, then replied, "I guess I was lucky."

"You servicemen get all the breaks while we civilians do all the dirty work," she wheezed at Marcus.

Marcus was slightly irked, "Just what do you do?"

"None of your business," was her reply.

"Daddy says she just sits around on her big butt all day, smokes cartons of cigarettes and drinks too much of his beer, while she listens to soaps on the radio or reads a dirty book. He says our home looks like Uncle Ned's pig pen," smirked the daughter as she cast her mother a denigrating look.

SWAT! Without even looking at her, the mother dealt her daughter a backhand slap across her mouth. Marcus was surprised and expected the little girl to emit a wild, calflike bawl. All she did was give her mother a vicious, snarling smile. "It's true," she said as she leered in triumph at Marcus.

Marcus thought, "Great Caesar's ghost, she must be used to such abuse." Realizing he was going to be across from the mother and daughter for the next two or three days depending on how the snowstorm now blanketing the west and midwest delayed the train's arrival in Chicago, he endeavored to defuse the woman's apparent irritation on having to ride backwards across country and having to sleep with her daughter in an upper berth. "I'll be glad to switch berths. I'll take the upper," he said.

"No, no," wailed the young girl, "I want to sleep upstairs. I won't sleep downstairs." She began to sniffle.

"Shut up, Verbena," said the mother.

"I won't. I'll tell Daddy you made me sleep downstairs, when he promised we'd sleep upstairs. I've always wanted to sleep upstairs on a train. Mr. sailor, say no."

For the first time the mother appeared uneasy. She cast a blistering look at her blubbering daughter, then glanced at Marcus. "We'll stay where we are," she growled, pulled a smudged paperback romance novel from her overnight bag and pretended to read.

Marcus could tell that the mother was fuming at him, her daughter and the world in general. The girl grinned at Marcus then looked out the window. Marcus, perturbed, also looked out the window and thought, "No introduction, no asking who I am, or my name. What a piss-poor trip this will be if I have to put up with this cow and calf combination for two or three days. Where did the little girl get the name Verbena? The Verbena I know is a lovely flower that grows close to the ground. Well, her name is accurate in one respect, she is growing close to the ground."

He heard two mournful power whistles as the train left the station in a smooth serpentine glide. The girl watched out the window for a few seconds then turned to Marcus and said, "Gee, its good to be going home." Her eyes beamed with genuine anticipation.

"You're so right, young lady. Where is home?"

"We live in a little coal mining town not far from Scranton, Pennsylvania," was her reply. "My daddy is a team boss in Mine Number Two and he's the union secretary."

Marcus believed the toughness of the two females had emanated from the male head of the family.

Her mother closed her book, arose, looked haughtily at Marcus, "Come on, Verbena, we're going to get something to eat."

"See you later, Mr. sailor," said the girl as she followed her mother toward the dining car.

Marcus waited until they disappeared, then arose, turned toward the club car and said softly, "Three such strange females in four days. I just can't wait to get home, back to normalcy." He was thinking of Mariana, Marla, his mother, and his two sisters.

□

He opened the door to the club car. The interior was even more swanky than it appeared from the outside. He observed that at the far end of the car was a crescent-shaped bar with a colorful hand-painted mural of the Rocky Mountains beneath the bar ledge. The mural stretched from one end of the bar to the other. There was no brass footrail. Obviously, he thought, you're not supposed to drink standing. Behind the bar was a dignified, gray-haired guy in horn-rimmed glasses wearing a tux, busy making drinks. Marcus noted that the interior car walls were walnut-paneled. Fairly close to the bar he saw a table occupied by five men: two servicemen, an army captain, a navy senior lieutenant, and three civilians. They were playing a card game.

Across the aisle from the card players were four or five low, empty, lounge chairs. From there, toward the front of the car, on each side of the aisle, were a series of low-backed booths with linen-covered tables and plush velvet seats, the same color as his Pullman seat. From where the booths stopped to where Marcus was standing, on one side of the aisle was a kitchenette, on the other side, a serving pantry and a lavatory.

Other than the card players in the club car, Marcus saw a young couple sitting opposite each other in one of the booths, holding hands across the table. They were whispering. In another booth, across and down from the card players was a gaunt, gray-haired man in an expensive, brown Harris tweed suit, smoking a cigar and reading a newspaper. He was facing the card players. Marcus watched as the gray-haired one with cold, blue-green eyes glanced at the card players. How delightful. What a relaxing place to pass the time on the trip home instead of sitting opposite the sullen cow and her tough calf. He showed his ticket to a steward who was working in the kitchenette area then ambled to a lounge chair opposite the card players.

From that point, he watched the game. A Mexican steward approached him. "Would you like something to drink or eat, Señor?"

"For the moment, a cup of coffee."

"Coming right up." The server left returning shortly thereafter with a cup, saucer, and pot of steaming coffee. "Sugar and cream are on the table," said the steward. He motioned to the small side table.

"I'll just take it black," answered Marcus. He was now seriously watching the card players and saw a challenge, concentrated, sipped his coffee for a while then put the cup down on the table, went to the bar and said, "Joe, I'll take a Scotch on the rocks."

"Yes, suh," was the calm answer.

When the drink was on the mahogany surface, Marcus looked at the bartender. Something about the man caught his eye. "Have I ever seen you before?" he asked. The man's coloring reminded him of someone. Who was it? But Marcus couldn't bring recognition from memory.

"I couldn't tell you where," the bartender answered.

Marcus took one more look at the bartender: Even that soft baritone voice. It was as if I have heard it before. He then half turned toward the card players, "You think they could make room for one more?" he asked.

"Sailor, I wouldn't do that if I was you," replied the bartender.

"Why not?" asked an amused Marcus.

"Because I've been watching, I think those cards are snake bit."

Marcus carefully scrutinized the bartender and wondered, "Does he know the meaning of the last two words of that comment?"

Marcus' hazel eyes were dancing. "How many times?" he asked softly.

"How many times what?" replied the bartender as he looked down, wiping the bar surface with a clean rag.

"How many times have those cards been snake bit?"

The server looked seriously at Marcus and quietly said, "Once."

"Maybe you're right," replied Marcus as he gazed with respect at the graying man behind the bar. "I think I'll join the fun."

"You better be very careful," half whispered the bartender.

"I'm a big boy, I can take care of myself." Marcus turned from the bar and started toward the table.

As the bartender's eyes followed Marcus, he whispered to himself, "Jesus, I am surprised that you are on this train. You didn't quite recognize me, but I recognized you, Marcus Bosconovich. You are one damned good cardplayer but you are heading into a game with stakes higher than you ever imagined. I wish you had stayed away from this car, this train."

While Marcus was in his lounge chair sipping coffee, he had observed the current dealer. The guy was tall, sharp-featured and sandy-haired. "Maybe about my age," thought Marcus. Marcus had watched the dealer snap the cards to the players. His hands were those of a pro. Marcus studied the face. It was expressionless except for a hint of a smile that curled at the edges of his mouth. His black eyes were cunning but his demeanor was pleasant, almost condescending. The deck he was dealing was cooked. Marcus, from where he sat, could just barely decipher the marked bicycles. He couldn't read the numbers but he could tell. Where had the cards come from? Were they the current dealer's? Was someone else at the table the prime or, despite the barman's warning that there was only one snake, was this a co-op between two players? He wondered as he watched from his seat, but wasn't close enough to tell. The army officer and the navy lieutenant are fair to middling players, apparently loaded with dough. Where are they heading? Home? They're playing too loosely to be artists at the game, five-card draw, nothing wild. Either they did not know the finer points of the game or their thoughts were more on getting home rather than getting well at the table. The guy to the left of the navy officer and to the immediate right of the dealer is older, about fifty. Marcus thought, it is almost as if he isn't there. He is quiet, serious, a cigarette dangling from the right side of his mouth, the smoke curling up between his horn-rimmed glasses, his gray eyes and never a wisp into either eye. He concentrated on his cards. Now and then he raised those beetle-browed, sharp eyes to look in the direction of the other players but apparently never at whoever was dealing. The chips stacked in front of him varied little from hand to hand. "He's a real pro," Marcus mused, "I wonder why he is in this game? He seems to be more of a watchdog than a player." The guy to the dealer's left was moon-faced, florid, short, loud, well-dressed, with a stogie stuck in his mouth. Tobacco ashes had spilled down over his expensive Italian tie. His beady black eyes danced constantly around the table. The smooth, glistening, rounded top of his bald head bounced the rays of the overhead light like tiny lightening bolts bouncing off a rock. On one hand, Marcus thought, the guy was in the drivers seat. But no, fatso dropped out, lost a bundle, pulled out nine fifty dollar bills and bought chips—five whites, five reds, then six blues. Marcus said to himself, "I wonder who set the price?"

Marcus, with drink in hand, now stood next to the current dealer, obviously the banker of the game, for behind him on a little table was a rack for the chips, red, white and blue. A number of chips were in each section.

He looked at the dealer and asked, "Is there room for another player?"

The dealer viewed the other players. "Sure," said the army officer, "Draw up a chair if you have four hundred and fifty bucks to spare."

"Hey, you two," said the dealer, pointing to the two officers, "Move apart enough to let him in."

The fat guy took the cigar out of his mouth and, with a twinkle in his eyes, said, "A rose between two thorns." There was a general guffaw around the table.

"Where are you headed, sailor?" asked the fat man.

"Home, Chicago," answered Marcus.

"Well, then," said the dealer, "You'll be around long enough to make a fair contribution."

"Maybe, who knows?" replied Marcus with a smile as he pulled up a chair, put his drink on a nearby small table, then reached for his wallet, took eight fifty dollar bills, two twenty dollar bills, one ten dollar bill and handed them to the dealer and banker.

"Five card draw, nothing wild, any pair to open, three's the maximum discard, table stakes and no limit if you ever feel that rash. In addition, aces swing high-low," said the dealer as he delivered the required chips to Marcus.

"Don't expect me to get rash very quickly," replied Marcus.

The older player, the one on the dealer's right, looked up from his cards. Not saying a word, he carefully studied Marcus.

The dealer announced, "I'm Henry Fosberg. This is Ray Baker." He pointed to the fat man on his immediate left. "Next to him is Navy Lieutenant Jim Holmes. On your left is Army Captain Tom Phillips. On his left is Jay O'Connor. Your name is what?"

"I'm Marcus Bosconovich, but you can call me Cooky B."

"Why?" asked fat Ray Baker.

"Because," said Lieutenant Holmes, "I'm sure he was a cook in the navy. Right?"

"On the button," replied Marcus.

"You ever played five card draw before, for table stakes, no limit?" calmly inquired gray-haired O'Connor.

"Oh, once or twice," Marcus replied then studied his questioner.

As Fosberg, the dealer, drew in the chips from the hand he had just won, he looked at Marcus and said, "Deal passes with each hand. We have two expanded decks, player to dealer's right shuffles the played deck, player to left of new dealer cuts for the current deal. Any questions?"

"Just a couple," responded Marcus. "Relief time, eating time, and quitting time?"

"Once you're in, anytime," said Ray Baker. "Let your constitution and your conscience be your guide."

"How about new decks?"

"Unfortunately," said Lieutenant Holmes, "Fosberg says he bought the last two decks aboard from the bartender shortly before the train pulled out. We'll just have to play with these. Any problem?"

Marcus had more than just a twinge of doubt at the veracity of that statement.

Again Marcus felt the steely gray eyes of O'Connor.

"No, I was just wondering about the rules of your game. I'm satisfied."

"Good," replied Fosberg. "Your deal, Fatso," as the navy lieutenant handed the cut deck to Baker.

"I'd rather be fat and happy than thin and dull like some people I've recently met," said Baker, then he grinned at Fosberg.

Fosberg cast Baker a glance.

The game went on and Marcus played carefully. He could read the marked cards as if they were dealt face up. In each suit the ace, king, queen, jack and twelve were clearly identifiable as were the sixes. Of the remaining cards, only one in each suit was marked. While he was playing, he studied the men around the table. It did not take Marcus long to determine that the two officers and fatso didn't know the cards were cooked. At first, he was not sure about Jay O'Connor or Fosberg. Their bets, raises, passes and calls were cautious, but seemed within normal play. Fosberg was constantly glancing around the table but in such an offhand manner as to kindle no questions from the other players. O'Connor seldom glanced up from his cards but when he did, it was swift and observant. Marcus became increasingly confident that he was a reader. The third hand was won by Lieutenant Holmes. There was four hundred in the pot. Marcus had contributed forty dollars until he dropped out. He knew exactly what Holmes held, a full house, jacks over tens. Fosberg was the caller. He had dropped one hundred into the game. He wasn't surprised at Holmes' hand.

Marcus finished his drink, ordered another cup of coffee and a club sandwich. A steward brought them and placed them on a side table. Marcus munched and sipped from time to time. The others ate sporadically the same way. Occasionally, one of the players would drop out for a hand to go to the lavatory. The game wore on. As it did, Marcus became aware that the real winner was Fosberg and Fosberg was also a reader but playing cagily so as not to unduly upset the other players. Jay O'Connor constantly held his own. Marcus could swear that the calm senior player held exactly the same amount of chips after hours of play that he had when Marcus entered the game.

Afternoon extended into evening, evening into night, no one had bet table stakes but the bets were climbing and the pots were growing in size. At 11:30 p.m. when Marcus walked to the lavatory, he thought, "If I get half a chance, I'm going to uncover Fosberg, the cheating bastard." While there, he reached into his money belt, took out two bicycle decks with the identical background as the decks they were playing in the game, drew from each deck the ace, king, queen, jack and twelve of spades then placed one of the sets in each of his winter blues pants pockets. In each pocket he also had a handkerchief. He returned to the table and shortly thereafter announced, "When the deal gets around to Fosberg, his will be the ultimate hand as far as I am concerned. I need some sleep."

"Okay by me," said Ray Baker. "There's always tomorrow." He was, up to this point, the real loser of the game. Marcus calculated Baker had lost at least eight hundred dollars most of it to Fosberg during the time he, Marcus, had joined the game. Time and again, Baker had bought chips from the banker, always in twenties or fifties. For some reason, Marcus felt Fosberg didn't realize O'Connor was also a reader. Marcus was now out of pocket sixty dollars, all by design. The game continued to Fosberg's deal.

On the ultimate deal, Baker opened the pot with a twenty dollar bet, drew two cards, and all stayed. Holmes drew three cards. Marcus drew two cards. Captain Phillips drew one card and O'Connor drew two cards. Fosberg drew three cards. After the draw, Marcus could tell Baker had three sixes, Holmes had two low pair, Marcus had zilch, not even a marked card. He was sure Captain Phillips had a low straight and Phillips did have the fourth six. O'Connor had a full house, tens over jacks, ten of spades and jacks of spades and diamonds missing. Fosberg had a full house, kings over aces, king of clubs missing and aces of diamonds and clubs missing. The betting started, Baker bet twenty dollars, Holmes raised him twenty. Captain Phillips stayed, Marcus stayed, O'Connor stayed. Fosberg raised a hundred, Baker stayed, Lieutenant Holmes dropped out. O'Connor stayed. Marcus raised a hundred on his unmarked cards. Fosberg gave him a sly grin. Fosberg raised him twenty. Baker stayed, Phillips stayed. O'Connor stayed. The betting began in earnest. Fosberg bet one hundred, Baker raised a hundred, Marcus raised him a hundred, Phillips dropped out, O'Connor dropped out. Fosberg raised a hundred. Baker stayed. Marcus raised a hundred with his unmarked cards. Fosberg wondered what the hell could the sailor have with those unmarked cards. He knew the enlisted Navy man couldn't have four of a kind. He had read the cards around the table and he knew the discards. Fosberg raised another hundred, then looked at Marcus. "What a bluffer that sailor is." Ray Baker, undaunted, raised a hundred. Marcus stayed. All remaining players were out. Marcus coughed slightly, reached for his handkerchief, wiped his mouth and with an expert unnoticed sleight of hand, switched the blue background, unmarked royal straight flush into his playing hand, put the handkerchief back in his pocket then raised Baker a hundred.

Fosberg said, "Table stakes, I'll match the table," and he pulled out a handful of crisp one hundred dollar bills, counted the chips in the center, moved in the balance of his chips and placed the bills on the table in front of him. He glanced at Marcus.

Baker stared at Fosberg. "I believe you, I'm out." He folded his hand and flipped it blue backs up on top of the discards on the table.

Marcus appeared to be studying his hand, then looked at Fosberg. After a slight smile, he said, "I wouldn't do that if I was you. I'm looking right down your throat."

Fosberg squinted at Marcus. "Just what could that bastard have?" Marcus reached for his wallet, put it on the table then reached underneath his t-shirt, opened a pouch in his money belt and pulled out a wad of bills. He slowly counted the pot including the chips and Fosberg's matching bills. He moved his remaining chips into the pot. "I'll double that bet," said Marcus and he placed the appropriate bills from his wallet and money belt onto the table.

Fosberg was thunderstruck. He believed Marcus, with no marked cards, couldn't have more than a low full house but something about the sailor's manner was serving as a warning, a clear-cut warning. What the hell could it be? He studied the table full of chips and bills. With a grimace he counted more bills and placed them on the table. He said, "I call."

Marcus spread his hand, ace, king, queen, jack and twelve of spades.

Fosberg was apoplectic, his breath came in short gasps. He just couldn't believe what he was seeing. He knew he had been had, but not how, and he couldn't show his cards. "I fold," he hissed, and with perspiration rolling off his brow he flipped his cards face down on top of the discards.

Jay O'Connor chuckled, then said softly, "I'll be damned."

"I've never seen that before," fat Ray Baker commented in unrestrained surprise.

"I doubt if you will ever see it again," said O'Connor and he continued to chuckle.

The two officers sat spellbound.

Marcus raked in the bills with both hands. He counted the chips. "Twelve hundred," he announced to Fosberg. Fosberg reached into his large billfold and started to count out hundred dollar bills.

"Not those," said Marcus.

"What do you mean, not those?"

"Man, they're too big for a sailor to handle. Maybe an officer can. But they're sure to cause trouble for someone like me. I've tried to cash "C" bills before. I'm serious," said Marcus, his hazel eyes were flashing as Fosberg looked at him in disgust. Marcus continued, "I know you've got more than a thousand in small bills. You took them during the game from the players around the table. I'll take those and the rest in "C" bills." The other players were watching the event with increasing interest particularly O'Connor.

"It's all U.S. currency. What the shit difference does it make?" asked Fosberg.

"I don't see why you mind then," said Marcus. "It'll make your wallet less bulky. I need the smaller bills."

There was silence as Fosberg was glancing at his wallet, so quiet that the sound of the car wheels speeding over the rail joints sounded like snare drumbeats as they reverberated through the club car.

"See you tomorrow, boys," said O'Connor. He pushed back his chair, stood but didn't leave. His eyes never left Fosberg.

Fosberg was now seething with anger, an almost panic anger, his cool manner was stripped. Fat Baker and the two officers watched with surprise, wondering what the outcome would be.

Without saying a word or looking up, Fosberg began to count the tens, twenties and fifties. When he reached nine hundred he said, "That's it. I've got to pay off the rest of the chips. You'll have to take the balance in hundreds."

Marcus coughed, reached for a handkerchief and while all the other players were concentrating on Fosberg counting his losses, Marcus gathered his winnings then flipped the cards, blue backs up to the discard deck as Fosberg continued to count his loss. Only the flipped cards weren't the winning hand shown by Marcus. He had deftly palmed his winning hand and returned his original hand as the down cards to the deck.

"That's fair," replied Marcus. He took the bills from Fosberg and the rest of the stake on the table. "I'll see you gentlemen tomorrow," he commented.

"You bet your sweet ass, you will," said Baker. He was now seriously studying Marcus.

Marcus arose, "Gentlemen," he announced, "It's been a lovely evening."

"For you," said Lieutenant Holmes, "Our time will come."

Marcus chuckled, "Could be," he replied. Fosberg paid off the rest of the players when they tallied their chips. As Marcus left the car, he noted it was empty except for the players. He was being closely followed by O'Connor. "You play one hell of a game, sailor," said the soft-spoken senior.

"You're no slouch either," responded Marcus.

When Marcus reached his berth, he turned briefly to O'Connor. "Good night, Sir, and thanks."

"For what?"

"For watching," responded Marcus.

O'Connor's eyebrows raised in mild surprise as he continued forward in the car. The other players passed Marcus without speaking. To Marcus, Fosberg appeared numb, almost as if he was in stark terror as he walked by.

Marcus entered his lower berth, closed the curtains, quietly opened his seabag, took out his blue Navy robe, toiletry kit and headed for the lavatory. He locked the door, took off his pants and blouse, reached into the pockets of his winter blues, took out the bills stuffed into his pockets and placed them in the stainless steel sink. Then he reached beneath his undershirt and unbuckled his money belt. Carefully, he distributed the bills in the pockets of the belt. He took the two Bicycle card decks from his money belt, tore them in shreds and flushed them down the commode. He replaced the belt around his waist, fastened it and said softly, "The bills are safer on me than in my wallet or pants. But, who knows how safe even that will be?" He brushed his teeth, put his robe on over his skivvies, gathered up his clothes and headed back to his berth. He noticed that the car silence was almost absolute. The heavy berth draw curtains deadened the sound of the sleepers, absorbed most of the track sounds. "In less than two days I'll be home," he thought as he crawled on his bunk, pulled the bunk curtains together, rolled his clothes Navy style and stuck them, his shoes and socks into the berth net. He pulled up the covers, relaxed and mused, "Not a bad day, but he hated for Baker to stay in the game. He was sure there would be repercussions of his actions by Fosberg, just what, he had no idea. He wondered what car Fosberg was in." Then he turned toward the car window with its drawn shade and thought of Mariana as he began drifting into dream time.

Suddenly a hand clasped over his mouth, a voice whispered in his ear. "Marcus Bosconovich, just keep quiet and listen. I met you this afternoon, in the card game, as Jay O'Connor. That's not my real name, my name is Clarence Waddell. I'm with the U.S. Secret Service. If you howl, we may both be dead in minutes." The hand came off his mouth. Marcus turned toward the voice. Waddell's head was stuck through the curtains. His hands appeared through the same opening and he flashed a small light on an ID card he held in one of them, then said in the same whispering tone, "Put on your robe, get your clothes and shoes from the net. Hurry, I'll carry your seabag, cap and pea jacket. Follow me. I promise it's for your benefit."

Marcus' heart was pounding, his adrenalin was racing. He liked the way he felt. Then he thought, "God, what a weird situation this is turning out to be. But the guy sounds convincing. He has made no threats, hasn't asked for money or flashed a pistol. Maybe he is for real, but why?" Already Waddell was heading to the front of the car. Instinctively, Marcus was sure something beyond his present knowledge was involved and that speed in following was an essential. He padded quietly behind the alleged operative Waddell. The Laredo Car porter was asleep in his chair compartment as they went by. Waddell opened the car doors as quietly as possible as the two men stalked through thirteen cars. Marcus had the strange sensation that he was floating through the dimly glowing entrails of the silver serpent. Not a word was spoken. Fortunately, the train was on straight track so Marcus had no balancing act to perform, no clutching of the curtains or holding on to wood panels to keep stride. He became aware someone was following him. He looked over his shoulder to see the bartender put a finger to his lips and with the other hand indicate that Marcus should continue to follow Waddell. Halfway down a chair car there was a steel door with only a round peephole in it. Over the door was a small sign, "No Entrance—Mail Car." Those passengers in the reclining car seats were asleep with UP (Union Pacific) blankets draped over them, and the car lights were low. Waddell stopped, pressed a hidden wall button and a small shaft of light shone momentarily through the peephole. The door opened silently and Waddell motioned for Marcus to enter. Marcus saw Waddell carefully study the sleeping passengers, then Marcus and the bartender, followed by Waddell, entered the compartment. The door shut silently behind the three. For a few seconds, they were in the inky blackness of a small cubicle. A door opened, opposite the one they had entered. Marcus walked into a lighted compartment. He blinked and thought, "This is no mailroon but some fancy living compartment."

He saw several large roomettes on either side of the car. Toward the front was a lounging area with comfortable chairs and a conference table. On it was some type of communications equipment, for what? Marcus had no idea. Seated at the table was a heavy-set, red-headed guy with his back to Marcus. He was apparently looking at currency laid out on the table. As Waddell followed by Marcus approached the table, the black bartender behind him tapped Marcus on his shoulder. Marcus looked over his shoulder, saw that the graying, thick head of hair, the sideburns, mustache, and horn-rimmed glasses were gone. "Greetings, Marcus," the former bartender said amiably.

"Holy shit," was Marcus' reply as he recognized his Cornell schoolmate. "Ronald Evans. So you were the bartender? You're as clever with disguise as you were with math. Yet, I thought I had seen you before. However you did it well enough to fool me. How are you? What in the world is this all about?"

"Damn, I'm glad Waddy got you here before anything adverse happened," responded Ronald Evans. "Drop your clothes in Roomette 4-C," and he pointed. "Then come on back and we'll introduce you to the problem. Afterwards we'll let you get some rest and fill you in on the details tomorrow morning."

As Marcus went to the roomette, he was not only surprised but delighted to see his former classmate. His memory surged and he recalled a day—a memorable day—several years ago. Earlier in that day not long before graduation from Cornell, he and Evans had attended a convocation in the university chapel. Both were inducted into Phi Beta Kappa, the national honorary scholarship fraternity. Marcus had seen Evans run on the Cornell track team, had been in several math classes with him but, at the time, knew him casually at best. That evening, there was to be a meeting of the local Phi Beta Kappa Chapter in a room at the Student Union building. The brick path from the road to the building was a good distance, about a block. In the cool, clear night, he and Evans approached the path from opposite directions, walking the road. They arrived at the path at the same time.

"Hi," said Evans.

"Hi, yourself," replied Marcus as both men started up the walkway. They had gone about twenty steps when Marcus stopped, looked at Evans and said, "You go ahead, I've had enough of this scholarship crap for one day."

"Where are you going?" asked Evans.

"Damned if I know, I just don't have the desire to act like a swell-headed highbrow when I know I'm not one."

"I'm with you all the way," replied Evans. That's when their real friendship began. The two men turned abruptly and walked silently down the walk.

When they reached the roadway, Evans looked at Marcus. "Which way?"

"Oh, I don't know, maybe a stroll by the lake wouldn't be bad. There's a new moon rising. It's quite a sight to see as the smiling imp peeks over the eastern rim of the tree-lined lake shore."

"Damn," said Evans.

"Damn what?" asked Marcus.

"What a contrast you are," replied Evans.

"How come?"

"The meanest son of a bitch I ever saw in a boxing ring, a scholar and a romantic rolled up in one. What drives you? What makes you so motivated?"

Marcus looked at his new friend. "You know, that's a fair question. I've never given it much thought." Momentarily he was silent. He heard the peepers by the lake, symphonically calling and searching for one and another. Every now and then one of the half-tamed mallard ducks, nesting in the weeds on the lake shore would let out a monotone "quack." To Marcus, the discordant "quack" was like a G string breaking in the first violin section of a big orchestra. The sound shocked the others in the section to momentary silence. A second or two later the section once again picked up the smooth flow of Debussy's "Clair de Lune," his mother's favorite, classical, musical composition, even if it wasn't Italian. Now he thought about Evans' question.

Marcus spoke, "I guess, first of all, my actions stem from my genes, something I fortunately or unfortunately was born with, inherited from my parents and forbears. Also, I guess it's my way of showing my love for my mom and dad, an appreciation of their sacrifices for me. Sometimes they don't see my motivation the same way as I do. How about you?"

"Man, until right now, I never gave genetics a thought. I don't even know who my parents were. I was raised in a Catholic orphanage in northeast Washington, D. C. The nuns were strict, but not strict enough. I had to learn to run."

"Why?"

"Because I was too black to be white and too white to be black. So there I was caught between two warring camps, even at the orphanage. It's been that way ever since. And I was determined not to be had by either side. I had to study. I had to run, that's the only way I saw out. It worked." He was quiet for a few seconds after the pause he said thoughtfully, "Now that you have mentioned it, I guess genetics played a part, a bigger part than I realized. I wonder who my parents and forbears were?"

"I don't know," said Marcus, "They had to have the right stuff or you wouldn't be where you are today. Not saying you haven't put what they gave you to good use. You have."

When he reached to the table the memory faded as Marcus concentrated on the present.

"This is Brad Comstock," said Evans, and red-headed, fair-skinned, barrel-chested Comstock arose from the table, turned to Marcus, held out his hand, then said with mock seriousness, "Smart with cards and math, heh?"

Marcus grinned at the stocky guy, shook Comstock's hand then asked, "What snake pit have I wandered into?"

"You haven't wandered into one. Waddy just rescued you from a nest of vipers," said Evans. "I tried to warn you. We are a part of a Secret Service team." Then he pulled out a chair.

Marcus sat, and his eyes were intently focused on his former schoolmate from Washington, D.C., ex-star half-miler and Phi Beta Kappa. Marcus wondered how long Evans had been with the Secret Service. He seemed very comfortable, at ease with his present post. "At first, I didn't know whether or not you knew the meaning of my question at the bar, before I entered the game," said Marcus. "When you answered 'One,' I was sure you were someone other than a mere bartender. But, I'll be damned if I could place you."

"Clever, wasn't I?" quipped Evans. "I knew who you were the minute I laid eyes on you and I just knew you would try to get in that game. I couldn't go further than to suggest that you stay out. Revealing who I was might have jeopardized our surveillance."

"What surveillance?" asked Marcus. "I had already determined the cards were cooked. I could tell that from where I sat after I entered the club car. I didn't then know who the cooker was. The setup intrigued me, offered a challenge I couldn't resist."

"You soon found out," responded Waddell.

"Yes. Only a cheap crook like Fosberg would use Bicycles. They are so easy to read."

"You're right," replied Waddell.

"I told you he was once a dealer. Now do you believe me?" asked Evans of Waddell.

"I do, I do," responded the solidly-built senior Secret Service operative. "I'm sure he didn't realize he wasn't just playing with a small-time crooked card player, and that his winning that last hand to stop Fosberg could have far more serious consequences than he ever dreamed of."

"What in the name of God are you talking about?" asked a concerned Marcus.

"My friend," said Evans, "So-called 'Fosberg' was not only the game banker, he is among the newest members of a ring of crooked dealers and counterfeiters that are working cross-country passenger service like you can't imagine."

"Him? He isn't that smart," quipped Marcus.

"I agree," said Evans, and he continued, "I'm sure he is a new tryout member. When you came into the club car, do you recall seeing a young couple in a booth holding hands, as well as a nattily-dressed gray-haired senior sitting facing us in a booth on the other side of the aisle from our table? They were the only other occupants in the club car at that time."

"I certainly do," answered Marcus.

"Well, we're sure they are also a part of the act. The gray-haired guy wearing the expensive Harris tweed, the one with the cigar stuck in his mouth, we know, though he doesn't yet know us. He's called Oren Leverbee, the coach, the watchdog. He's reputed to be a feared underworld killer of the first order, formerly with a New York mob. Just who he was watching we're not sure but we suspect he was there to observe the game, protect his employer's interest if their initiate didn't give a first-rate performance—and, thanks to you, he didn't."

"You mean Fosberg?" asked Marcus.

"Yep," replied Waddell, "And the young couple holding hands in the other booth, we saw them in deep conversation with Leverbee several times."

"Are we talking about the same couple, the tough-looking little blonde with the thin guy who was letting his brown hair grow but didn't quite cover his ears, the guy with the lower part of his left earlobe missing like someone bit it off in a fight?" asked Marcus.

"The same," said Waddell. "They're tied into this racket in some fashion. We'll try our best to find out about them when we reach a regional office."

"How?" asked Marcus.

"Well, first of all, I got plenty of snapshots of them as well as everyone else who came into the car," said Evans.

"I didn't see you take a picture during the whole time. And I was facing you from across the game table," replied Marcus.

"I didn't take them with a Brownie if that's what you mean. I had a lapel buttonhole camera that can take scads of shots. The control was in my tux jacket pocket. I even got three or four of you, right good too. They've all been developed. We'll use them as soon as we get to an office."

Now Marcus was truly interested. "You're saying there's a real con team on this train?"

Comstock, who had been quiet during most of the conversation, spoke up. "You better believe there is. That's why Waddy came for you as soon as we considered it safe for him to do so. Evans was his backup to make sure your move was covered. Those slick rascals are not just conning the passengers with a crooked card game, they are paying off with counterfeit 'C' bills."

"I saw those bills. In fact, I've got several. They looked okay to me, I'm pretty good at phonies."

"They do look good, they should, they're made from true plates—a little old—retired—for some reason not destroyed then stolen," said Waddell.

"Stolen from where?" asked Marcus.

"The Security Room at the Bureau of Printing and Engraving in Washington, D. C.," replied Waddell. "Only the paper reveals the bills are not true. It took us quite a while to even determine that."

Marcus reached under his t-shirt, unbuckled his money belt and placed it on the table. Then he opened a belt pouch, took out all of the "C" bills. "Gosh," he said, "I've got at least six or seven good ones mixed in with the phonies. I can't tell which are which."

"I can," replied Comstock. He took a jeweler's eyepiece from his pocket, adjusted it. Then with a small pair of tweezers, picked up and carefully examined each piece of currency. "Ours, yours, ours," he said as he scrutinized the bills, and continued until he had examined all of them. "Those seven are yours, genuine. These fifteen are ours, counterfeit, we'll examine and test them later," said Comstock.

"For what?" asked Marcus.

"Among other things, for fingerprints," said Waddell.

"Gee, mine may be all over them," responded Marcus.

"We already have yours," said Evans. "They will be easy to eliminate."

"How in the world did you get my prints?" asked a surprised Marcus.

"From your first drink glass. I just knew you would get in that game and knowing you, I had a damned good idea that something unusual could happen before the game was over."

"What should I do with the rest of the money from that hand?" Marcus asked as he carefully studied Waddell.

"Keep it. You earned it, even if by sleight of hand. Fatso Baker could care less. He knew he was being taken by somebody. He'll be delighted to learn who you are and he'll keep his mouth shut. The two servicemen shouldn't have been in the game anyway. As for me, serves me right. I should have had matching bicycles on me, instead of your having them. Damn, what a pickle that would have been with both of us, at the same time trying to unveil that crooked bastard," replied Waddell.

"And what a lovely mess that would have been," said Evans. The three lawmen were consumed with laughter.

"My God," said Marcus, "I'm damned glad you didn't." He was now worried about the entire evening.

"Relax, Marcus," responded Waddell, and he smiled at the Navy cook. "By the time you entered the fray, I knew you were a reader. I could have stopped the game at any time."

"How did you know I was a reader?"

"Evans signaled to me and a little later sneaked me a note identifying you. You were really the guy in the middle."

"Oh, boy," sighed Marcus.

"I suggest we call it quits for tonight," said Evans. "Get some rest, Marcus. Tomorrow, at breakfast, we'll fill you in as far as we can or are permitted to."

Marcus looked at the three men with increasing respect. "Thanks. I'm beginning to believe I may owe my life to your efforts."

"Who knows? The show is only beginning. I don't blame you for what you did tonight," replied Waddell. "You took one hell of a chance."

"Hindsight is better than foresight And you know what? You're right, but that Fosberg was such a cheap phony," Marcus' eyes were beaming with the thrill he was now enjoying, "I couldn't resist the game and doing what I did. I was interested in seeing how the game would play out. I had no idea it would end like this. I hope I haven't jeopardized your surveillance efforts," he said, then headed for his roomette. After he opened the door to this sleeping quarters, he looked over his shoulder, called out, "Once again, guys, thanks for your efforts, I am grateful."

When Marcus had closed the door, Evans turned to his two cohorts and after a mischievous smile, "I told you he is a regular guy even if he is a math wizard and a cardshark. That's not all, he outranked me in scholarship and was the cream of middleweight boxers in the Ivy League. He won the championship for us in his senior year."

"Well, well," chided Waddell, "That's interesting."

"Oh, come on, Waddy, the guy hasn't even gotten out of the Navy yet," said Comstock.

"I didn't say anything but 'that's interesting,'" replied Waddell.

"Bull," added Comstock. "We've been with you long enough to

know what your remarks mean. You have him in the palm of your hand."

"Good night, boys," said Waddy. A sly smile lit his face as he headed for bed.

Evans turned to Comstock. "I'll bet you a buck that somehow Waddy will have a copy of Marcus' background—college resume, employment records including his dealing days and his naval personnel folder in the very near future."

"No bet," retorted Comstock as the two men turned in for the night.

Marcus readied for bed. Before pulling up the covers, he reached into his seabag and took out his notebook. Propped up with pillows, he wrote for quite a while, notes of the events that had transpired since his last entry. Then, replacing his notebook, he daydreamed, fantasized about his returning home. Just before he drifted off to sleep he was aware that once again he had met some more unusual, interesting characters in this thrilling adventure called Life.

CHAPTER 6

Shortly after Marcus had been escorted to his safe haven in the so-called "mail car" by Waddell and Evans, there was a knock on the door to Roomette 5 in the "Wyoming Car," the car next to the club car. "Mr. Weaver, this is Leverbee. We need to talk now," said a low voice.

"Just a minute," replied Michael Weaver as he was called. He arose and opened the door. His shapely, peroxided, blonde girlfriend, in the lower bunk, pulled the bed covers up to her neck as the door opened. Leverbee entered, closed the door and squeezed into the one small chair in the roomette.

"We have a problem, a real problem," he said.

"About what?" shot back Weaver. His agitation at being interrupted in nonconjugal coitus was evident as he wrapped his purple satin robe around his slender body and sat at the foot of his girlfriend's berth.

"For the last hour I've been sitting on my bunk worrying about what happened in the club car after you two left. I think I should tell you, Fosberg the initiate, has fucked up. I told you in Frisco we shouldn't have taken him on. He has no real smarts. On the last hand of the night he lost a bundle, good money and ours."

85

"How?"

"In my opinion, he was outsmarted by that wavy-haired, cocky sailor."

"Just how in the hell did Fosberg lose with those marked cards?"

"To someone who could read the cards as well as he could and knew how to take advantage of what he read."

"Was he a Fed of some kind?"

"I doubt that. I watched him carefully during the game. He knows his cards, also I'm sure he was a reader but that dumb bastard, Fosberg, never knew it until it was too late. I tried several times to signal him but either he ignored me or forgot the signals."

"What's the Navy guy's name?"

"I didn't get it. He was seated too far away from me. When he came into the game, he announced it just once. The only comment I clearly heard was, 'Because he was a cook in the Navy, Right?' And that came from the Navy lieutenant in the game. He had a voice like a fog horn, even if he had tried to whisper. Fosberg should know."

"How much did our guy lose?"

"As well as I could tell, something in excess of three thousand."

"On that one hand?"

"Yes, on that one hand and about fifteen hundred was in our 'C' bills."

"Where's the Navy guy's bunk?"

"I don't know but Fosberg might. Our "Man," if that's what he can be called was getting so nervous over the way the game ended that I left the car before he did. I was afraid I would explode or Fosberg might give us away if I stayed there. And to make matters worse I'm sure the older guy in the game was some kind of Fed. I could just sense it. He played like one, slyly observing every damn move that was made by anyone at the table. However, I'm positive Fosberg never realized there was a Fed in the game, or he would have played the entire night differently than he did."

The girl in the bunk broke in, "I was facing Fosberg until we left. I could see him pretty well. He was a Nervous Nelly the whole time we were there. It's a shame we didn't stay until the game was over."

Weaver looked at his girlfriend. "Lorraine, you're nuts. If we had made any move and a Fed was at the table, all hell might have broken loose." He hesitated, stared at Leverbee. Weaver was in a cold fury, but in a calm voice he said, "Leverbee, if you believe there was a Fed in the game and I accept your assessment, I think you should question Fosberg for all he is worth. He shouldn't be worth much when you finish." Then, with that same tone, he said, "The boss can't afford giveaways."

"I understand," answered Leverbee. He looked down at his supple hands admiringly, flexed them, reached into one of his tweed jacket pockets with one hand, pulled out a pair of black kid gloves, then with deliberate slowness, he put them on, pulled them taut and gently caressed one gloved hand over the other as if he was caressing priceless objects of art.

Lorraine, watching from the lower berth, shuddered ever so slightly.

"I'll find out from Fosberg if he knows where the sailor's bunk is," said Leverbee. "After I finish with Fosberg I'll have a little talk with one of the Navy's finest. I'm pretty sure we can get all the money back one way or another."

Weaver was steely eyeing Leverbee. "Take care of Fosberg. Report back to me what you learn from him. Just don't go near the sailor's bunk until after we have discussed the matter. Something doesn't smell right about the whole episode."

"You're right, Boss," replied Leverbee and he left.

"That damn, dumb, dealing jerk," said Lorraine.

Leverbee walked through the cars toward the head of the train until he came to Roomette 6 in the "Diablo Car" stopped and knocked softly.

"Who's there?" asked a shaken voice.

"Leverbee. Let me in."

The door opened. Gloved Leverbee entered, closed and bolted the door. He turned to Fosberg. "What the fuck happened?"

"Its…its…the damnedest thing I ever saw."

"Tell me," said Leverbee and the icy draft exhaled by the gloved visitor made Fosberg shiver.

"Well, on the last hand, on my three-card draw, I held a full house, kings over aces. I had the kings of spades, diamonds and clubs, and the aces of spades and diamonds. I knew what everyone around the table held after their draw, all except the sailor. He didn't have a marked card. Whatever he had, had to be low. He couldn't have had four of a kind or a straight flush. After the first bet, that bastard started to run up the bets. I finally bet table stakes. He was the only one left in the game and smugly says, 'I wouldn't do that if I was you. I'm looking right down your throat.' Then he doubles the bet. For the first time, I had an odd feeling, I could tell something was wrong, really wrong, so rather than raise him, I called. Then, that son of a bitch lays down a royal straight flush. The cards were Bicycles, just like we were playing unmarked. I realized too late that he was a reader and I had been had. I dared not show my hand so I folded. How he did it, I don't know."

"Where are the cards? Did he throw in his hand?"

"Yes, they're right over there," Fosberg pointed to the blue-backed deck in one of the two deck slots in the round chip rack.

Leverbee took the deck, riffled them quickly then said, "There's no unmarked royal straight flush in the deck."

"Don't kid me, man," replied Fosberg. He took the deck and riffled carefully. His Adams apple began to rise and fall almost in rhythm with the clacking rail joints. He was rapidly becoming panic-stricken. "How did he do it?" he whispered.

"Shit, you are a beginner compared to him. It had to be sleight of hand. Did you notice any unusual hand movements toward the end of the game?"

"No, he just covered his mouth with his hands and handkerchief when he coughed once or twice."

"You, you simple-minded jerk," said Leverbee. Now his eyes were two narrow slits.

"What's his name?"

"His name?"

"Yes, his name?"

Fosberg was in absolute terror. "His name is...is Cooky whatever."

"Cooky whatever? That's no name, only a part of a nickname. What's his real name?"

Fosberg cast a glance at Leverbee's gloved hands. They appeared to him like talons on a giant falcon, slowly folding, unfolding. He was on the verge of fainting. "Something like son of a bitch."

Leverbee said with steely coolness, "Calm down, think."

"I can't remember. I just can't remember," said Fosberg and his neck muscles on the right side twitched as if he had been stricken with some kind of nervous tic.

"By any chance, do you know where he bunks?"

"I do remember that. I saw him stop at bunk 17 in the Laredo car as I was on the way to my roomette. The dirty bastard."

"How about the gray-haired older guy in the game, the one on your right with glasses?"

"What about him?"

"What was his name?"

"I do remember his name, Jay…Jay O'Connor. He was the fourth one in the game."

"How much did he lose?"

Momentarily Fosberg was relieved, his tension lowered. "Nothing," he said.

"How much did he win?"

Now Fosberg's nervousness mounted again. He looked at the floor. "In addition to the four hundred and fifty he put in the game he won twenty bucks. I paid him off last."

"He spent over six hours in the game and only won twenty bucks?"

"Yeah, why?"

"Did it ever occur to you that O'Connor was a reader, was a Fed and was watching you like a hawk?"

"Hell, no. He said he was an insurance broker."

"Just how many guys, good card players would sit around, blow an evening and part of a night for a lousy twenty bucks?"

"How was I to know?" and Fosberg's anxiety was soaring.

"You claim to be a pro?" said Leverbee, calmly smoothing his gloves.

Fosberg, almost numb with terror, murmured, "I didn't know. I just didn't know."

"How about my signals to you?"

Fosberg's eyes were owl wide. "Shit, I forgot all about them. I wondered what the hell those motions of yours were."

Leverbee drew a .38 caliber pistol from his left shoulder holster, reached into a jacket pocket, calmly took out a silencer and attached it to the adapter on the pistol. The right side of Fosberg's face twitched violently. He opened his mouth as if to speak.

"You utter a peep and you will suffer more than you ever imagined a dumb son of a bitch like you could. Turn around," said Leverbee quietly but very convincingly.

Fosberg, gasping, unsteady on his feet, slowly turned and stopped. Leverbee grasped the pistol by the silencer extension, skillfully dealt Fosberg a smart tap with the pistol butt at a certain spot behind Fosberg's right ear. The initiate card shark collapsed to the floor, unconscious, without even exhaling a sigh. Leverbee took off the silencer, replaced his pistol, effortlessly lifted Fosberg onto the lower bunk, turned him on his back and with those black talons, he choked the remaining life from the inept unconscious card crook. Just to make sure, Leverbee placed the berth pillow over Fosberg's face, took Fosberg's belt from his pants, wrapped it around the pillow and Fosberg's head, then tightened the belt securely. The killer stepped back, quietly admired his work, stripped the clothing from Fosberg, counted the remaining funds the dead dealer had in his jacket and stuffed them into his, Leverbee's jacket pockets. He put the dead man's clothing and all Fosberg's gear into Fosberg's suitcase. Leverbee drew from one of his pockets a short length of cord, tied Fosberg's hands behind his back, took the roomette key off the stainless steel sink and with total nonchalance he opened the door to the corridor. After making sure that all was clear he locked the door from the corridor side. With suitcase in hand, he returned to Weaver's roomette. Then knocked on the door.

"Who?" asked Weaver.

"Leverbee," was the calm reply.

Weaver opened the door. Leverbee entered and sat in the same small uncomfortable chair. After placing Fosberg's suitcase near the stainless steel sink, he delivered the reclaimed funds to Weaver. "Fosberg has decided to take a long trip to where it is hot, very hot. He didn't need his clothes to go there so he gave them to me," said Leverbee.

The blonde squirmed, tittered nervously.

"What did he say before he said goodbye?" asked Weaver.

"Not a hell of a lot, but a little. He was scared shitless. I'm sure he knew what was going to happen sooner or later. He knew he had really screwed up. He couldn't think of the sailor's name, just something about a cook. He did remember passing the guy at berth No. 17 in the Laredo car and he did remember the grayhead's name, Jay O'Connor. I'm just sure that bastard is some kind of Fed. I doubt that O'Connor is his real name."

"You could be right," replied Weaver as he reached up with his left hand and scratched his left ear, the one with part of the lobe missing. He thought for a few seconds then commented, "Get that damned sailor and take him to Fosberg's roomette. I want to talk to him before he joins Fosberg." Weaver hesitated, "I think we can make it look like that Navy jerk was lured into Fosberg's roomette and they killed each other even if you have to redress that dead prick."

"Smart, smart, smart," said Leverbee.

"Convince him to come quietly. I'll meet you there."

"No trouble, Boss, I will."

Leverbee walked swiftly through the cars to berth 17 of the Laredo car. He parted the curtains to 17A and took a peek. "I must be going blind," he mumbled to himself. He parted the curtains wider and saw the berth was empty. He looked at the clothes net, it also was empty. There was no sign of a suitcase, a seabag, or any kind of clothes carrier. "What the shit?" he said softly. "It's as if he disappeared into thin air." He closed the curtains, stepped one foot up on the lower bunk, pulled himself up, peeked into the upper berth 17B and quickly closed the curtain. As he stepped down, he shivered slightly, then whispered, "Jesus, two of the ugliest I've ever seen and I've seen a lot." He went to the lavatory in the car and opened the door. The room was empty. Now Leverbee's adrenalin was pumping and he sensed trouble, real trouble. He walked rapidly to Fosberg's door, knocked and hissed, "Quick." Weaver sensed the nervous tone, promptly opened the door.

Leverbee entered Fosberg's roomette, closed the door. While still clinging to the door knob to steady himself as the train went around a tight curve, he said, "There's no sign of that damned sailor and all his clothes are gone."

"What?"

"You heard me right, he's gone, not a sign of him."

Weaver, seated on the end of the berth that held the cooling body of Fosberg, was silent for a couple of minutes, then said, "Lets go back to my quarters, I want to check something." They left the roomette and Leverbee locked the door.

They entered Weaver's roomette. He went to the hanging locker, reached into his suitcoat, pulled out a schedule of the City of San Francisco and studied the timetable. He looked at the blonde in the berth, "Lorraine, get your ass out of that sack. We've got to move and move fast."

"Sure, Punkin," she replied.

Weaver turned to Leverbee. "Go pack your gear and bring it here. We're going to get off at the next stop: Omaha, Nebraska. That will be within two hours. Before we leave we're going to send a message to that Navy bastard if he's around. Where in the shit can he be? The train hasn't stopped once since the game broke up."

Leverbee left to do his boss' bidding, "I wish I knew the name of that sailor. It sure would make things easier," Weaver said over his shoulder to Lorraine as they were dressing. "But I dare not awaken the porter to try and find out. He might get a little nosy. Jay O'Connor," he mumbled as he pulled out a small note pad from an inner jacket pocket and wrote the name on a page.

"Hon, what are we going to do when we get to Omaha?" asked Lorraine.

"First, I'm going to find us a decent hotel room, then call Robin Yeager in Chicago and see if he can put a tail on that blonde wavy-haired navy bastard when he arrives in Chicago."

"S'pose he's not on the train when it gets to Chicago or Robin can't find him?"

"Quit your s'posin," he replied then stopped, looked at Lorraine. "If Robin can't find him and tail him, there could be real trouble down the road somewhere. Just where that somewhere will be, I have no idea." As he was tying his shoe laces he said, "Tomorrow morning I will call the gallery in Georgetown. After that the three of us will catch a train, taking the southern route home. If there was a Fed in the game, he may notify his buddies on how long Leverbee, you and I stayed in that club car. If he finds out what has happened on this train I'm sure he will call ahead to Chicago. Someone might try to put us under surveillance. I won't let that happen."

"Punkin, you're smart, damned smart" said Lorraine. She came over and planted a kiss on his cheek. "That's one of the reasons I like you." Michael Weaver beamed.

Leverbee returned with his packed gear to Weaver's roomette. "Let's go to Fosberg's digs. You untie his hands and remove the pillow then we're going to wrap him in a blanket, take him to that Navy bastard's berth and leave him there stark naked with no ID," said Weaver, and he continued, "That's going to be a message for someone, including the smartass, seagoing punk, wherever he is."

"Good thinking," replied Leverbee. "He may even get the blame for the stuffing."

"Leverbee, you carry the body after you wrap him in a bunk blanket. I'll follow you, so if someone should be up and see us, I'll say our friend passed out from drinking too much. You are carrying him to his berth."

The deed was done quickly and quietly. No one was up or about. Leverbee, still gloved, returned the blanket to Fosberg's berth, tidied up the roomette area, left, locked the door from the corridor side and rejoined the twosome in Weaver's roomette.

"Mission accomplished," said Leverbee.

"Whew, I'm glad that's over," sighed Lorraine. "Now, if we only could find that sailor," she said as the threesome made ready to leave the train.

□

Before dawn, the City of San Francisco stopped at Omaha, Nebraska. Ignatius Pearsall was the conductor on duty. He watched from the station platform as the passengers debarked. He saw the unholy trio leave the train, have a red cap pick up their luggage and head for the station exit. Pearsall glanced at his watch: no need to wake Waddell now. By walkie-talkie he would call him in the early morning and tell him when the trio left the train. When all was clear Pearsall, with his little lantern signaled the watching engineer, reentered the train. The silver serpent sped eastward into the waking hours.

□

At 10:00 that morning the phone rang in the basement of the International Etching and Art Gallery just off M Street in the Georgetown section of Washington, D.C. In a sound-proofed basement office, Warren Cahill picked up the phone. "Cahill here."

"Warren, this is Michael, we're in Omaha, Nebraska."

"How did the sale of the etchings go in Frisco?" asked Cahill.

"Fine. Beaton is still a genius. Not a soul could tell they weren't the originals."

"Why are you in Omaha?"

"We had a problem with one of our new employees on the way back. Just a little change in plans."

"So, the jerk didn't measure up?"

"You could say that. How is the operation?"

"Splendid, Boss. We're on eight trains, not including the City of San Fran. The dealers are smart. We're averaging a total, better than a hundred thou a week in exchange plus our share of the games' take. When do you expect to be back? By the end of the week? Okay. I'll await your regular nightly call from now on at what time? Seven p.m.? Good, I'll be seeing you whenever."

Before Cahill could hang up Weaver said, "Wait a minute, Warren. I've been thinking. You had better notify the 'main frame' on each train as soon as possible that when any member leaves the train and reaches his digs at the end of their current run, to hole up."

"Why?" asked Cahill.

"Because I have a hunch there was a fed of some kind on our train and in the game. If that's true he'll be notifying his buddies of what happened on the San Fran. You can bet your sweet ass, there will be surveillance on most all cross-country passenger trains."

"What service would the fed be from?" inquired Cahill.

"I'll lay you odds he was a Secret Service operative."

"Well, what are your orders, Boss?"

"Have our leaders instruct each team member to lay low, tell them to take it easy until they receive their next instructions from me. I'm already working on a new MO. It will be complete by the time I return to D.C. And, it won't require so much travel."

"Suppose some of the boys get antsy, want to leave?"

"Convince them it's better for their health if they stay." Weaver hesitated then said softly, "There's always the watchdog."

"I understand, Boss. You will call regularly at 7:00 p.m.?" again asked Cahill.

"On the dot, unless the train we will be on is late," replied Weaver and he hung up.

Warren Cahill blinked owl-like through his thick glasses and pondered, "What a setup for Michael and me. It just couldn't be any better than this. I have only been out of Allenwood for a year after a four-year hitch for skimming. Again I am riding on easy street. That Michael is one slick dude. Just how in the hell did he find old Wilfred Beaton, former Boston Academy of Arts instructor, engraver, etcher extraordinaire, alcoholic, genius with a Boston accent so thick you could cut it with a butter knife. And the poor drunken bastard is locked up in that hole in the wall, so-called apartment, just down from my office." Cahill knew Beaton, formerly an employee of the U.S. Bureau of Printing and Engraving, was the engraver of the "C" bill plates now in the soundproof print room next to his office. That office was accessed through a wall panel in his room and that heavy panel was solid oak. Only Weaver knew how to open the panel. There was a hidden electrical switch in his office. Weaver and Beaton operated the presses under tight, soundproofed security. "The product my God, it is beautiful, so authentic. You just couldn't tell it from a real "C" bill," thought Cahill.

CHAPTER 7

Marcus was awakened by Evans banging on his door. "Wake up you double-dealing rascal. Isn't there anything that disturbs your soul, your sleep?"

"Just you banging on the door, Ron," replied Marcus as he looked at his watch. It read 9:30 a.m.

"Well, we've got a number of things to talk about. It's ten-thirty a.m. where we are. Breakfast will be on the conference table in ten minutes."

"I'll be there," answered Marcus.

☐

Around the table sat Comstock, Evans, Waddell and Marcus.

Waddell spoke, "Earlier this morning the train stopped in Omaha, Nebraska. Pearsall reported to me that Leverbee and the young couple got off there."

"Who is Pearsall?" asked Marcus.

"Ignatius (Iggy) Pearsall. He's one of us, but is presently employed under cover, by Union Pacific as a conductor on this train."

"How did he report to you? Did he come into this car?

"No, by walkie-talkie," replied Waddell. It was obvious to Marcus that the calm, restrained senior operative was in charge.

"Why did they leave, if you know?" asked Marcus.

"We honestly don't, could be several reasons. One, to report to their boss what happened in the game. Two, to find out who you are. And three, heaven forbid, because of what might have happened to Fosberg."

"Why that last comment?" asked Marcus.

"Because Fosberg didn't leave with them and his roomette is locked according to Iggy. We'll check on that a little later. Let's eat."

For a brief period there was silence as the four men ate breakfast. Then Waddell resumed the conversation. "Thank God everyone was asleep when you, Evans and I waltzed through the train last night. No one is supposed to use the so-called 'Mail room' door except in a true emergency. We considered your plight to be one."

"How do you generally get from this compartment into the rest of the train?" asked Marcus.

"We have a schedule of every station on the route. By walkie-talkie, we determine where we should be—here in conference and communication or in the train for surveillance. When the train stops at a scheduled station or one requested by us we make such changes as are agreed. The only agent to spend full-time on the train is Iggy. He's the best at really being a conductor."

Evans spoke up. "Waddy, I don't think we should go all the way to Chicago, particularly with Marcus aboard. I'm sure Leverbee or whoever controled the con crew aboard will have managed someway to call ahead and someone will pick up Marcus' trail as soon as he leaves the train. That could be disastrous for him. Marcus isn't hard to describe and his navy uniform is a standout, like a firing range dummy."

"Damn, I never thought about it like that. What am I supposed to do?" asked Marcus.

"We've got plenty of time to make our plans but you're in far greater potential danger than you may have imagined. We just wanted to acquaint you with the facts as we see them," said Waddell.

"Man, you could be right. I've been in the Navy too long. I would have thought about the episode much clearer and acted differently if this happened at the casino."

"Time and place have a lot to do with thinking and reacting," said Waddell. "You're in the civilian world now, also not in the best element of that either."

"I hope you're not talking about us," said Evans. He guffawed. So did the others.

Marcus changed the direction of the conversation. "How about Fatso Baker at the card table?" he asked Waddell. "I hated to see him lose a bundle on that last hand. The officers didn't lose much."

"Don't worry about Baker. His loss last night was like your losing a nickel in a slot machine," replied Waddell.

"And what's that supposed to mean?" asked Marcus.

"He's the CEO and largest stockholder of one of the major munitions companies in the U.S. In addition, he holds a fistful of Union Pacific stock, is on the board of UP, travels first-class free and you can bet your ass he knew he was being taken—maybe not how. Of all the players at the table, it was you he was interested in. I watched him when the game was over. I could tell he was wondering how you were going to dig yourself out of the hole you made by winning the last hand. I'll bet he's making quiet inquiries right now as to your whereabouts. He just couldn't make up his mind whether you were a good guy or a bad guy. He has the instincts of a ferret or he wouldn't be where he is in his business."

"I'm relieved," said Marcus. "I really didn't want to take his money. He'd lost quite a bit during the evening."

"Don't worry," reiterated Evans.

As the foursome was finishing breakfast, a buzzing sounded from the speaker of the Base Station on the table followed by, "Screech, this is Peahead." Marcus looked at Evans.

"That's Pearsall calling Waddell," said Evans. "Screech for screech owl because Waddell is so calm, controlled. It's Pearsall's favorite nickname for Waddy. They've been together for years."

Waddell pressed the sending button. "Go ahead Peahead, what's the problem?"

"Plenty. The Laredo, second car forward of the club car, is in an uproar."

"Why?" asked Waddell.

"Because there's a dead body in 17A."

"That's my bunk," said a surprised Marcus.

"I'm sure it's Fosberg," said Pearsall.

"Who found him?" asked Waddell.

"Jose, the porter."

"Where are you now?"

"In the club car john. I locked the door when I came in."

"Why did the porter find him?"

"Well, some loud-mouthed cow who had upper berth 17B bellyached that the damned sailor below her was sleeping too late. She wanted him to get up so her riding seat would be available to her and her daughter. When Jose stuck his head between the curtains, he saw it wasn't the sailor but some guy he had never seen before. He called me. I investigated and found Fosberg—ice cold—dead and stark naked."

"Damn," thought Marcus, "someone else sees her as a cow too."

"Well, did you cover him up?" asked Waddell calmly.

"First thing," responded Peahead.

Evans and Comstock tittered.

"Can you tell how he died?"

"Sure, Screech. There are glove marks on his neck. His color indicates he was strangled and suffocated. No one heard a sound during the night. I'll bet the body was moved to that bunk from Fosberg's roomette in the Diablo car. I've a feeling somebody is sending somebody a message. I'll use the master key to check his supposed sleeping quarters but I'll bet my next raise there will be no ID."

"What do you propose to do after that?" asked Waddell.

"I have talked to Frank Essig, the Chief Conductor. He is going to make a stop at Clinton, Iowa, bring in the authorities and turn over Fosberg's body to them. I'm sure they will call in the F.B.I. God only knows in what state he was killed."

"Good work," said Waddell.

"Good work, my ass," responded Peahead. "Now that damned mooing female in 17B is raising hell about getting the body off the bunk so she can have her seat. She says she knew that sailor was a killer from the moment she laid eyes on him. She is demanding we search the train for him."

"Tell her politely to go screw," said Waddell.

"Ah, Screech, you know I can't tell her that. I've let her and her daughter go to the club car. That's easing her pain."

"Splendid. How are the rest of the car passengers?"

"Antsy, but waiting to see how things play out."

"Iggy, keep the curtains shut on 17A, assign a porter to keep everyone away from the berth and keep me posted," said Waddell then he added, "Out." The radio went dead.

There was silence for a few moments. "Boys," said Waddell, "When the train stops at Clinton, Iowa we are going to get off. Everybody change to conductors' uniforms. They're in the hanging locker. There's one in there that will just about fit you, Marcus. When all of you finish changing, pack your regular clothing in your suitcases. Marcus, there's a couple extra suitcases in there." He motioned to locker 22. "Repack your gear in them, including your seabag."

Marcus was confounded at the swiftness and completeness of Waddell's orders. "That guy is just a little short of a genius," he thought. It was almost as if Waddell knew he, Marcus, was going to be on the train as well as what would happen. "I wonder how many contingent plans he has stored away in that facile mind of his," mused Marcus as he took the conductor suit handed him, went to his roomette to change and repack. When he reentered the lounge area of the car, the others had completed redressing and were sitting around the table.

Marcus couldn't help but guffaw as he looked at them. "You're one sorry-looking conductor threesome," he said, and his hazel eyes just danced.

Evans laughed, then said, "You didn't get a swell head over your outfit either. The cap is three sizes too big. Let me have it, I'll pack the lining with toilet paper so it will not drop to your ears."

"Okay, boys," said Waddell, "I've radioed ahead. In addition to the authorities and an ambulance greeting the train, I have arranged for a public service car to meet us at the station. I know it's cold as hell outside and there's ten inches of snow on the ground but after our meeting with the authorities we're going to rent an auto with a driver and have him drive us to Chicago. I can't risk us leaving the train at the Chicago terminal."

"What about my family?" asked Marcus. "They and my girlfriend are going to meet me when I arrive."

"We'll arrange for you to call home from Clinton. Make up a good story. You met a buddy. The train stopped. You two got off to stretch your legs and suddenly the train left. Just make it plausible. You'll catch the next train, even if it's a local. Tell them not to meet you at the train station. You will be home as soon as you can," said Waddell.

"My family will accept it. But, my girlfriend, who wrangled the ticket for me is going to be damned upset—even when she sees me."

"Lie like you were married," said Waddell with a smirk.

"I've no experience at that," commented Marcus.

"At what, lying?" jibed Evans.

"No, at marriage," responded Marcus, then he grinned at Evans.

□

The four men made ready to leave the train at the Clinton City station. As they debarked, Waddy turned to Marcus, "What's your street address and home phone number?" Marcus gave him the information. Waddy wrote it down in a small notebook. "Thanks," he said then a slight smile lit his face. Evans looked at his boss, next to Marcus and thought, "You don't know it, old friend, but you've just been hooked."

Marcus stepped from the car platform to the station floor. He heaved a gentle sigh of relief and whispered to himself, "Whew, I was not only ingested but I was damn near digested by the serpent. Thanks to Evans and his buddies, that whole episode for me has turned out kinda' like Jonah in the belly of the whale."

There was a large, black sedan bearing the city logo on the driver's door waiting for them outside the station. Waddy walked over to the driver's side, motioned for the driver to lower the window. He did.

"We're the ones you're waiting for, take us to police headquarters," Waddell said. He turned to his uncomfortable threesome, "Grab your suitcases, we're going to change in the police locker room after meeting with the Chief."

In short order, the four conductor misfits had walked up the granite steps of City Hall and were heading down a corridor to police headquarters. Waddell turned to Marcus. "Clifford Baynard, Chief of Police, together with one of his deputies will be in the Chief's office when we get there. The deputy will take you to a room where you can call your family. The rest of us will be meeting with the Chief for about a half hour. When that confab is over we will meet you out here in the corridor. Then we'll change to our regular clothes and be on our way. But, no talking in the rental auto about what has happened, just small talk. All rental car drivers have big ears and it's going to be a long, cold drive."

Marcus met the deputy, a lank, Midwestern sourpuss who escorted him to a vacant office, pointed to the phone on a desk. In a flat, nasal tone, he said, "Be our guest." Then the deputy left.

"Thanks," replied Marcus. He pulled up a nearby chair, sat, got the long-distance operator, gave her his home phone number, and waited. The phone rang, Marcus heard his mother's lyrical voice, "Bosconovich house, Marla, speaking."

"Hi, Mom, it's me, Marcus."

"You calling from the train?"

"No, I'm at a phone in Clinton, Iowa."

"What are you doing there?"

"Right now, I'm calling you," he responded and guffawed.

"Don't smart apple your mother. Why are you in Clinton?"

"Well, I met a guy. We got off to stretch our legs and the train left without us. I'll take the next local whenever that is. But, don't come to the station to meet me. I'll be home as soon as I can. Please tell Mariana for me. Is she there?"

"No, she and your sister Irma, have gone to a Marshall Fields special sale. They said they needed to pick up a few things. But Mariana is going to be pretty upset when she hears what you have done."

"Mom, I couldn't stop what happened, believe me."

There was something about the tone of that statement that rang true. "Something has occurred," she mused to herself.

"You all right?" she asked.

"Yes, Mom, I'm fine. I'll be home as soon as possible."

"Maybe it's good you called. I just heard the radio news say that about fifty miles east of Clinton there has been a tremendous snow and rock slide that has blocked the UP tracks to Chicago. I'll tell Mariana you called because the train had to stop in Clinton and wait until the slide is removed and the rails repaired."

"No wonder Dad married you. You not only have the angles and the curves, you figure each angle, then drive safely around the curves."

"To hear you talk, one would think you come from an Irish background," jibed his mother.

"Bye, Mom, say hello to the family for me. I'll be there soon. I love you."

"Take care, Bambino mio. Ride the wind with your head up." The phone went dead. She fathoms my every tone, thought Marcus. He hung up his phone and went into the corridor to wait for the surveillance threesome. Not long thereafter, they emerged from the police chief's office. Waddy looked at Marcus and said, "Everything is taken care of. Let's go to the police locker room and change to our regular clothes. Damn, the crotch in these trousers is so tight it's almost rupturing my nuts. Boys, drop the monkey suits in the locker room. Marcus, change your gear to your seabag. I've already made arrangements to have the conductor uniforms and the suitcases you used taken back to the mail car before the train leaves. And it won't be leaving for quite a while. There's been a hell of a snow and rock slide onto the UP tracks, west of Chicago."

"I know," said Marcus.

"How?" asked Waddell.

"My mom told me about the slide when I talked to her by phone a few minutes ago."

"So, you didn't have to lie after all?"

"I did, I didn't know about the slide but she covered for me," replied Marcus.

"Some people get all the breaks," said Evans.

"That includes both of us," responded Marcus. The two men smiled at each other.

CHAPTER 8

Evening approached with a sodden, gray blanket quietly and swiftly covering the sky. A new snowfall was sweeping in from Canada as the black, rental sedan pulled up to the marquee of the Drake Hotel in Chicago. Waddell turned to Marcus on the back seat, "You don't mind taking a cab home from here I hope. I know you can afford it."

"No, that's okay," replied Marcus as he got out of the car. With the aid of the driver he retrieved his seabag from the rack on top.

Waddell rolled down the front window, "You're not going anywhere for the next five or six days are you?"

"No," replied Marcus. "I'm going to spend some time with my family and girlfriend, get released from the Navy, maybe spend a couple days surveying the job market here. After that I'm going to New York for a little R and R."

"Well, if something should happen before I call you and you decide to go to New York, call me before you go. I'll be at this number during the daytime for at least a week. You can reach me later by calling the number on the face of the card." Waddell showed Marcus his business card, turned it over, indicated the local telephone number, handed the card to him, then said, "Please not a word of this episode to your family until I say so."

Marcus nodded in agreement.

Evans hollered from the back seat, "See you soon, buddy," and waved.

Marcus waved back and wondered, "Is that a farewell or a message?" He hailed a cab, slung his seabag onto the rear seat, got in, gave the cabby his address. The ride homeward in the cab triggered past memories for Marcus, among them his mother's oft-told story of how she immigrated to the United States, and met Sergio, his dad. Marla was sixteen when she left Bergamo, Italy, with her uncle Dominic Cavozzi, his wife, Lucia and two daughters. After their arrival in the U.S. they all settled into an apartment in "Little Italy," an area on the south side of Chicago.

Before coming to the U.S., his mother had attended a parochial girls' school on the outskirts of Bergamo. In school she had taken English as a second language and by the time she immigrated to the U.S. spoke it well. For as long as she could remember, she had looked forward to a musical career as a soprano.

Marla's mother died suddenly when she was fifteen. As a result of her mother's death, her father fell into deep despair. In the process he lost his job at the winery. She and her father had been temporarily forced to live with relatives. When her Uncle Dominic decided to bring his family to the U.S., he inveigled her father to let Marla come with them at least until Marla's dad could get back on his feet.

Upon settling in Chicago, Marla obtained a job at La Provincio, a restaurant that featured Italian music during the evenings. In the morning, she, as a part-time student, attended voice classes at the University of Chicago. In the evenings, she was a waitress and singer at the restaurant. About a year after her arrival in the U.S. and while at lunch in the student cafeteria, she sat next to a handsome, solidly built, quiet brunet. She accidentally dropped her luncheon fork onto the floor by his chair. He reached down, picked it up, wiped it off and returned it to her. He had the loveliest smile. "Thank you," she said, and that's when she met Sergio Bosconovich, a senior in the university's school of education.

She learned Sergio had been born and raised in Chicago and that he was five years her elder. His ambition was to be a high school teacher of mathematics. He realized his ambition. Marcus, sitting in the cab, knew he had derived his love of math from his dad. He also knew that Sergio, during his high school days, had been quite a wrestler as well as a good student.

Six months after Sergio met Marla, they were married. Shortly thereafter, his mom gave up her ambitions to be a professional singer and opted for a career as a loving wife and mother. But Marcus's family's home had been filled with music. His mother still sang in the St. Mary's church choir and in a neighborhood chorale. His sister, Bianca, a well paid bookkeeper, could play a mean jazz piano, mostly by ear. Irma, his youngest sister was the real musical talent of the family. She had been studying the cello since she was six years old. She, with her mom and dad, had attended a Chicago Symphony concert and heard Pablo Casals, the famous Spanish cellist as the featured soloist on the program. From that moment on, her quiet drive had been to master that instrument. By the time Marcus joined the Navy, she was playing in local ensembles and loving it.

Marcus had no talent as a musician but he enjoyed music, particularly the big bands. From the time he had been permitted to have a radio in his room at home, he, over the years, had listened to many of the late-night broadcasts, headlining among others the dance bands of Guy Lombardo, the Dorsey Brothers, Ted Fiorrito, Hal Kemp, Isham Jones, Harry James, Duke Ellington and Glen Gray. The different sounds of those musical groups were a source of never-ending pleasure for him. They conjured up all kinds of daydreams. As a result of his love of the big band sound he had learned to dance at an early age. In high school, even in college, he, with the right partner could cut a mean rug whether it was swing, big apple, jitterbug, or some new evolving dance craze. He got a thrill from dancing just as he did from his gymnastics in high school or boxing in college and later.

Marcus's memories faded and he was brought to the present when the cab slid a little on the new falling snow as the yellow turned from the boulevard onto Marcus's home street. The cab driver who had been silent until then turned his head slightly, said to Marcus, "The whole block must have been waiting for your coming home to celebrate Christmas and The New Year."

Marcus looked, his eyes teared just a mite with excitement and thanksgiving. Besides the usual Christmas wreaths on the front doors and the chains of running cedar wound around many of the front stoop railings, on his family's side of the block were small, white paper bags spaced near the curb about six feet apart, each partially filled with sand and into that sand a candle had been placed. The light from those candles through the bags added a welcome glow, gave a delicious spicy scent to the block. He didn't tell the driver that Marla, his mother, had started the extra seasonal touch years ago. It had been adopted by all the homes on his side of the block for over five years. The bags were generally removed the day following New Year's Day. Then he wondered, "What day is it? My God, its New Year's Day." So much happened during the last thirty-six hours, he had forgotten all about New Year's Eve. He had spent it on the train.

"They're not there just for me. They're there for the spirit of Christmas and the New Year. We've been doing it on our block for quite a while," said Marcus.

"Geez, it's kinda' pretty, nice. I'll have to tell my wife," responded the driver.

The cab stopped at the corner row house, Marcus' family's home. He got out, paid and tipped the driver, slung his seabag over his shoulder then said to the cab driver, "Have a good New Year."

"Thanks, sailor, same to you," and the cabby drove off.

Marcus walked up the five steps to the overhead-lighted stoop. For some reason, those steps made him short of breath. Until that moment, he never realized what it really felt like to come home. He rang the door bell. The door opened.

"Holy Christmas — WOW," and, with that exclamation Mariana in a red sweater and blue jeans jumped at Marcus, wrapped her arms around his neck, her lithe legs around his waist, placed her head on his shoulder and let the tears of rejoicing flow.

Marcus dropped his seabag, clutched a railing to keep from being bowled over, wrapped his arms around his soaring eagle companion and his tears almost matched hers.

Bernie, his sixteen-year-old kid brother burst on the scene, seeing Marcus, he yelled, "Mom, Dad, he's here, really he's here." He hugged his brother and Mariana. The doorway was filled with his parents. Mariana untangled herself from Marcus but kept an arm around his waist.

His mother placed her hands on his cheeks, kissed him and said softly, "Thank God, thank God, you're home, safe." She stroked his head and shoulders.

Marcus' dad placed a strong arm around his returning son, kissed him on his cheek and, with hidden emotion, said quietly, "Welcome home, Son. It's so good to have you back."

Marcus could hear feet pounding down the stairway from the second floor. His two sisters, Bianca and Irma, rushed through the hall to the door. They were not to be denied. They pushed their parents, young brother, and Mariana aside and both grabbed at him. They were weeping with joy, speechless at first. Then blonde Bianca spoke, "You weren't expected until late tomorrow. The rock slide hasn't been removed yet. How did you get here?"

"Santa brought me in his sleigh," he replied then grinned.

"I don't give a damn who brought you. We've got you at last," responded Irma as she wiped away tears from her tender, brown eyes with the back of her hand. The two girls hugged their brother and kissed him on his cheeks.

The family, including Mariana, surged into the hall, then into the living room, where a bright log fire was burning in the fireplace. Marcus saw the Christmas creche on the mantel over the fireplace as it had been at this time of the year ever since he could remember. Only sixteen-year-old Bernie was a little behind the rest of his family. He was having a bit of trouble lugging his brother's heavy seabag.

"This is a real unexpected surprise," said his mother.

"A most pleasant one," said his dad as he looked at his son with quiet pride and relief, then he sat in his favorite, overstuffed, brown, leather-covered chair.

"Gee, Brother, you look great, really," said Bernie.

Mariana couldn't help but smile at Marcus' younger brother for those were her sentiments to a tee. "God," she murmured to herself, "Marcus is more handsome than ever and more self-possessed than I've ever seen him."

Bianca, much like her mother, only slenderer, disengaged herself from the family group and headed for the hall clothes closet. Marcus called out to her, "Hey, Sis, where are you going? I've just gotten home."

Bianca turned to him, her dark, blue eyes sparkling, "To my

apartment. We didn't expect you home today. I've got to go. Vincent will be picking me up there at seven o'clock. We're going out to supper."

"Your apartment? Don't you live here?"

"Not any more, big brother, I have my own digs at Shore Towers."

"And who is Vincent?" asked Marcus.

"Vincent McQuire, the guy she is going to get hitched to," responded Bernie.

"You, you're going to be married?" asked Marcus.

"Surely am in May," and Bianca flashed a little diamond engagement ring.

"Holy smoke," said Marcus, "How things are changing."

"Even little girls grow up," said Marcus' dad and then smiled wistfully.

"He's a wonderful man. I worried about her, if she would ever find Mr. Right. But, she knows what she is doing. He's lucky, so is she. They're a good match. Bianca, you better hurry, dear, or you'll be late," said Marcus' mother.

Bianca took her coat from the closet, put it on, came over, gave her mom and dad a good-bye kiss, then walked up to her older brother. She put her hands on his shoulders, tiptoed, kissed him gently on his lips, drew back and looking him squarely in the eye, she said, "He's much like you. You'll like him."

"If he truly loves you, I know I will," replied Marcus. Bianca left.

Mariana's eyes sparkled as she looked at her returning poet and mused, "As powerful a guy as you are, you are by nature the most gentle, considerate human being I have ever known."

Marcus' mother, Marla, hurried to the dining room and added another place setting to the dinner table. Her eldest son was back, thank heavens. "Bring that other dining chair for your brother," said Marla to Bernie. He quickly complied. She beckoned to her daughter, Irma and to Mariana. "Please help me bring in supper." She then nodded to Irma, "When we eat, you sit on that side of the table with Bernie so Mariana can be next to Marcus."

Shortly thereafter, Marla stuck her head into the living room where Marcus, his dad and Bernie were in conversation, "Marcus, Bernie, go to the kitchen and wash up, supper is ready."

Marcus felt a thrill, he was really home. As he left the kitchen and entered the dining room, a chair between Marcus's mother and Mariana was waiting. "You sit there," pointed his mother. "Lets be seated," she said. Then she sat, looked with glowing pride at her gathering. She reached out, took Bernie's outstretched hand and with the other clasped Marcus's hand. "Join hands, bow your heads. Now, Sergio, my dear, will you lead us in a thanksgiving, such a real New Year's blessing," she said quietly.

Marcus reached out and clasped Mariana's outstretched hand. He didn't hear much of his father's blessing because holding back his emotions all but deafened him. They surged like a roaring tide in his ears. Mariana sensed how Marcus felt. She felt it, tightened her grip on his hand, squeezing hard to suppress the outward portrayal of her inner feelings. She need not have worried so about control of her emotions for Marla's tears were dropping unashamedly into the serving of potato soup in front of her.

When Sergio Bosconovich said "Amen," it was repeated by all and napkins dabbed the tears around the table.

Marcus's mother looked at him, smiled, "I'm so glad Mariana published your poems. They're lovely. I don't know where you get it from but I thank whatever ancestor provided the background."

"Some of them are kinda' horny," chimed in Bernie.

"Bernie," said his mother, "They're not horny, just romantic."

"Same thing," replied Bernie and his eyes twinkled as he looked at Marcus.

"Enough, Bernard," said his dad. "Let's change the subject." Sergio looked at Mariana. "Excuse our young son please, his manner of speech in some ways is not yet adult."

Mariana was all but convulsed as she tried her best to hold back her laughter. She half hid her mouth with her napkin, coughed and said, "That's okay, I understand." Marla winked at Mariana.

Marcus sat grinning, like the proverbial Cheshire cat, realizing how like Mom Bernie is, only young and rough around the edges.

"Let's eat," said Marcus' dad and they did. When supper was being concluded, Marla turned to her young son, "Bernie, when you finish, take your brother's seabag to his study on the third floor."

"Sure, Mom, I better do it now or I'm liable to forget." He left to fulfill the mission.

"Marcus," said his mother, "Mariana is using your bedroom.

You'll have to use the sleep sofa in your study, the front room. You two will have to share the connecting bath. Your old bed is gone, I gave it to the Salvation Army."

Marcus wondered why in the world did she get rid of it. Bernie came bounding back into the dining room and again took his seat.

"What's wrong with it?" asked Marcus, "I was raised in that bed."

"Well, son, it wasn't really a bed but a big old cot. The mattress never did fit right. Besides, after you entered the Navy and when Lucia, Uncle Dominic's wife died and he went to live with his daughter Isabella, he gave me the Cavozzi family bedstead. Its been in our family for generations."

"It cost a fortune to have the springs and mattress made for that monstrosity," said his dad.

"You should see it," said Bernie. "It's almost as big as a boxing ring. The curved, wooden headboard and footboard make it look like one heck of a big old-fashioned sleigh."

"It's very comfortable," said Mariana and she grinned at Marcus.

"Thank you Mariana, it's one family heirloom I want to keep. Marcus' room and bath will serve as our guest quarters when you're gone for good, Marcus," said his mother.

"Too big," responded his dad soberly. Then he turned to Marcus. "Son, have you given any thought as to what you want to do when you leave the Navy?"

"I hope you don't go back to work at the casino," said his mother.

Marcus smiled. "That was just an adventure but it did give me time to try my hand at poetry."

"Marcus wouldn't have trouble getting a job in New York with any number of good publications I know of. Fact is, I'm going to talk with him about that later," said an interested Mariana.

"Good," replied Marla, "It's time he settled down." She smiled knowingly at Mariana.

Sergio, still a solidly-built man in his late fifties, a Liberty High School math teacher, arose, so did Bernie. "I'm coach of the high school wrestling team. Bernie's in the 135-pound class. We have a team meeting tonight, no workout, just some strategy talk," Sergio said to Marcus, then turned to his wife. "We'll be home early, about ten o'clock."

"See you tomorrow morning, brother," said Bernie, and the two left.

Marcus, Marla and Mariana cleared the table, washed and wiped the dishes, put them away, then went to the living room. Marla and Mariana sat on the sofa, Marcus was in his dad's lounging chair. He turned to his mother, "Dad looks just fine and, my God, how Bernie has grown."

"He has," responded Marla, "He's doing well at school, but he's going through the trouble stage. Girls—they seem to gravitate to him."

"It runs in the family," said Mariana, her eyes twinkling. Marcus scowled.

"And his mouth," continued Marla, "He has a sense of humor but it's too raunchy for your dad. Many of Bernie's humorous comments bother him. When you get a chance talk to your brother, tell him to calm it down a little, just a little. He has yet to listen to me."

"I will, Mom. Don't worry, he'll come out on the right side. He's just beginning to feel his—ah—oats," said Marcus.

Mariana was delighted with the interchange between mother and son and thought, "What a lovely relationship the family has." At that moment from upstairs came the solemn strains of a cello. Mariana realized that Irma had quietly disappeared, almost as soon as supper ended. Mariana thought. "Except for her, she is the quiet one, and golly, she has reason to be, but how long must it last?"

Marla listened, then turned to Marcus, "You know, Irma now plays in the symphony. But, that's not helping much. I wish we could get her to go out more. She really needs to."

"Isn't Irving Feldstein home? He entered the service so early, I just supposed he was home from the Army. What happened between Irma and Irving?" asked Marcus.

Before Marla could answer, he turned to Mariana. "Irving is a quiet one like Irma. They've been good friends and more almost since the day they were born—about the same time. He lives next door."

"I know," replied Mariana, her eyes portraying a look Marcus couldn't at that moment fathom.

"Did," said his mother.

"Did what?" asked Marcus.

"Did live next door. He was killed in the Battle of the Bulge," she said softly.

"Oh, no," whispered Marcus. He remembered the last time he saw Irma and Irving together, and they were together. He had returned home one night after a date not long before he left to go back to Reno, Nevada and his work at the casino. His mother had told him previously that Irving was going to leave the University of Chicago. He had been drafted and was going into the Army. Marcus then realized that Irma had a pained expression, really an aching expression in her eyes for several days prior to the time his mother told him Irving was leaving. He understood that his sister was genuinely in love with Irving and he with her but there had never been any talk of marriage. They were too young.

After returning to his room that night Marcus had stepped out on the upstairs, covered porch off his bedroom for a look at the clear, full moon-lit night before he retired. While standing on the upstairs back porch he happened to look down into the Feldstein back yard. In an open space among some heavy-leafed bushes, he saw Irma and Irving, fully clothed, lying on a blanket. There was no wild episode ongoing. They were wrapped in each others arms, two adult human beings, affectionately and almost desperately holding each other. He just couldn't look any more. He didn't want to invade their privacy. Now, he realized it was as if they knew what was going to happen. "Oh, shit," he said, looking down at the floor and forgetting that his mother and Mariana were in the room.

"Marcus!" his mother admonished sharply.

Mariana reached over, gently put her hand on Marla Bosconovich's arm and shook her head quietly from side to side.

"I'm sorry," he replied, "I know Irma is hurting so. I don't know what to do."

"Except your just being you, her caring brother, you can't do anything that will really help. She has to," said Mariana.

Marcus looked wistfully at Mariana, nodded in acquiescence and said softly, "You're right."

"What a fine woman Mariana is. I hope Marcus truly recognizes it," thought his mother as she looked first at her son and then at his girlfriend.

Marcus, his mother and Mariana engaged in light conversation for quite a while. Finally, Marla spoke up, "I've had a long, fulfilling and exciting day. I'm going up, relax and read in bed, hopefully until your father and Bernie return. They're like two kids when it comes to wrestling. They're worse than you were, Marcus, at your high school gym team meetings. They never come home on time from one of those gatherings." She hesitated, looked with affection at them. "Besides, you two haven't had a moment alone. Good night, dear ones." She arose, blew each of them a kiss.

"Good night, Mom, it's great to be home."

"Good night, Marla," said Mariana. "You've provided a lovely evening."

Marcus' mother smiled at the twosome over her shoulder then went upstairs.

Mariana looked at Marcus, patted the sofa cushion beside her, the one his mother had just left. "Come sit where you belong," and Marcus needed no further bidding. He took her in his arms, tenderly kissed her eyes, her mouth. She responded with fervor, fervor from a year and a half of longing. He finally drew back and with those hazel eyes sparkling asked, "Is Uncle Dominic's bed big enough for two?"

"Who needs a bed?" queried Mariana and the sparkle in her eyes matched his. "But, to answer you, yes. Bernie is right. That bed is nearly as big as a boxing ring. We might get lost in it."

"Never," replied Marcus. "But, before we go to bed, I've got to take a shower. I really had some sweaty moments on that train. I know I stink."

Mariana sensed a problem but let it pass. "Marcus Bosconovich, you never stink, I love every aroma from you, but if it makes you feel better, take a shower—not a cold one." Then she giggled. Taking his hand, the twosome climbed quickly to the third floor.

□

Marcus came out of the bathroom freshly showered and in his PJ bottoms. His bedroom was dark except for the glow of the street light that filtered in from the windows to his bedroom screened porch. He looked at the bed.

"It does look like a big sleigh," he said.

"Yes, it does, Darling," replied Mariana as she lay in the enormous antique bed. "But, where are the horses?"

"Oh, we'll just pretend they're galloping."

"That won't be hard to do," quipped Mariana. She burst out laughing and held out her arms to Marcus. In a twinkling, off came the PJs and he was in bed.

"Oh, my God," she said, "It has been so long. I was afraid you might never return. I would feel even worse than Irma does if that had happened."

Marcus wrapped his arms around her and she drew him close to her, as if to enfold all of him in her. His lips sought hers in unrestrained passion and their tongues fought to possess each other. Suddenly, she drew back in mock seriousness. "What balloon ride are you planning?"

Marcus looked at her in amazement. "What did you say?"

"What balloon ride are you planning?"

"What in the world are you talking about?"

"This," she said, then reached down and started to roll back the condom he was wearing. She had felt it on her groin.

"Gee, that's for your protection."

"Do you always take a bath with your socks on?" she jibed.

"Look, I was only thinking of you."

"Well, don't," and she continued to furl his flag.

Marcus was now becoming really perturbed. She laughed quietly, kissed him on his forehead. "Darling," she said, "I want you not some rubberized covering."

"But, Mariana."

"No buts," followed by the soft, gentle voice he loved. "I'm in love with you and sure I'm Catholic, but not a dumb zealot. When I knew you were coming home, I went to a gynecologist who fitted me with a diaphragm. I'm using it tonight. I truly want you, all of you. I love you so much, but any family we have will be mutually planned, I hope. If only I could express how I feel, like you do with your poetry."

"Oh, my God, Mariana, you've expressed it by your action better than any poet ever could."

They were on fire with their passion, but there was a mutual feeling of unity that surmounted their eroticism. She turned onto her back, spread her legs, bent her knees and, as he kneeled between them, she pushed his wavy hair from his forehead with one hand. With the other, she helped guide his sensitive friend into her moist opening. "Beloved," she whispered to him, "Welcome home." And she threw all restraint to the winds. Her arms wrapped around his neck. Their mutual rhythm increased in intensity. The horses were galloping. She pulled her mouth away from his and moaned, "Now, now, please now." Marcus was ready. She felt the surge within her and he felt the emission. For both it was ecstasy.

"Oh, Marcus," she whispered, "It is worth all the waiting and I'm not through yet."

"Neither am I," replied a gasping Marcus. "But, it will take me a little more time than you," and he guffawed.

He was now beside her. "I know how to handle that," she said, then reached down and started to caress his moist, limp friend. She leaned against him pressing her breasts against his chest. Their tongues again met. She leaned back and with loving tenderness, said, "Raise up, let me draw my left leg up under you. It will be more comfortable for both of us." He did and then he caressed her version of his best friend. She raised her right leg over his left thigh. "Now," she said, "I want you again but we can take our time, know the real meaning of union." Once more he was a part of her. Her blue eyes beamed at him. "This is as it should be and I hope forever."

"Oh Mariana, it couldn't be better than this," gasped Marcus.

She looked into those lovely hazel eyes and replied gently, but meaningfully, "Oh, yes it can, and will be if we truly love each other. It takes a while for any two people really in love to learn how to satisfy each other physically, emotionally and spiritually. But, oh, what a beginning we have made." She felt the increasing hardness of her future mate. He began to thrust and she responded. Both of her arms were again wrapped around his neck, her breath came in gasps as she neared another orgasm. "My beloved, are you ready?" she whispered.

"Whenever you say," he responded breathlessly.

She answered excitedly, "Now, and I want all of you." She pressed against him as hard as she could. He came, she moaned and reached orgasm, pressed, released, pressed again, then went limp. "Thank God you're mine and I'm yours," she said ever so softly.

Marcus caressed her face, her breasts with loving gentleness. "I've come home to so much more than I ever dreamed of and I've dreamed a lot. I not only love you, I'm in love with you," and he smiled.

Mariana returned the smile, kissed him on his cheek. "Can I have my leg back?"

Marcus guffawed, "For now," he replied.

Mariana withdrew her leg, stretched it and heaved a sigh of womanly contentment.

"Turn away from me, let me cup you like two old married people," he said.

"I'm afraid I'll go to sleep if I do that. What if your mother or a member of your family should see us, find us here?"

"That won't make any difference, we're going to be legally married soon."

Mariana turned, looked at him. "Is that a proposal?"

"Could it be anything else? I'm already married to you, you to me and you know it."

"Good night, my beloved husband," she said, kissed him on his cheek, turned her back to him, nestled against his chest, and drew his hand over her, onto her breast. She sighed, kissed the back of his hand. In no time she was fast asleep.

Never in his life had Marcus felt so fulfilled. Mariana really was his wife in every way, but by law. He wanted no other. He was in love and knew he was loved. What more could a guy ever ask for?

Then, for a brief spell he felt sorrow. Sorrow for Sam. He thought, "If only she could have grown up normally and found a guy she could truly love, live with. I know it would not have been me. But, I am damned glad I had the experience with her rather than what I set out to do. I would now be ashamed to be with Mariana if I had found a dirty screw that night. Marcus Bosconovich, you are still one lucky bastard." With his arm over his beloved Mariana, he too drifted off to a needed and restful sleep.

During the night Marcus awakened to go to the bathroom. When he returned, Mariana, aroused, turned to him, "Let's try again," she said. And they did, so successfully. Quickly thereafter both dropped into deep sleep.

$$\square$$

Mariana awakened the next morning refreshed and full of piss and vinegar, as Marcus would say. She looked at her sleeping, beloved dreamer and husband, for truly, he was her husband, kissed him on his cheek, slid out of bed, took her shower, quietly dressed then hurried down to the kitchen to help Marla with breakfast. She could hear her future mother-in-law singing softly as she was preparing the meal. Mariana entered the kitchen.

Marla looked up and smiled. "You had a nice night." It wasn't a question but a statement.

117

"Yes, I surely did," replied a grinning Mariana.

"Do you truly love him?"

"Why do you ask? You know the answer." Her eyes danced with joy as she looked fondly at her future mother-in-law.

"Has he asked you to marry him?"

"What is she driving at?" wondered Mariana.

"Yes," she answered.

"What did you say?"

"Marla, you know darn well what I said."

"Well, what did you say?" and Marla was laughing quietly.

"I said yes."

"When?" asked Marla.

"Soon. As soon as we can set a sensible date."

"Now," said Marla, "Now, I can talk to you like a future daughter-in-law."

Mariana was slightly perplexed.

"Do you remember I told you to try not to roll over on the right side of Uncle Dominic's bed?" Marla could hardly contain herself, keep from bursting out laughing.

"I vaguely remember something like that."

"Thank God you didn't remember it last night."

Mariana just couldn't figure Marla. She looked questioningly at her.

"The flooring in Marcus' bedroom isn't quite level. Every time someone moves on the right side of that bed it sounds like Bernie riding a pogo stick on the third floor. It reverberates to the second floor. Heavenly days and nights, it is loud."

Mariana began to get the drift of Marla's conversation. She started to giggle.

Marla continued, "The rhythmic pounding so excited Sergio for the first time in ten years, we did it twice last night. It was lovely."

Mariana exploded. She laughed until tears came. Then she hugged Marla and thought, "What a lovely, natural woman you are. I would be your friend if there was no Marcus. You are younger in spirit than I."

Marla looked with serious affection at her future daughter-in-law. "You be careful my lovely child you're not married yet."

Mariana, looking into Marla's eyes, quietly said, "Yes, we are in every way except for that little piece of paper. I promise we'll have that soon. And yes, I am being careful."

Marla couldn't help herself. She wrapped her arms around Mariana, gave her a loving hug, stepped back and said, "Thank God you found him. He will need you more than you ever imagined. You're good for him. I only hope he makes you happy. My daughters I love because they're mine. You I love because of who and what you are whether or not you marry Marcus." She kissed Mariana on her cheek then said, "But, I pray to God you do."

She looked over her future daughter-in-law's shoulder. "Oh, my, those scrambled eggs are going to be hard as rock." She hastily took the skillet off the stove. "Go, sit down at the table. I hear the rest of the family straggling to breakfast. I'll serve it."

Mariana went light-hearted from the kitchen, sat in her designated seat and watched as her future-in-law family came in for breakfast, "What an unusual, delightful family. I wish I could say the same for mine," she reflected.

☐

Breakfast repartee was light but constant. Always in the background was a hint of the night music from the third floor. Marcus grinned, said nothing. From time to time, Mariana giggled but gave no explanation. When breakfast was over, the family pitched in removing the dishes from the dining room to the kitchen. As they finished, Marla turned to them and said. "All of you get out except Marcus. I want him to help me wash and dry."

"I'll help," said her husband.

"No, you won't," replied Marla. "You heard me." The family members left the kitchen, except for Marcus. He knew his mother wanted a private confab. He looked at her with love and pride, "Though mom is a little plumper now she is still a truly beautiful woman. So much of it comes from inside. In that respect, she is so like Mariana," thought Marcus.

Marla reached out, closed the door to the dining room, then turned to her son.

"Do you love her, not just with that thing," and she pointed, "But from deep in here and here?" and she pointed to her breast and then her head.

Marcus knew that as lightly as she asked the question she was genuinely serious. "Yes, Mom," he answered, "With every bit of me.

There are times when I am truly surprised how well she knows me, almost my every thought."

"She does," said Marla and continued, "Have you asked her to marry you?"

"I have."

"And, what did she say?"

"She said yes."

"I know," said his mother, "I just wanted to hear it from you. Marcus, you are a grown man. You've been graced with a good body and mind. That can be either a help or a detriment. You're the one to determine that. There are all kinds of adventures through life but thrill-seeking doesn't make for a very stable life or love. And your gambling work, though you made good money was for you thrill-seeking, I can tell. I was afraid you'd fall into the hands of crooks, the mob, but I know you haven't." She stopped and looked seriously at her son. "Mariana knows you haven't also. You were flirting with danger the whole time."

Marcus looked at his mother. "I'm ready to settle down but I've got to pick my own career."

"I like that," said his mother, "I know Mariana well enough to say she will never stand in your way whatever your endeavor may be. She'll be a good support and don't you forget it. She is, without doubt, one of the finest women I have ever met barring nobody.

"At times she may appear a little positive, that's the business side of her. But her love for you is so very adult and real. She's amazing. I love her not only because she loves you but for what she is and she knows her own faults. She's human. You be good to her—real good to her, do you hear me?"

Marcus smiled. "I knew you liked her the minute I heard your voice in the background on her call to me in Frisco. I'll never knowingly let either of you down. Yes, I'll do my damnedest to be good to her."

"I believe you, my first *bambino*," then she caressed his face. With her right hand she reached inside the neckline of her dress, into the crevice of her full bosom and pulled out a little black ring box. She held it in her hand, opened it for Marcus to see.

"Holy Christ," he gasped, "It is gorgeous. I never saw it before. You've never worn that ring."

"No. I love what your father has given me during the years." She held out her left hand with the small diamond engagement ring in a Tiffany setting and her wedding band. Then she held out her right hand with the small emerald surrounded by diamond chips. "I would never want to hurt his feelings because underneath that rugged exterior, he is so sensitive. This ring was my mother's engagement ring and her mother's. How far back it goes, I don't know. But, you, as my oldest son, I want you to give it to Mariana if she will accept it as her engagement ring. I don't mind your telling her where it came from. She can have it sized to fit her finger. If she won't take it, I will understand. Here," and she handed the ring to Marcus.

For a moment Marcus was speechless then asked, "How long have you had the ring?"

"My father gave it to me when I returned to Italy as he, in the early 1930s lay dying. My mother had died years before but he just couldn't part with it until he knew he would soon be leaving this mortal coil. The ring was his constant reminder of her. Your dad knows nothing about it. I've never told him and have kept it safely hidden. Mariana deserves the ring. She'll know the value, which by the way is almost as much as this house. I've had the diamond appraised."

"How can I ever thank you, Mom?"

"By really making her happy. Don't give it to her in the presence of the family. Just give her the ring in private. She'll understand."

Marcus hugged his mother with more emotional strength than he realized. He released his hold. She gasped for breath.

"Look, I'm not young like Mariana," she gasped. "I know you love me, but don't squeeze me to death." She breathed deeply to refill her lungs.

Marcus guffawed.

"Go on out, join the family, I'll do the dishes. Just keep your mouth shut about this conversation," said his mother.

Marcus left the kitchen. His feet hardly touched the floor. "How lucky I have been all my life," he murmured as he went into the living room. Mariana wasn't there. "Where's Mariana?" he asked.

"Ah, she's gone upstairs to clean her teeth and take a..."

"Bernard!" loudly exclaimed his father.

"Take a glass of water," said Bernie smugly.

Marcus went to the third floor. He looked. Mariana was in his bedroom, in front of the dresser mirror, just before putting on her lipstick. "Hon," he said, "When you finish, come into the study. I want to talk with you for a few minutes."

"Sure," responded Mariana. Even before she had come upstairs after breakfast, she had decided the time was ripe for her to talk quietly, seriously with him. When he asked her to come into the study, she decided not to put on the lipstick, then walked into Marcus' mental playground. He patted the sleep sofa cushion next to where he sat. "Close the hall door and come sit beside me where you belong," he said, mimicking her invitation of the evening before. She joined him. He turned her face to his with those hazel eyes flashing, and calmly asked, "Will you marry me?"

"I thought we settled all that last night?"

"Just answer me yes or no, will you marry me?"

She could just see the devil in those flashing eyes. She wasn't sure what was to follow. "I don't believe you want me to say no," she kidded.

"Please," he begged, "Just answer yes or no."

"Yes," she said, kissed him gently on the cheek, drew back and waited.

He pulled the box from his pocket, opened it, took out the ring, "Hold out your engagement ring finger, let's see if this fits."

She held out her finger and, much to Marcus' surprise, the ring slid on as if it had been sized for her.

"Great Caesar's ghost," gasped Mariana. "Where in the world did you get that?" Marcus was surprised for Mariana seemed to be in real shock.

"Why? Does it make any difference?"

"Do you know what you have just put on my finger?"

"A ring, an engagement ring."

"Oh, Marcus," she said. "This isn't just a ring. It's an exquisite, large, antique, European-cut diamond, in a platinum Florence mount. This ring is worth a fortune."

Marcus was flabbergasted. "How do you know?"

"Well, my family and relations are not exactly destitute. My great uncle Flavion McClaron is still alive in Rotterdam, Holland. He's a diamond merchant. We have several books on diamonds and mountings at home. He gave them to my dad a long time ago. Every year Flavion comes over to sell to the diamond market, Tiffany's and others. Being a gal, I was naturally interested in such things. I'm no gemologist, but I have read about and can recognize certain basic cuttings and settings. This gives me the shivers." She held the ring up toward the ceiling light to see the prismatic effect. "Really, Marcus, where in the world did you get it?" She looked at him, read his expression. "Oh my God, beloved, it was your mother's."

"And her mother's and her mother's," replied Marcus. "My dad doesn't even know she had it. She just couldn't tell him when she returned from her father's funeral in Italy years ago. I want you to have the ring, so does she."

Mariana put her hands to her face, wept quietly. Then she reached into her jeans pocket, pulled out a kleenex, wiped her eyes, blew her nose, turned to Marcus and said, "I'll cherish the ring like no other gift in my life." She put her arms around his neck, pulled him to her and they kissed with a depth of feeling that left passion in the gutter. When she drew away, she told him, "Marcus, I'll wear the ring every day of my life but I insist on having it appraised, then I shall carry a rider on my insurance policy. Do you realize this is the kind of jewel that real thieves look for? When my mother sees this she'll want to mud wrestle me for it. I'm not kidding, Darling, this is the kind of ring that makes women wear gloves when they go out in public, not just eye-catching, it's breath-taking. Your mother,"—she stopped, sighed, looked at Marcus, then said, "You can't understand but I already love her more than mine, much more." She looked at the ring, her eyes clouded, "We are two of a kind, I won't flash it, I dare not."

She arose, "Excuse me a minute, I'll be right back." Mariana left the study, went through the bathroom to her suitcase in Marcus' bedroom. She returned shortly with a small folder then sat next to her love. "Marcus," she said, "We've got to talk business for a moment." She brought out two sets of documents, each containing six pages, flipped to the last pages, took a fountain pen that had been clipped to the folder and gave it to him. "Sign both of these right here," and she pointed.

"What in the world are those?" Marcus asked.

"Just sign them, then I'll tell you."

"Tell me first."

"You do trust me, don't you?"

Marcus frowned, looked at her quizzically. "Certainly, Darling," he said in a rather tentative voice.

"Well, sign them."

He did, not having the slightest idea what he had signed but he was perturbed at Mariana's apparently complete change in demeanor. Then he looked at her. "What are they?"

"The contracts for the royalties on your poems," she said sweetly. "Here," and she handed him a certified check from The Purple Canary Press for twenty-two thousand dollars.

"Holy smoke! What is this for?"

"Seventeen thousand for your royalties and five thousand for your poetry prize. I was afraid you wouldn't sign the contracts if you knew what they were. I have to be as fair with you as I am with any other poet or writer I publish."

"I don't want—I don't need…"

"It's not a question of want or need, my beloved, you've earned it. I've made my fair share from the sale of the books. You and the other two poets have made the book possible and successful."

Marcus was looking at her in an almost befuddled manner. He'd never given a thought to making money from the poems. He had written them because he had to. Something inside compelled him to struggle, to try. Yet even when they were finished, there was always something about them he thought he could and should change for the better.

She was once again the soft, loving creature he adored. "My beloved dreamer," she said, "I know you didn't expect a cent from them. Like the rest of you they are far better than you realize. That's one just one of the reasons I love you so and always will."

Marcus swept into his arms the wellspring, the source that triggered the creative juices of all types within him. He was truly aroused. He untwined his arms, got up, walked to the bathroom door to the bedroom, locked it from the bathroom side, returned, locked the study door to the hall and turned to Mariana. "I'm going to unfold the sleep sofa and you better get that thing-a-ma-jig-diaphragm."

She grinned then started taking off her blue jeans. "I knew I had to have the business talk with you alone. I didn't have the slightest idea about the ring. But I hoped my talk with you would end as you have just suggested. I put that thing-a-ma-jig back in when I came up to brush my teeth." Already she was out of her jeans, panties and slipping the sweater over her head. Marcus lost no time. His clothes flew off.

He was sitting on the edge of the sleep sofa finishing taking off his shoes and socks when he felt her warm breasts against his back. Her arms wrapped around him as she leaned over his shoulder. "I love you so unashamedly, unfettered by false modesty that I just ache thinking about it and you," then she giggled softly. In her lovely, soft voice she continued, "We're only physically young once. For how long that will be, God alone knows. I do want us to have so many wonderful memories of our youth that they will truly keep us young at heart forever." She pulled him back, down onto the sofa bed and almost instantly was on top, straddling him. All of her was inviting him in. He lovingly accepted the invitation and entered with youthful passion.

He gazed into those lovely blue eyes looking down at him, caressed her firm breasts, leaned up and kissed her hardened nipples, dropped back onto the bed then with increasing excitement said, "Marcus Bosconovich, you are lucky, so very lucky."

"So is Mariana Lucas Bosconovich," said his love. She leaned down and tenderly kissed him on his lips. Then she pressed her groin against his, again, again, again. They were in Shangrila.

□

The phone rang. "I'll get it," said Bernie. He went into the living room, picked up the phone from the table. "Bosconovich residence, Bernie speaking. You want to speak to my brother? Just a minute."

His mother was standing by him. "Who is it?"

"Some guy named Waddell wants to speak to Marcus. I'll go get him."

His mother took the phone, put her hand over the mouthpiece. "No you won't. You stay right here." She took her hand off the mouthpiece. "Mr. Waddell, this is Marcus' mother. He's busy right now. Can he call you back in thirty minutes?" She listened. "Fine," she said, "I'll give him the number." She hung up the phone, turned to her young son, "Bernie, Marcus and Mariana are discussing some important business. They'll be down shortly."

"Like the business they discussed most all last night?" he asked.

"Not exactly," said his mother, "They've got some things to work out."

"I hope they don't work them out on Uncle Dominic's bed. They're liable to bust the ceiling in my bedroom if they do." He left the room giggling.

His mother watched him go and couldn't help but laugh also. "You're one observant, growing-up rascal," she said to herself.

Then she decided the time was now to have an adult talk with her young son. "Bernie," she called, "Come back for a moment." Bernie reappeared. "Sit beside me, we've got to have a little chat." Bernie saw she was serious, sat beside her.

"Yes, Mom."

"There is a time for jest and humor, and you do have a wonderful, slightly raunchy, sense of humor. And there are times for thoughtful consideration. Your brother has come home unscathed from one of the most horrible wars in human history. He has come home to a woman, an adult woman, regardless of her beauty and youthfulness. He loves her, she loves him. They are most fortunate to have found each other. Do you understand me?"

Bernie was awed and thrilled that his mother would at last treat him as if he really was growing up, not the smart alec kid he seemed most of the time.

"I know that, Mom, I really like her. I think she will be good for Marcus or I wouldn't kid about it. I don't mean any harm. I'm proud of them both. But you've got to admit that damned bed was disturbing last night."

"Yes, it was," and she grinned momentarily. "Your time will come in the future. If you're as fortunate as Marcus, I will be doubly thankful. If you're as honest and straightforward about a loving relationship with some girl who will be your wife, you will be as blessed as Marcus and Mariana. Not all life is soundless, sightless or secretive. Some evidence of unity between a loving man and woman is always apparent even if it is no more than your dad and me holding hands in the living room. That's not dirty. Neither is sex by loving couples. Your brother and Mariana are going to be married soon. 'Screwing around,' as you call it is dirty. However, true love between a man and woman does include sex. It's one of the great unifying parts, the glue that helps hold them together through life. And there will be troubled times for them as there are for all of us. We're human and imperfect. A great deal of hurt that happens in life can be healed by two people in love. Part of that healing includes lovemaking. It's not just for the conception of children. That's not exactly the church's view, but it's mine, I've lived by that view. Your father and I have had a wonderful loving life. Want to make fun of that?"

Bernie looked at his mother in awe. "No, no, no. I hadn't given it much real thought before. And I do begin to understand what you've told me. In the past I've thought around the edges of what you were talking about. But you've put it to me for the first time in a grown-up way. I know you and Dad love each other. I am comfortable with that knowledge and proud to be your son. When you say 'love,' I know it means more than sex. How much? You are the first to help me understand. I'll kinda' have to grow into that understanding. You've really helped to direct me. But can't I kid about it just a little. To me, kidding about their mutual affection just a little makes the true meaning of love more honest, natural and open not hidden or dirty."

"You are maturing, my little one. Yes, you can kid just a little and knowing you you will. Please think twice before you do to make sure you're advocating love not belittling life."

"I'll have to do some thinking on that too," replied Bernie.

She kissed him on his forehead. "Go down into the basement and get the other snow shovel. Then go help your dad. The walkway and sidewalk are covered with eight inches of new snow. You think about what I've said while you are shoveling."

Marla arose, went about her household chores. Bernie sat and contemplated for a few seconds. When he got up to get his parka and gloves, he said to the room, "Marcus and Mariana are lucky. I wonder if someday I will be as lucky." Then, as he headed for the basement steps, he started thinking about the next wrestling match.

☐

Marla was puttering around the living room when she heard Marcus and Mariana coming down the stairway. She went into the hall, waiting for them. When they reached the first floor level she said, "Marcus, a Mr. Clarence Waddell telephoned a few minutes ago. He would appreciate a call from you. Here's his number." She handed him the note paper on which she had written the number.

"Who is Mr. Waddell?" asked Mariana.

"A guy I met on the train coming east," answered Marcus. "He's staying in Chicago for a few days."

127

Mariana was carefully studying her lover, her husband-in-fact. Something about his tone of voice bothered her. As casual as his reply had been there was just a trace of tension in his whole demeanor.

"Did you play cards on the train?" she asked.

"Sure did."

"With him?"

"Yep."

"Do you owe him some money?"

"No, Dear, not a cent."

"Does he owe you any money?"

"Not a dime."

"Well, why is he calling you?"

"We became friends. He said if he had the time we might have lunch together during his stay. He really is a regular guy. I'll call him in a few minutes."

Marla and Mariana exchanged glances.

"Did any of the other card players stop over in Chicago?" asked Marla.

"Really, Mom, I have no idea. But, Waddy and I kinda' hit it off together."

"Sounds reasonable," said Marla and she headed into the dining room, from the dining room to the kitchen.

Mariana's blue eyes were anchored on Marla. "Excuse me," Mariana said to Marcus. She followed Marla, caught up with her in the kitchen. "Never, never in my life did I expect anything like this," she said and raised her hand with the exquisite ring.

Marla smiled. "You will have earned it if you truly love him and stick by him. He does love you dearly. But because of what nature gave him in both mind and body he doesn't view the world like most of us even like most men."

"Thank God," replied Mariana, "I know that."

"At times his outlook on life might be really troubling," said Marla.

"At times all life can be," responded Mariana.

"Oh boy, how right you are. But my dear child he doesn't know that yet."

"Maybe you're right, Marla. I'll just have to wait and see. Regardless of what happens I'll still love him."

"I know that and so does he." Marla kissed her future daughter-in-law on the cheek. "The ring is where it should be," she said and left the room to continue her chores.

Mariana went in search of Marcus and heard him talking on the den phone.

"When?" he asked. "Sure, Waddy I can meet you at the hotel grill at noon day after tomorrow. Thanks for calling. I'll see you."

Mariana, standing nearby, asked "Am I included?"

"Nope, just boy talk," and he smiled a beguiling smile at Mariana.

"I'm going to call my dad and tell him we're engaged. Then I'm going to call my office," said Mariana.

"Be my guest," replied Marcus. He arose from the chair by the phone, kissed Mariana on her cheek, grabbed his pea jacket and said, "I'm going out to see how Dad and Bernie are coming along with their snow shoveling."

☐

When Marcus came in from aiding to remove the snow from the sidewalk, Mariana helped him out of his pea jacket. She said, "Darling, there are some problems at my office. I really should return to New York tomorrow. I've already called and gotten a plane ticket. The flight leaves Munie at ten a.m."

"I wish you didn't have to go but I understand. Never did I expect such a New Year's present, you being here with my family."

"I love you. I love them. I wouldn't have missed your homecoming for all the tea in China." She leaned over, kissed his ruddy cheek, made so by the cold outside and the exercise.

"I'll be in New York by Wednesday or Thursday of next week. I'll call before I leave here," responded Marcus.

"And you'll be staying at my place. I've got plenty of room. Two bedrooms and two baths, a mother-in-law arrangement, one bedroom and bath on opposite sides of the living room. The setup looks so prim and proper, twin beds in each."

"That'll take some adjusting after the Cavozzi sleigh," said Marcus.

"We'll adjust," and Mariana laughed, then kissed her beloved. He responded, passionately.

She gently pushed him away. "I believe you would do it right here in the hall."

"Might try," he responded then relaxed with a grin.

"I'll meet you at the airport if you let me know the flight." She was quiet for a few seconds observing him, then, "There are some major publishing reps I want you to meet. Each knows your work and is interested in discussing with you the possibility of your joining their respective staff."

"Gee, that's thoughtful of you. I will meet with them. I've got a few irons in the fire also. I need to settle down to a permanent job. It's a requisite before we get legally married and I want to do that as soon as possible if not sooner," he paused, then guffawed.

"We don't have to wait on your getting a job before we legally tie the knot. Both of us have funds. Take your time. Find the right one."

"Maybe we don't but I do. I've never given a thought to not pulling my weight in any union we have. I wouldn't feel right if I didn't contribute my just share to our financial worries. Call it male ego or whatever."

"Marcus, you are just someone so different than I've ever known. And its those differences that are endearing. Okay."

Marla came into the hall from the living room. "I heard the last remarks of you two. I'm so sorry you must leave tomorrow Mariana. I can't remember a more joyful holiday. To top it off, Sergio and I will be hosts for this evening, call it a little engagement announcement party. All of us, Bernie, Bianca and Vince included are going in town to Dominicas for supper and from there we have tickets to the Chicago Symphony at University Hall. Your sister is playing. The Chicago Chorale will be there too. The program will be primarily a Christmas program but it ends with several works by Debussy, 'L'Apres midi-d' un Faune,' 'La mer' and 'Clair delune.' Please don't let me down. This may be our last chance to be together until you two are married."

"How lovely and thoughtful," responded Mariana. "Marcus and I look forward to the evening with all of you. We appreciate your invitation."

Marcus was now a de facto husband, what else could he say? So he just smiled and nodded affirmatively.

CHAPTER 9

Marcus, in the big sleigh bed, came awake early in the morning of the day following Mariana's return to New York. He turned to look at his soaring eagle companion and remembered, she was gone. Immediately he became restive even though he was in the bosom of his loving family. He knew he was ready for a family of his own. He dressed quickly then went downstairs to make a cup of coffee. Marla, by nature an early riser, was in the kitchen as he entered. She cast him a wary look. "Already lonely?" she asked.

"How in the world did you know that?"

"Because I'm your mother," was her straightforward answer.

"Yes, I'm lonely but in addition, I am going in early to the Navy Release Center. Then I'm going to have lunch with Waddell and after that I'm going by Marshall Fields to get some new clothes. I'll be back by supper time."

Marla continued to eye her son, "You better consider a size or two larger. You've put on a little weight." She was quiet a couple of seconds then, "Take your time, don't jump if he offers you some kind of job."

"I have no idea that he is going to offer me a job. Why did you say that?"

GRIFFIN GARNETT

"Oh, just a mother's intuition," responded Marla. She didn't tell Marcus that Mrs. Feldstein called yesterday to say some government fellow had dropped by her house and asked about Marcus, his character and reputation. He apparently had also talked to a couple of other neighbors. Was it because of Marcus' gambling or was it about a job offer? Marla couldn't tell which but she hoped with all her heart it was a job offer. That's why she said what she did.

After a hot breakfast prepared by his mother, Marcus went to the coat closet beneath the stairway to the second floor, took a dark blue knit scarf from a hook and draped it around his neck. He put on his Navy peacoat and rolldown winter deck cap. His mother had followed him into the hall silently watching as he prepared to go out into the natural deep freeze. She walked up to him, raised the collar of his peacoat to cover his cheeks against the cold and said, "Sniff, taste before you bite the apple. It could be green and mighty sour."

Marcus kissed his mom, smiled in acknowledgment of her hidden approach and replied, "I promise I'll not commit to any offer today, if there is one." Then quietly he closed the front door as he left.

He headed for the bus stop and had to concentrate on his footing. Though snow had been shoveled from the sidewalks, a sheet of ice a half inch thick was in place of that snow. He wasn't used to frigid weather. He had just returned from a lengthy period in the tropics. He had no galoshes or boots. By the time he had walked a hundred yards toward the bus stop, he wondered where his feet had gone. He couldn't feel them walking at all and yet they were. Even with a pair of his dad's mittens on, his fingers ached. He stuck his hands in the deep folds of his peacoat pockets. Each time he inhaled, a colony of stinging ants seemed to be walking down his throat towards his lungs. When he exhaled it was as if a steam engine was snorting, trying to get started.

On reaching the deserted bus stop he looked up the empty avenue and thought, "No telling how long I will have to wait because the kitchen radio had announced that the buses were running on no regular schedule, slipping, sliding, fender benders and resulting traffic snarls are this morning's norm. What a hell of a place to freeze—at a Chicago bus stop." But, Marcus was lucky. Shortly thereafter an almost empty bus slid to a stop. Marcus sighed in relief, entered and before too many skids, arrived at the corner near the

132

Naval Release Center. His feet were again his. For whatever reason probably including the snowstorm which had ended the day before, the Center was almost empty of returning navy men seeking to be released from active duty. Marcus soon completed his physical discharge. All went well. He decided not to stay in the active reserve, arranged for his severance and accumulated leave pay. He left the Center a warmed, free man, a civilian. He felt both excited and a bit sad. Excited that he could now get on with his life, find a job and marry Mariana, saddened by the fact that a bothersome, yet adventuresome tour of duty was over. He had seen a part of the world he had only dreamed of, enjoyed his shipboard life and its challenges, had time to write many poems, and had met so many interesting characters, among them Greg Morgan, first his exec, later his skipper. Marcus learned from his shipmates that the slim, confident, CO was a native Virginian who, prior to his entry in the Navy, had been a capable trial lawyer in the northern part of that state. He couldn't help but chuckle over the memory of their first meeting when he returned the gambling money he had taken from the crew. He knew he had piqued Greg's curiosity with his poems. But Greg never let on. Neither did he.

Marcus left the Naval Release Center. He still had time to kill before meeting with Waddell, so despite the cold, blustering wind blowing in from the lake, the extending threatening icicles that hung everywhere from roofs, gutters, trees, power lines, telephone lines, even from doorways, where heat had seeped out between the top of the door frames and building sidings, he decided to walk to the Drake Hotel. He figured he could make it almost as quickly on foot as he could by cab, street car or bus, for traffic was still snarled by the remnants of the last heavy snowfall. Though the thoroughfares had been cleared of most of the snow, the freeze had kept the streets sheets of glass despite or maybe because of the constant traffic.

Marcus wondered as he walked. "Why does Waddell want to see me? I know nothing about the crooks the Secret Service have under surveillance. I know nothing about the art of snooping. Yes, I do know cards and how to tell if they are cooked. I can tell almost by instinct, who is cheating in a game and how. I like the challenge, the thrill of a good card game. In most of them, I can mathematically figure my odds by the time the last card is dealt and the first round of bets have been made. Do I want to again engage even if legitimate in a job that demands my knowledge, my dexterity with cards?"

"My mother has warned me about thrill-seeking and I know Mariana sides with her. Shit, I have never consciously thought of my life that way. Yet, why else have I so constantly tried to keep my body in good shape, my mind so alert? Not because I seek to extend my life but because I love searching and finding, the challenges, the thrills of life, then meeting them head-on.

"The physical challenges I have met and, if not conquered, I even enjoyed the failures because they were to somebody better than I am, I respect that. The mental challenges are more confusing, the results not quite as clear. I am intrigued by math and even the card games. There I am pitting my knowledge, my intuition against that of another human being, much like a physical challenge. But then my love of poetry is another matter. Sure math plays some role in the symmetry of the art, yet my desire, my urge to express myself in that form comes from where? It is almost as if from another person, one I do not understand clearly. The more I search and try to look into myself and find the source of that drive the more confused I seem to be because in my attempts at poetry I am never the clear winner or loser. I am constantly struggling to master the art. To me, the results are disappointing. If Mariana hadn't persistently encouraged me I might have said to hell with it and abandoned my poetic efforts. Now I am hooked. Just what the ultimate effect on me those efforts will have, I don't know, but for the first time my subconscious self is really looking at my conscious, confident physical being and there are problems."

When he arrived at the hotel marquee, he was instantly the surface Marcus. He found his train acquaintance in the lounge-grill. As he approached, Waddell arose from the table for two, extended his hand. "I'm pleased to see you again, Marcus, I hope your return home and the holiday have been all you envisioned them to be."

"And a lot more," replied Marcus. "I hope you've been enjoying yourself during the same time."

"I have. Aimee, my wife was able to join me here. We've had a delightful time when I've been off duty. Would you like a cocktail before we eat?"

"Sure. Scotch on the rocks."

Waddell ordered the drink.

"How'd you find your family and girlfriend?"

"Couldn't be better, I'm happy to be home."

Waddell stirred his vodka and tonic with a swizzle stick, looked at the glass then at Marcus. "I know you had a double major at Cornell, math and English. I know you got your masters in math and became a card dealer in Reno. I know that you were an outstanding middle-weight boxer at college and in the Navy. I was surprised to learn that you are a published poet." He paused. "With all that background, including your spat with Mariana Lucas why did you become a cook in the Navy?"

Marcus looked at Waddell and wondered, "The guy is certainly thorough, but why?" "I just didn't want to be an officer in the armed forces—too restrictive—too out front. Cooking was a challenge, something new and I would have time," —Marcus stopped, looked at his delivered drink.

"Time for what?"

Marcus responded, "Time to keep in physical shape, time to study people, their reactions, time to work on my poetry and think."

"Think about what?"

"Where in the hell you got all that information about me and why?"

Waddell was not the least perturbed by the last remark and question. He continued, "Did you get released from the Navy?"

"This morning before I came here," replied Marcus.

"Well, what are your plans for the future?"

"At the moment I'm not sure, something in the field of applied math or go with a publication in New York. You know my girlfriend has a small publishing outfit there."

Waddell grinned. "Yeah, I know. Ever given a thought to making a career in the federal government?"

"No."

"Ronald Evans has a high regard for your capabilities and honesty."

"So have my parents and girlfriend."

"Are you going to marry her?"

"You bet I am. Just as soon as I have a permanent job."

"Would she object to your being with the finest agency in the U. S. Government, the Secret Service?"

"I've never even thought about it, never discussed that subject with her."

"Well, think about it, talk it over with her on your next trip to New York but no one else not even your parents."

"Are you serious in offering me a post in that agency?"

"Serious enough for me to have your collegiate record, including comments from your masters professor, a recommendation from the hotel chain, a copy of your Naval record and to have had a chat with several of the families in your home neighborhood. You'd fit, fit well."

"How do you know?" asked a surprised Marcus.

"Because I've seen you in action, alone and in company. You would like the Service. Let me tell you just a little something about it. Later when you join, you'll get a lot more. The Secret Service became the first federal law enforcement agency. It was in 1865 that Hugh McCulloch, then Secretary of the U.S. Treasury, told President Lincoln that counterfeiting, particularly counterfeiting of paper money, was almost ruining the federal financial system. At that time, one in every three pieces of U.S. paper money was counterfeit, a forgery. The national banks were then separately issuing their currency backed by gold reserves. The bills were easy to copy and counterfeit. President Lincoln agreed and on April 14, 1865 earlier during the day on which he was shot at the Ford Theater, he approved of the plan to establish the agency. The Secret Service was written into law by Congress on July 5, 1865. On that date William Woods became the first chief of the Secret Service. His primary objective was to restore public confidence in the money of this country. He employed ten full-time agents, then called 'operatives' to do the job. Later more operatives and part-time employees called assistant operatives were called in.

"For a number of years the Secret Service was the only federal law enforcement agency and was intermittently employed for other purposes, including gathering of intelligence. In 1908 the Justice Department organized the Bureau of Investigations. That investigative department later became the F.B.I.

"Subsequent to 1894 when the Secret Service uncovered a plot to assassinate President Grover Cleveland, the Service was used to protect the president on an ad hoc basis as threats against the life of the president were uncovered.

"In 1902, a year after the assassination of President McKinley, the public demanded protection for the president. President Theodore Roosevelt assigned secret service agents to provide round-the-clock protection for the president. In 1906, Congress passed an act under the Sundry Civil Expense Act providing funds for the protection of the president. In 1913 those funds were extended to include the vice president, in 1917 to include the president's immediate family. In 1922, President Warren Harding established the Uniformed Branch Division to protect the White House and other buildings that dealt with the business of the president and vice president. In 1930, President Herbert Hoover constituted the Uniformed Branch Division as a part of the Secret Service. That house protective force is presently made up of detailees assigned from the Metropolitan Police Department of the District of Columbia.

"The training of new operatives of the Service is carried out by in-house training received from experienced members. However, in D.C., learning the use of firearms is under the guidance of U.S. Coast Guard instructors. Regular practice sessions are held on the firing range in the basement of the Treasury Building."

"That's quite an education in a thimble," commented Marcus. He was curious.

"In view of your background, your talent with math and cards and your physical abilities, the Chief would put me in charge of your initial training. We really need your services in the matter you endeavored to solve on your own."

"Not very smart was I?"

"All depends upon how you look at it. Not with what we know. You were in a dangerous spot. Thank God you realized it before it was too late. You do have cool guts and the right instincts."

"What happens, God forbid, if something adverse should occur to me in the line of duty?"

"You are protected by health insurance, life insurance, disability retirement, real disability retirement. In addition, U.S. Government sick leave and annual leave are pretty generous. I'm no mathematician like you but I have figured that my retirement benefits beat those of any industry I know of—by a mile—except for Congress."

"Where would I be stationed?"

"There are a number of posts but in all probability New York or

Washington. However, if you come with us in the near future, you will be on the road a good bit until we clear up the present unpleasantness you know about." Waddy became quiet.

A minute went by then Marcus' first remark was from an oblique angle, "Fosberg wasn't his real name was it?"

"No. To tell you the truth we don't yet know his baptismal name."

"And Leverbee wasn't his real name either?"

"Right again, but we do know, or think we know his given name. He has used many aliases."

There was another brief period of silence followed by Marcus' question, "I gather from your previous remarks you would want me to work with your team on the present con and counterfeiting case?"

"Yes, you would fit well into our ongoing operation."

Marcus wondered how. He looked searchingly at Waddell. "You don't mind if I ask you a couple questions that have piqued my curiosity?"

"Not at all. Fire away," answered his interested host.

"Ronald Evans had on a disguise, really a clever one. Why didn't you, particularly since you were the only Service player in the game? I would think there would be more reason for your not wanting to be recognized than him. True, you had a fake name."

"Marcus, the logic of your math comes through clear as a bell," his host replied. "I don't usually play the game. I'm a background artist, been in the Service long enough to call the shots from somewhere on the sidelines. On that last trip from Frisco to here, Comstock the usual game player had his hands full working on some small bills we ran across in Frisco. We needed to know as much about them as we could as soon as possible and he is our paper expert. I agreed, at the last minute to take his place when we learned there was to be a game in the club car. Comstock is also the disguise specialist on my team. You're right, I should have made some type of alteration in appearance but I had no time to do so once we knew the game was starting and Evans, acting as the bartender, suspected we might be on to something. Our trip coming out to Frisco was a waste of time and government money but the return one sure as hell wasn't." Waddell's face lit up with a satisfied smile.

Marcus understood.

"I'm going to New York in about a week. I'll talk it over seriously with Mariana. I just can't do it by phone. After our discussion I'll make a decision and let you know within two weeks from now. Where will I be able to reach you?" asked Marcus.

"Just call the number on the face of the card I gave you. Leave them the number where you can be reached. I'll get back to you as soon as possible."

"Anything else you need from me?"

"Nothing. Just keep your nose clean until then, no gambling, no private eye investigation. Keep out of trouble and enjoy your upcoming weeks of R and R."

Marcus was still trying to get some real emotional reaction from Waddell. "I may look at other job possibilities."

"You won't find any as challenging, as thrilling, as my offer can be. Maybe someday you will be guarding the president of the U.S."

"Is that a thrill?"

"No, it's a challenge, but you wouldn't be ready for that for quite a while."

"Good," replied Marcus. "I think that would be damned confining, meticulous."

"It is. You understand already."

The two men were quiet for a brief span sipping their drinks.

"How long have you been married?" asked Marcus.

"Been married for twenty years."

"Any children?"

"Only one, a daughter, Anna. She was killed in an auto accident just before the war."

"I'm sorry. I didn't mean to arouse bad memories."

"That's alright Marcus you didn't arouse them. They're there constantly just under the surface. It takes far less than your honest question of interest to bring them above ground. Gradually Aimee and I are dealing with our loss like adults but it's a long trip."

"I'm sure it is," replied Marcus. "I hope I never have to face it."

"Have more than one if you can. That will lessen the hurt."

"Mariana and I plan to," responded Marcus.

Lunch arrived and the two men ate silently each closeted with the thoughts their preluncheon chat had sparked.

"Where do you call home?" queried Marcus as they finished their meal.

"Washington, D. C. I was born and raised in the Georgetown area, an unusual place where poverty sits on the lap of wealth and politics."

"Did you go to school there?"

"Surely did. Jackson Elementary School, then to Western High School and from there to George Washington University in D.C. I am a graduate in criminology. One way or the other I've been in law enforcement ever since."

"Were you married when you took your first job in police work?"

"Was indeed, Aimee and I were married just after I graduated from G.W. She was at that time, a junior at a teachers college in town. She is used to law enforcement work. Her dad was a detective, a lieutenant on the D. C. Police. She knew what to expect. We've had a good life together, kinda' rough on her at times. But she rolls with the punches." He was silent, pondering for a few seconds. "God knows what I would do without her," he said softly. That was the first real indication Marcus observed of any depth of feeling by the senior operative. "Odd, he is so controlled," thought Marcus.

Waddell continued as if Marcus' entry into the Service was a foregone conclusion. "I suggest you might get a job with your future wife's publishing company, like a roving publicist, marketing her books, pay would be nominal, say on a commission basis. That would cover your tracks on undercover work. You don't plan on publishing any more poems right now, do you?"

Marcus was surprised by the guy, he hesitated then replied, "Not at the moment."

"Good, because if your name became too well known or your picture was pasted all over book covers you wouldn't be very useful in certain undercover work, like for instance, the present problem my team is working on. And we may give you an alias from time to time."

"Hell, I have no idea whether or not I'm going to join 'your team' or any government team. This is my first talk with you on the subject."

"I know, I was just thinking out loud. It just might work best that way." Marcus realized that quiet Clarence Waddell was no fool in his approach. He wasn't just thinking out loud, he was planting a seed Marcus knew Mariana might be willing to accept. Just how did his new friend know that much about her?

"Where do you live now?" asked Marcus.

"Same house I was raised in, on 28th Street in Washington, D.C. I am an only child. When my parents died, I inherited the home, been there ever since. I couldn't have a better place, value is going up every year, especially since old man Hollerith, the founder of IBM, has bought the whole block above us. The area is quiet, near downtown. Montrose Park and Oak Hill Cemetery are at the top of the hill. Got everything my wife and I need. In addition we have some land and a shack out in Dunn Loring, Virginia. It's only a hop and skip over Chain Bridge. We love flowers and vegetables. Gardening is our release from life's problems, like poetry is yours. We find time for it. You can too. Now back to your job."

"No more talk about the job. I'll let you know, Mr. Waddell," responded Marcus. He arose and those hazel eyes were disturbed as he reached out and shook Waddell's hand. "Thank's for the lunch and the offer."

"It's been a pleasure, Marcus. I'll await your call."

The two men parted.

□

Just as the street lights came on, Marcus got out of the cab in front of his family's home, laden with his purchases from Marshall Fields. He stooped a little so the boxes on top of the Leaning Tower of Pisa wouldn't tumble and rang the door bell. Bernie opened the front door, grinned, then said, "I didn't know Santa made second deliveries."

"Not usually," replied Marcus, "But while I was getting some new civvies I realized he did miss the Bosconovich chimney. The falling snow blinded his view. Please help me bring these into the house." One of them started to slide. "Grab it," said Marcus, "It's yours." Bernie reached quickly. Marcus continued, "I didn't have time for Christmas shopping in Frisco. With Mariana here and the way things happened, I did my Christmas shopping this afternoon—just a little late."

"Man, you didn't have to get us anything. Your getting home with no holes in you was the best gift you could give us."

"Bullshit!" said Marcus, "Sounds nice, but remember I am also a Bosconovich. You hide that gift of yours after you've opened it and

141

help me hide the rest of the gifts before mom hears us. I'll lay odds that maybe not tonight, but no later than tomorrow night at the supper table mom will say, 'Marcus, Dear, did you have a nice Christmas day? Did you think of us?' We both know what that means."

"For a buck?" queried Bernie.

"You're on," replied his brother.

The next evening at the supper table, after Sergio had offered his usual thanksgiving, Marla turned to her eldest, "Marcus, your New Year's Day homecoming was a surprise and a continuing delight. Did you have a nice Christmas day? Did you think of us?"

Bernie, laughing, slid out of his dining chair, went around and slapped a dollar bill down on his brother's empty dinner plate, then together guffawing Bernie and Marcus went to get the family gifts Marcus had bought at Marshall Fields.

Marla smiled in satisfaction. Sergio looked slightly befuddled.

CHAPTER 10

Brian O'Flanagan Lucas, the youngest son of deceased Boston Harbor longshoreman Kevin Lucas, now owns Finley & Finley, the oldest and largest wholesale produce broker on the Boston Harbor scene. When younger, Brian had neither the desire nor the build for being a lifelong longshoreman. He was not power-built, squat and broad-shouldered like his Irish father but was more like Arlene, his Celtic background mother—lean with black wavy hair. As a young teenager he was skinny but not quite awkward. His blue eyes were observant and many a time were his source of salvation from possible serious injury as he hauled boxed Finley & Finley produce by hand dolly from the store bins to the shipping nets. He started when he was thirteen years old, in the afternoons after school. In the summers, he worked full time, sun up until dark, with only a thirty-minute break for a bag lunch. Each of his four older brothers worked at some effort the same way. It was just expected and the norm in order for the Lucas family of eight to live above poverty level.

By the time Brian graduated from high school, and he did well, he was lithe and strong. His center of gravity was such that his effortless natural, erect carriage gave him an air of born, gentle nobleness that was eye-catching to all who saw him. However, it was his face that defined him. He was high cheekboned like his mother and his light skin always seemed to be tinged with a stubble, even when freshly shaved. Those features, together with his piercing light blue eyes gave him an apostolic appearance of constant focus and concentration only relieved by the impish glance that from time to time came from those blue blazers. Through some hereditary trait when he smiled there was a pleasant symmetry to his countenance. He revealed a glistening perfect set of white teeth not milky-yellow, not askew or with one or two missing like most of his friends and family.

The two Finley brothers, original owners of Finley & Finley, were no fools. In Brian, they saw a fresh face for their business and they trained him slowly but well. First he delivered to the most disgruntled local customers. Brian learned the problems concerning produce marketing including condition, count, spoilage and lateness of delivery. He learned to assuage customers by replacement, switching, verbal understanding and sympathy for their problems, if nothing more. Several years later, he delivered to the larger, more sophisticated clientele. He gave no thought to college, he was being educated in a trade, a coming industry. He became knowledgeable and reveled in his chosen occupation. During many evenings at home, he read prodigiously about the produce business. He obtained books on the subject from the public library, found old trade papers, magazines that covered all aspects of his life's work: crop costs, effects of weather, shortages, futures, national and international trading rates and timing. He seldom went out on dates, there just wasn't that much time. He knew what he wanted to be, someone other than a local produce delivery man. He observed the office routines, soon learned the method of buying future and current produce, became acquainted with shipping procedures and billing. The Finleys, more and more, began to feel his presence and his efforts. Their customers, both foreign and domestic took a shine to the charismatic, focused, noble-looking Irishman who really was learning and loved the business of being a middleman. Other area produce wholesalers began to cast their eyes on young Lucas but the Finleys knew. They made sure he was theirs.

Joe Finley, one of the two owner brothers, had no children but a bitchy wife. Frank, the other brother, had a lovely Hispanic, alcoholic wife Eleanora and three children—two boys, Tim and Algernon neither of whom had the slightest interest in the wholesale produce business and a younger daughter, Karen.

Karen had gone, as a day student, to a parochial academy in Boston. How she got through the school, Frank, her father, could not fathom, for she never cracked a book. When home, she spent most of her time either on that damned new gadget, the telephone, or out on dates. Upon graduation from parochial school she was accepted and enrolled in Radcliffe College for young ladies. Frank, the pragmatist he had become, was sure that at college Karen must have majored in men. She wasn't smart but she was clever. He figured his daughter must have slept with most of her male professors for her to obtain the grades she made. To his surprise she graduated from college then returned home to enter the so-called social scene.

Shortly after Karen graduated from college, Joe Finley died. His wife had predeceased him. Frank became the sole owner of Finley & Finley. In no time at all he made Brian Lucas an equal partner in the business.

Without any nudging from her father, Karen saw her future in Brian, just five years her senior. He was then adultly handsome, smart, knowledgeable in the wholesale produce business and acceptable in almost any social arena. In addition, he was making real money for the firm and himself. For Karen, the snare was easier than catching an unsuspecting fly on fly paper. Brian was frequently invited to have dinner with the Finleys. Karen and Brian went regularly to the Boston Symphony using the Finleys' season tickets and to the ice hockey games at the Garden the same way.

Though knowledgeable, astute and forceful about business, Brian was gullible around women. He had no real social or sexual experience with them but he was delighted to be in the company of his partner's daughter. He liked her cleverness, her articulateness and, last, but not least, her body, small, trim and neat. Her black eyes, much like her mother's, were dark pools of almost hypnotic suggestion. Her lips were wide, warm and inviting. He could tell by looking. To him, she was a siren wrapped in the finest ladies' apparel Boston could offer. The first time he saw her nude on her parents king-sized bed, when her mother and father were away on a South

American cruise, my God, he lost his breath from excitement, desire, and almost fainted. Man, did she know how to answer that desire. While her parents were away on that trip, she taught him much, so much he could hardly wait for the Finleys' return so he and Karen could get married. During the waiting period, Karen was grinning, grinning like the proverbial Cheshire cat who played constantly with her cornered mouse but waited until her family gathered before she truly attacked him.

In his office, Brian, now sixty years of age, swivelled in his enormous olive green, leather-covered executive chair and remembered that first time he saw Karen nude, as if it was this morning, not even yesterday. He no longer gasped in excitement. His brow furrowed in disgust at that unwelcome memory and more.

Yes, he was Finley & Finley. His father-in-law had died years ago, after Brian's daughter, Mariana, had been born. Frank Finley, at his death, was wealthy, had willed his share of the business to Brian. Brian, now sole owner of the business, had more funds and investments than were reasonably necessary for him and his family to lead a happy, comfortable life. Was his life really happy or comfortable? He pondered as he remembered.

Frank had, in his will, provided a trust for his wife, Eleanora. She was now in a retirement home, and seemed to be enjoying her life. She was an ageing, lovely, alcoholic whose ability, even in the retirement home, to find spiritus frumenti in other residents living areas, was second only to a pure-bred bloodhound's ability to sniff and locate escaped felons. On her death the corpus of her trust would go to Karen.

Tim Finley and Algernon Finley, the two older brothers of his wife Karen had been provided for by separate trusts set up in Frank's will. The brothers would only receive the annual income from their respective trusts. The National Bank of Boston was the trustee in each. On each son's death, the corpus of his trust would go to his children, if any. That was the devil in Frank speaking through his will, because Tim was a Catholic priest, Algernon was a closet queen, and Frank knew. If the deceased sons had no children at the time of their respective death, then each son's respective trust would terminate and the total trust assets would go equally to the daughters of their sister Karen. If there were no daughters, then to Karen's sons, share and share alike.

146

Karen's share of her father's estate was also left in trust. She was to receive only the income, unless she suffered an illness requiring hospitalization. In that event, if necessary, the trustee could invade the trust corpus for medical and hospital expenses. The income was to be paid to her at least annually, more frequently if the trustee so chose. Much to her anger and chagrin, her father had named him, Brian, trustee. He knew why his father-in-law had named him as trustee. It was an obligation he, Brian, assumed with a heavy heart. On Karen's death, the corpus was to be distributed equally to any of her children surviving her, if none, it was to go equally to the children of Tim and Algernon, again the devil in Frank speaking. If all the foregoing failed, then to Radcliffe College.

Five years after his father-in-law's death, Tim, the priest, was accidentally killed near Faneuil Hall while trying to break up a fight between two rival youth gangs, many of whose members were parishioners of his church. It was a sad ending.

Tim had no children so his trust corpus went to Mariana, Karen's only daughter and Karen fumed.

Algernon died not long thereafter of pneumonia preceded by a strange, debilitating illness. He had no children, so his trust corpus also went to Mariana. By the time she was twenty-one years old, Mariana was a young woman of considerable means. Few, if any, of her friends knew it. She invested and used her money wisely. She had inherited Brian's financial shrewdness.

Mariana's two older brothers resented her independent wealth. Sean, five years her senior, the wandering, woman chaser, the true son of his mother, was openly honest and told her he was envious. Tully, two years older than Mariana, was surly, devious, even underhanded. He had tried various ways to obtain funds from her accounts but had failed miserably. In the process he had completely alienated any remaining sisterly feelings Mariana may have had for him. All this Brian knew and reflected on.

On that winter day in early 1946, as Brian sat and slowly swung his chair from side to side brooding about his past, present, and future he was heart sick had been numerous times before, particularly when he thought about his two sons. Were they really his? His memory drifted back to his earlier discussions with his wife. The times of his sons' conceptions as alleged by Karen didn't seem to jibe with nature's calendar or the few times they had been together as a married couple, through no lack of interest by Brian. Karen had insisted and he had, with reluctance accepted her explanations. According to Karen, Sean had been born one month premature and Tully was two months premature, however, to him they both appeared full-term, healthy baby boys. He guessed that doubt was the reason for the rather distant attitude toward his two sons. That, and the fact neither son resembled any member of his family or his wife's family, didn't bear the traits, good or bad, of either side.

He continued his swiveling and his heart soared with love and affection when he thought of Mariana. She was his daughter. He knew it. He and his wife had been guests of the United Fruit Lines on a sixty-day, almost world-wide cruise. The freighter merchantman accommodated forty passengers. No luxury ocean liner could have provided the meals, the stateroom and the services offered by the cruising freighter. The sights the Lucases saw, the strange and exotic ports of call the ship visited on this, the Lucases' first cruise, he would forever remember. But the brightest of all those memories were the two times, early in the cruise, the only times on the cruise when he and Karen were together as man and wife. The dates and nature jibed. Upon Mariana's birth, the various segments of the Lucas family bestowed her with gifts, piles of them, for girls were a rarity in the Lucas clan. Beyond all that, she was a real Lucas. As she grew, she was almost a female clone of him: slim, erect, pale blue eyes, wavy black hair, alert and with the same earthy but honest directness that was his. He worshiped her.

He remembered how Karen fretted, felt challenged by her daughter from the day Mariana first popped into view. Karen began hovering over her sons but was distanced from her daughter from the day of her birth, never breastfed her though she had an ample supply to the extent they frequently ached and almost leaked. Brian knew that she obtained a breast pump, pretended she was nursing Tully as the milk flowed to the jar. That was as close as she would ever get to suckling his daughter. Mariana, as she grew, sensed her mother's coolness toward her and she often wondered why. In her inexpert, youthful ways she tried to narrow the gap to get closer to her mother but to no avail. So, Mariana, with her natural positive outlook on life, didn't let it bother her too much, didn't fret over it, because there was

Dad. And he was always there for her. He sighed then mumbled, "Always will be."

When Mariana was two years old, the family moved to a lovely home on the hill road that led up to the Wollaston, Massachusetts reservoir. The gray, shingled house was a sprawling, comfortable home. The screened back porch looked out over the grove of birch trees toward Wollaston Beach.

In the summers, Brian frequently took Mariana to the beach and to his country club pool. He had taught her to swim by the time she was five then turned her over to the club swimming and diving coach. Tom Eberling took a liking to the skinny brunette. It wasn't long before he was teaching her to dive. He could tell that what she lacked in compactness of body, she offset by a growing gracefulness. She could be a champion diver someday if she maintained her determination.

The Boston schools, whether public or parochial, in Brian's opinion weren't good enough for his daughter so after discussing it with her, sent her to one of the ranking private boarding schools in the country not far from Boston. She came home frequently to be with him. Most of those times her mother was in Florida, abroad, or traveling with friends. Mariana graduated from the boarding school with honors and went to Radcliffe College as had her mother. She distinguished herself there academically, majoring in journalism and in addition was the star of the diving team. In her senior year she was the editor of the school magazine and became focused on the field of publication. Like her dad, she could focus on and drive toward a goal. He alone attended her graduation but that was enough for her. She had brought honor to his name as well as hers.

The one thing that had worried him about his daughter was her relationship with men. Until she graduated from college she hadn't let her hair down and talked with him about her dates, her boyfriends if any. One night shortly after their return from her college graduation she met him for dinner at his club. When she walked into the mixed lounge to join him, most of the male eyes in the room that weren't blinded by glaucoma or some other eye defect just naturally gravitated toward her. He looked at her and didn't blame them. She was truly a beautiful young woman: tall, lithe, graceful and with a natural ease of manner that made anyone who met her feel they had known her for years. At supper that night he had inquired, "Honey, you've never mentioned a boyfriend? Do you have one?"

She heaved a sigh then said, "Dad, I'm glad you asked me. I've been a little reluctant to talk about that, your being a man but here goes. No, I don't have a particular boyfriend now. I've had boyfriends, experiences and chances. I've learned. When the right guy comes along you'll be the first to know." He understood. Nothing more need be said.

Mariana, with her mind set on the publication business, began to look for opportunities. Boston just wasn't the place for her. Through a couple of former collegemates, she learned of a failing small publishing house, the Purple Canary on 63rd Street in New York City. So, off she went to the Big Apple staying at the Barbazon Plaza Women's Residential Hotel. Quietly, she investigated the small press and determined that, though she would be one of the few women running such an endeavor in New York City, she could make a go of the business what with her contacts and her Dad's. So, after considerable haggling with the aesthetic male owner, and with Brian's approval she bought the little publishing house.

Mariana was establishing her business with him providing her the middleman expertise he could plus a loan which she had recently repaid in full. He didn't want her to initially use her money. In addition, he wanted her to feel what it was like to be financially obligated. He had told her, "The publishing business is a middleman business much like my own. I am the middleman between the growers, buyers and consumers. You are the middleman between the writers, bookstores and the readers. The only differences are the products and method of advertising and selling. Same game," then he explained in detail. How quickly she grasped the concept and with the aid of his business acquaintances was successful from the start. Brian knew she had made numerous contacts with men—good looking, ugly, intelligent, scheming, the whole gamut same as in any middleman field.

Mariana couldn't make it home for this Christmas 1945. She had told him by phone that she was going to attend a convention of small presses in Philadelphia, Pennsylvania right after Christmas. The planning for that business trip would take her through Christmas. She would be in Philadelphia starting December 26, staying at the Pennsylvania Hotel. She would call him when she returned to New York and they would make plans for a delayed holiday get-together.

This morning, out of the blue, as he sat remembering and swiveling, she had called him to say she was in Chicago, Illinois and engaged to, of all people, a Navy cook. At first he was aghast. Then, in that lilting voice of hers, she had said, "Not just any old Navy cook but one with a master's degree in math from Cornell and one of the three poets in my recently and profitably published volume, *Poems by Three Pacific War Poets*. I'm at his parents' home in Chicago. I'll be back in my office on Monday. Call me when you are coming to New York. I want you to help me plan my wedding."

He had replied, "I have business in New York City on Tuesday of next week. Please meet me for supper at 6:30 that night in the Astor Grill."

"I'll be there, I love you," she replied and hung up the phone.

What he didn't tell her was, the business he had was finding out about the cook, her new boyfriend, her fiance. His wholesale grocery business could stand for him being away for almost any length of time and besides he was at loose ends. Karen, his wife was in Florida; Sean, the skirt-chasing son, was skiing with a babe somewhere in Maine; and Tully, who apparently worked for some art gallery in Washington, D.C. never visited him and was seldom even in D.C. God knows where he spends his time, mused Brian.

He had no dalliances though Marjorie Hempstead a long-standing acquaintance of his and his wife's had been in love with him for years and he knew it. He considered dalliances difficult to handle. They kept him from concentrating, doing his best in business. So his physical and emotional outlets were his bridge games at the club, an occasional light workout in the club gym, his nightly bourbon and water after supper as he slumped in his Barco Lounger in the den, listened to music on the radio and reminisced before he retired.

Brian stopped his swiveling, looked at his watch, punched the intercom button on his phone, said to his secretary, "Priscilla, I need a little vacation from the office. I'll be away for about a week. I'll be home for the next three or four days. After that I will be in New York at the Astor Hotel. Tell Alfred to take over for me. I'll call you and pick up any messages before I go to the Big Apple. Just keep things moving." He hung up and headed home.

In his den the next morning, after reading the morning paper, Brian was looking forward to seeing his daughter, even hearing of her love affair. He missed her so during the just-past empty Christmas holiday. He was alone and lonely. Mariana had told him the name of her husband to be, Marcus A. Bosconovich, certainly not Irish, he thought and he remembered she had told him that Marcus graduated from Cornell before he went into the Navy. How long before the Navy had he finished college? Brian wondered. He was interested, became focused, so he set the wheels of background checking in motion. He called his credit company, then his friend, Albert Insbrooke, Professor of Horticulture at Cornell, and asked for a scholastic and personnel profile on Marcus. The professor agreed to do so promptly, thinking his Boston acquaintance was considering the young man as a potential employee. Brian called his neighbor, Admiral Bralle and asked if he could obtain a summary of Marcus' naval record. Four days later, just before he was to make his trip to New York, information poured in about Marcus A. Bosconovich. He read the reports and was surprised. He really wanted to meet his daughter's intended. What an unusual, nonconforming, brilliant, young man and by no means destitute. However, he sensed trouble because his daughter's husband-to-be was not only a scholar, he was a powerful athlete. He knew those two characteristics seldom went together compatibly. No wonder his daughter was intrigued. He was, just reading about him. Was he really good marriage material, good enough for his daughter? He put all of Marcus' personnel information in a folder and placed it on top of his clothes in his suitcase. He would have time to study the folder contents more carefully and to make calls, if necessary, when he had reached his room at the Astor Hotel, his favorite hostelry where Vincent Lopez the diminutive jazz piano virtuoso and his band were headlining in the grill, had been for sometime. For years, he and Karen had made the Astor their New York home when he was in that city on business or pleasure.

$$\square$$

Ensconced at a table for two, along one wall in the swank Grill Room, Brian told Ernst, the maitre-d', "My daughter is joining me. Please escort her here."

"It will be a pleasure Mr. Lucas," responded Ernst. When he, with a broad grin, returned, followed by Brian's stunning-looking daughter, the maitre-d' pulled out the chair opposite her father and he motioned to Mariana. "Please be seated, Miss Lucas." He then turned to Brian. "Escorting your daughter wasn't just a pleasure but a rare delight," he said. He turned back to Mariana, "You have all the fine features of your father. He's good looking. On you, they are beautiful. Have a nice meal," he said, then he motioned for the table waiter.

"Gee, he's smooth," said Mariana.

"As silk," responded her father. "He's right, you know." Brian Lucas beamed at his daughter.

Mariana giggled that soft responsive way she had done ever since he could remember, particularly when, after putting her to bed, kissing her first on her cheek, then on her ear, and whispering huskily, "Dive for the sky and your dreams my blue-eyed colleen."

The duo ordered drinks: for Brian, his usual bourbon and water, for Mariana a glass of Bristol Cream. When they were delivered, he held out his glass, Mariana touched it with hers. "To your future. May it always be as happy as now."

"What an odd but lovely toast," replied Mariana.

"Honey, the first awakening of true love forms one of the happiest memories in any life, man or woman."

"You know, you are quite a guy as well as being my dad."

"Tell me about Marcus. How and where did you meet him?"

Mariana proceeded to tell her father of her evolving love for Marcus, even of the spat that caused the breakup just before he enlisted in the Navy, the letters he had written, the poems he had sent with the letters, how she was able to get them published, how she had established contact with his family, her trip to Chicago and staying with his family. She told him of her awaiting Marcus' return at his family home, her feelings for Marla, Marcus' mother. She then raised her left hand and showed him her engagement ring.

"Holy Christ," gasped Brian.

"Those were my sentiments exactly," she replied and grinned. Two couples seated at the next table heard the remarks, saw the ring as Mariana's father, holding her hand, studied the shimmering jewel. The two girls' eyes bugged with awe and jealousy. Their dinner partners squirmed uncomfortably.

"Honey, how in the world could he afford such a gem?" She told him the story of the ring. When she finished, he said, "His family is damned near as intriguing as Marcus. What an unusual clan. Maybe things will turn out okay after all."

Mariana drew back her ring hand, looked seriously at her father. "And, what did you mean by that crack? You didn't have any right to seek a background check on him. He's not going to be one of your employees."

"I didn't say I had made a background check on your intended."

"I know you, it was as clear as if Marcus' resumè sheets were spread out on the table in front of you."

Her dad looked at her and after a faint smile said, "Damn, we're too much alike. I knew, however I worded it, you would know, just by the manner in which I spoke."

"Yep."

"Yes, Mariana, I did invade your privacy. I did investigate Marcus, and no, maybe ethically I shouldn't have. But, I love you, I wasn't inquiring for your sake. You've made your decision and you are the one who should truly know him. I made the inquiries for my sake, to try and determine how I would view him and not be bowled over by some charismatic, slick rascal who might have wrongfully set your hormones spinning."

Mariana's eyes were two blue flames. "There have been times, and this is one of them, when, if I were a man, I would smack the crap out of you. I should leave this moment but I won't because I love you and I know you love me. However, now and then, your blunt approach infuriates me."

"I'll accept that," said her dad then he added, "You didn't let me finish."

"Finish what?"

"Marcus' resumès: collegiate, credit and naval reveal to me, without my even meeting him a most complex personality, brilliant scholar, athlete, dreamer, decent, caring, and somehow a money maker."

"You've got him right so far," said Mariana.

"Wrap it all together and you have a powerful personality who has apparently never known real adversity even though he is a thrillseeker."

"That last part, what did you say he is?"

"He is a thrillseeker, almost by nature. I've known a couple like him in my lifetime."

Mariana studied her father carefully. Then she looked down at her drink and turned the half empty glass of wine around and around. After a brief silence, two pairs of honest, blue eyes met, one older, experienced and wise, the other young with vision of the future.

Softly she replied, "I know that. His mother knows that and I hope he is beginning to understand it also. Whether he can channel that part of his being into a positive part of his life, God only knows. But, I truly love him. He is, by nature, one of the most decent, gentle, considerate persons I have ever met. Underneath all of that drive is a dreamer with more potential creative poetic ability than any person I ever expected to meet, much less fall in love with. And, it's that part of him I hope I can help to reach its potential. Whatever happens, I understand him, even his frailties, and he understands mine. They're the same as yours, our positiveness, our bluntness, our intense focus, sometimes to our detriment. He loves me in the way I, as an adult, want to be loved. We are right for each other."

"That's why I said 'maybe things will turn out all right after all.' I know you. And he, besides being complex seems to be a decent guy and has some funds and investments stashed away. How he made them I don't know, but I can guess," said her dad.

"He's got twenty-two thousand more than your figures show," said Mariana.

"How so?"

"Because that's what I paid him for the royalties and the prize one of his poems has earned. And you know what? He could have cared less. He's never inquired if I have money, who backs the Purple Canary or how I am able to live in a swank two-bedroom, two-bath co-op overlooking the East River in New York."

"He's a gambler, a confident one," said her father.

"No, he's a mathematician."

"All good gamblers are."

"How do you know?"

"Because to a lesser extent, all successful middlemen are good mathematicians and gamblers, even you."

Mariana's blue eyes were saucer round. "I never thought of it that way."

"The difference, my dear daughter, is that we offer a product, a legitimate product to the public and after figuring the odds we gamble that the public will accept it, like it. For Marcus it's difficult, his resumès, his athleticism and his masteral thesis when considered together, indicate a guy who lives to gamble, not just on cards, gamble for the thrill of gambling, not necessarily offering a product to the market, except for his poems. Yes, if you could help make his creative writing or his poems the product and he is thrilled and maintains the direction of those efforts, you would have won one hell of a triumph for your man. I love you as my wonderful daughter. I would be thrilled for you if you and Marcus succeed. Does he have a job yet?"

"No, he's coming to New York in a few days. I've already inquired about opportunities for him. There are several openings into which he would fit well."

"Don't push too hard. I can tell he won't stand for that. Suggest, nudge a little but let the decision be his or you'll never make it together."

"Golly, Dad, that's exactly what his mother has told me and I agree."

Brian reached across the table, took his daughter's ringed hand, kissed the palm of it, closed her palm and released her hand. Mariana's eyes clouded, she looked down at the table then said softly, "Damn, why can't Mom see you as I do. She wouldn't let you out of her sight if she did. I know you ache from loneliness. I've seen it in your eyes for years. If you won't divorce her at least find a friend to share some of your loneliness." She looked at her dad with a trace of tears in her eyes.

"You are one observant woman."

"I'm your daughter."

Brian Lucas' blue eyes beamed at his daughter and there was a tired sadness about his whole body. "It's too late, way too late," he said.

"Never," said Mariana, then her voice dropped to the soft, gentle tone, "Marjorie Hempstead has been a widow for five years and she has been in love with you for five years before her bum of a husband died. She still is. Her children are grown, gone. She is rattling around in that big house on the bay shore. She is as lonely as you are. I know you genuinely like her but for some damned fool puritanical reason you refuse to even acknowledge her as a friend. Call her, go see her, ask her out for dinner. Do any darn thing the two of you feel up to.

You've got a right to a life. Let's be honest, Mother doesn't care what you do so long as she has her money. Not only does she have hers, but in addition, you give her more than is good for her and I know you won't stop."

Brian's eyes were wide with astonishment. Now he was the child and she the adult. "How in God's name do you know all this?"

"Because I'm your daughter and I have watched carefully over the years. I care for you as my father just as you care for me as your daughter."

Brian had to breathe deeply several times to hide the emotions that surged within him. What she had told him was bluntly right just as he had told her. Now there was an outlet and escape from it all. "Nola," the signature theme of Vincent Lopez and his orchestra lilted through the grill. The first dinner dance set of the evening was underway.

"Would a beautiful young lady like to dance with her grumpy old dad before we order?"

"That would be the best aperitif I could think of," responded Mariana as she led the way to the dance floor.

□

Supper conversation was light. As they were drinking their demitasse Brian looked at his daughter and asked her, "Have you given any thought as to when and where you want to be married? And do you want a big or little wedding?"

"I can't give you a date at this moment but we want to be married as soon as Marcus settles into his civilian job. I don't think it will take him long to find one. Where do I want to be married? I've given that some thought too. Most of my friends are no longer in Wollaston. They're scattered to the four winds. Mom is never home, neither are Sean or Tully. My peers are here in New York. I know Marcus' family will come wherever we are married. What do you think?"

"I understand what you are saying. Do you go to church here?"

"Sure, fairly regularly to mass at Saint Timothy's. I know Father Edwards, the associate priest."

"How about Marcus? Is he Catholic?"

"He was baptized and confirmed in the church and is registered as a member of Saint Mary's in Chicago, has been since he was thirteen. Is he Catholic? Well, let's put it this way. I'm far from being a devout parishioner, haven't been in a confessional booth in a long while but I doubt that Marcus even knows what one is. His beliefs, at least what I've heard him express, are nonconforming as to the postulated teachings of any denomination I know of. Yet, even those beliefs reveal a certain spirituality that is hauntingly uplifting, beautiful, a part of his being a dreamer."

"I haven't the slightest idea what you are talking about," said her father. "Technically is he qualified to be married in the church?"

"Yes."

"That's what I really wanted to find out. You will let me know well enough in advance so I can round up as much of our clan as possible."

"Dad, you know I will and I'll be talking with you regularly as I always have. Thanks for a lovely dinner. You will escort me down the aisle and give me away, won't you?"

"Now, you've made my evening," said her father as he arose. "I'll walk with you to the cab stand in front of the hotel."

They stood, she kissed him on his cheek, placed an arm through one of his and the look-alike couple, one older, experienced and sadder, the other younger and full of visions were an eye-catching duo as they gracefully left the grill room.

CHAPTER 11

Alice-Lee Taliaferro lounging comfortably on her new sofa in the living room of her apartment put down the book she was reading, turned and, leaning on the near sofa arm looked at Samantha who was sitting at the dining room table, in deep concentration, writing a letter. "I know it's none of my business but you are so serious who is the letter to, your family?" she inquired.

Samantha, her black eyes gleaming, looked at Alice-Lee and said, "Never. It's to Marcus."

"Marcus? I thought you didn't want to see him again?"

"I didn't say that. I said there was a reason, a good reason I couldn't, shouldn't see him again. I learned he checked out of the Huntington two days after we said goodbye. That was more than ten days ago. I have his family's address and I promised I would keep in touch with him. He has a right to know why I did what I did, why I sent him away."

"He's not the only one," responded Alice-Lee. She waited for an answer. For some reason she felt uncomfortable concerning any hidden revelations that might emerge.

Samantha's eyes clouded, she gulped once or twice, smiled

whimsically, then whispered, "I've got no more than six months to live."

"What? What did you just say?" Alice-Lee arose from the sofa and headed towards her friend.

"You heard me. I've got no more than six months to live."

Alice-Lee stopped, stared aghast. "Who told you that? How do you know? That's preposterous."

"No, it's not preposterous. I wish it was. Dr. Embers, Chief of the Oncology Department at San Francisco General Hospital told me so after you had gone home." Samantha looked with sympathy at her tall, sleek, almost always under control friend. She wasn't now. She appeared horror-stricken. "I have a type of lymphatic cancer, probably resulting from my Christmas disease and the increasing failure of my immune system. There is no known cure. The cancer is spreading," said Sam hesitatingly.

"Why didn't you tell me before?"

"Because I didn't find out until after you left for the holidays. So much has happened since the night I came over here I thought I better wait.

"You knew I hadn't been feeling up to snuff when you left. A couple of weeks before you returned to Richmond for the holidays I went to my physician, Dr. Pebbles who took some tests. As a result, he sent me to Dr. Embers, a renowned oncologist. Embers took another battery of tests including a couple of biopsies. All the results weren't back before you left but just before Christmas he called me in for a consultation." Her eyes clouded with tears and she gasped at the memory of his gentle demeanor then the startling, numbing revelation he gave her. "Oh God," she said, "I was and am scared out of my wits. I don't want to die so soon." Placing her elbows on the table, she dropped her head into her hands and wept unashamedly. Alice-Lee bent over, exhaled as if someone had kicked her in the belly. She straightened up, walked quickly to the table, grabbed a chair and brought it alongside of her friend. Then she, with tears of surprise and terror streaming down her cheeks, wrapped her arms around Samantha and hugged her to her bosom.

"Maybe he made a horrible mistake," she said.

"Not a chance," replied Sam soberly. "The tests and diagnosis were reviewed by several other leading, local oncological diagnosticians. They agree."

"Oh, Sam, Sam, Sam, you are the most gutsy person I've ever met.

Christmas disease all your life, now this. So that's why you sent Marcus away?" said a tearful Alice-Lee.

"Yes, plus the fact that I knew Marcus did not and should never love me. Underneath that romantic, blithe surface appearance of his is an innate decency that might have compelled him to stay and try to aid me regardless of the consequences. He revealed so much of himself the night I first met him. I was damned selfish when I found out how much I could trust him. Truly, I do love him like no other love of my life. It goes way beyond sex. He was my only real glimpse at what life could have been if I was well and had found the right person. For me it was a lifetime spiritual experience, relationship. I'll never regret it. I owe him so much more than he will ever understand. I told him I would write to him and asked that he respond. This is my first letter to him. I'm revealing the truth."

Alice-Lee released Sam, looked at her and those misty gray-blue eyes of hers spoke an affection that made Sam smile. "I'm glad I met you and have you for a friend. It's one of the crowning events of my life," said Alice-Lee.

"Thanks," said Sam. "Now you know. Let's change the subject. If I think about it too long at any one time I go into almost uncontrollable hysterics. I've some life to live yet. I'll finish my letter to Marcus later. Tell me who your column for tomorrow will be about."

"Screw the damned column. Let's go out and get drunk, stinking drunk, so we can try to forget this slimy orb called Earth at least temporarily."

Sam felt sorrier for her friend than she did for herself. She knew Alice-Lee was hard to shock but Sam's disclosure seemed to have hit some hidden release button of emotional depth in her friend. "I'll go," said Sam, "But, as you know, I don't dare to get drunk, shouldn't touch a drop of liquor, so the doctor says. It could hasten the end. Where shall we go?"

"Someplace where you and I know no one and no one knows us. Where they don't care, won't even touch you if you get potted and fall flat on your face."

Sam's smile was a little bitter, a little twisted. "I know such a place. I've been there twice, once while I was in hell. The other time while I was in heaven."

"Strange, you were in hell then in heaven at the same place?"

"Yep. Where I first met Marcus and where I had my goodbye drink with him. It's called the Shanghai Lounge and Seafood Grill. They have wonderful chocolate milkshakes there."

"Ugh! The very thought of a chocolate milkshake makes me nauseated," said Alice-Lee.

"You don't have to have one. The bar is fifty feet long, with every drink known to man. And, the decor is something to behold."

"Sounds uplifting," said Alice-Lee with a smirk as she walked to the hall closet and grabbed her and Samantha's winter coats off the hangers.

"On the mural above the bar mirror you'll see more astounding objects for uplifts than you've ever seen before," said Sam giggling.

"I can't wait," replied Alice-Lee as she handed Samantha her coat. The duo left the apartment. Alice-Lee checked the door to make sure it was locked.

"Let's take a cab," said Samantha, "particularly if you're set on drinking."

"Smart idea," responded Alice-Lee as they headed for the elevator.

□

Cherrie, Queen of the Evening, was on her throne and saw Sam and Alice-Lee enter the lounge: What an odd couple, kinda like Miss Mutt and Miss Jeff and they're not even queer. She continued her stare as the duo walked by her headed for the bar. Suddenly, she said softly to no one, "Holy shit, I don't know the black-haired little one, but the tall, slinky blonde I've seen before in the newspaper society pictures. That's Alice-Lee something or other. She's the society columnist for *The Chronicle*. Just what in the hell are they doing here? Slumming?" Cherrie watched with increasing interest as the short and tall of it sat on adjoining seats at the bar. When fat Gene, the barman placed their drinks on the mahogany surface, she saw Alice-Lee reach out, take the jigger of whiskey, down it like a roustabout, then took only a sip of chaser, "She's been to a bar before but what the hell is the little one drinking? Some horrible brown-looking, thick liquid in a tall glass. Something new every day." Suddenly her reverie was broken.

"Hi, Cherrie, got a little time?"

Cherrie looked up at silver-haired Charlie Langsdon, smiled and said, "For you always, Charlie."

"How about taking the night off?"

"Just what are you suggesting?"

"Well, Emma has gone east to see the kids. She forgot we had tickets to the Barber of Seville for tonight at the Opera House. Let's drop by your place, you can change from that damned costume you're wearing, toss the wig and get into some real clothes. I know you have them, I've seen you on some of your occasional trips home." He looked at his watch. "If we hurry, we can reach the Opera House before the curtain goes up on the first act."

"Charlie, are you sure you want me to go with you?"

"I wouldn't be here asking if I didn't. No one will know who you are."

"You and dad were the closest of friends and you are the only person from the neighborhood I've ever seen here. I've often wondered how long ago did he tell you?"

"Years ago, just before your brother Malcolm had polio. I have told no one, not even Emma. I guess I'm the only one in the neighborhood who really knows. I'll never mention it."

"Thank you and God," said Cherrie. She arose, grabbed her fake fur, then accompanying her aristocratic-looking companion, headed for the door. Several of her colleagues looked with veiled jealousy as Cherrie left in the company of the handsome gray-haired guy. They entered his car at the curbside and drove off.

☐

Charles Langsdon was nervously sitting in his auto which was parked in front of Cherrie's rundown apartment building. "My God, how can she stand this place," he said to himself, then waited with all doors locked. Suddenly, out of the building swept a stunning, middle-aged brunette in a formal, black evening gown covered by a mink stole all exactly appropriate for the opera.

She approached the passenger side front door. Charlie had to look hard before he recognized Cherrie to be Shirley. He quickly reached over, unlocked and opened the passenger door. "I'm ready," said the aristocratic-looking, full-bosomed woman.

"Shirley," he said, "I had to look twice. It's so hard to believe and understand."

"Even for me," replied Shirley. "But that's how it is. You are not only my dad's good friend, you are also mine. I'll never forget your thoughtfulness." The handsome couple headed for the opera.

☐

Later that evening, Sam in near exhaustion, managed to help thoroughly soused Alice-Lee into the apartment elevator and from there to their fifth floor apartment. Sam just couldn't get Alice-Lee any further than the new sofa in the living room. And Sam was getting irritated with her lanky, drunk friend draped over her shoulder, like Sam was half carrying, half dragging a limp rolled up rug. She deposited Alice-Lee on her new sofa, heaved a sigh then said caustically, "Now let's see if you can keep from ruining your newest acquisition." Sam, fatigued, stumbled off to bed.

CHAPTER 12

The day before he was to leave for New York and in the morning mail a letter arrived at the Bosconovich home addressed to Mr. Marcus A. Bosconovich. The handwriting was neat. To Marla it looked quite feminine, even if the return address was Sam Kingsbury of Sealcrest Apartments, San Francisco, California. Around noon that day Marcus returned home after getting a haircut followed by shooting a few rounds of pocket billiards at Lacy's. The house was vacant except for his mother. She saw him as he entered the front door. "There's a letter for you on the glove table in the hall. It came in the morning mail from Sam Kingsbury," she said.

"Thanks," responded Marcus as he hung up his new parka in the hall closet.

"He surely has lovely handwriting almost like a girl's. Where'd you meet him?"

"In Frisco, at a bar one night during the time I was trying to arrange to get home," was Marcus' reply. He walked to the table, picked up Sam's letter, folded it, put it in his shirt pocket, then said calmly, "I'm going up to my study and read for a while."

"Lunch will be ready in twenty minutes," said Marla.

"Don't bother about any for me, I had a sandwich and a beer at Lacy's."

And Marla thought, "Sandwich and beer? That's not enough to hold him until supper time. I wonder just who that letter is from and what it says."

Marcus reached his study, flopped onto the sofa bed, propped his head up with pillows against the sofa arm, opened the envelope, took out Sam's letter, began to read:

January 16, 1946

Dear Marcus,

I have started this letter a dozen times and each time I finish the opening sentence, I realize how inadequately it expresses what I want to say. So, accept my limitations. I must tell you there are now times when I am as selfishly happy as I never expected to be in this life. Those times are the memories made by you.

It didn't take me long to reach Alice-Lee Taliaferro's apartment the night I left you. Hers will be my permanent residence until I have to leave. My street address is on the envelope of this letter. When I arrived at her apartment, sat on her new sofa and stuck one of my hands into my coat pocket, guess what I found? No, it wasn't just money but another pocketful of understanding I never expected, didn't truly merit. The next morning, when I found your poems the end of the rainbow in my big suitcase, I knew I was right and that I had met the one person who truly made the loveliest dream of my life come true.

I remember reading some philosopher who wrote that all moments of happiness are brief flights from pain. How I love those flights that you have made possible for me. Behind them, I confess is a consuming anger for what I have endured and know I must face in the nearing future. Why me? I frequently doubt that there is a god, at least a so-called god of love. Maybe there is an unidentifiable creator, but of what?

Here I am a woman, a flawed woman, as you already know. What you didn't know is that within the week before I met you I had been diagnosed by the best oncology team in the Frisco area as having a terminal illness, a type of lymphatic cancer, maybe brought on by my lifelong hemophilic condition and a poor immune system. My oncologist has gently yet positively advised me that I have no more than six to eight months left in this camouflage cover—my body—until now, not a bad-looking body, as you have told me.

I dread, abhor the thought of being someone's—anyone's—your obligatory responsibility. I sensed that you, being you would have unhesitatingly made my burden yours had you known my true condition.

There is no way I could reciprocate, not during the short time I have on this spinning, dizzying planet that's why I discouraged you from a closer friendship or relationship because I do care about you so much. Now you know.

There are constant questions that burn like fires within me. Why was my mother a carrier? Who did she inherit it from because Christmas disease is primarily a female, inherited fault? Was it because of some sin my forbears had committed and the result of that sin is being visited on generations after? Yes, I am angry at my parents for letting me be born. They knew. And so does the creator—God—whatever name the I am is called. Why wasn't the illness visited on my sisters instead of me?

Marcus, I am telling only you of my feelings. My mother died when I was fifteen. My father and sisters, I cannot yet tell you what I think of them. I would rather roast in so-called hell before I confide in any one of them. Alice-Lee now knows my terminal problem. She was shocked initially but she is strong emotionally and so very pragmatic. She'll be a real help during my last days for she is my constant anchor to reality.

I must tell you that I no longer read the Bible. If it is the word of the creator, it has been filtered and refiltered through imperfect man. The written result, to me, emphasizes the narcissism of mankind, not the spirituality of a loving creator, at least not the loving creator I had long ago conceived of.

I go to no church or organized place of worship for the mouthings of the so-called "men of the cloth," including my father often make me want to puke. They preach doctrinated theology, platitudes garnered initially from inside ivy-covered, cold cathedrals and through politicized teachings of the so-called "New Testament." What the hell do most clerics really know about pain, constant pain and suffering from childhood on—like mine? Not even you can imagine it. The few who do know and try to bring it into some kind of spiritual perspective are seldom listened to.

From some mysterious, unidentified voice within me saying this is the one, some strange revelation of trust I saw in those hazel eyes of yours, I have trusted and loved you in the broadest encompassing definitions of those words in the English language. The very moment I met you I knew that my consuming dream could come true—to live, be accepted, understood. I had to trust you to really live for even so short a time. All of your actions even to the end of the rainbow in my suitcase have enabled me to make flights from gnawing pain to highs of selfish happiness I never expected.

Now, to the mundane. I know you wondered where I had squandered what funds I had saved. I will tell you. Through a girlfriend at my former job, I learned her mother was dying of cancer. The mother's last days were being spent in a type of hospice which, according to my friend was quite different from the average elephant dying ground our society is so used to accepting. The "House of Eternity" is run by a little-known order, Sisters of the Spirit. The hospice is located north of Saucellito on a bluff overlooking the Pacific Ocean. I rented a car and drove out to take a look. What I saw was to me comforting, none of the usual church trappings but the place has an air of almost mystical spirituality. Though the buildings overlook the ocean, the site is not barren and rocky. It is nestled in a grove of beautiful, towering evergreens. Much of the structures are glass-enclosed, even the individual, residential rooms have enormous windows so that nature seems to be quietly walking into each room. For me, unidentifiable serenity permeates the entire scene.

There is a dining area overlooking the ocean. That room adjoins a covered porch with the same view, a view where many days the ocean seems to calmly climb beyond the sky and at other times, the sky and sea brawl and claw at each other in a breath-taking manner. There are several rooms for prayer or quiet reflection. Those rooms are relatively bare. In each there is a table against a wall, a few comfortable chairs, kneeling pads on a soft, dark green carpet There is one closet to each such room, and in that closet are the symbols of every religion I have read about and others completely unknown to me. Those symbols can be used by an individual or small group so desiring them. If requested, a minister, priest, rabbi, shaman, or any spiritual leader may visit with you, either in your private room or in one of the meeting rooms. Guests of residents are permitted at any time the resident elects.

The one consideration that I didn't fully comprehend at first, but now do, is that there are no mirrors anywhere. No patient is obliged or challenged to look at his or her deteriorating image. If you are vain enough you may have your own hand mirror. Most residents don't.

All of the Sisters are registered nurses trained in hospice care. Their dark green robes further the illusion of bringing nature into the compound. The Order is medically served by a nearby community hospital.

After a couple of visits, I have reserved a room at The House. The financing is simple. I have placed my funds in a special kind of savings account with a bank not far from the retreat. It handles all of the hospice's financial arrangements. Those funds will earn interest. When I am no longer able to physically maintain myself and upon the written certification by my oncologist and a medical committee at the local hospital, I will move to the retreat. My funds will be drawn against by the Sisters on an agreed monthly basis. The hospice will provide for all my needs until I depart this mortal coil. If I die before the funds are completely utilized for my care I have the right to dispose of the remainder in any manner I select. I have chosen to give those funds, if any, to the Order. If I should outlive my finances, the Order will continue to care for me until I die. That's why I had no real money when you asked me. And I have provided in writing that no heroic measures be taken to keep me alive. Damn, I will have suffered enough in this life, just let me go. Where? I have no idea, but it can't be worse than what I will have lived through. So much for my problems.

Tell me of your trip home, your family and the lovely girl in your wallet. I envy her. If she truly loves you I wish I could be her friend because I admire and respect her for finding you.

At present I go to work regularly. However, when I reach the apartment at each day's end, I am increasingly exhausted. Tonight I am tired so tired I cannot continue this letter. I'll mail it in the morning on the way to work and I'll write when I can even without receiving a reply, for just thinking of you when I write helps to ease my agony.

Please, Marcus, write.

Samantha, the Swallow

In the warm silence of his third floor study Marcus rose from the sofa, walked to the window, looked at the bare maple trees that lined the street. After reading Sam's letter, the trees appeared to him as ungainly, prehistoric, unidentified skeletons, suddenly frozen in place as if they had been trapped in motion by a withering icy blast shouted by Old Man Winter when he was the caller playing the childhood game "Red Light." Marcus shivered slightly and mused, "Death I have thought of, because after life, death. But dying is something else. I have given little thought about the process though I have for years seen it in many forms: in beach landings as some unidentified bastard gasped his last on a strange beach; fish flopping with lips pursed and gills expanding and contracting in a desperate manner as they lay dying in the bottom of the skiff when Dad and I fished in Lake Erie; and the annual flowering plants in Mom's backyard garden quietly dropping their blossoms, slowly yielding to nature's demand. The process of dying has never been so intimate before." He vividly remembered Sam. For a brief period he not only saw her but was her and, he murmured, "My God, I have never before in my life felt such suffering, never imagined it could exist." As he sheepishly crept back into himself he felt ashamed for he had never before experienced that horror. Then he thought, "How can I claim to be a poet of love, hate and life without experiencing the feeling of dying for isn't that where life begins?"

While Marcus stood by the window absorbed in those thoughts he saw two pigeons huddled close together on the telephone line that led from his family home to the pole by the most grotesque of trees. "Life goes on," he mumbled. His thoughts were interrupted by the gentle voice of his mother. She was standing in the hall doorway to his study.

170

"Are you sure you won't join me for lunch? I have sauerbraten your favorite." Her eyes studied him tenderly.

"No, Mom, I'm really not hungry." Marla knew he wasn't, just why she didn't know. She left silently.

Marcus went over to his desk, sat, pulled out a sheet of typing paper. After carefully lining it up in his typewriter, he typed, thought then typed some more:

21 January 1946

Dear Sam,

To me you are no swallow, no small, insignificant split-tailed little yellow-breasted bird, that seemingly darts purposelessly from one point to another. To me you are a dark, blue-flamed comet that seared across my sight and mind, disappearing so suddenly and leaving forever imprinted within me, the warm, pinkish glow of your trail—trust.

Yes, I could feel the heat from your hidden anger, I suspected there was a health problem of deeper concern to you than your Christmas disease. I had no idea as to the origin if that is the sole origin of your anger. For some strange reason, I doubt that it is. I promise never to reveal your full answer. My relationship with you, though brief, goes far beyond the experience of a casual sexual encounter. The effect on me of our meeting really goes beyond my ability to adequately express, even consciously understand. Why your trust? Maybe it is a trust I had subconsciously dreamed of but never expected. And, it was there so suddenly in reality. Just as suddenly you were gone, leaving a glowing, disturbing memory, one I'll never forget.

Concerning your anger at whoever or whatever created you, me, all life on this earth, I do not fault you for your honest, outright expressions of pain and bitterness.

Until I met you, I have given little conscious thought that the condition of my body, my outlook on life, wasn't the norm for everyone. Now I sometimes feel ashamed for having so much. From time to time, I get a glimpse of reality and I realize that I am selfish, unduly selfish, concealed by charismatic ego. Then I feel guilt and that guilt expresses itself in concern for others. But the continuing pain you have endured with more grace than I have ever before witnessed is beyond my understanding. Yet,

171

I conceive of something far greater than all men, all matter, that understands all creation including our diverse imperfect being and accepts our frailties, even your pain. For whoever or whatever created the universe in whoever's or whatever's process of creation, in Christianity, God is the given name. For me, attempted definition trivializes the enormity of my concept. To think that God created man alone in his image, I agree is the narcissism of man. Everything the creator created is in his image. For me, he is all images. Why he created man seemingly so imperfectly I don't know. And theologians don't know either, therein enters belief. Maybe God didn't want the competition of a perfect creation. Then where would God be? So, for me, the plan or plans of universal creation are far greater than the present conglomerate mind of man can comprehend, but I believe a master plan or plans, at least for this planet, is life, life as we see it in many diverse forms. Why life? To serve the creator, maybe time and time again. And the recognition by the creator? I do not know the plan or plans of recognition but, here I go again. I believe ultimately all creation is the creator's and will be accepted by the creator in a love for which there is no current human definition or understanding.

So I say honestly, I sympathize with you but I do not really comprehend your pain for I have never suffered as you have. I do understand your refusal of going further in our relationship. I don't know how I would have reacted if I had known earlier the magnitude of your problems. However, by your letter you have cemented the most unusual friendship I have ever experienced.

I do understand why you had no funds when we met. I do not understand your relationship with your family. In your next letter, please tell me more.

I admire your choice of a place to die. Please send a photo of it if you have one as I want to endeavor to experience the spirituality it brings you.

I arrived home recently and Mariana (the girl in my wallet) was here. Generally speaking my family is well but my sister Irma is still in shock over the loss of her boyfriend who was killed in the Battle of the Bulge. She, in her way, is struggling

172

to come to grips with that reality just as you are endeavoring to understand and to come to grips with yours.

Mariana and I intend to be married as soon as I find a permanent job and we can make the necessary wedding arrangements. You are also right, I haven't told her of our meeting. I don't know how to explain it to her partly because I do not know how to explain it to myself. I found something so entirely different than I expected.

I am job searching. What it will be, I don't know yet, but it will have to offer a real challenge physically and mentally. I'll soon make up my mind.

Keep the mail coming my Goddess of Spirituality. I'll respond even if ultimately I have to tell Mariana and take the consequences.

Ever,

Marcus

Marcus took an envelope from the drawer, addressed it simply to Sam Kingsbury, c/o Alice-Lee Taliaferro with her noted address, placed the letter in the envelope, sealed it, stamped it and stuck it in one of his pants pockets. He would mail it later in the afternoon. He made a mental note to get a new notebook from the corner drugstore when he went to mail Sam's letter.

Marcus arose, went to his bedroom closet, took the two full notebooks from the bottom of his seabag and brought them into his study. For a few minutes he thumbed through them, then sat and wondered when he would really get the time to dream and put those thoughts and events into poetry. He heaved a sigh, folded Sam's letter to him and placed it inside the cover of Notebook #7. He walked to a side of the room where a small slide-bolted door opened into the empty attic space. He unbolted and opened the door. With the aid of the light from his study dimly shining into the area, he crawled out on two ceiling beams. When he reached a certain point, he reached down beneath the insulation padding and brought up a rectangular, metal box, large enough to hold a number of notebooks. Then he reached up, retrieved a small key hanging from a nail in a roofing rafter, opened the box and put the two notebooks into it. He carefully relocked the box, hung the key where only he knew of its location, replaced the box under the insulation and made sure the area looked undisturbed. Slowly he backed out of the unfinished space, shut and slide-bolted the door. That little steel container had been his Pandora's box since he had first started to take notes for his poetry. Not even his mother knew it existed. He brushed the dust and cobwebs from his pants and sweater. Damn! now he was hungry. So he ambled downstairs to rummage the refrigerator for something that would hold him until supper.

☐

Breakfast at the Bosconovich house the next morning was a more reserved gathering than usual. Marcus wasn't hungry, he was leaving for New York within two hours. Inside he had a strange feeling, stranger than when he entered the Navy, like he was leaving a loving nest, a haven, never to return to the same relationship that had nurtured him all these years. From now on, he was truly on his own, not even the masculine warmth and comradeship of his former shipmates. He was excited because he would be with Mariana, but he was saddened.

Bernie at the breakfast table looked at him with little brother affection. "I'm gonna miss you as I've never missed you before. Why? Wish I knew. Maybe it's because I'm beginning to grow up. I really like what I see when I look at you. Say hi to Mariana for me. And, good luck! Call me in an evening sometime when you haven't anything else to do and let's shoot the bull."

Marcus quietly gulped then said, "I sure as hell will, Bernie. You have my word."

Irma quietly arose from the table and holding back her tears came around, kissed her brother on his forehead. Then, with no words, she quickly climbed the stairs. To see any loved one leave was more than she could yet cope with. Such leaving shrieked to her of her loss and she had yet to put that loss in a dimmed memory.

Marla watched her children's expressions of filial love and affection. She was proud, also saddened. Her eldest was truly leaving the nest. They all knew it. Mother of Mary, she, Marla, knew it. She couldn't help how she felt. She loved him more than the rest and one reason was because he was strong and brilliant and good as he is, he's the most vulnerable of all. "Mariana," she begged silently, "He's yours now, love him as I do, for his trials are just beginning."

Marcus' dad had taken the morning off from teaching. "Son," he said and his eyes beamed with pride and affection, "We better get going. You're supposed to be at the airport forty minutes before flight time. I don't want to rush. The roads are still slippery."

The two men were silent as they drove to the airport. Each was remembering his version of Marcus' family life to the present. For each of them, there were hidden thoughts and memories of Marcus' growth from childhood. They provoked a silence of mutual love and respect.

When they reached the passenger terminal entrance at Chicago Municipal Airport, Sergio stopped the car, both got out. Sergio opened the trunk and helped Marcus deliver his traveling gear to the flight-cap. They then engaged in a bear hug. "If you ever need me, call. I'll be available," said his dad as he released Marcus.

"You know I will," responded Marcus. He kissed his dad on his cheek. "I love you," he said.

His father couldn't respond. He knew he would cry if he spoke. With a forced smile he left, looked over his shoulder, waved to his son, climbed into the driver's seat of his car and slowly drove away from the terminal. Marcus waited until the car was swallowed by the airport traffic. "You are still one lucky bastard, Marcus Bosconovich," he said and his eyes were full of tears. He headed for his flight to New York. Suddenly he remembered—he had forgotten to pack his Pandora's box with his other gear. It was still in the attic.

CHAPTER 13

On their way home from LaGuardia Airport, as she slowly turned her auto from the slick street into the driveway of the underground garage area of her apartment building, Mariana commented to Marcus, "This has been a rough winter." She stopped, rolled down her driver's side window, held out her sensor, aimed it and clicked. The garage door grudgingly began to roll up.

"Sure has been, but you're one of the lucky ones that has an in-building parking space," responded Marcus.

"That's because the building is on a hill and whoever converted it from a factory into an apartment building had the smarts to make the lowest level into parking that could be entered from the street. But it costs."

"I'll bet it does," replied Marcus.

After parking in her allotted space, Mariana helped him by taking the smallest suitcase to the elevator. He lugged the other two big ones and a Val-pack. As the elevator rose, Mariana said, "There are three residential floors with only five units to a floor. Mine is the one on the top floor, directly opposite the elevator."

When they arrived Mariana crossed the hallway, unlocked the

door and beckoned Marcus to enter. He hesitated. "You go first. You're the lady of the house," he said.

"I've seen it before. You haven't," and she waited for Marcus to enter. He passed through the front hall then gasped.

"What the hell is this, a convention center?" he asked, dropping his gear on the parquet floor and staring around the room in awe. "These ceilings must be fifteen feet high." Then his eyes settled on the large, rectangular fireplace in the center of the room, the glass doors on two opposite sides were open. The four-sided, copper-sheeted, slanted top, which reached up to the square black metal chimney pipe bounced streaks of soft yellow glow from the ceiling-mounted track lights. Gas fire logs were burning in the fireplace. "Have you taken up the art of glass blowing?" he asked as he looked at the unusual fiery centerpiece.

"I guess whoever rebuilt this place ran out of money when they reached this floor so they just improvised," replied a smiling Mariana.

"You know better. What a masterful design," and his gaze continued around the room. "Gee," he said, "You could put the entire first floor of my family's home into your living room."

"This whole place couldn't touch one room in your family's home."

"Why not?"

"Because, Darling, family love and unity just swells each of those rooms to a size I've never seen before."

"Give us time, Beloved," he said, then came over and enfolded Mariana in his arms, giving and receiving a homecoming kiss. When he drew back to catch his breath he looked over her shoulder to a Baldwin grand piano not too far from a garden scene mural wall. He noticed a sterling silver-framed photograph on the piano. It piqued his curiosity. Taking Mariana by the hand he walked over to the piano, picked up the photo and recognized his bride-to-be. "This must be your family," he said.

"It is, all except for my brother, Tully, just two years older than I. Usually I keep it on my dressing table. Since I've spent such a lovely time with your family, I thought you should at least begin to know mine, if only through a picture. I put it on the piano this morning before I drove out to meet you."

"When was the photo taken?"

"Just before Sean left to join the Army in 1942. That was one of the few times in the past ten years we've been together, except for Tully. Winsome, the housekeeper at my parents' home in Wollaston, took it. This is my dad, Brian," and she pointed to a handsome gray-haired guy seated on a love seat.

"My, gosh, now I know from whom you get your looks. He's handsome, but you." He looked fondly at Mariana, "You're just beautiful, much more so than in that picture."

"You better had be prejudiced." Mariana smiled, kissed him on his cheek and continued, "This is my mom." Marcus saw the small, attractive-looking brunette who sat with an air of disturbed arrogance. Her unwrinkled face was mask-like. "If she cracked a smile, her face would disintegrate worse than Dorian Gray's. She's had at least three facelifts and just can't stand looking older than me," said Mariana.

"Tell her to quit. She doesn't have a chance."

"Prejudiced again but I love it," replied Mariana as she tightened her free arm around his waist. "This is Sean, my older brother, standing with me behind the loveseat.

"He bares a real resemblance to your mother."

"In more ways than you can imagine," replied Mariana.

"Your other brother, Tully, where was he?"

"Who knows? He has an apartment in the Cathedral Towers and works for some kind of art gallery in Washington, D. C. We hardly ever see him or hear from him. At least I don't. And I don't care to."

Marcus sensed a real problem between Mariana and her younger brother but decided not to further inquire at the moment.

"Now that you've met my family, at least most of them, grab your gear and let me show you where we really will live." She picked up the suitcase she had been carrying and said, "Come on, Love, I've got plenty of closet and bureau space in my bedroom." Marcus stood for a minute more, gazing at the warm, comfortable living room scene, the soft Chinese antique rugs on the floor, the grouping of seating arrangements with sofas and wing chairs in comfortable conversation pits, the exquisite paintings, modern and antique that seemed to flow in harmony around the walls of the room, the large French doors that opened onto a balcony and viewed the East River, the reading nook at one end of the room with built-in book cases, filled with hardbacks of most genres read by modern man and the two lounge reading chairs nearby. "What exquisite taste she has," he thought. "I really wasn't expecting this."

"Come on Marcus, you've got to hang your suits and put away your shirts before they get all rumpled," Mariana called out over her shoulder.

Marcus picked up his gear and followed her into the master bedroom, her bedroom. When he entered, he was again surprised, then thought, "How big these rooms are and the beautifully covered twin beds. This place must have cost a fortune."

"That closet is for your suits and hanging clothes. I put my summer clothing in the other bedroom closet." Mariana pointed to a large walk-in closet. Then she pointed to the lovely antique six-drawered maple chest on stand. "You can have the top three drawers. I'll use the lower drawers and those in my dressing table."

Marcus looked at her, "Gee, she's got it all arranged and it's lovely. But, what will happen when I tell her about my discussion with Waddell?" He was disturbed, sat quietly on one of the single beds watching her. She turned toward him, came over, sat beside him, placed a hand on his knee, looked at him seriously. "Wanna talk?" she asked quietly.

"About what?"

"Whatever is on your mind."

"Nothing's on my mind. I guess I'm a little tired from the excitement of anticipation and the trip."

"Bull! I know you, Marcus Bosconovich and I love you. Want me to start?"

Marcus looked at Mariana. He had sensed an underlying uneasiness in her since she had met him at the airport. Now he could see worry and a little fear in those lovely blue eyes. "What in the world are you talking about?" he asked.

"For starters, Waddell." she replied.

"Waddell? What do you know about him?"

"He's been here."

"In this building, in your apartment?" Marcus was bewildered by the turn in the conversation.

"Yes, Beloved, in this apartment, in my living room, a few days

179

after his conference with you. He wasn't rude or crass. He called and said he would like to speak to me here, in private, about you. I agreed, so he came by and we talked."

"You never mentioned him in our phone conversations."

"No, that conversation was too important to discuss over the phone. I knew I had to wait until I saw you. You didn't mention your meeting with him in our phone talks either."

"He had no right to do that," and Marcus' mounting anger showed.

"Darling, he had every right to come by. I appreciate him doing so. Are you seriously considering his offer to go with the Secret Service?"

"Hell, Mariana, I've hardly gotten in town. I haven't had a chance to discuss anything with you and you ask right out of the blue, am I going with the Secret Service?"

"Marcus, I knew something was bothering you from the moment I picked you up at the airport. Waddell's disclosure has been bothering me. I presumed your problem was the same as mine— Waddell's offer. Am I wrong?"

Marcus looked into two inquiring blue eyes, his agitation began to melt. "No, Hon," he said softly, "Just pissed off that he has spoken to you before I got a chance to talk about it face to face with you. What did he tell you?"

"Not a great deal about the duties of the Secret Service except the members guard the president and his family, the vice president and his family, are responsible for nabbing counterfeiters of U. S. currency, paper money, coins and government notes and bonds. What was disturbing were the questions he asked about me, us, if I married you."

"What kind of questions?"

"How would I feel if you had to guard the president or his family. How would I feel if you had to go undercover and I didn't hear from you regularly, maybe for two or three weeks at a time. He also said there was some danger in the job."

"What did you say? What were your answers?"

"Well," Mariana hesitated, looked seriously at Marcus, "I told him that if, after you and I had discussed the matter thoroughly and you are determined to enter the Service I would accept the risks as a part of your job."

"Is that all?"

"No, not exactly. I told him I thought you had far more to offer the public through your knowledge of math and poetry than being the bodyguard for anybody less than Jesus Christ."

"My God, what did he say to that?"

"He laughed and said, 'You could be right. Let's see how it plays out.'"

"Did he say anything else?"

"Nothing, except you are one charismatic guy and a damned good card player. That's how he met you. I know he conferred with you at the Drake Hotel in Chicago and he made you an offer to join the Service, didn't he?"

Marcus looked at Mariana. "Yes, he did, and I told him I would talk over the matter with you before I seriously considered his offer. I was going to investigate other possibilities before I gave him an answer."

"He told me that. I'm glad you did. Why are you even thinking about the Service, with all the other possible openings through your math and poetry?"

"The offer pays pretty well. There's a good retirement program. I can still work on my poetry in my off time."

"Under the stress of that kind of occupation? No way," said a positive Mariana. She looked at her beloved, those blue eyes digging deep. "What else, Marcus? Tell me."

Marcus sighed then said, "I may owe my life to him and one of his associates an old schoolmate of mine."

"That episode happened on the train, on the way home didn't it?"

"Yes, Honey, it did."

Now Mariana was curious, truly curious but she knew she had to tread lightly because, if there was something Marcus really wanted to tell her he would have told her before now. "Can you tell me what happened on your way home?"

Mariana looked at Marcus. She saw worry and doubt, serious doubt in those hazel eyes—a look she couldn't remember having seen before. For some reason she felt as if someone had poured ice water down her back. She almost gasped aloud. "Never mind, Darling," she said then patted his knee.

"All I can say right now, Mariana, is that I was very foolish. I wish I had never been on that train."

"You mean you wish you hadn't come home to me at your family's house in Chicago?" Mariana was upset, tears filling her eyes.

"No, no, that's not what I meant, just that particular train and what happened on it."

"Well, what did happen?"

Marcus looked down at his wiggling feet. "I beat a crooked card player at his own game. Waddell was also in the game, knew quite a bit more than I did about what was really going on, later that night, he and Ron Evans saved my life, I'm sure."

Mariana knew from Marcus' attitude he was basically telling her the truth, but not all the details. She dare not dig further because she knew she would, at the present, get no more answers. She placed an arm around his waist, leaned her head on his shoulder, and said quietly, "Thank God for Waddell." Inwardly she ached, for she knew Marcus had again acted the thrill- seeker. Maybe for the first time he had really bitten off more than he alone could handle and now realized it. Worse, she believed that Marcus felt a real obligation to Waddell and Evans, whoever Evans was. That didn't come lightly from Marcus. He must have gotten himself in a real pickle. She said, "Come on, I'll help you unpack, then I know a little French restaurant on 63rd Street where we can have lunch, sit quietly and discuss our future."

"Thanks, Honey. I'd like that." Marcus again knew he was genuinely loved. As he unpacked, his heart ached about the decisions he would have to make. When he had finished unpacking he walked up to Mariana, folded his arms around his beloved and kissed her tenderly, trying to will away the decision problem. In her, there was no problem, come hell or high water, she loved him whatever his decision.

She responded with real passion. Then she drew back. "Come on, Bambino mio, let's get a cab and go out for that lunch. We're just beginning to find out what life together is really like."

For the first time in two days, Marcus relaxed. "Maybe she would understand if I decided to enter the Service," he told himself. He hoped she would see that endeavor as a legitimate challenge not just him on a new, thrill-seeking adventure. Despite what Mariana has said, if Waddell could find time for his gardening he could find time for his poetry.

Once they were seated in the quiet reaches of Quo Vadis, at a corner table for two and had ordered their preluncheon drinks, Scotch on the rocks for Marcus, Bristol Cream for Mariana, she said, "Let's talk about our wedding. I know you will find a good job before long. You've already got one offer."

"Fair enough," replied Marcus. "Where do you want to be married?"

"Here in New York, at St. Timothy's Chapel not far from my apartment. I've already discussed the wedding with my dad."

"That's fine with me," replied Marcus. He was ready to tie the knot legally anywhere; Buddhist temple, the Cathedral of St. Johns, or the Clerk's Office of the New York City Municipal Court. He was married. All he wanted was the official public stamp of approval. Mariana knew his approach, respected it but she wanted the imprint of a real church ceremony, not only for society's sake, but for hers. That was the way she had been brought up. Also, that was the way her dad wanted her to be married.

"I don't want a big wedding, just my family, your family and a few good friends," she said.

"That suits me to a tee," replied Marcus. "When?"

"Well, I have already talked to Father Edwards. He's nice, young, our age and he is willing to waive the bans providing we meet with him for three sessions of premarital counseling."

"He's our age, single, but wants three sessions of counseling us?"

"Yes, what's wrong with that?"

"Don't you think it should be the other way around?"

"What are you talking about?"

"Supposedly he's never known about sexual love, or close relationships with a woman. He's married to a church institution and he is going to counsel us on how to live together?"

"Yes, Marcus, be understanding. He's going to chat with us primarily on Catholic doctrine."

"I understand. I understand, but it's kinda hypocritical. Neither of us truly follows the tenets of our supposed religious denomination. Yet, here we are, really married, committed, but must seek society's stamp of approval and listen to doctrine."

"Is that so hard to understand?" asked Mariana. "There have to be some guide posts every society lives by, even in the jungle, or things would be an unregulated mess. Only if conglomerate man was perfect, or very nearly so, could he live a communal life of anarchy — politically, morally or socially."

Marcus looked at Mariana with affection. "We've taken some of the same classes, I can tell," he said.

"Yes, and we won't be hurt by attending those sessions. We really might learn something, including the right or wrong sacrifice Father Edwards has made for his beliefs. If he is true to his tenets, he will, in my opinion miss the greatest love of all, creation. All living creatures, whether by instinct or purposely serve the creator, God, whoever that may be. I think that in human beings loving creation is the greatest expression of service to God above any denominational edict or belief."

"And you say I am the long-winded one?" Marcus looked at Mariana with pride and respect. "You're right. We'll go. Maybe we will learn a good bit. When do you want the ceremony?"

"Let me look on my pocket calendar for various reasons." She pulled the little card from her wallet, thought and then said, "How about the second Friday in March?"

"Fine with me."

"I know my dad will want the reception dinner to be at the Astor Hotel."

"That's right expensive."

"He can afford it."

"Gee, who's going to make all the arrangements?"

"Dad and I. No sweat. You just give me the names and addresses of your guests. We'll follow through. However, it's up to you to find places for them to stay overnight if need be."

"Mariana, I hate for you to go to all that trouble."

"Making those arrangements isn't trouble. I'll only be married once in public. I look forward to doing so," and she beamed.

When they finished lunch and were leaving the restaurant, Mariana said, "Marcus, when we get home I have a list of several publishers who would like to talk with you about job possibilities. Will you call them and make an appointment with each?"

"Sure, Hon," he said, but underneath that calm commitment was the gnawing knowledge that he was merely assuaging Mariana's wishes. For some undefinable reason he really was interested in Waddell's offer to have him join the Secret Service.

When they reached Mariana's apartment, she said, "Why don't you go in my—our—bedroom, use the phone extension on the bed table and arrange for some interviews. I have to finish reading a romance manuscript before making a final determination to accept or reject."

Marcus took her fur coat and his new winter coat, hung them in the hall closet. He also took the proffered list from Mariana, went into the bedroom, slipped off his shoes and sport coat, crawled on her bed, turned on the reading light. With his back up against the headboard, he began to make calls. Mariana retired to her reading nook, took the manuscript from a folder, began to read and make notes concerning the material. The remainder of the afternoon passed as quietly as a cat in a warm empty house, surreptitiously hopping up on her absent mistresses bed, walking to the center of the new, soft quilt, curling up, then snoozing and fantasizing about whatever cats quietly fantasize about.

Mariana finished her reading and it was dark outside. She arose, looked into her bedroom, the reading lamp above the bed beamed down on Marcus. He was sound asleep. Her eyes shone like soft blue lights as she watched him, and muttered, "No wonder you are your mother's favorite. Not only are you her eldest son but you really do fit that song, 'You Must Have Been a Beautiful Baby.'" She approached the bed, turned off the reading light, kicked off her shoes and crawled onto the bed beside Marcus. "Move over you big lug," she said softly. He didn't budge. "Move over," she said louder, "My behind is hanging over the side of the bed." Marcus rolled over towards her. Mariana slipped off the edge of the bed and landed with a loud thump, butt first on the floor. He came awake with a start.

"What the hell's going on?" he asked as he reached for the reading light.

"I was just trying to crawl in beside you to take a snooze too," lamented Mariana. "That bed's too small for the two of us. It's out of here tomorrow." She arose from the floor rubbing her rump. Marcus let out a guffaw.

"It's not too small for some things, but it isn't the most comforting for just snuggling."

"Well, I like to snuggle after some things," and Mariana giggled, then said, "I'd rather have the Cavozzi heirloom than these dinky beds."

"I'll call Mom, maybe she'll mail it to us."

"Don't you wish?"

"Hon, shall we do some things, eat, and then sleep in the separate beds, or shall we eat, do some things, then sleep in the separate beds?"

Mariana's eyes sparkled. "Let's just do some things, and some things, then sleep wherever. We had a big enough meal at lunch today to carry us until breakfast." Marcus had already anticipated her answer and was busy shedding his clothes. They did sleep in separate beds for that one night.

The next day Marcus gave Mariana her first wedding gift, a king-sized bed with a headboard that matched the room decor. He bought it but she picked it out. He disassembled the twin beds and lugged them to her storage area with the help of Henry Dimond, the apartment concierge. Mariana and Marcus were beginning, even now, to settle into a joint life.

During the week, Marcus dutifully went to the interviews he had arranged on the afternoon of his arrival in New York.

Early in the evening, after his first interview when Mariana returned from her office and before she and Marcus went out to supper, she asked, "How did your day go? Who did you see?"

"First I saw Dale Morris at Scribners."

"What was the result?"

"Oh, she'll let me know in a couple days."

"What kind of work was discussed?"

"Poetry review."

"You don't sound very enthusiastic about the possibility."

"Well, Hon, to tell the truth, I don't think I would fit in, too confining, too narrow an area to cover, not much of a challenge."

Mariana studied Marcus. "That would be a good beginning spot," she said. "You would have time to work on your poetry."

"Not there."

"Why not there?"

"The place is as dull as dirty dish water. All they wanted to discuss was form, style and how much the job paid. That's just not my speed," replied Marcus.

"Well, what would be your speed? What would challenge you?"

"I don't know. I'm not yet sure. I'm going to finish the interviews before I make a decision."

"Sure," said Mariana. But she watched his every expression, the slight hitch of his shoulders as he talked and she knew him well enough to know he wasn't telling the whole truth: True, none of the entry-level openings will have the challenge, the thrill you seek in life unless you have become really dedicated to poetry or creative writing in some form. Oh, God, I love you so, I hate to see you enter the Secret Service. But, if that's what your heart dictates, I'm with you all the way regardless of where it leads.

□

By Friday noon of that week, Marcus had completed his interviews. At 2:00 p.m. he met Waddell at a Secret Service office not far from Times Square. When he entered Waddell's office, the senior operative arose from behind a desk, came around and shook Marcus' hand vigorously. "Have you made up your mind?" he inquired.

"Subject to Mariana's approval and after we are married, if you still want me, I'm interested," said Marcus.

"You sure? Have you investigated other opportunities?"

"I have, for now I'm sure. Only time will tell if I'm going into the right slot."

"That's an honest answer," said Waddell. For the first time he wondered whether he had oversold Marcus on the idea. Maybe the guy was more sensitive than he thought?

To Marcus the new line of endeavor was a challenge, a thrill of the unknown. That concept overpowered all other instincts or reasoning — and this would be a venture of legitimate service. He just knew Mariana would accept his choice.

Waddell then spoke in a businesslike manner. "I expect you to get married in not more than a month and report for duty here not more than six weeks from now. Come back this coming Monday, we will swear you in, get all paperwork completed and have you take your physical. From Monday on, until you report here for work under my supervision, I will, from time to time, give you reading material on the Service and I will give you the background of your initial assignment for you to study at home. You will be on the payroll after you sign up."

"Thanks," responded Marcus. "I look forward to working with you." Marcus started to leave.

"By the way, I do suggest you make a surface arrangement to be a roving publicist for your wife's publishing house. For the time being that could be the safest cover for you I can think of."

Marcus looked at Waddell. "Are you sure that will work?" he asked. "You've made that suggestion before."

"Talk it over with Mariana before you come in Monday. I think she will agree."

Marcus closed the door to the office, left the suite and headed to Mariana's apartment.

He arrived at the apartment building, pressed the code numbers and the front door opened. He entered the elevator. As it rose, he wondered how he would break the news to Mariana. He had a reluctance to even tell her. He unlocked the door, walked through the front hall into the huge flowing living room. At the far end near Mariana's reading area, a track light shown down on a small end table alongside Mariana's reading chair. A note was propped up on the table against an empty coffee mug. Marcus went over to the table, picked up the note. It read:

> Beloved,
>
> I know where your heart is. Take Waddell's offer. You now
> will need quiet space, even away from me, if you are truly going
> to reflect and try to do what you really do best. Go look in the
> far bedroom. I'll be a few minutes late in coming home. I have
> a staff meeting this afternoon.
>
> Mariana

Marcus was nonplussed. He hadn't said a word all week about the Secret Service. How did she know? He walked to the bedroom and opened the door. "Oh, my God," he said, then he almost choked as he gulped. He was standing in his third-floor study of his family's home. How did she do it? The off-white of the walls, the big convertible sofa bed with the muted peacock design on the light tan background, the oak roll-top desk with its row of pigeon holes, the typewriter, the gooseneck desk lamp with the red shade, the big, padded-arm swivel chair that could be adjusted to unbelievable heights, the old Bokharra rug with its geometric patterns, even the natural-colored, leather-covered easy chair. They had to be his. How did she get them from Chicago without his knowing? And, where was the tasteful bedroom furniture that had formerly graced the room? For the first time he wasn't at all sure he had done the right thing by taking Waddell's offer. The reason he had that feeling, he just didn't know. It was an elusive one.

CHAPTER 14

On that blustery March Friday afternoon, the swirling, chilling winds in Times Square added impetus and briskness of step to the homeward-bound TGIF crowd as it began to scurry for the subway entrances like many irritated prairie dogs rushing for tunnel openings as they sought to evade the jaws of the coyote clan closing in on them. The constant b-e-e-e-e-p of the taxis sounded harsher, even more frantic than usual. In contrast, there was a hushed, uncertain silence in the small nave of Saint Timothy's Church only a few blocks removed from the hustle and bustle of the center of the Big Apple.

Bernie Bosconovich, in his first rented tuxedo, but not one whit ill at ease, stood alongside his older brother, Marcus, at the foot of the chancel steps to the altar. He was Marcus's best man in the wedding about to commence. The nuptial affair was to be a small, intimate gathering. On the groom's side of the center aisle was the Bosconovich family including Marla, Sergio, Irma, Bianca and her fiancee, Vincent as well as Dominic Cavozzi, his two spinster daughters and the Feldsteins, the senior Bosconovich's next-door neighbors. On the bride's side were Arlene Trimble, Jack Willingham and Ernestine Smithers, three of her staff members. In addition to them, her maid of honor was Katherine Rogers, her former college roommate, now associate editor of The Purple Canary Press. Mariana's mother was somewhere in South America. The wedding invitation apparently never reached her.

Shortly before the ceremony commenced, two men quietly entered the church and sat in the last pew on the bride's side. Marcus, from the front of the chancel, saw them, was surprised and pleased — Ron Evans and Clarence Waddell. Mariana must have invited them. "Damn, she is smart and considerate," thought Marcus.

The ceremony began. The organ boomed Lohengrin's "Wedding March." Katherine Rogers, in a pale blue, three-quarter length, taffeta dress started down the aisle with her maid of honor bouquet demurely held at belly button height. She wondered, "I've done this so many times before, when will it be my time to make the trip, and it really counts." Next, Mariana in her lovely white, silk, ankle-length dress, her head draped with the simple, sheer, white lace veil, appeared angelic to Marcus, and she just seemed to float down the aisle on the arm of her father.

Bernie stood on tiptoe, whispered to Marcus, "Damn, she truly is beautiful." Marcus grinned and nodded in agreement. Then, both noticed a handsome, tanned young man and attractive young woman enter the church and come as close to the front as they could get on the bride's side. Marcus recognized the guy from the picture on Mariana's piano, her older brother, Sean. At least he had the decency and affection to come to his sister's wedding, thought Marcus.

☐

The ceremony was ending and after Father Edwards said, "You may kiss the bride," he took a step closer to the couple, said so softly only they could hear, "If I had found someone like Mariana, I probably would be standing where Marcus is standing instead of where I am." Marcus and Mariana beamed at the gentle man of the cloth, for he, in their private discussions before today, had already proven to be a real friend.

Just before Mariana and Marcus started up the aisle to leave the church, Marcus saw, for the first time, a serene, silver-haired, tastefully dressed woman standing at the far end of the pew immediately behind his family. She looked with affection, concentrating her gaze on the back of Brian Lucas. He must have felt the concentration because he turned his head, looked over his right shoulder at the attractive middle-aged woman. Their eyes met. He nodded his head ever so slightly. A lovely smile and slight blush lit up the face of the woman. Who was she, Marcus wondered? Mariana grinned at her father then at her father's friend.

□

The wedding dinner held in a small dining room adjoining the Astor Grill was, in the beginning a rather restrained, sedate affair. This was the first meeting by and between the two families. Though Mariana and Marcus had tried to previously arrange family introductions, the course of events had not lent a helping hand. Not until the group arrived at the hotel and were met by the photographer that Brian Lucas had engaged did the families begin to meet and greet each other.

After the various photos had been taken, it was meal time. Mariana had seen to the seating placement cards. She knew Evans and Waddell could not attend the dinner. Her dad was at one end of the table, Sergio Bosconovich was at the other. Mariana was seated next to Marcus and across the table from Marla. The remainder of the dinner guests were seated as best she could arrange in a hurry, this in view of the fact that her brother Sean, and his companion of the moment hadn't sent acceptances to the wedding. Marcus noticed that the comely gray-haired lady he had seen at the church was not one of the supper guests.

Father Edwards asked the blessing and the meal began. Dinner talk was careful, courteous. When the time came for the toasts, the champagne glasses were filled, Brian Lucas and Sergio Bosconovich gave proper toasts to the just-married couple. There was still an air of unfamiliarity that threaded the after-wedding dinner. Then, to the surprise of all, Bernie clinked a knife on his champagne glass which contained just enough of the bubbly for him to follow through. He arose with the dignity and confidence of an accomplished after-dinner speaker. His black eyes were sparkling, not from drink but from the humor and caring within. He held up his glass, glanced around the table to make sure he had everyone's attention. "He's a cool, smart youngster," thought Brian Lucas.

"To my brother and there can be none better and to Mariana, my friend because she loves my brother, I want to make this toast. It may be old to some of you but it's new to me. Just before our trip here, I found it in a little book in my high school library. The book is titled, *Toasts for Most Occasions.*" Sergio looked puzzled. Marla looked across the table at Mariana. Both were bemused because they were not sure just what would come next. Marcus grinned. He knew it had to be a doozy. Brian Lucas was fascinated by the youngest member of the Bosconovich family.

"To Mariana and Marcus on their continuing sleigh ride through life."

Mariana and Marla began to titter. Sergio was more nonplussed than ever. Bianca's fiancee cleared this throat. Bernie, with a showman's composure, continued, "Here's to the couple in sweet repose." Marla coughed then brought her napkin to her mouth to restrain her belly laugh. Mariana's cheeks were puffed out as she endeavored not to explode. She knew what was coming next, at least most of it.

"Tummy to tummy and toes to toes."

Now, even Brian Lucas' belly was rising and falling in a convulsive manner, holding back laughter.

Bernie continued, "Ah, for a moment of love's delight. Then back to back for the rest of the night. Good luck to a wonderful couple, my brother and my new sister-in-law." With that, he raised the glass to his lips and downed the champagne. Then, with an impish smile and dignified grace he sat.

Marla and Mariana whooped. Laughter filled the room. "Here, here," were the responses. Glasses tinkled, were emptied. Even Sergio was rolling with guffaws. "What a discerning young rascal you are," thought Brian Lucas, "someday you'll sway an audience for whatever cause."

The underlying restraint in the room was broken. Now the wedding celebration was truly under way.

During the merriment, Marcus excused himself to go to the men's room. Brian saw him and followed. After their ablutions, Marcus held the lavatory door open for his father-in-law. Brian looked at Marcus and said, "Thanks Marcus, let's go over to those two chairs in the alcove and chat for a few minutes." He pointed.

Marcus responded, "Sure, I would enjoy that."

When they sat, Brian studied Marcus a few seconds then said, "I regret I haven't had a chance to talk with you before the wedding, just what are you going to do with your life now that you are out of the Navy?"

"Straightforward and blunt, even more so than Mariana," thought Marcus. "Mr. Lucas, I wish you and I had been able to talk before Mariana and I were married today. We tried to arrange it but you were so busy, something always seemed to get in the way."

"I'm not blaming you, Marcus. Our lack of prior conversation was my dereliction, not yours. But, I am interested for both of your sakes."

"Mariana and I have agreed that, for the present, I will be employed as a publicity rep for her press, the writers and poets she represents. That will give me time to work on my poetry."

Brian was quiet for a brief period, his eyes seemed to bore into Marcus. "Do you really expect me to believe that explanation?"

"It's the truth. Ask Mariana."

"I will, and even if she says the same, I won't believe it," was the caustic reply.

"Just why do you say that?"

"Because I've studied your resumès, all of them and I have talked with my daughter. You're no Mister Sweet Salesman. Though you are a capable poet as far as I can tell you're not dedicated to the art. That's not all, something tells me you're not dedicated to anything but thrill-seeking, primarily because of what nature gave you, a powerful body, a quick mind, aided by your knowledge of math and card-playing ability."

Marcus was beginning a slow boil because whether his new father-in-law was right or wrong, he Marcus was offended by the tactless statement made by Brian Lucas in this, their introductory conversation.

"Mr. Lucas, you may have all of my resumès but you don't know me at all. I think you are being pretty presumptuous in your comments. I love your daughter with all of me. I would never knowingly lead a life that would in any way jeopardize our chance for a happy future together-and that includes gambling—cards— whatever. I am going to be the publicist for her firm's authors and poets. I will continue my poetic efforts. That's all I'm going to say on the subject—take or leave it." Marcus started to rise.

Brian held out his hand, motioned him to sit back. "Son," he said, "Take it easy. I believe you believe what you say is the truth. But is it? Only time will tell." He stopped, looked with apparent calm acceptance at his new son-in-law. "I can tell you love her and she knows that, but be careful with that God-given drive of yours. Keep it channeled for a worthy goal—a long life of increasing happiness for you and my daughter together. We'll talk some more from time to time. And I'll be glad to eat crumbs from the floor at your table each New Year's eve that I am wrong." Brian arose, stuck out his hand and the two strong men shook hands. They then strolled back to the festive occasion.

□

Mariana and Marcus had planned a ten-day honeymoon trip. First they were going to drive to Savannah, Georgia spend a couple days there, then they were going to fly to the Bahamas for the rest of the honeymoon. But with the advent of Marcus' new job, they changed their plans almost on the eve of their wedding day. They would stay in New York for a couple of days, relax, go to the Metropolitan Museum, Carnegie Hall, take a leisurely boat trip around Manhattan, have dinner at the Manhattan Press Club of which Mariana was a member. None of these events had Marcus ever experienced. He was excited about them. Then, they would drive to Washington, D.C. and spend a week there. Neither of them had ever visited the nation's capital, the headquarters of Marcus' new employment. There was much to see there also. The weather cooperated, the days were clear, brisk, and the evenings were cool and starlit. All in all, this was a most appropriate time and place for two such different personalities to continue to meld. They did at a loving pace.

One night while they were staying in the bridal suite at the posh Hay-Adams Hotel across Pennsylvania Avenue from the White House, and as Mariana crawled into bed, Marcus was already there propped up by pillows, writing in a notebook.

"Darling, what are you doing?" she asked.

"Just making notes for the future," was Marcus' reply.

"Future what?"

"Future writing—poems."

"I've never seen you do that before," said Mariana, a little curious.

"I've generally made those entries while you were studying a manuscript. The notes form the background, the basic concepts for my poetry.

"Except for the time I was in the Navy, I've been periodically making them since my first days at the casino."

"Why didn't you make them in the Navy?"

"Well, I wrote most of the poems you published while sitting in the open forward gun turret on the four-sixty point five. There, I had an unobstructed view of the sea in almost every direction. It was quiet in an inspirational way and I could see beyond the horizon into imagination. I used the notes I had scribbled before I entered the service."

"You know, I think your poems are lovely but you haven't answered my question."

Marcus looked tenderly at his wife. "I guess I don't consciously know all the reasons why I didn't continue my notes during that time. But, the main reason was the realization that, though I was willing to serve my country, I was at that time, serving a failure of man."

"A failure of man?" queried his wife.

"Yes, Mariana, in my opinion war is an acknowledged failure of man. How little we are removed from so-called red-blooded, carnivorous animals that the ultimate way to survive is by killing. Who knows how many brothers, husbands, fathers, my ship and I aided in killing, even if they were Japanese. And, who knows, anyone of them under different circumstances could have been my friend. I didn't know them and they didn't know me. I just couldn't make notes about such things."

"You could have been a conscientious objector," said a serious Mariana.

"I could have been, but I guess I am one of those unthinking animals that wants to survive. I wanted my family and you to survive. Putting patriotism aside to me was instinct not thinking that enabled me to handle the service. Sooner or later, I would have been drafted anyway. And there was just one basic unspoken hope among all of us. If we succeeded, maybe, just maybe, western man would have a chance to progress however he defines progress."

"How rough on you your tour of Navy duty must have been," said Mariana. Her eyes beamed respect for the honesty of her mate.

Marcus smiled, then said, "No, Dear, it really wasn't. I didn't think much about it, I just followed my survival instincts and training except in that gun turret where I dreamed into poetry."

"How lovely," murmured Mariana. Now she was beginning to have an increased understanding of the man she truly loved. He soon turned off the light and all was well.

□

"My, it's good to be back here," said Mariana as she unlocked the apartment door.

"Surely is," replied Marcus as he entered and gazed with appreciation around the lovely living room. "No place like home." He walked over and gave his wife a loving kiss. She responded.

That night as she climbed into their king-size bed, Marcus had preceded her and again was writing in his notebook. Looking at him, she said, "Gee, it's great for you to be making those notes. I can't wait for your next poems."

Marcus smiled then answered, "In a corner of the attic at my family's home, I have hidden a metal box with seven filled notebooks. They, together with this and future notebooks form the background of the poems you have published and what I hope to do in the future. On our next trip to my family's home, I shall retrieve them, bring them here. I hope to use those notebooks in the near future. In the excitement of leaving home and coming to New York, I forgot to bring them."

"Oh, Beloved, I'll call your mother tonight and have Bernie find the box, send it to you. You should have your notebooks."

Marcus was serious as he looked at his wife. "No, only you and I know they exist. I alone know where they are. When I retrieve the box, I shall do so without my family ever knowing it was there. I'll get it soon. Please don't mention the notebooks or the box to my family. My life is in there. If, God forbid, I should die before we go back to Chicago, the notebooks are yours and yours alone to do with as you wish after you have read or attempted to read them, if you can find them."

"Are they a diary?" asked Mariana in open amazement.

"Not in any acceptable reader form, but to me they are the key to my poetry and reveal me as I truly am," Marcus replied.

"Darling, you know I will honor your request. I appreciate your confidence, I do love you so." She reached over and caressed his cheek. Shortly thereafter, Marcus padded out the room with the notebook in hand. She heard him rummaging somewhere in the distance and heard a drawer in his desk slam shut. He returned, snapped off the bedside lamp and slid into bed beside her. Soon, with youthful passion, they where again united. This time, now that they were truly married, Mariana was the planner, attempting to live up to her belief that, in human beings loving creation is the greatest expression of service to God. She didn't tell Marcus. She wanted to surprise him later. She just knew he would be pleased.

CHAPTER 15

The morning after returning from their honeymoon, Mariana went to her office and Marcus started the day in his study reviewing the material Waddell had given him. After a scrounged lunch from the fridge, he went back to his task. During the late afternoon, he opened a recently received, bulky, manila envelope. In it was a file marked "Confidential." The file contained a document written by Waddell outlining the nature of Marcus's first assignment. He read it. Sure enough, he was to be a member of his new boss's surveillance team, endeavoring to help identify and bring to justice the gang of crooked card players and counterfeiters who were causing real problems for many banks, scammed victims and most of all, the Secret Service. That security organization was apparently catching holy hell from top government officials for not being able to quickly identify the leaders, the brains of the illegal operation and to pinpoint where the presses and the operational headquarters of the funny money group were located. Among other items in the file for Marcus's review were a number of snapshots of some of the alleged members of the illegal society, at least two photos of each suspect. Waddell's instructional letter contained a request that Marcus commit to memory the image of each miscreant. Among them, Marcus recognized the photos of Henry Fosberg, Oren Leverbee, the tough-looking little blonde and the thin, dark-haired brunet, the one with part of his left earlobe missing. No named identity had been given to those two. But he remembered seeing them in the train club car. Marcus studied their photos carefully and wondered what role they played in the scheme. They seemed so insignificant. As he was finishing his snapshot review, he heard the apartment entrance door slam shut. Mariana sang out, "I'm home, Dear. Where are you?"

"In the study," replied Marcus. He quickly gathered the investigative material, placed it in the confidential file and began sliding the file into the large manila folder. She breezed into the room. Marcus arose from his desk chair. They exchanged a warm kiss. Then Marcus turned, finished shoving the file into the manila folder, tied the string on the cover of the folder, put it in the top drawer of his desk and with his arm around his wife, as they left the room, he said, "Let's go to Quo Vadis for supper."

She smiled, nodded in agreement, then asked, "Been working on your first assignment?"

"Surely have. How did you know?"

"I saw the word 'Confidential' on the file as you slid it into the folder. I guessed that's what it was. Don't worry, I promise I'll never touch any of your job material. Just don't leave it lying around exposed, I might take a peek," she said and grinned.

"I won't," he replied and was comfortable with her response. They soon left for supper at Quo Vadis, their favorite eatery.

□

Cradled in a big wing chair in front of the lowered blaze in the fireplace, the couple listened to the late evening broadcast of Glen Gray and his Casa Loma Band. "Smoke Rings," the band's signature song, announced the end of the program. "My, what a lovely way to end a day after such a nice meal," said Mariana as she, nestled in his arms, leaned up and kissed his cheek.

"Couldn't ask for more," responded her husband. "For some reason, I really am sleepy, ready for bed."

Mariana sat up, looked around the dimly lit room and seeing a light on in Marcus's study, said, "You go ahead. I'll be right there as soon as I turn off the light in your study and get a little glass of milk from the fridge. That helps me get to sleep quicker when we don't do 'some things.'" She rose and headed for the study. Marcus guffawed and, as she rose, slapped her caressingly on her fanny. He headed for the master bedroom. Once there, he started to undress. Mariana walked into his study. As she reached for the wall switch to turn off the overhead light she caught a glimpse of something white under one of the casters of his desk chair. She walked over to the chair, pushed the leg roller off the object, obviously a snapshot, back up. She reached down, picked it up, turned the little photo face up, gasped and whispered, "My God, how did that photo get here? Who took it? Why?" She turned off the light, headed to the kitchen. She remembered that Marcus had been hurriedly closing a file marked "Confidential" when she entered his study before they went out to supper. She was truly upset, bewildered, "Could the photo have come from that file? Should she give it to Marcus? Or, wait and see if he inquired about it? Anything she did might lead to trouble, maybe agonizing trouble for her family, particularly her father." The snapshot, she was almost mesmerized by looking at it, was a recent photo of her brother, Tully. It was a view showing the left side of his head, revealing the partially missing earlobe. "Could he be one of the suspects in Marcus's first case with the Secret Service?" she pondered, as she hastily tucked the snapshot into a pocket of her sport jacket.

Mariana wandered unsteadily into the kitchen, almost as if she were sliding on slimy, spilled boiled okra and the thought of that made her nauseous. For the moment, she forgot what she came for, then remembered the milk. "It won't make any difference if I drink a gallon of the stuff. I'll never get to sleep tonight," she thought as she, with a trembling hand, poured milk into the fruit juice glass. "Damn it," she said as the milk flowed over the rim of the little glass onto the sinkboard. She stopped, grabbed a kitchen towel and cleaned up the mess. With forced composure, she headed back to their bedroom. Marcus was in bed, sound asleep. She gulped down the milk. Afterward she took the snapshot from her pocket, placed it, back up, on her dressing table. Taking her fountain pen from her jacket pocket, she wrote a question on the back of the photo, placed the little picture in the third drawer of her jewelry case underneath a mishmash of earrings, bracelets and clips. The case was sitting on her dressing table. Mariana cast a look over her shoulder at her sleeping mate, closed, locked the jewelry case, and hid the key on a little hook imbedded on the back of the frame of her wall-hung dressing table mirror.

She changed into her PJs. Just before getting into the king-size bed she looked at her beloved dreamer. "Oh, Marcus," she said softly with real anxiety, "Just where are we heading now?" then crawled in beside him hoping to relax and sleep. But sleep wouldn't come and the photo brought disturbing memories of how Tully her brother lost that part of his ear. She was five and he was seven. They had to stay indoors because it was a blowy, rainy Saturday. "Brutus," a collie, was the family pet. She loved the dog. Everyone in the family liked Brutus, except Tully and Brutus sensed Tully's dislike of him. Brutus generally was friendly, "Even unfortunately to strangers, he isn't much of a watch dog. He likes everybody," her dad had said. The one person Brutus stayed away from was Tully. When the rest of the family weren't around, Tully taunted, teased and hit at Brutus. Mariana had caught him in the act once or twice. Tully claimed the dog had snapped at him and he was just paying him back. Mariana knew Tully's statement was a fib.

On that Saturday morning, Mariana was sitting on the living room floor of her family's home looking at the bright multicolored characters in a large Mother Goose story book, just learning to put together letters, making words, real words. Brutus was lying beside her with his head partially on her lap. He was snoozing. Tully entered the room, walked rapidly around the oval carpet twice, then came over, sat on the floor on the other side of Brutus and squirmed. Mariana paid no attention to him. She was enthralled with her endeavor. Her brother became irritated at her lack of attention to him. Suddenly he reached down, took hold of Brutus' tail and bent it with his two hands. Brutus came awake, looked up and growled. Mariana remembered looking at her brother and saying, "Tully, don't. That's mean." Tully smirked at her, held a part of the dog's tail between his hands, leaned down and bit it hard. Brutus howled. In a flash, he whirled around, snapped Tully on his ear and Tully was still biting. Her brother let loose and screamed, holding his badly bleeding ear. Karen, their mother, rushed into the room. Tully ran to her, yowling, "That dog bit me for no reason." Mariana was petrified. She said nothing. Her mother rushed Tully to the doctor for some emergency repairs to her brother's ear. A small bloody part of his earlobe was lying on the living room rug.

Brutus, whimpering, had slunk under the sofa. Mariana had a hard time coaxing him to come out. When he did, he was shivering as if something horrible had happened and was happening. He was right. When her mother returned with Tully, his ear was bandaged. She had Winsome lock Brutus in the pantry until her dad returned that night. When he came home from work, her mother, almost hysterical, met him at the front door and right off insisted that they have Brutus destroyed. According to her, the dog had, without provocation, attacked Tully. Mariana remembered she couldn't help from blurting out, "It wasn't Brutus's fault, Tully started it."

"That's a lie," shouted Tully and he glared at his little sister. "I was merely sitting by him, stroking his tail when he just whirled and bit me."

"That's not true," yelled Mariana. "Look at Brutus' tail. I'll bet you will find Tully's teeth marks on it. He bit Brutus's tail."

Mariana's mother was seething. She came to her son's rescue. "Tully doesn't lie. Mariana has a vivid imagination She has an undue affection for that vicious animal."

Her dad went to the pantry, patted the dog, then carefully and gently examined his tail. Brutus whimpered once when her dad apparently found a tender spot on the dog's tail but he could see no teeth marks. He left Brutus in the pantry, came back to the living room. The little piece of Tully's earlobe had been previously picked up and thrown in the trash by Winsome. He turned to his son, "Are you sure you didn't bite Brutus first?" he asked.

"You don't believe me?" whimpered Tully.

"I'm ashamed of you, Brian," said Karen. "Mariana was engrossed in her Mother Goose, she didn't see what happened. I want that dog put away now!"

Mariana knew she had lost the battle to save her pet. She left the living room weeping and furious. That night Brutus was gone, so was any real affection she had for her brother. Could he now be involved in something so serious, his actions would be the subject of investigation by the Secret Service? She found that hard to believe and harder still that Marcus's first case on his new job just after they had been married would involve her brother Tully. She thought, I'll just wait for a while before I mention any of it to Marcus. She tried to put her brother out of her mind for the rest of the night. Not too successfully. Her sleep was filled with wild dreams, nightmares, all seeming to swirl around Tully.

CHAPTER 16

The next day Marcus reported for work under Waddell in the New York City field office. There was a conference. It included the ranking operatives of six teams that were riding the rails and monitoring the transcontinental passenger routes from the east coast to the west coast, from Canada to the Gulf of Mexico. The meeting was held in the conference room. Marcus soon realized that Waddell was not only the team leader of which he, Marcus, was a member, but his superior was now the coordinating officer of all six teams.

Waddell spoke, "There have been instructions from the Chief that, at present, we are not to nab and arrest the individual con artists we have identified until the complete *modus operandi* (MO), the bosses and the location of the press or presses that print the counterfeit bills have been determined. For us to now nab the crooked dealers and their support members might chase the top guns underground and thwart the Service's endeavor.

"In addition to your team reports which I have received and will be sending to headquarters with my summary, let's discuss briefly where we are and where we should be headed."

Bill Whitehead, lead operative on the New York to Miami run, spoke up in a husky voice, "I can't speak for others, but we have, up 'til now identified most of the crooked bastards that have been working the Florida run. We don't have enough men to put a constant tail on each suspect. However, another problem has been trying to identify the bagman or bagmen. Who distributes the C bills and collects the scam proceeds? When and where? We've had one hell of a time trying to find that source. Someone is or some ones are slick. If we could determine those runners maybe we could trace their steps to the brains of the operation."

The other leaders nodded in agreement. "But," said Whitehead, "That's not the main problem."

"What do you mean?" asked Waddell.

"Since Friday a week ago, all of the suspects on our train have disappeared, one by one, as if dissolved into thin air."

"Same here," said Operative Alvin Smith, lead on the Dallas run. The others agreed.

Waddell was upset. "You mean those con teams are no longer on your routes?"

"That's correct," said Smith. "On our run from Cleveland to Dallas ten days ago those rascals began leaving the train, one at a time, at various stops. We didn't have the men to follow them but we did notify the nearest field office sending them copies of their photos. Not one of the suspects was on the train during our return trip."

"It's almost as if they had been tipped off that we were on their trail," said Whitehead.

Marcus stared at Waddell. His leader seemed not a whit perturbed. "Could be they have been called in for a meeting," said Waddell. "Or could be I screwed up."

"You screwed up, how?" asked Whitehead.

"Some time ago, on our last run from Frisco to Chicago, and at the last minute, I had to enter the game on the City of San Francisco. Even though I used a fake ID, I used no disguise. The way the evening ended might have led their leader onboard to realize there was a Fed in the game. Most of the con team on our run left the train in Omaha, Nebraska around two in the morning."

"You say most, what do you mean by most?" asked Smith.

"Someone murdered their game player that night on the train before they left. I feel sure it was one of the trio that got off at the Omaha station."

"Why would they kill their own shill?" asked Williams.

"Because he really did not know how to handle a game in which he lost a pot full. His pals were afraid he might talk if he was cornered by the law," answered Waddell.

"How in the hell did he lose so badly? Generally, the team works on counterfeit payoff anyway?" queried Smith.

"Gentlemen, I am not at liberty to divulge any more information at the moment. Don't worry. Just keep alert. Each of your teams will make one more run. If there are no marked games and bad C bills passed we know they will have changed their MO.

"There's one thing we do know. Whoever heads the ring is avaricious and thinks big. He or they can't stand being idle very long. A new method of operation will evolve soon. In the meantime we can digest the forthcoming report on the evidence that's being turned over by us to the FBI lab. Already, we know who makes the paper the bills are printed on. The manufacturer has agreed to put a new hidden date marking on all future C bill paper runs. A large amount of similar appearing but entirely different grade of paper is sold to the government through D.C. procurement channels as well as to leading office suppliers and stationers in the northeast area. It is not uncommon for private contractors to try and match government stationery paper—anything to curry favor. Maybe we'll learn more."

After a brief discussion of technical matters, the meeting ended. Waddell and his group remained in the conference room. When the last of the other leaders had gone, Waddell turned to the members of his team. "There are a number of loose ends for us to tie up here at the office. It will take us a while. However, you will leave two weeks from this coming Friday on another trip west first by New York Central to Chicago then by Southern Pacific to San Diego and back."

"What do you mean, 'you,' shouldn't that have been 'we?'" asked Comstock.

"No, I meant the three of you to be joined by Peahead when you entrain in Chicago. I have been ordered to remain here and coordinate the efforts of all six teams. Ron, you will be the operative in charge, still the barman. Brad, you are the player. Marcus, you are the representative of your wife's publishing company, the club car game watcher. Here are your purported ID cards." Waddell handed Marcus a complete new set of identification including a social security card, New York driver's permit and Purple Canary business cards all bearing the name Wesley Young.

Marcus looked at the set, momentarily surprised and stunned.

Before he could say a word Evans spoke up, "Welcome to fantasyland. None of us openly carries our true identity on this operation. You know our real identities because of what happened on the City of San Francisco. See," and Ron pulled out his wallet. To all intents and purposes, he was Leon Applewhite. "We carry our real identities here until we need them." Ron took off his right shoe, carefully pulled up a sole insert. Underneath the insert was his Secret Service ID card. He turned it over. On the back were two phone numbers. "The top one clears through this office. The lower one, when used correctly, reaches the Intelligence Office in Washington, D.C. During the week, we'll instruct you on the correct use of the card," said Evans. "Here's your sole insert and Service ID."

Marcus was now more surprised than ever. He took off his right shoe and tried the insert. It fit perfectly. "How in the hell did you know my shoe size?" queried Marcus.

Evans smiled and said, "The night you slept in the 'mail car.' Waddell came into your roomette while you were sleeping, took the size and imprint of your right shoe inner sole. He was sure, even then, that you would come with the Service."

Marcus looked at Waddell. Waddell was watching Marcus with the eyes of a cheetah. "You're not only quiet, confident and smart, you have the balls of a brass monkey," said an agitated Marcus.

Waddell relaxed, merriment danced from those gray-blue eyes. "You have to have them in this sport. Yours are just as hard as mine or you wouldn't have gotten in that game on the train."

"What in the hell is Mariana going to say when I tell her?"

"Ask her if she has a new sales rep by the name of Wesley Young."

Marcus's mouth dropped open in awe at the nerve, the ingenuity of his new boss.

Waddell grinned, then said, "I asked her shortly before your honeymoon. At that time, I requested her not to tell you for your own good. I said I would tell you when the time was ripe. I had my reasons, I can tell by your expression and reaction that she didn't tell you. Marcus, I promise never again to confide in your wife and request that she keep it a secret. I have found out all I need to know. You, my friend, are married to a very lovely helpmate. I can trust her as she trusts you. There may be times in the future when I have to call her but it will involve no secrets to be kept from you—I promise. However, there will be times when she must keep your missions private—if she knows."

The others on the team were intently watching Marcus.

"I appreciate what you've said. And, yes, I married a wonderful woman. I've known that from the start of our relationship. All I ask, Waddy, is that you never knowingly put Mariana at risk." Marcus still wondered how in the hell Waddell was so confident that he, Marcus, would come with the Service.

"Agreed," said Waddell then he smiled at Marcus.

Comstock and Evans relaxed. The test was over.

Waddell spoke, "Marcus, you're damned observant, knowledgeable and clever with cards but I know you've had no training with side arms. Until your team trip, Ron, among other instructions, will be giving you an intensive course in weapon handling. He'll take you regularly to the nearby N.Y.P.D. range for pistol practice and technique. In addition, Brad will help you with the simple elements of disguise. Your instructions for disguise on your upcoming trip will be given in your orders." He stopped, looked seriously at his little group, then continued, "Gentlemen, there will be no private quarters on the Empire State Express. You will be bunking, upper and lower, in Pullmans until you reach Chicago. The Southern Pacific trip will have the 'mail car.' Ron, as the leader, you have your instructions. Marcus, keep those keen eyes open as to all who enter the club car particularly those in the game and keep in touch with Ron. Finch, just don't lose too much. It's not your money." The threesome tittered. "Ron, from now on, it's your deal, take over. In addition to the odds and ends of office reports we have yet to complete, you will have ten days to prepare for the run. When you see Peahead, tell him this is his last cushy trip to the west coast. I'll see each of you when you return, good hunting." Waddell arose and left the conference room.

Evans turned to Marcus, "When you read your instructions, you'll realize that Waddell is a quiet wizard. The details of his orders will amaze you."

"He has already amazed me more times than you know," responded Marcus.

Comstock left to do more paper research. Evans took Marcus in tow to the secluded, underground range not far from the office.

When evening fell with the first target practice session ended and as they walked to the subway, Ron said, "Leave your true identification papers at home from now on. Hide them in a place only you and Mariana know of." He looked again at Marcus. "Relax, you're not carrying a hot potato under your jacket also you are not an army sniper looking for an enemy. Only in last-ditch, self-defense or defending a required subject will you ever use it. I've had mine for over four years, never drawn it yet. Half the time, I don't have to wear it. You'll learn."

"Right now that revolver feels like I am carrying an exposed machine gun."

"I understand, but with your build and the fit of your jacket, no one will ever know it's there. Just think of it as a fountain pen in an extra pocket."

"That will take some thinking," and Marcus smiled feebly.

On the subway headed for home, Marcus, for the first time, began to realize that his newly chosen occupation wasn't a thrill-seeking adventure but tedious hard work demanding concentration on details, even more so than in his poetry efforts. "This is not what I expected," he said softly as he exited the subway stairway to the street and started his walk home.

☐

That evening during supper at home, Mariana asked, "Hon, how was you first day?"

"Quite different than I anticipated. For a while I will be learning how to handle a pistol, use disguise, interview suspects, and God knows what else. On Friday two weeks from now I leave with the team on another run, this time to San Diego. We'll be gone between two and three weeks. I'll keep in touch. The team will be in San Diego for at least five days. I'll call regularly while I'm there. Both Waddy and Evans have assured me I will have time to be your rep while I am in San Dieg."

Mariana was quiet for a few seconds, then said, "When you're in San Diego there are a number of bookstores I would like you to visit. Before you leave, I will prepare a sheet with names and addresses and give you a number of book lists to discuss with them. They can either order direct or through my distributor for that region. In addition, I'll furnish you with publicity info on the lead volumes. In the meanwhile, I will drop those stores a note that you will be by in the near future. Just make sure you introduce yourself to the store representatives as Marcus Bosconovich. I will have laid out the background work before you get there. Also remember, you are Wesley Young in your work with the Secret Service. We can talk by phone about any store problems."

Marcus smiled feebly. "I hope I have done the right thing," he said.

"At least, you've taken the first step," said Mariana. "Beloved, I think that it is in the right direction. But, whether it is the road you really want to travel to the future, only you can tell and you have to give the effort time. You know I'm with you."

"I know that, I've always known that. But, for me, the future isn't as clear as it once seemed to be."

"Marcus, my darling, the real world ahead is never as clear as the one you see when you look back over your shoulder. Just handle it the best way you can. That's all any of us do. If you do your dreams will be the richer for those efforts and your poetry will have ever deeper meaning. Don't let everyday life smother those dreams."

"I won't, you have my word. Thanks for your understanding."

To Marcus the supper tasted better, the rooms seemed warmer, more pleasant and the thrill of living was back, particularly living with Mariana.

CHAPTER 17

One morning in late May, Michael Weaver had just returned home from an extensive trip setting up the new MO for his organization and picked up the accumulated mail from his Cathedral Towers apartment box (Number 16). All of the apartment house mail boxes were on the wall of the main corridor on the same side as the elevators. He also picked up the mail for the efficiency apartment next door to his (Number 18). He had the keys to both mailboxes, was entitled to receive and read the mail from each. The Number 18 box held, among other items, a large brown envelope addressed to Mr. Tully Lucas. On the face of that envelope was stamped "Don't Bend or Fold, Photo Inside." He knew from the return address on the envelope that whatever was enclosed was from the produce firm of Finley & Finley in Boston, Massachusetts.

Weaver took the mail from the boxes to his apartment. After getting a cold beer from the fridge, he flopped into his reading chair in the living room, turned on the nearby standing lamp, and started to open the mail. He decided to first tackle the large, flat envelope addressed to his alter ego. On opening the envelope, he saw a note accompanying an eight by ten inch photograph. The note read:

Dear Tully,

Though you didn't attend your sister's wedding, I am sending you one of the photos taken right after the ceremony. As you can see, your sister was a beautiful bride. Her husband is no slouch in looks either. His name is Marcus A. Bosconovich which you should know from the wedding invitation Mariana sent you. In addition to writing poetry, he will be a traveling publicist for your sister's publishing house. I think you should send her an appropriate gift.

Write when you can.

Love,

Dad

Michael looked at the young bride in the photo. Damn, she does look lovely, but he hated every inch of her even in the bridal gown. Then he glared at her new husband. He blinked, looked again, blinked again. "I must be losing my mind," he said, "I see his face on almost every guy I look at." He held the picture at arms length and squinted. Again he closed his eyes and felt as if a surge of electricity was charging every nerve ending in his body. He opened his eyes, with the photo still at arms length focused on the smiling groom, shivered in excitement and fear, fear that he was seeing an image that wasn't there. He reached over to the phone on a table near him, placed a call. When a male voice answered, Michael spoke in an excited high, almost female, voice. "Leverbee is that you?"

"Who are you?" answered a resonant male voice.

"Oren, it's me Michael."

"What in the hell has happened to you?"

Michael gulped, calmed a bit, then in a more normal tone replied, "Got a frog in my throat. But jump in your car, get your ass over here as soon as possible because I've got something unusual to show you."

"Can't it wait until after supper. I was just going out the door to get a bite to eat?"

"No! And if it is what I think it is you'll be as excited as I am."

"Okay. I'll be there in less than ten minutes."

"Thanks," said Michael and he hung up the phone. He was quivering with excitement, rage. He arose, started walking around the edge of the large oriental rug in the living room as if he was leading a nervous race horse by headstall around the paddock before the big race. Only he was the race house but who was leading him? When he was excited, he could feel the headstall but he could never see the walker at the end of the halter.

Some unseen hand always seemed to be leading him when he was excited, had been doing so ever since he was a youngster, like the hand that led him to get even with his sister by biting the tail of her dog, getting even with her for being dad's favorite and she was dad's constant favorite. As always, he had that weird feeling — maybe Brian isn't my dad. Now, if what he had seen was true he could really triumph more than he ever dreamed of. Suddenly, he had to urinate so he raced to the bathroom and wondered, "Why is it that whenever I become excited I have to piss? No one but Lorraine knows I wear protective pads to help from revealing my weakness at stress time. If she ever dares to open her mouth about my problem and I find out that will be the last time she will ever again do so."

Returning to the living room, Michael Weaver took the wedding picture of the couple and placed it on the fireplace mantle, just underneath the original, framed etching of Henry Clay, his favorite. Once more he resumed his pacing around the fringe of the rug until the front door bell rang. Now, he was calmer, walked to the door, opened it. Seeing Oren Leverbee, he said, "Welcome to the house of revelations."

"What the shit are you talking about?" inquired Leverbee.

"Take off your raincoat, drop it on that chair," and he pointed, "Then look around the room and tell me what you see."

Leverbee placed his coat on the chair, looked casually around the room, smirked and said, "I see a lot of expensive furniture but no taste," he answered.

"Look again."

Leverbee again looked, this time he was observant with two beady eyes that had been trained for years to see the smallest details. Finally, his eyes moved to the mantle, passed the photo, then stopped. He looked back at the picture of the newly wedded couple, took two steps forward and with both hands took the photo from the mantle, squinted and brought the picture closer to him. "Where in hell did you get this?" he asked.

"That's the sister of my friend next door and her new husband."

"His sister?"

"You heard me."

"And that bastard is her husband?" he nodded toward the groom in the photo.

"So, you recognized him also. I thought I might be hallucinating. That's why I asked you to come over."

"He's the Navy jerk who swindled Fosberg. What's his name?" asked Leverbee.

"Marcus A. Bosconovich."

"That's him, that's him. When I asked Fosberg his name, he said, 'something like son of a bitch.' I thought he was nuts. He almost had it right, poor bastard. Where are they now?"

"Right this minute, I don't know, maybe on their honeymoon."

"Where do they live, if you know?"

"In New York City, in her apartment, I guess. She's a small publisher there. According to my friend's father, that jerk is a poet. He will be working for her as a publisher's rep."

"After all the trouble he has caused us. I'd like to get my hands on him," said Leverbee.

"Calm down, Oren. If her dad is right, we may be able to parley this photo into something really big."

"I'll wager he's no more poet or publicist than I am. I'll bet he is taking your friend's sister for all she's worth and doing a little quiet gambling on the side. He's just a born gambler, I could tell."

"My God, I hope you are right. However, remember someone else was in that game on that train. He is the one who caused me to change our MO. I wonder if the damned poet was a part of his operation?"

"Not a chance, my friend. That guy is just a thrill-seeking gambler, looking out for numero uno. The main thing that has bothered me about him is how he got off that train—disappeared."

"That's been bothering me also. Believe you me I intend to find out. We'll just take it slow and easy. We've got too much at stake for a knee jerk reaction. Now I have a way to begin our search to find him. You've answered my question. Supper is on me, let's go to Napoleon's. It's got the best coq au vin in town."

□

That evening, the men sat opposite each other at a table for two in a quiet corner of the upscale dining room on Connecticut Avenue in D.C. enjoying their meal. Michael looked at Leverbee and said, "I put out a tracer on O'Connor. You're right. He is a fed, a long-time member of the Secret Service, I'm sure his real name is Clarence Waddell. Why in the hell he had no disguise is beyond me."

"Emergency," said Leverbee. "He probably was placed in that game at the last minute like a substitute."

"Who was the leader?" asked Michael.

"Damned if I know. It certainly wasn't the black bartender. He was too old and dumb and it wasn't fatso. He was just a wealthy blowhard having fun. It could have been the fed."

"There are a couple other items that worry me, big time."

"Like what?" asked Leverbee.

"Well, if we recognize Bosconovich, I'm sure he could recognize us—you—me."

Leverbee was quiet for a few moments, then replied, "Maybe so. But, will we ever see him again? And why?"

"Oh, we might run into him at some odd time. For what reason, who knows, except I would like to throttle the son of a bitch."

"I can understand that desire," said Leverbee. He felt a little disturbed. "I doubt that the sailor ever saw us," he said, then inquired, "Is that the only item?"

"No," replied Michael, "I am sure that my friend next door sent a photo of me to his sister long before she met that seagoing prick, sort of a long-distance introduction."

"Why?" asked Leverbee.

"Oh, he's kind of a romantic bastard, likes to play the matchmaker."

"Well, he didn't do very well by you. She married that slimy seagoing cook." Leverbee pointed to Marcus' picture.

"I know. If she showed him my picture and he recognized who it was, he might try to do something about it."

"Why, what would he do? He doesn't know you from a sack of salt. You weren't in the game. You, Lorraine and I were just in the club car. Shit, he'll never think there was a tie-in. How could he?"

"You're right. I'll skip it. Somehow just seeing that photo made me nervous."

"There are more important items for us to talk about," said Leverbee. "Here are the reports on your new MO." Leverbee handed a set of papers to his boss. "As requested by you, each major USO

Club in San Francisco, Miami, New York, Chicago and Dallas is now well-covered. We've rented a room in the designated hotels on the list. Each is as close as we could get to the respective USO Club.

"Lorraine is meeting each leader, making new distributions and picking up our proceeds from past events. The shills visiting each club are good. For the time being however, they are playing it carefully as you suggested only five suckers to a game in the hotel rooms. The limits are low. I think there will be less chance of successful surveillance than ever before. That was one damned good idea of operation you concocted after the City of San Francisco problem. Lorraine will arrive from her collection trip within the next four days. She tried to reach you earlier today but you were out so she reported to Cahill and he told me to tell you."

"Thanks," said Weaver, "I'll be glad to get the proceeds. We need them. And I'll be happy to see her again."

CHAPTER 18

The next morning, Michael Weaver, after arising and thinking about the events of the previous evening, was excited, had already gone to the bathroom once. Then he went to the apartment next door. At 9:30 a.m., he placed a long distance call from that apartment. Someone on the other end answered, "Finley & Finley."

"I want to speak with Brian Lucas," said Weaver.

"Who's calling," a female voice asked.

"His son, Tully."

There was silence of a few seconds then, "Hi, Tully. It's good to hear from you."

"Good to hear your voice too, Dad. I just returned from an extended business trip and found the wedding picture of Mariana and her new husband you sent in early April. She looks lovely."

"Indeed. She was a beautiful bride," answered Brian. He wondered just why in the hell Tully was calling to say that his sister was beautiful. Brian knew the two hated each other.

"Have you sent her a gift yet?" asked his dad.

"No, but I will in a couple days. Where are they living now, so I'll know where to send it?"

217

"In Mariana's apartment in New York. Is that the reason for your call? To tell me your sister was a beautiful bride and to check her address?"

"No, that's only part of the reason I called."

"What's the rest?"

"Well, I showed the wedding picture you sent me to a friend of mine, a private investigator in our office building. He thought he recognized the guy."

"Why would he know Mariana's husband?"

"Because if he is the guy my friend thinks he is, he's no poet but a petty gambler, a card shark that he stumbled across sometime ago."

Brian was stumped, aghast. Certainly he had never told Tully about Marcus' background. How did Tully know Marcus was good at cards?

"I don't understand," replied Brian cautiously.

"I didn't think you did. I know Mariana and I don't get along well. But I would hate to see her tied to some no-good gambler who might be taking her for all she is worth."

"So would I," answered Brian.

"Dad, I think I should fly up and discuss the matter with you. I don't like to do it on the phone."

Brian was intrigued. Maybe Tully wasn't so bad after all. Sibling rivalry wasn't an unknown factor in most families. And Tully was Mariana's brother. There had to be some filial connection.

"When would you like to come up?" asked Brian.

"I'll meet you in your office at ten a.m. this coming Friday if it's okay with you."

Brian glanced at his calendar. It was clear. "I'll be waiting for you, see you then. Thanks for calling."

After Tully hung up, Brian was agitated, wondered how in the world Tully knew about Marcus. He called Mariana on her private office number.

She picked up the phone, "Mariana," she said.

"Hi, Honey," said her dad.

"Oh, how lovely to hear from you so early in the day."

"Always the right words."

Mariana giggled, then asked, "What's on your mind? There has to be a special reason for you to call before noon."

"You're right, Mariana. There is. Not long after your wedding, I sent Tully a wedding photo of you and Marcus. I also suggested he send you a wedding present."

"You might as well have suggested that he jump off a cliff," was her tart reply.

"I understand," said Brian, "But I received a disturbing call from him this morning."

"Why?"

"Because, he said he had just returned from a business trip and found in his mailbox the wedding picture of you and Marcus I had sent earlier. He showed it to a friend of his who recognized Marcus."

"So," said Mariana. Now she was curious.

"His friend, a private detective, said he recognized Marcus as a crooked gambler he had met on an occasion."

Mariana was alarmed, defensive. "Where did Tully's friend meet him?"

"He didn't say. Tully is flying here Friday. I am to confer with him in my office at ten a.m."

Mariana was silent. She was remembering the snapshot of Tully she had found in Marcus' study.

"You still there?" asked her dad.

"Yes, I'm here, just thinking how in the world Tully could know that Marcus is good with cards."

"I really have no idea. I certainly haven't talked to him about Marcus. I was calling you to find out if you had recently talked to Tully or have any idea how he got the information."

"None," replied Mariana. "God knows when I last talked to Tully, it was long before I met Marcus. I'm sure Marcus is no crooked gambler even if he is knowledgeable with cards."

"I hope you are right. Is he home with you?"

"No, not presently. He's on a business trip for me, why?"

"I just wondered if Marcus was home with you."

"You're wondering a lot more than that. Like it or not, I'll tell you once more he's no crook. I am sure of that. I've got to go, I have an author's agent waiting in my reception room." She hung up her phone. She knew her father wasn't convinced that she had married the right guy.

Brian was worried by Mariana's agitation.

CHAPTER 19

Tully arrived at the Finley & Finley office suite on time and was ushered into Brian's office by Priscilla White, Brian's secretary. She cast a wary eye at Tully as she opened the door to his dad's office. She hadn't liked the young son for years, not since he was sixteen, when she, upon returning from a quick trip to the ladies room, had caught him dumping her desk glass jar of jelly beans into his jacket pocket. As she entered the room, he quickly placed the lid on the jar, sat it on her desk and said, "I just took a couple. They looked so good." The jar was almost empty. She had refilled it earlier that morning. She didn't say a word in reply but by her looks he had to know she knew he was lying. She was positive this present visit, like all others, meant trouble. It always did when Tully came to see his dad. The last time, more than four years after he moved to D.C., was to wheedle a couple thousand dollars out of Brian allegedly to cover the costs of an abortion for some hard-nosed bitch in Washington, D.C. Priscilla, observant as she was, was sure the whole deal was a concocted story and that Tully and his paramour, whoever she was, were in cahoots, needed the money to cover some crooked debt or scheme.

How did she know as much as she did? Well, she was the one who cut the check for Tully. After Brian had delivered it to his son and Tully left, she had asked Brian to what account should the check be charged. He had been quiet for a minute or two, "To mine," he had said. Priscilla, having been Brian's secretary for twenty years and his friend, had finally dug out of him what the check allegedly was for, then promised never to tell and she hadn't. Tully made her blood boil for she knew Brian had spent thousands of dollars on him endeavoring to have his son educated, first at Choate School for Young Men, then two years at MIT and finally for two years at the Boston School of Fine Arts where Tully apparently excelled in the art of etching. Shortly after finishing art school, Tully moved to Washington, D.C. and became employed by some art gallery that specialized in etchings. He hadn't darkened his dad's office door since the abortion affair.

Tully approached his father's desk, attempted a smile which his father saw as a humorless grimace, then Tully said, "Hi, Dad, it's good to see you again. You look well."

Brian looked calmly almost coldly at his son, shook Tully's extended hand and replied, "How goes it with you?"

"I'm still slaving for the gallery. I guess it could be a lot worse."

"It mustn't be all that bad. You've put on a few pounds and you are wearing a Hart Schaffner and Marx."

Tully slouched into a chair on the opposite side of the desk from his father, responded, "Still the observant one, you introduced me to that line. You've been wearing that brand for years."

"Well, I can afford it."

"How do you know I can't?"

"Tully, you're right. I don't really know what you can afford. The fact is right now I know very little about you. You've never given me the opportunity to do so. Except when you've needed money, you have avoided me as if I stunk like a skunk. Why now?"

Tully boiled inwardly for he knew his father was bluntly right. Again the grimace then, "I guess I'm growing up a bit. I don't need money—not right now anyway. I really came because of Mariana."

"I remember what you said on the phone," said Brian as he intently studied Tully. "Why the sudden interest?"

"My interest isn't that sudden. We are a family after all, aren't we? I may be a little jealous of her financial condition. But, I would hate worse to see the money leave the family. She may need it one day."

Brian was irritated because some of the feelings Tully had expressed were his also. "Son," he said, "I do worry about your sister. I don't know how much she really knows about her husband. In my opinion, he is quite a complex character."

Tully was really interested. This was the true reason he had made the trip. "What do you mean by complex?" he asked.

"Well, Marcus is a Phi Beta Kappa graduate from Cornell, has his master's degree in math and is a published poet. Your sister included his works in her book, *Poems by Three Pacific War Poets.*"

"I had no idea," said a concentrating Tully.

"That's not all," responded Brian, "He was champion middle weight boxer at college and a finalist in the U.S. Navy 7th Fleet boxing tournament during the war. I have to admit, he not only is a damned good-looking guy and he has funds."

"Holy crap, I had no idea."

"In addition," said Brian, "His master's paper is an interesting read, entitled "How to Gamble Right." After Marcus left Cornell and until he entered the service he was a house dealer at a Reno, Nevada gambling casino. He is from Chicago. His parents still live there. They are most pleasant. To me, Marcus is an enigma."

Tully's mind was whirling with what he had just learned. "So, my friend was right when he said he had met Marcus and that Marcus was a crooked gambler."

"Not so fast," replied Brian. "Two and two only make four."

"Unless they are put side by side, then they make twenty-two," replied Tully.

"Son, you are jumping at big conclusions. How do you know Marcus is a crooked gambler?"

"Because my friend was in the club car of Union Pacific's finest streamliner, the City of San Francisco, coming east earlier this year when he watched a card game. He's sure Marcus was in that game."

"So what?" asked Brian.

"My friend who knows cards is also sure that the cards used in the game were marked. He is dead certain that Marcus knew the cards were marked. My friend said Marcus walked away from that game with a bundle. The memory of that slick card shark just stuck in my friend's mind."

"Did your friend do anything to let the others in the game know that Marcus was a crooked gambler?"

"No," replied Tully, "Because my friend was afraid there was at least one other game player in cahoots with Marcus, and he wasn't sure that some of the other occupants of the car were not members of the illegal activity. He didn't want to get in any trouble."

"Tell me, Tully, you say your friend is a private investigator. Why was he on that train?"

"Oh, he was just returning from Frisco where he had followed a wealthy, cheating husband and his lady friend from D.C. They were passengers on a westerly run of the same train. My friend had taken pictures of them during their trip. He represented the wife of the guy. He was gathering material for her pending divorce proceeding in D.C."

"And you say the private investigator has offices in the same building your gallery occupies?"

"That's right. I have his card. I'll give it to you before I leave. You can check his references. He's a member of the National Association of Private Investigators. By the way, is Marcus at home now with Mariana or is he supposedly on the road as her business rep?"

"I'm not sure," responded Brian. And he wasn't. He realized he had not doubted for one minute that Marcus worked for Mariana whatever his other activities might be. Now he wondered why he hadn't checked to find out.

"Maybe I'll have my friend try to find out if Marcus really does work for Mariana."

"Tully, that's not such a bad idea. Let me know what he finds."

"Would you cover his expenses say up to five hundred bucks?"

Brian was quiet, looking intently at Tully. "Yes, providing you give me his card and he is legit."

"Sure," replied Tully as he handed his father the card. Brian looked, studied it. The card read: " Paul Cavalier—Private Investigator," same address as Tully's, but Suite 403, a telephone number and finally: "Member of the National Association of Private Investigators."

"I'll check him out. I know the Association," said Brian.

"I was sure that you did," replied Tully. He again forced the grimace.

Brian looked at his watch then at Tully. "Son, I've got a business appointment in Quincy, Massachusetts at noon. I hate to break up this meeting but I have to go."

"That's alright, Dad, I knew you were busy and had slipped me into your schedule. I've got a couple other matters to tend to while I'm here today. In addition I've got to catch the 5:00 p.m. train back to D.C. Please keep in touch with me about Marcus and Mariana. I'll let you know what I find out."

For some reason, Brian felt that Tully had already found out more about Marcus than he expected to. Maybe he, Brian had shot his mouth off more than he should have. But what he knew was available to any businessman. "So long, Son," he said, "Don't forget to send your sister a wedding present."

"Don't worry, I won't. By the way, Dad, do you know if Mariana has a family photo of all of us?"

Brian pondered briefly then replied, "Not to my knowledge. The copy of the last group photo I sent her did not include you. God knows where you were at that time. It was just before Sean entered the Army. Why?"

"No real reason. We have her wedding picture, but she has none of her whole family to show Marcus," said Tully.

I guess you're right but that's your fault not mine," replied Brian.

Tully left the room quite satisfied. As he sauntered down the hall toward the elevator, he began to worry, "Just who in the hell is Marcus Bosconovich and how did he disappear on that train?" he mumbled. Before Tully took the elevator to the building lobby he had to stop by the men's room to relieve himself. He was excited.

□

Two days later, as Leverbee and Michael Weaver were again seated in Napoleon's having supper Weaver spoke, "I had a long talk with my next-door neighbor. He was in town overnight and gave me some interesting information on his sister's husband that bastard Bosconovich."

"Like what?" asked Leverbee.

"Well, first of all, he is no simple crooked card shark."

"What's that supposed to mean?"

"He's an honor graduate from Cornell University, has his master's degree in mathematics, is a recognized poet and was a collegiate champion middle-weight boxer. In addition, before he entered the Navy he was a house dealer at a Reno gambling casino."

"Christ, I had no idea," said Leverbee, "But I told you he was smart. Where is he now?"

"Apparently he is a publicist for my friend's sister, the publisher and working on his poetry."

"Shit, that just doesn't sound right. That jerk has too much energy to be tied down to such a job."

"I agree. That's where you come in."

"Just how, Michael?"

"By helping me find out what that bastard is really up to. I want to find out how he left that train and why."

Leverbee looked questioningly at Michael wondering why the serious interest. "Hell, Michael, we could be sticking our nose into a bucket of crap. Why bother with the jerk?"

Michael was irritated. "I'll tell you why and I've thought it through carefully. First, Waddel, the Secret Service operative, was in that game. That damned sailor stole a potful from Fosberg. If you think that Waddel didn't know what was happening you're dumber than I think you are. I am sure that Waddel has communicated with Bosconovich. Waddel may be the one to have caused that Navy jerk to disappear, how and for what reason I'm not sure."

Now Leverbee was genuinely interested. "Damn, I never thought of it that way but you could be right," he replied.

"I gave your PI card to my friend next door and he gave it to his dad. Since then I've heard from my neighbor. His dad may get in touch with you to have you find out if Bosconovich is really employed by his daughter as a publicity rep. Whether or not he calls I think we ought to try and find out."

"That shouldn't be hard to do," responded Leverbee.

"I agree. Start on it tomorrow. You have enough contacts with the powers-that-be, particularly the New York City Employment Commission to determine if that crooked sailor is on her payroll."

"I'll report to you as soon as I have an answer," responded Leverbee.

"Good man," said Michael Weaver.

The two men finished their supper, then parted.

The next morning, among other items Leverbee checked, was Tully Lucas, Michael Weaver's next-door neighbor. Sure enough he was for real. He had a social security number, a District of Columbia driving license and banking connections in Massachusetts that were hard to identify or tie down. Just to make sure, he checked Michael Weaver's background. He was for real also. He had a social security number, a D.C. driver's permit and his bank accounts were in D.C.

"I wonder what the tie-in is?" he murmured after reviewing the material. "Until I find out differently I'm satisfied with my deal with Michael." Later that day, he started to seriously investigate whether or not Marcus Bosconovich was employed by the Purple Canary Press.

CHAPTER 20

Three days later, Michael Weaver and Oren Leverbee were seated in Weaver's office at the gallery.

"What have you found out?" asked Weaver.

"Well, first of all, Marcus Bosconovich is on the payroll of the Purple Canary. He has a pittance of a base salary plus some type of commission. Just what he really earns we won't know until his next tax return is filed."

"I was hoping what my friend said was in error but I guess not," was Weaver's response.

"The Purple Canary must be doing quite a business," continued Leverbee.

"Why do you say that?"

"Because almost at the same time Bosconovich's wife hired her husband, she also hired another rep by the name of Wesley Young and he's hired strictly on a commission basis."

Weaver was quiet scribbling odd figures on a pad. He looked up at Leverbee. "My friend says his sister was born making money. I'm inclined to believe him."

"Maybe so, maybe not," said Leverbee, "What troubles me is that the second new employee could be a front, a fake."

"For what?"

"Well, let's suppose Bosconovich's wife knows her husband is a gambler, a crook and a successful one. She might have agreed to give him a cover, a fake ID while he is on the road to gambling ventures. She could be the cover for a share of his take and this could happen while he, in his real name, is on the road as her legitimate publicity rep."

"Damn, I never thought of it that way," said Weaver. Suddenly he rose from his chair and said, "S'cuse me. I'll be right back." In a minute or so he returned. "What a relief," he said as he tightened his belt. "What you said just before I left the room gave me an idea. What if that bastard Bosconovich has in some way been induced by Waddell and is now part of the Secret Service, his wife knows it and is cooperating with the Service by not only giving him a job but also a fake ID to use when he is undercover on a Secret Service operation?"

Leverbee was flexing his hands, thinking. He stopped, looked at Weaver and said, "It's a possibility but I doubt that is so. However, I'll have my sources check and see if they can find anything that ties Bosconovich or Young to the Service."

"The boss would appreciate that," said Weaver.

"I know damned well he would," replied Leverbee, his piercing eyes bore into Weaver's. At that moment there was a knock on the door.

"Who is it?" asked Weaver.

"Lorraine," was the answer.

Leverbee rose, "I'll be going. I'll get back to you in three or four days and report what I find out."

"Okay," was Weaver's response. "Come in, Lorraine," he called out. She entered as Leverbee left.

"Hi, Oren," said Lorraine as she passed Leverbee in the doorway.

"See you later, Lorraine," was his reply.

Lorraine closed the office door.

"My God, its good to see you again," said Michael Weaver as he stood, came around the desk and kissed her fervently. She responded then lugged a big brief case onto his desk.

"You better had say that." She smirked, opened the brief case and said, "Look what Mrs. Santa Claus brought."

Michael looked into the suitcase and saw the wads of currency in banded stacks. Alongside of them, in an open envelope, was Lorraine's report neatly handwritten. "Two hundred thou of good old Uncle Sam's money," said Lorraine.

"Not a bad exchange and yield," replied Weaver as he looked with admiration at his bag-lady.

"The only base that's not doing well is Miami," said Lorraine. "I'm afraid someone is taking more than his share—skimming."

"We'll have the watchdog make a little trip shortly. I'm sure that will be remedied. Where is your gear?"

"In the suitcase behind the front counter in the gallery. No use lugging it in here."

"You're right, grab a chair for a few minutes while I sort the take. I'll put one-third in Riggs Bank, one-third in American Security and one-third in the National Savings and Trust. That'll keep each account in range. I'll make the deposits before the banks' closing time on the way home today."

"Let's do it Michael, I'm pooped. Changing costumes as well as making sure I wasn't followed by anyone is tiring. The train schedules have been hellacious. I didn't sleep a wink last night on that trip from Miami. The roadbed was so damned rough, I felt like I was trying to sleep on a huge electric vibrating machine and those two rowdies in the roomette next to mine, hell, they partied loud most of the night."

"I'll be ready to go in a few minutes. You just sit and relax," said Michael. Lorraine Driscoll dropped exhausted into the easy chair in a corner of Michael's office, was asleep in no time. He looked up from writing the deposit slips when he heard her soft snore. "Really, she is better than I deserve," he thought. "She has proven herself to be damned honest, but why?"

When he was ready, he gathered the deposits, went over and tapped her lightly on her shoulder. "Wake up, Babe, I'm ready to go."

She came to with a start and stretched, "Oh Michael, I was having the loveliest dream. We were lying on a warm, sandy beach that went on forever, just you and me. The ocean was so silent, so calm. We had no cares."

"Maybe that'll be true before too long," he replied. "Come on, I have to make these deposits before the banks close." Lorraine pushed up from her chair, retrieved her suitcase from behind the counter and followed Michael out of the office back door to his car parked in the small parking area at the rear of the gallery building.

Before long the deposits were made and the twosome had wended their way to his apartment. After they entered, Michael closed the door, turned her to him and kissed her with fervor. She responded briefly, drew away and said, "Michael, no more tonight. I'm too tired to eat, let alone make love. I've got to get some rest." Michael persisted, drew her close again. Lorraine's black eyes narrowed, her body stiffened. "Listen, you selfish bastard, I deliver your bogus bills, I collect your crooked money and I give you my body when I'm not completely exhausted. What the hell more do you want from me? I'm not some knothole in a pet log of yours."

Michael relaxed, knew she was right for she was the only person in his life who seemingly dedicated herself to him. He lifted her right hand, kissed the back of it gently then said, "Go on to bed, Princess, you've more than earned your keep."

Lorraine's whole body relaxed, she looked at him with a strained but tender expression on her face. "Goodnight, Punkin," she responded and entered the bedroom with twin beds.

□

That night, after a pick-up supper in his kitchen, Michael was disturbed. He couldn't wait the three or four days he knew it would take Leverbee to determine just what Marcus was really up to. There was an urgency that he find out immediately what was Marcus' MO and why? He could just feel danger approaching. He wondered, "Could Mariana be the real source of my troubles? Maybe she knows more about my occupation than I think she does. She had to be acquainted with that bastard Bosconovich before he came east on the train. She published his poems before the war ended. Is she using Marcus to get even with me?" That blond punk had already caused big trouble. The next move by those two could be disastrous for him. They had to be stopped.

He prowled, circling and circling the living room rug. He stopped, went to his desk and wrote a note to Lorraine. He took it to the kitchen and propped it against the sugar bowl on the table where she would be sure to find it in the morning. From the hall coat closet he took his dark blue trench coat and a matching short-brimmed fedora. After shutting off all the lights except the night light in the hall and peeking into the bedroom where Lorraine was snoring softly, he made sure the safety latch on the apartment door worked. For some strange reason he didn't want to leave Lorraine unprotected. He left the apartment, quietly shutting the door. From there, he went into the apartment next door. Half an hour later, when he emerged, he no longer was the same Michael Weaver but a blond with hair down to his shoulders, his ears completely covered. His bushy, blond eyebrows were encircled by a pair of gold-rimmed glasses. A blonde moustache graced his upper lip and he was at least one inch taller. He thought, "No one, not even his relatives or Lorraine would recognize him." With a weekender traveling bag in hand, he left the apartment, entered a waiting taxi and was on his way to Union Station.

□

Lorraine awoke the next morning with an empty feeling not from lack of food even though she was hungry. She just sensed it when she looked over to Michael's bed. Not only was he not there, the bed hadn't been slept in, hadn't been disturbed since it was last made up. She was instantly wide awake. "Punkin," she called, "Are you in the living room?" She, in her PJs, raced into the living room, saw it was empty then hurried to the kitchen and saw the note.

Dear Babe,

After reading your last report, I have decided to make a quick trip to Miami to check on our staff in person. I will call you here at 6:00 p.m. three days from now not before. Work with Cahill and Leverbee. No outside collection trips until I call. Don't tell them where I have gone. Keep a weather eye on Cahill, he is a weak reed.

Your Punkin, Michael

"Oh Jesus, what is that fool up to now? He should have talked to me before he left. Why didn't he tell me where he would be staying? And why do I care anyway?" she mumbled, as she nervously set about getting a light breakfast before she went to the gallery. How she hated to deal with that cold bastard, Leverbee and his slimy cohort, Cahill. Why did Michael keep leaving her in such stressful situations? But when she was at the gallery there were always legitimate sales to make and she liked that.

□

231

As dawn broke, blond Martin Strange entered the Lexington Hotel in New York City where he had previously made a reservation by long distance phone. He registered and promptly went to his room. He briefly contemplated going down to an early breakfast, decided against it, undressed, took off his blond wig, eyebrows and moustache, took two sleeping pills and shortly thereafter, Michael Weaver dropped off to sleep comforted by the thought that his plans were complete. Soon, very soon, he would have eliminated the main roadblocks to being successful, very successful.

CHAPTER 21

Michael Weaver awoke around noon, showered, shaved, put on his well-concealing disguise. Afterwards he dressed meticulously. He was now Martin Strange, a natty Fifth Avenue stroller, a young member of the moneyed crowd about to engage in the day's business. Today, he would begin to learn about two of his clients, their every move. After a leisurely lunch in the hotel coffee shop, he went to a public phone in the lobby and placed a call. A pleasant female voice answered, "The Purple Canary, Rachel Ingalls, receptionist, speaking."

"May I speak with Mr. Marcus Bosconovich please?" asked Strange.

"I'm sorry, sir, he is out of town but he will be back in two or three days."

"Are you sure he'll be back then?"

"Not more than three days from now. Can I give him a message from you?"

"Thanks, but no. I'm an old Navy pal passing through town. I just called to say hi," and Strange hung up the phone. He walked confidently from the hotel, hailed a cab and was driven to within a block of Mariana Bosconovich's apartment. He left the cab, paid and tipped the driver and made as if he was going to enter the nine-story building where the cab had stopped. He watched out the corner of his eye when the cab disappeared, he strolled to the immediate vicinity of Mariana's apartment building. He began to make mental notes of the surroundings. He had never been there before. From across the street he watched the front entrance and saw several individuals leave the premises. He was lucky, a trades vehicle drove up and parked in the allotted space in front of the building. The driver got out, went to the door. It was locked. He looked, found a button and pushed it. From where Strange stood watching, he saw someone inside approach, open the glass door, converse briefly with the tradesman, then let the guy, carrying a large box into the building. "So much for security," thought Strange. He walked from the front of the apartment house around the corner of the building observing a large garage door, obviously parking for the building. He could see the electric eye that was the sensor for the automatic door opener. It was just above the upper left corner of the door frame. A little to the left of the garage door was a single, heavy metal door. He checked it, a safety door for fire or other exit, he determined, but there was no way anyone could enter that door from outside street level. He noted there were three levels to the building not including the parking level. "On just what level was Mariana's apartment?" Strange asked himself. Though he had her street address and apartment number, he did not know on what floor her unit was located. He couldn't risk guessing. He crossed the street in front of the apartment house, leaned against a street light pole as he scribbled his notations in a little notebook. He also made a small diagram of the apartment building, noted the curb parking sign in the vicinity and the parking times printed on the sign. Tomorrow, he would begin the nitty gritty work to determine just when Mariana left the apartment and when she returned. So much for today. He did not want to be seen as someone loitering in the neighborhood. You never could tell when a busybody might be staring out of a window. So, he walked to Lexington Avenue then caught a cab back to his hotel.

That night after supper he went to Radio City Music Hall to see the movie and watch the Rockettes perform on stage.

□

Early the next morning, Martin Strange, rented a car and arrived at six a.m. in the immediate area of the Bosconovich apartment. He parked where, from the curbside view across from the apartment house he could observe the front of the building as well as the garage entrance area. He had already determined that all apartments had some frontal view of the East River. He saw the lights come on across the front of the building as the various tenants arose. He noted when the lights were turned low or off. He observed the residents as they left the front entrance of the building and the autos as they left the garage. He could read the license plates with his binoculars as the cars came out of the garage then turned to the right or left when they entered the street. Success at last as he saw Mariana Bosconovich leave the garage in her Jaguar convertible with the top down. The time was 8:27 a.m. He looked back at his notes. He believed it was she who had turned out the lights on the third floor center area at 8:20 a.m. but, just to be certain, he would watch for her return home in the evening.

Pretending to be a literary agent, he, in the afternoon, called the Purple Canary Press from a public phone booth inquiring as to when Mariana generally arrived home. He was told between 4:30 and 5:30 p.m. By 4:00 p.m. he had found a parking space not quite as good as the morning one but adequate. He watched. At 4:45 p.m. she pulled up in the driveway, aimed her sensor and the garage door rolled up. The Jag entered the garage and the door rolled down. Sure enough, in about five minutes, lights came on in the third floor center area facing the river. Martin Strange had his answer.

That evening he went to a second-hand clothing store not far from his hotel, bought a tan windbreaker and a New York Yankee baseball cap. Now he was ready, excited and damned glad he was wearing the protective pad.

Early the next afternoon, Michael Weaver sauntered to the Central Florist just a few doors from his hotel, paid cash for a dozen red roses, had them boxed, took a small sender's card and, after writing on it "From Marcus with love, I'll be home soon," he placed the card in the box with the flowers and took the flowers to his hotel room.

At 5:00 p.m. Michael Weaver placed the elements of his disguise into a shopping bag. He slipped on a dark blue turtleneck shirt, put on his suit coat and topcoat. Next he picked up the bag and the box of flowers, opened the door of his hotel room, peered into the corridor. Making sure no guests were strolling the hall, he walked to the inside fire escape stairway, quickly descended the five flights to street level. He walked from the street level fire escape door to a corner drugstore, put his parcels on the outside of the phone booth, dropped a coin into the phone slot and placed a number with the operator. The phone rang followed by, "Mariana Bosconovich speaking."

In a disguised voice, Michael Weaver said, "Mrs. Bosconovich, this is the Central Florist on Sixth Avenue. We always call before we deliver. Will you be a home this evening around 5:45 p.m.?"

"Why, yes indeed. I'll be here."

"I hope your husband hasn't returned from his trip."

"No, he hasn't. Why?"

"The flowers are from him."

"That thoughtful guy. I'll be delighted."

"See you then," and Weaver hung up the phone. A big grin lit his face, a ferocious grin.

Michael walked to the nearby parking garage, entered his rented car then drove near Mariana's apartment. He parked on a side street in an area of closed shops, not far from the apartment. In the car, he took off his topcoat and suit coat, put on the second-hand parka, making sure it hid the holster. Reaching into the shopping bag, he brought out the disguise elements, properly donned them and the Yankee baseball cap. Again he was Martin Strange. He was feeling exuberant. He knew it would work. He carefully placed the suit coat and topcoat into the shopping bag and put the bag on the floor between the front and rear seats of the car. Confidently, he drove to the front entrance of the apartment house, stopped in the area for "small package delivery." He picked up the box of flowers, left the car, headed to the apartment's main entrance. Once there, he rang the bell. Henry Dimond, the concierge appeared, smiled when he saw the floral box and opened the main door. "Mrs. Bosconovich is waiting for the flowers," he said, "I'll take them to her."

"No, my friend, I'll do that. She has to open them and make sure they are in good condition. Then she has to give me a receipt, company policy, you know."

"Okay," said Dimond, "Not a bad idea either. Her's is the apartment just opposite the elevator on the third floor." Dimond motioned to the elevator.

"Thanks," said Strange as he walked to the waiting elevator. When the elevator door opened on the third floor, Mariana Bosconovich, svelte in her business suit, was standing in the doorway to her apartment, a big anticipatory grin was spread across her face.

"Oh, I'm excited," she said. "Henry Dimond called to say you were on your way up."

"Do you mind if I step inside and have you make sure the flowers are in A-one condition? That's company policy. After that, I'll get you to sign the receipt."

"Not at all," said Mariana. She took the box, put it on a table by a sofa and started taking the lid off. The florist delivery man, without her noticing, quietly shut and bolted the front door.

After she removed the lid, turned back the green tissue paper lining, she looked at the roses and was just a bit surprised. "The flower shop must have run out of the others," she said softly, then leaned down, sniffed and exhaled in pleasurable satisfaction. "They look lovely and smell heavenly. I'll sign the receipt," she said as she raised up to face the delivery man. There was a weird, foreboding silence about the guy. Those beady eyes staring out at her from underneath the blond brows seemed to spit darts of venom. She was frightened as she signed the receipt that had been stuck onto the boxtop. "Here," she said, "Take it and leave, please."

He stood as if entranced, continued his glare at her, then around the apartment. She started to move. "Don't take a step and don't reach for the phone," was the harsh command. The florist delivery man stepped closer. In a twinkling, a revolver was in his right hand, pointing at her.

"Oh my God, what is this?" she muttered.

"Nothing will happen if you answer a few questions I have, but if you move a step, it will be your last."

"Why the questions? Who are you?"

Slowly she was sensing she knew this odd individual but from where?

"Makes no difference. When will your husband return? Tonight or tomorrow?"

"My husband? What do you want with him?"

"Just answer my question," he said, then gave a little involuntary hunch of his shoulders.

Mariana's eyes widened in surprise, then horror.

"My God, Tully, it's you. What has gotten into you and why the disguise?"

"How could you tell?" he asked. His eyes widened.

"No matter how you tried to cover up, after a couple of moves, I couldn't help but recognize you. I've known you since I was first able to remember. None of those memories are worth a damn, just irritating."

"What a loving sister I have," said Tully in mock sweetness.

"And what a bastard of a brother I have, now holding a gun on me. Why? I haven't the faintest idea."

"This isn't about you. It's Marcus, the prick you married."

"Don't you wish you were half the man he is?" she taunted.

"Shut up. Don't talk to me that way or I'll splatter your brains all over your exquisite carpets and be happy to do so."

Mariana realized her brother was out of control, slightly, if not seriously demented. She would have to play her role carefully or he might really hurt her. "Just what do you want with Marcus?" she asked calmly.

"Where is he now?"

"Returning from a trip to San Diego."

"Why San Diego?"

"He is on a book rep tour for my company, the authors and poets I publish."

"Is that all?"

"That's all, as far as I am concerned."

"You know he is a graduate in math from Cornell and was a card dealer in Reno."

"Of course I know that. I met him in Reno but he is much more than a card dealer. He is a mathematician, also an excellent poet. I have published his poems."

"So Dad says."

"When did he arrive home from the Pacific?"

"Arrive where?"

"Stateside."

"Damned if I know. I greeted him at his family's home in Chicago in early January this year." Now Mariana was beginning to be filled with real apprehension. She remembered the photo she had hidden in her jewelry case.

"Why do you want to know? What does he mean to you?" Mariana's ice cold blue eyes were boring into her brother's.

"On what train did he come into Chicago?"

"How in the world would I know. I wasn't there. I didn't meet any train. Just what are you trying to find out from me? I welcomed him home when I answered the door bell at his parents house."

"When?"

"What the hell business is it of yours when I met him?"

"Plenty," replied Tully. "Is he working with Clarence Waddell as a Secret Service operative? And is his job with you a front, a cover-up for his real endeavor?"

Mariana gasped, looked at her brother in concealed horror. "Tully, damn it, look at me carefully. Do I look like a complete nut to be involved in any such wild scheme. Why in God's name are you asking such questions? Point that thing away from me, it frightens me." She reached out to turn the pistol away.

Tully jerked, the silencer-equipped pistol fired a soft z-a-t, Mariana tumbled and sprawled on the oriental rug, face down, in the rough shape of a swastika. A pillow of the sofa on the other side of the room shook. An expanding crimson stain crept from beneath her chest onto the rug, beyond her body. Tully was startled, momentarily numb, he didn't really know if he intended to shoot her or if she had hit the pistol and it just went off. My God, he never really expected it to happen this way at least not until he found out about Marcus. He knew no more now than he had learned from his father. He would really have to be careful if he was going to eliminate that Navy bastard. Now he had to.

He looked down at his sister, felt no shame or sorrow, didn't know if she was dead or alive for she had not moved since she fell. He squatted and with one black, kid-gloved hand felt for a pulse beat in her left wrist. There was none. Again he felt for a pulse beat on the right side of her throat. There was none also. Just as he was about to stand up, he spotted Mariana's engagement ring on her extended left hand. "What a rock!" he thought. At that moment, the idea hit him: her death would appear as a robbery by the florist delivery boy. He just knew Lorraine would love the ring. She liked flashy ornaments. He took out his handkerchief, carefully removed the ring, wrapped the handkerchief around it and replaced the handkerchief in his pants pocket. He straightened up, looked around the room, took the greeting card from the flower box, tore it into pieces. He walked to the kitchen and dropped the paper bits into the wastebasket. He felt giddy but excited and peed in his pad. He walked over, took one look at the flowers then left the apartment quietly shutting the entrance door. He walked down the stairway to the first floor, saw no one in the lobby and left the building. He entered his car in the service area, glanced at his watch. Only twelve minutes since he had arrived at the building. "Not bad," he muttered as he slowly drove away. A couple of blocks later, as he continued his slow pace, he saw what he was looking for—an unlighted alley with open trash receptacles along one side. He turned into the darkening lane, went a few yards, stopped and switched off his headlights. Inside his car, he reached into the back and retrieved the shopping bag. Quickly, he shed the windbreaker, cap and changed into his suit coat and topcoat. He removed all of his disguise. Placing the disguise material on the windbreaker, he rolled the windbreaker into a tight bundle. With the driver's side window down, he started the car and as he slowly drove alongside one of the big open trash bins, he reached over with his left hand, picked up the bundle from the front passenger seat, reached out the driver's window then dropped all of the disguise into the stinking contents of a bin. He switched on the headlights of the car as he turned from the alley into the street. Now, he was again Michael Weaver. He would get to Marcus Bosconovich on his next big move but he had to plan it very carefully. At the moment he knew he should return immediately to D.C. and to Lorraine.

CHAPTER 22

That same evening, Evans' team, including Marcus returned to New York from their trip west, left Grand Central Station and headed for the New York office. The entire venture had been dismal, boring, not a sign of a con team on the run to San Diego or on the return. There had been a couple of interesting card games with Marines returning from San Diego but all legitimate, no problems other than a couple of master sergeants getting a little too much of the vino and wanting to fight the war over again. Those episodes were easily handled by their Marine buddies either in or out of the games.

Marcus had visited Mariana's listed stores in San Diego. He was surprised to find out how well many of the Purple Canary books were selling, even the volume with his poetry. But other than make a few notes in his hotel room, he didn't have the quiet time to work on his poetry except during the last night of his hotel stay he had started one, "The Comet." The memory of Samantha was the basis for that effort. He wrote the first line, "Far beyond sight, the comet sears across the void that is all time and mind." No further could he construct.

Shortly after the team had reported into the New York office,

Marcus went to a desk phone and called Mariana's apartment number. No answer. He was perturbed for it was well after her usual quitting time. So, he called her office. No answer there either. Where could she have gone? Shopping, he hoped.

Marcus joined the other members of the team and Waddell in the conference room. The debriefing was short and sweet. It was obvious from Evans' report when viewed in the light of the reports from the other teams that the counterfeiting masterminds had changed their MO. Waddell was sure of it.

As the team was preparing to leave the room and return to their respective residences, Waddell came up to Marcus. "Mind if I join you? Aimee is back in D.C. I owe you and Mariana a supper for my earlier intrusion on your good faith. I only hope I don't interfere with her supper preparations for tonight. You did call her yesterday when the train stopped in Chicago to let her know that you'd be home tonight, didn't you?"

"Surely did," responded Marcus, "I suggested to her that we should eat out tonight because the train might be late in arriving. She agreed. She will be delighted to have you join us."

On the way out of the office building front entrance Marcus turned to his boss. "Waddy, I've got to drop by next door to the "Shoppe-de-Fleurs" and pick up the dozen white roses I ordered this evening before I came into our building. I'm going to take them to Mariana as a little homecoming gift."

"White roses?" inquired his boss.

"Yes, they are her favorite and mine."

"Aimee prefers red ones," said Waddell.

In a couple of minutes, Marcus returned with a floral box under an arm. He hailed a cab. The two men were soon at Mariana's apartment. Marcus rang the door bell. No answer. He took out his key, unlocked the door. "You go first," said his boss.

As Marcus entered the hallway, he had a strange foreboding feeling. From the hallway he could see that the gas fireplace was burning full blast. The living room lights burned brightly as if someone had recently entered the apartment. He called, "Hi, Hon, I'm home. Waddell is with me." He waited, no sound. Waddy entered the hallway behind his junior employee. Marcus took three steps into the living room, looked in horror, dropped the box of white roses on the floor, then bellowed, "Mariana." He rushed and knelt by the prostrate form of his wife.

Waddell saw and yelled, "For God's sake, don't touch her. Where is the nearest phone?" Marcus pointed. Waddell grabbed the phone, called the operator and said, "Get an ambulance to the Somerset House, third floor apartment 301, then call the police."

"Immediately," was the answer, "And who is speaking?"

"S. S. Operative Waddell," was his reply, "Hurry." He hung up the phone. He walked to Mariana's fallen body, reached down and felt for a wrist pulse, there was none. Then he felt for a neck pulse, none. "Better my prints than yours, if an investigation is made," he said, as he gently felt an arm, a leg. He could tell she had died very recently.

Marcus was faint. He kneeled on all fours, shook his head, shivered, looked at his fallen eagle companion and broke into a moan, almost a howl of pain.

Waddell's stomach was in knots, but he had to remain calm for both of their sakes. He stood, then stooped down, placed his strong arms under the shoulders of swaying Marcus, closing his hands together in front of his employee's chest, he said, "Marcus get up. I'll help, but you can't stay there. Lets get you to a chair." He lifted, lifted almost dead weight. Marcus' face was gray, he was gasping for breath, his strength completely drained by the first great shock of his life. Waddell dragged him to a large lounging chair and tenderly lowered him into it. He looked at his ashen-faced young friend. The senior operative reached out and dealt his young subordinate a stiff slap across his right cheek. "Don't you dare faint on me now. It could mean your life." He tilted Marcus's body forward. "Put your head between your knees, breathe, breathe deeply." Marcus felt the sting of the slap, heard as if a voice was calling him from a distance. "Do you hear me Marcus? Do you hear me? If you do, nod your head." Marcus nodded feebly. "Thank God," said Waddy. "Now breathe deeply, please."

Slowly Marcus complied. Little by little some strength again flowed through him. Marcus opened his eyes, looked up at his boss and feebly said, "Thanks."

"Now, lean back in that chair. I'm going to get something to prop up your feet." He spied a large hassock halfway across the room, hurried to it and rolled it to where Marcus sat. Placing the hassock in front of Marcus, he propped Marcus' feet on the brown, round seat. Waddell's eyes shown with compassion, concern. "I didn't slap you to be nasty," he said, "I was afraid if you really went into deep shock, something serious might happen. I would never forgive myself."

"No need to explain, Waddy. I understand. In fact, I was and am ready to die. Nothing in my life has ever hit me like the sight of her lying there." Marcus shuddered but was able to stop the reflux before it filled his mouth.

"Marcus, I am positive she is dead. And I'm sure she was shot. I can see the hole in the back of her jacket where the bullet came out, as well as the blood stain on the rug. I know it is grim and I hate to have you look at her, but if you can, you should before the police arrive. You might see something none of them would notice. I'll help you up. If it makes you sick, just puke wherever, but not on her. Please, please don't touch her."

Marcus again shivered. With the help of the senior operative, he arose, swayed toward his deceased wife and stood close to her body. He looked, tears surging, almost blinding him. He wiped them away, looked again. "My beloved eagle," he moaned, "Why couldn't I fly away with you?"

Waddell strengthened his grip around Marcus' shoulders. "Marcus, is there anything you see that is different?"

"Different, Jesus, she is dead," he mumbled. "That's what is different." He started to turn back to his chair, stopped, again looked down at his deceased wife. "Holy shit," he said, "Her ring is gone."

"What ring? Her wedding band is still there."

"The engagement ring I gave her before we were married. It has been a treasure, an heirloom in my mom's family for generations. It is no ordinary little engagement ring. It's worth a fortune."

"Did Mariana wear it all the time?"

"Never took it off."

"When was the last time you saw it?"

"After I kissed her goodbye at the station and as I got on the train, she waved to me, I saw it then, couldn't help but see it."

"That's one hell of a help, Marcus, but don't tell anyone, not yet."

"Why not?"

"I don't want it known publicly. I'll tell you when."

For the first time, Waddell saw the box of red roses sitting on the table near the sofa. "Marcus," he said firmly, "Did you order another box of roses for your wife at anytime on your way home?"

"Never," was Marcus' moanful reply. He looked at the box on the table. "Where in the hell did they come from?"

"I have no idea," replied Waddy.

Waddell had hardly finished his remarks when there came an authoritative knock on the door. "Police," a heavy masculine voice said.

"Just a minute. I'll be right there," replied Waddell. He hurried to the door, opened it and admitted the two officers standing there. "Come in," he said.

The two plainclothes men showed their badges. The heavyset redhead said, "I'm Sigmond Lester, lieutenant homicide. This is my partner, Alfred Rich, also lieutenant homicide. Who are you?" he inquired of Waddell.

"I'm the one who put in the distress call," He stopped, stared defiantly at the officers. "In public, so far as you are concerned I'm Jay O'Connor, and he handed Lieutenant Lester a New York driver's permit with his photo on it. "But," he said, then reached down, took off his right shoe, and took out his true identity. "I'm really Clarence Waddell, a senior operative of the Secret Service, currently working out of the New York field office."

"How do I know you're not lying?" inquired a rather disbelieving Lester.

"Call the office and ask for my identity. Here's the number."

"Who's the New York office senior operative, the area chief?" asked Lester.

"Donald Ankers," replied Waddell. "He once was a partner of mine."

Lester relaxed, smiled, held out his hand, "He has been a long-time friend of mine. I've heard him mention your name many a time. You're Waddy."

"Sure am."

"Who is this guy with you?" and he pointed to Marcus.

"Marcus Bosconovich, husband of the deceased woman and a junior operative under me."

"Did he call you before you called us?"

"No, he has just returned from a mission to California. He stopped by the office for a debriefing before going home. He, his wife and I were going out to supper together. This is what we found when we entered the apartment."

Lester looked around the room, saw the box of red roses then the white ones scattered on the floor. "Gee," he said, "Someone sure in hell loves roses."

Waddy scowled at the detective and replied, "Marcus was bringing the white ones home as a gift to his wife. He dropped them when he saw his wife on the floor. We have no idea where the red ones came from."

"Al," said Lester to his associate, "Pick up the white roses from the floor. Take them into the kitchen. Find something to put them in."

"Sure thing," replied Detective Rich and he immediately complied.

The lead detective looked sympathetically at Marcus. "Don't get up," he said as Marcus started to stand. The detective went over, shook Marcus' hand. "What a hell of a greeting you've had." He then patted Marcus' shoulder, looked at the distraught figure in front of him, "Ache, hurt you're bound to. I assure you, we'll leave no stone unturned bringing the culprit to justice whoever he or she is," he said.

The door bell sounded. Detective Lester opened the door. The New York Police Department crime lab crew was there, photographer, fingerprint specialist, the whole schmeer.

The detective walked over to Waddell. "I think you should take your friend into the bedroom. He may not like what he sees when we roll her over. Tell him we will have to take her body and there will be an autopsy. He can claim her body from the morgue in a couple of days, we won't take long. There has to be a complete investigation. Anything odd about this event?"

"Not to my knowledge," replied Waddell. "If anything turns up, I will let you know immediately."

"Thanks," said Lester. Then he hollered to his buddy in the kitchen, "Hey, Rich, have you found anything to put the flowers in? We've got to get moving on this investigation."

"Yeah, I'm coming. I'm coming," responded Rich. "Just hold your horses, I had a hell of a time finding something big enough to hold them."

Waddy walked over to his junior operative. "Come on Marcus,

let's go into the bedroom. I've got to tell you what the procedure will be. Also, they have to take Mariana's body for an autopsy."

Marcus arose as if sleepwalking, stumbled into the bedroom, then dropped into a lounge chair. His boss followed him into the room, closed the door. "Marcus, my good friend, what has happened is not your fault. Some thief must have spotted your wife's ring, stalked her, found where she lived and the only way he could get the ring was by killing her."

"If that's the way it happened, I shouldn't have given her the damned ring. It is my fault," Marcus then sobbed.

"She loved you. She died loving you. You didn't kill her. She knew that before she died. We'll get the bastard. I swear on my life, we will," said Waddell as he gripped hard Marcus's hand.

Marcus appeared absolutely numb, unresponsive. Waddell continued, "They have to take your wife's body for an examination by the coroner. It will be released as soon as the autopsy is complete. I'm staying here tonight. When the crowd leaves, you should call her parents and yours to let them know what happened," said Waddell calmly, but firmly. "You've still got a life to live."

"What life? How the shit do you know?" Marcus' eyes were fierce, almost those of a predatory animal. Waddell didn't flinch. His eyes bore into Marcus' with a deep, gnawing sadness.

"Remember, I've been most of your way," he replied quietly.

Marcus' whole countenance relaxed, tears streamed down his cheeks. "Oh, Jesus," he said, "How will I find a way?"

Waddell was quiet, watching his junior's every move. He made a decision. "Marcus, you're a man, a strong man inside and out. Each of us has to find our way the best we can. It takes time, time and trying my friend, really trying. The medics are in the living room now, I'm going to get a sedative for you. They always carry them." Waddell left the room.

Marcus flailed viciously at the bed pillows. "That cowardly bastard, whoever he is, I hope to God I catch him. So help me, I'll kill him inch by inch and revel in his pain," he blubbered then moaned, "Mariana, Mariana, why not me?"

Waddell reentered the room, gave Marcus two white pills. "Get on the bed. Swallow them whole and drink this glass of water." Marcus abjectly obeyed. In no time the pills were doing their job, Marcus was out like a light. Waddell took off Marcus' shoes, squared him in the bed then covered him with an afghan that was folded at the foot of the bed. Standing by the bedside he said, "You do love her, just as I love Aimee. I understand your hurt but as dim as it seems now you have a future ahead, hopefully a challenging one. You must realize that. She would want it that way. Rest, my young friend, the fight's just beginning."

Waddell left the room and walked to the living room. The homicide group, with Mariana's body in a body bag and on a gurney, was preparing to leave. Lester looked at Waddell, "How's he doing?"

"As well as can be expected. The guy's only been married about three months," replied Waddell.

"We found the spent bullet from a .38 caliber pistol. It was lying on the yellow sofa," and Lester pointed. "The shot apparently hit the sofa pillow, didn't penetrate and dropped down on the cushion. From that we have determined Mrs. Bosconovich was standing facing the hall when the shot was fired. There is no evidence of bruise or contusion, no evidence of struggle on her body that we can see. From the powder burns on her suit jacket, she must have been standing fairly close to her killer. I wonder if she knew the culprit?"

Waddell was truly surprised by the last question. "I hadn't thought about that before," he responded. Now he would think about it, give the idea serious thought. No stone would be left unturned. "Do you know how the killer got in the building?" asked Waddell.

"My partner, Rich, has begun his investigation. Right now he is downstairs talking with Henry Dimond, the apartment concierge. I'm sure it involves those flowers on the table. We'll take the red roses and the box for a complete exam. I'll let you know what we find out."

"I appreciate that. I will reciprocate," replied Waddell.

"When can your man stand a little interrogation?"

"In a couple of days. I'll call and make arrangements."

"Thanks, Waddy," and Lester prepared to leave. He looked down at the blood-stained throw rug on which Mariana had died. "I think you would be doing your friend a favor if you rolled up that rug and sent it to the cleaners before he awakens. We've got all the evidence from it we need."

"Good idea, I'll do so as soon you leave," responded Marcus' boss.

248

Waddell was sitting quietly on a sofa drinking a hot cup of tea he had made in Mariana's kitchen. "Maybe it was a robbery gone wrong or maybe it was something more," he thought. Marcus' name had only been announced once in the game on the train. He had remembered it, doubted the others did. Yet could be. Fosberg was dead, maybe he had talked before he was killed. Even at that, how could they have traced Marcus to his wife's apartment—and then killed her? He couldn't fathom it yet, however a warning bell was ringing in his subconscious. He wouldn't let Marcus out of Secret Service sight until he had more evidence of what was behind the killing. Either he, Evans or Comstock would be with Mariana's distraught husband until a clear view of the killing had surfaced, maybe even after that.

After scrounging a supper from Marcus' fridge, Waddell called the New York field office, gave a phone report then called his wife Aimee in D.C., told her his return would be delayed, just how long he didn't know. He also told her as much of the episode as he thought she should know. He ended his conversation with her by saying, "I love you, Honey. I would have reacted worse than Marcus if it had been you."

"Take care of yourself for me, beloved," was his wife's response, then she hung up her phone.

CHAPTER 23

Marcus awoke groggy, confused, turned to look at Mariana. She wasn't there. He remembered. "Oh my God! To think she will never be there again and it is all my fault. I never should have taken that ring from Mom. In these days and times, it was too much of a challenge for some thief to resist, probably on dope at that."

His despondency deepened. He arose, sat on the side of the bed and gazed, at nothing. There was no room. He was sitting on a bed in the midst of nowhere. Fog swirled in every direction. He had no desire to challenge it.

Suddenly a face appeared. "I heard you thrashing around, coming to. How do you feel this morning?"

Marcus, confused, looked and saw it was Clarence Waddell. "Waddy, what the hell are you doing here?"

"What any friend does for another," was his calm response.

Marcus shook his head from side to side, trying to brush the cobwebs away. "Have you been here all night?"

"Sure, your sofa in the den is very comfortable. Come on, breakfast is ready in the kitchen."

Marcus looked at himself and realized he was still fully clothed. "I don't want to eat. I just want to starve and die," he mumbled.

"Cut the crap, Marcus. The longer you feel sorry for yourself, the worse it will be to meet reality. Meeting that bitch is going to be hard anyway you cut it. But you've got to try."

"Why, oh why did it have to happen to her? Why not me?"

"Only providence knows, yet maybe someday we'll find out, but we can't do it without living—trying."

Marcus looked solemnly at his boss. "Don't talk platitudes to me." He stopped. After a sad smile, he said, "You're right. That's what Mariana would have said also."

"Marcus, you've got to call and tell her parents and you should call yours also."

"Oh, man, that's going to be rough. Her dad thinks I'm some kind of thrill-seeking card shark, I guess I have been. He doesn't know what I really do for a living. I've kept my mouth closed, so did Mariana."

"You let me handle that angle when the time comes. He'll soon understand."

"And my mom is going to think the same."

"When all is clear, I'll see that she knows the truth. However, you've got to tell them of Mariana's death before they read it in some newspaper or hear it on the radio. First, come on and try to eat just a little."

At the kitchen table both men were quiet but Waddell, as inconspicuously as possible, watched Marcus' every move, saw the tears streak his face, saw him shiver from time to time and noticed that his hands trembled as Marcus handled a spoon or raised toast to eat. "The poor guy is really suffering tortures of the damned. Despite the powerful body and blithe outward appearance, Marcus is far more sensitive than I first thought him to be. I should have known because I've had read his poems, liked them and was moved deeply by several. I'll have to watch him more closely," muttered Waddell.

After a few bites, Marcus pushed his chair back and said, "Now I'm going in to face hell. You don't mind if I shut the bedroom door while I make those calls?"

"No, Marcus. I appreciate your desire for privacy."

Waddell washed the breakfast dishes then sat and listened to the kitchen radio. Sure enough there was news of the murder on radio station WABC. While he was listening, the apartment bell rang. He went to the door. Henry Dimond, the apartment concierge, was standing there looking upset. "There's a bunch of reporters and photographers clamoring to get in the front door. They want to talk to Mr. Bosconovich. What should I do?" he asked.

Waddell saw a pad and pencil on the living room table. He took the pencil and hurriedly scribbled on the pad. "Marcus, I'll be right back. The news vultures are at the front door. I'll ward them off for now. Sooner or later they'll corner you, but we must talk before they do."

Waddy went to the lobby, opened the front door, told the newsmen he was a close friend of Bosconovich and that his friend was in no condition to hold a news conference at the present time. Besides, until the police had completed their initial investigation, Marcus had been ordered by them not to say a word about the event to anybody. The disgruntled pack were starting to argue when Lieutenant Lester appeared with a uniformed police officer. The group grew silent. Lester looked at them, one he knew. "Haskell," he said, "We'll let you know when you can speak with Mr. Bosconovich. Sergeant Riley will be on duty here to see that the victim's husband has his privacy, at least for the time being. Give the guy a chance to get over the shock. How would you feel if you were him?"

"You will let us know?" called out one reporter.

"Yeah, but you'll be hanging close by and know anyway," was Lester's retort. The reporters left.

"Have you found out anything?" asked Waddell as they walked to the elevator.

"Some," said Lester, "As of yet it leads to nowhere except you and your associate are in the clear. We checked his story and yours. The two of you were giving me straight talk."

"Shit, I told you that last night."

"I know and believed you, but I had to check."

"What else have you uncovered?"

"Where is Marcus?" asked Lester.

"In the bedroom telling her parents and his what has occurred."

"Let's wait until he finishes his calls. I want him to also hear what I've learned. Got any hot tea?"

"On the stove," said Waddell. "Mugs are on the second shelf in the cabinet to the left of the stove." Lester strolled to the kitchen.

□

The bedroom door opened, an even more disheveled-looking Marcus walked into the living room and flopped onto a sofa opposite where Waddell was sitting.

"Rough?" asked Waddell.

"More than you'll ever know," responded Marcus.

"Lieutenant Lester is in the kitchen getting a cup of tea. He'll be here in a minute to tell us what he has learned."

Marcus nodded his head in acknowledgment.

Lester entered the room, mug in hand, saw Marcus, quietly came over and sat beside him on the sofa. "I know it's a bitch to go through even though I've never been there, thank God. I do have some information," he said.

"Let's hear it," said Waddell.

"First, Henry Dimond, the concierge, told us that late yesterday afternoon, after Mrs. Bosconovich had returned home from work, she called down to say that flowers from the Central Florist on 5th Avenue were being delivered to her and to let the delivery boy in when he came to the lobby door. Soon, a guy with a blond flowing hairdo, blond eyebrows and a blond moustache appeared. He was wearing a tan windbreaker and a New York Yankee's cap. He had a large box of flowers from Central Florist for Mrs. Bosconovich. Dimond offered to take the flowers but the delivery boy said it was the florist's policy that he, the delivery boy, would give her the flowers. He said she had to check them to make sure they were fresh and then give him a receipt. So, he let the guy in. Dimond says he called Mrs. Bosconovich to let her know the florist deliveryman was on his way to her apartment, then Dimond went to the basement storage area. He doesn't know when the delivery man left. When he came up from the basement to the lobby about twenty minutes later, he looked out the front door. The florist car was gone. He said the car had no sign on it like most delivery vehicles. That's all he knew. So we checked the Central Florist. They have no such delivery man. All their vehicles are small, black panel trucks with their name and phone number painted in gold-colored letters on each side.

"One of the clerks at the florist did remember a walk-in, a dapper-dressed guy wearing a dark fedora that matched his trench coat. The guy bought a dozen roses. The clerk recalled that the man had shoulder length, dark brown hair. He also had bushy brown eyebrows. The clerk remembered that the guy paid cash for the flowers, took a greeting card on which he scribbled a note and placed it in the box just before the clerk put the lid on it."

"How tall did the clerk say the guy was?" asked Waddell.

"About five foot eleven or six feet."

"How many other customers ordered a dozen red roses that day?"

"I asked the same question," replied Lester. "Their records showed several, but they were phone orders. None was marked for delivery to the Bosconovich apartment."

"Were there any other pickups?" asked Waddell.

"A couple, but they were to old customers. The shop knew where those flowers were going."

"Maybe so, maybe not," said Waddell.

Lester looked quizzically at Waddell and Marcus. "What bothers me is, if it was the brunet guy who bought the roses, why would he change his appearance? What was he after?"

Waddell looked seriously at the lieutenant and then at Marcus. "Sigmond, I'm going to give you the only clue Marcus and I can figure, but you've got to keep it quiet, make a thorough investigation before you let it be known publicly, promise?"

"I do," said a sober Lester.

Waddy spoke, "When we found Mariana's body on the floor and after Marcus' initial shock, I asked him if he noticed anything about his deceased wife that was different, anything before the homicide crew arrived. At first, he was so numb at the tragedy that he could hardly see, but he tried and suddenly he said to me, 'Her ring is gone.' I asked him what he meant because she was wearing her wedding ring. He then told me he had given her an heirloom engagement ring. It had been in his mother's family for generations and was worth more than he ever imagined. His wife knew the value because her great uncle is a diamond merchant. She had, over the years, perused some of the gem books her uncle had given her father."

"Holy Christ," said Lester, "Did she wear it regularly?"

"Always, except when she bathed," said Marcus. "I wish to hell she hadn't, but its too late now."

"What a motive, someone could have been stalking her for weeks," said Lester. He looked at Marcus, "Are there any pictures or descriptions of that ring?"

Marcus was thoughtful for a brief space, then replied, "I'm not sure, but she did say she was going to carry the value of the ring as a rider on her jewelry insurance policy."

"We'll get to that as soon as we can," replied Lester.

"Remember what I asked you?" queried Waddy.

"More reason than ever to keep it quiet until we have all the information about the gem," replied Lester. Then he looked at Marcus. "Your wife's body will be released tomorrow. I suggest you start making the appropriate arrangements."

CHAPTER 24

Marcus made his agreement with a New York City undertaker for the preparation and shipment of Mariana's body to the funeral home in Boston as requested by her father. Brian Lucas had made provisions for a "Mass for the Dead" to be held at St. Mark's Catholic Church in Wollaston. His daughter would be buried in the Lucas family plot in the cemetery on the outskirts of the town. Mariana's father had insisted and Marcus was in no condition to deny the request. Marcus was still walking in fog. When he went to the morgue to obtain the release of Mariana's body, Waddell went with him. While Marcus was executing the release paperwork with one attendant, another attendant put a hand on Waddell's arm and beckoned him to step to a far side of the room. Waddell did so. During the conversation, the senior operative's eyes opened wide in surprise. He stared at Marcus with increased worry and sympathy, nodded his head in acknowledgment then left the attendant and returned to the side of his young associate.

With all arrangements completed, they left the morgue. Waddell looked at Marcus and remarked, "It's such a nice morning, let's walk for a while before we catch a cab to the office."

"Sure," replied Marcus. His thoughts were elsewhere, not on the morning.

They had walked for about a block in silence when Waddell eased closer to Marcus, stuck an arm through one of his and said quietly, "I didn't know you were planning a family so soon."

Marcus at first didn't comprehend what Waddell had said, continued walking then suddenly stopped as if he had hit a wall. "What was that you said?"

"I didn't know you were planning a family so soon."

Marcus grasped the meaning of the statement. His eyes were saucer round, filled with such fright and sorrow that Waddell's heart ached for his young employee. "Oh, my God, no," said Marcus, his breathing came in erratic, moanful gasps and his legs buckled. Waddell's hand tightened on Marcus' arm as he kept his young friend from staggering to his knees.

"Keep walking," said Waddell, "You've got to keep walking." After a few seconds, he continued, "I can tell you didn't know, and maybe she wasn't sure either. But, according to the coroner, Mariana was at least six weeks pregnant."

"She never told me but every now and then I caught her sly glance as if she was saying, 'I know something that you don't.' Oh, Waddy, where will this end?" Then Marcus' face turned to stone, cold fury. "That son of a bitch, I'll tear him, torture him in the worst way my mind can conceive of if I ever can lay hands on him. This is the end." A change in demeanor swept over Marcus, a change that Waddell found deeply disturbing as if some demon had been released, taking over Marcus. The expression in his young operative's eyes bothered Waddell. This wasn't the blithe-spirited, energetic, romantic, young man he knew, even in sorrow. Those eyes were the eyes of a predator, a killer. He had seen such eyes before.

"Marcus, right now it's very rough for you. However, there will come a time when, in the due course of life, the memory of this episode has to fade if you are to have any real future at all."

"Shit," was Marcus's single word reply.

The duo walked silently for a block, then Waddell hailed a cab. Once they were in the cab, he turned to Marcus and said, "No need of your coming into the office today. I'll drop you by home so you can get ready for your trip to Boston. Where will the service be held?"

"In Wollaston, Massachusetts, at St. Mark's Catholic Church. She will be buried in the family plot at the cemetery on the outskirts of town. The service will be held this Friday, two days from now at 10:00 a.m."

"I'll be there," replied his boss.

Marcus made no answer.

The rest of the drive to Marcus' apartment building was in silence. When they arrived, Marcus got out. "Thanks," he said and without looking at Waddell he headed for the front door. The cab started to pull away.

"Wait," said Waddell to the driver. "I want to make sure he gets in." The driver stopped the cab. Waddell studied every move, every attitude of Marcus' body, as his young operative walked with steely vigor toward the building and then thought, "No, Marcus, no. Don't lose the dream that makes you you. The world's not quite as rotten as it appears to you now." "Let's go," he said to the cab driver and the senior operative headed for his office.

□

The train arrived in Boston. Marcus got off, went forward to the baggage car, watched as Mariana's coffin was taken from the car, placed on a dolly and taken to a waiting hearse parked near the loading platform. Then with no show of any feelings, as if he was a robot, Marcus left by cab and soon arrived at the Parker House Hotel. He entered and told a desk clerk he had a reservation.

The clerk scanned the list, looked at Marcus, "Your brother Bernie has already arrived. He changed your room to a double. He'll be staying with you if you don't mind."

Marcus smiled and replied, "No, I'm delighted he did it." Marcus signed in, picked up his gear and headed for Room 607 and knocked. Instantly the door opened. A serious Bernie threw his arms around his brother and kissed him on his cheek.

"Man, its good to see you again," he said.

"You too," replied Marcus. As cold as he felt, he fought back tears.

"I'll take your luggage," said Bernie. "You can have the bed by the window." He pointed, then took his brother's foldpack, put it on a luggage rack at the foot of the bed.

After depositing the luggage, Bernie sat on his bed, "Take a load off, relax for a few minutes and tell me what happened if you want to."

Marcus looked affectionately at Bernie. "Gosh, he is growing up fast," he thought.

"Bernie, I still can't believe it. I'm walking in the damnedest fog." Then Marcus proceeded to tell what he and Clarence Waddell had walked into when they arrived at Mariana's apartment. When he finished, Bernie looked at him, "What a hell of a deal to come home to," he said.

"The worst in my life," answered Marcus. "Never again."

Bernie was quiet for a few seconds then spoke, "Waddell, isn't he the same guy who called shortly after you arrived home?"

Marcus was now seriously eyeing his brother. "Yes, he did," Marcus replied. He volunteered no explanation.

Bernie was inquisitive. "And he was the guy with you when you found Mariana?"

Marcus nodded affirmatively.

"He certainly has turned out to be a good friend. Why was he with you that evening?"

Marcus was surprised at the depth of Bernie's inquiry. "Waddell, Mariana and I were going out to supper together. He met me in town just after I returned from a book tour in San Diego. He'll be here for the funeral tomorrow," replied Marcus.

Bernie just knew Waddell was playing a bigger role in Marcus's life than his brother was willing to divulge. But why? And he knew his brother well enough to realize Marcus would tell him no more at the present.

"Brother," said Bernie, "Dad is down with a bad case of flu, Mom was afraid to leave him. Vince, Irma and Bianca are on a vacation in Canada. Irma is still depressed, so the family decided the trip might do her good that's why I'm the only one here. This was my first real train trip alone. I loved it. The "Empire State Express' is one comfortable ride. Man, there were some gorgeous babes on the trip, a little too old for me, but they were awesome to look at."

For the first time since Mariana's death Marcus let out a hearty laugh, "You're some rascal. Look, but don't touch," he said.

"Never fear, never fear, brother, I know my league," and he smiled in return. Now he was serious. "Mom is really broken up over Mariana's death. She cried most of the day after you called."

"I knew that would happen," replied Marcus somberly.

"And, she's upset with you. Somehow she thinks you may have caused Mariana's death, but she won't explain."

"Maybe Mom's right, indirectly, who knows? I don't." Marcus' hazel eyes bore into his brother's. "Bernie, I'm going to tell you something only Waddell and I know. You have to promise not to tell a soul — no one. For the time being it's just your and my secret — from Mom, Dad and the girls.

"I promise, cross my heart." Bernie made the sign.

"Whoever killed Mariana stole the engagement ring I gave her, stole it right off her finger."

"You mean that rock you gave her before she left to go home. I saw it. It was like Gibraltar."

Marcus nodded, then softly said, "It was Mom's. She gave it to me to give to Mariana. The ring had been in her family for generations. It was very valuable."

"Mom never told Dad she had the ring?"

"No, Bernie, she hasn't. She said to have done so would have embarrassed him. She never told him and she never wore it."

"Now, Mariana's dead because of that ring?" asked Bernie.

"Who knows, but it could be. The police are looking into the matter. They have asked me to be quiet about the ring. I wish to God Mom had never given it to me."

"I understand, but she had no idea such a thing would happen."

"I agree. For now no word about it — you promised."

"Have no fear, brother. If Mom found out that the ring might have caused Mariana's death, that knowledge could destroy her, sure as hell. Jeez, I'll never say a word. You needn't worry about it. By the way, Dad said to tell you he loves you and if you really need him to just call. Flu or no flu, he will be wherever you want him."

Tears filled Marcus' eyes. "I know that," he replied, "This is one battle I've got to fight on my own."

"Damn, I'm glad it's not me," said Bernie as he looked with deep affection and respect at his older brother. "Shouldn't we try to get some supper? I understand from the check-in desk that the Parker House Men's Grill has excellent food."

"Let's do," replied Marcus and he forced a feeble smile.

☐

During supper Bernie carried the conversation. He knew he had to. He told of his latest wrestling matches, how he had won three but lost the city championship when he got careless. He said the loss had taught him a real lesson. He told Marcus about his new girl friend, Hilda. She was stacked, smart, played a mean game of girls basketball and was a Lutheran. That last item was the only thing that displeased Mom. Marcus couldn't help but chuckle. As Bernie was running out of conversation, Marcus looked at him somberly, "Bernie, tomorrow might be a rough day for me. Mariana's dad still thinks I'm some kind of card-playing jerk, a crooked gambler. I know he thinks I caused her death."

Bernie's black eyes beamed, "Screw him. He has only met you once or twice. I've known you all my life. Just what you really do for a living besides write poetry, I don't know. But, I know its nothing crooked. You're just not made that way."

Marcus' hazel eyes were full of tender affection and tears, "Thanks, Bernie." Then he added, "I know two secrets are a big burden, but I've got a favor to ask. Again, nothing is to be said to Mom or Dad about it until I say so."

"You're on," responded Bernie.

"You know the little door in my old study at home, the one that goes into the unfinished attic?"

"Sure," replied his brother.

"Well, if you crawl out on the two ceiling beams that lead outward from the door, about eight feet, reach up and on one of the roof rafters you'll find a small key. When you find the key, reach right down from there between those two beams, feel underneath the insulation. You'll find a locked metal box."

Bernie's eyes were bugging. "And so?" he asked.

"Get the box and key. The box contains nothing but notebooks— mine. Mail the box and key in a package to me at Mariana's apartment. Do it when no one is around. Mom doesn't even know about it."

Bernie looked quizzically at Marcus. "What's in those notebooks?"

Marcus looked down at the table and quietly said, "My life."

"Your diaries?"

"Sort of."

"I promise," said Bernie. He was growing by the minute with the trust and confidence his brother was placing in him.

Marcus reached into his wallet and took out a twenty dollar bill. "This is for your trouble, the cost of mailing. Send the package first class to me at Mariana's apartment."

"I'll do it as soon as I get a chance after I return home. And I'll be mum."

Supper ended. As they rose Marcus said, "Let's take a walk, I need a little exercise to settle that meal. It was good. I've put the cost on my room bill."

"Thanks," said Bernie. "But, Dad gave me enough money to cover my expenses."

"Keep it, I can never repay you for coming." The two brothers left for an evening stroll before turning in for the night.

□

Waddell was waiting for Marcus outside the church. He was pleased to see him accompanied by his younger brother. He knew that Marcus felt isolated not only from most of his family but from members of the Lucas family. He realized that the vast majority of the mass attendees were friends of the Lucas family or Mariana's friends from college and her business. None knew him, Bernie or Marcus. Waddell could just sense that to most of the mourners, he, Marcus and Bernie seemed to be an unholy trio, not representatives of the holy trinity. Marcus, without going into any preliminaries, introduced "my friend," Waddell, to Bernie. For some strange reason Bernie and the senior operative were comfortable in each other's company, kind of like a loving uncle and nephew.

Marcus, Bernie and Waddell were ushered up the center aisle to a front pew. On the opposite side of the aisle Marcus saw Brian Lucas, Sean Lucas, his girlfriend, the one who attended Mariana and Marcus' wedding. In addition there was a dark-skinned woman in her late fifties as well as several employees of the Purple Canary Press, including Katherine Rogers, Mariana's associate editor. He could tell the church was filling in on both sides of the aisle. Marcus saw a calm, attractive, silver-haired woman, tastefully dressed enter from a side aisle and sit on the far end of his pew. She looked steadily in the direction of Brian Lucas. Finally, Lucas looked in her direction. Momentarily their eyes met, then Brian Lucas looked away. It was the same woman Marcus had seen at the wedding. Mariana's mother was nowhere in sight.

The service began. As Mariana's casket was wheeled to the front near the altar stairs, Marcus' vision became blurred. He heard little of the litany. He was remembering a lost life and he saw Mariana's face on every stained-glass female figure even Mary's, the mother of Christ. Clouds seemed to envelope him. He was in space, soaring as an eagle, a lone desolate eagle. Despite Bernie's nudging, Marcus just couldn't go up and participate in the Eucharist. Bernie caught Waddell's glance as the senior Secret Service operative indicated to Bernie not to insist that his brother partake of communion.

Bernie and Waddell noticed the odd glances of various mourners as they gave Marcus the fisheye for not being a communicant at the Eucharist for his deceased wife. Bernie and Waddell felt Marcus was suffering tortures of hellacious guilt, accepting a conclusion that he was responsible for his wife's death, true or not and that he deemed himself unworthy of partaking in the flesh and blood of Christ. They felt that many of the churchgoers reasoned Marcus was a cold-blooded killer and had no interest in Mariana's entering the heavenly kingdom that included Brian Lucas who sat glowering at his son-in-law.

The mass over, the funeral procession wound its way to the cemetery. On that clear, June day, as the burial service was ending, the priest uttered the words ashes to ashes, dust to dust, and sprinkled the coffin top with dirt. Marcus tearfully looked up from the coffin. He peered through the wrought iron fence to a field beyond the cemetery boundary. He saw a sight that made him gasp, a farmer sowing a late seed crop by hand. The seeds softly drifted to the recently tilled loamy soil. The chaff lazily drifted away toward the hill beyond. On that hill, the bluets were still blooming, the exact color of Mariana's eyes. Marcus wept silently for the sowing and the hill color symbolized to him the new life she had entered alone — quietly he raged over his loss and he was cold with fury.

When the burial was completed, Marcus and Bernie said a few polite words to the grieving members of the Lucas family and to a devastated Katherine Rogers, Mariana's associate editor.

Brian Lucas looked at Marcus, first with hatred, but, observing the depth of obvious sorrow that enveloped his son-in-law, he wondered: What is it about him that appears so genuinely devastated? Inwardly he winced at this own feelings of momentary sadness for Marcus, bastard that he was.

Marcus, Bernie and Waddell did not go to the wake to be held at Brian's house after the funeral. Their invitation, if that's what it could be called, was meant to be rejected. The unwelcomed trio headed to their hotel preparing to leave.

When Waddell reached his room, he telephoned the field office in New York. Ron Evans answered his call. "Ron," he asked, "Have you found anything new in your investigation of Mariana's murder?"

"Yes, just one interesting tidbit. I rummaged around Mariana's apartment. In a trash can in the kitchen, among a lot of crap I found pieces of a Central Florist card and pasted them together. In someone's handwriting it read, 'From Marcus with love, I'll be home soon.'"

"Who's handwriting?" asked Waddell.

"Damned if I know but I've handled the reconstructed card carefully. I immediately turned it over to the file for investigation."

There was silence for a few moments on Waddell's end of the line then he spoke, "Ron, I've got a hunch that Mariana's death was no stalking robbery gone wrong."

"Why, boss?"

"Because of that card. Someone knew Marcus was out of town. I surmise that someone also knew that he was supposed to be returning home soon."

"Waddy, how in the hell would that person know?"

"I suggest you check the Purple Canary, find out if anyone called shortly before Mariana's death requesting to speak to Marcus. I don't care what the answer is, you get over to his apartment, get in anyway you can and wait for him. You stay with him like a leech, day and night, until we get some kind of inkling about who is shadowing him and why."

"I'm on my way. But, Marcus is going to be damned curious as to why I am at his place."

"Tell him, tell him all you know and that I have ordered you to work with him trying to find a reason for Mariana's death. Besides, in his condition, he may need an extra trigger hand. He's not his usual observant self. I'll try to reach him before he leaves the Parker House Hotel."

"Gotcha, boss." Evans hung up his phone.

□

When Marcus arrived at the apartment, Henry Dimond was lounging on the sofa in the small foyer. He saw Marcus enter.

"Mr. Bosconovich, you have a guest in your apartment, a Mr. Ronald Evans."

Marcus was surprised because Waddy had said nothing to him about Evans being at his apartment. "Thanks," was Marcus' reply. As he headed to the elevator, he looked over his shoulder. "How did he get in?"

Henry replied, "He had a key."

Marcus reached the apartment floor, left the elevator and saw Ron standing in the doorway. As he approached, Ron held out his hand. "Henry called to say you were on your way up."

Marcus shook Ron's hand, studied him seriously and asked, "Why are you here?"

"Come in and I'll tell you. It's quite apparent Waddy wasn't able to reach you before you left your hotel." Ron sat on a sofa beside his friend, told him what information he, Waddy and the police had been able to put together. "In addition," he said, "I'm going to stay around here for a while just to lend a hand when I can. I know none of your family has come to help. Mariana's old man thinks you're scum. So does the staff at the Purple Canary. In addition to your little brother, you've got to have someone on your side to help out right now. And I've known you since a moonlit night way back when."

Marcus looked at his friend. Though there was a constant cold fury boiling inside of him, his eyes shown with true compassion. "Now I know how you must have felt much of your life," Marcus said softly.

"At the present time, it's not me who has to be considered. It's you. There are a number of things you have to do. Did Mariana leave a will and if she did, where is it?"

"Yes, she did. It's in our safety deposit box at the Chase Manhattan branch just up the street. Both our wills are there."

"Well, sometime today or tomorrow, you ought to get her will, see what it says and have it probated."

"I hate the thought of that, but you are right."

"I think you should make an inventory of her belongings so you can follow the terms of the will, whatever it says. When you finish those chores, we'll discuss whether you should stay here even if the will says yes."

"Why in hell should I move from here if the will says yes?"

"Let's talk about it later," said Ron.

"No, dammit, now," and Marcus' agitation was apparent.

Ron remained cool, "Because if someone is after you, this place isn't the easiest castle to defend."

"Who in the shit cares?"

"I do, your brother Bernie does, so will the rest of your family and Mariana's family when the truth is told. In addition, the Service has an obligation to you. Also, Waddy cares. He's not just a damned good agent, he truly admires you, your guts and has much more than Service respect for what you are enduring. You've got to come to earth, this isn't just some bad dream. It's a part of life you've got to face and now, if you're the man I think you are."

Marcus looked with respect at his friend. "You're not just a mid-distance runner, you are a damned good long-distance runner—a real friend, thanks. Lets have a light drink first, then get started on the inventory in the apartment. All of it is hers, even in the den. I'll start in the bedroom. You start in the den."

Marcus rose, went to the small bar at the far end of the living room, poured a light scotch for himself, bourbon for Ron. Seated on the sofa, each sipped silently. Ron, as unobtrusively as he could, studied Marcus. Marcus was somewhere off in space studying an unidentified figure, his enemy, Mariana's killer. Finally Ron said, "That was nice. Now lets get to work. Have you an extra notepad and pencil?"

"Plenty," replied Marcus. He rose, went to his study, returned with two small composition notebooks and pens, gave one of each to Ron.

"Fine," said Evans, "Just the thing." He took the proffered pad and pen then headed for the den. Marcus sighed and went to the bedroom. He decided the first items that should be inventoried were her jewelry. He looked on her dressing table and saw the three-drawered jewelry box. He knew she kept much of her costume jewelry in there, maybe others, he thought. He tried to unlatch the box catch only to find it was locked. He had no idea where the key was so he reached onto the dressing table, took a pair of heavy scissors that were lying there. He pried with a snap, the latch flew open. He raised the lid and saw the top layer, all kinds of necklaces, most obviously accouterment for certain evening wear. He pulled out the second drawer, there were watches, several of them, one or two diamond-studded. He opened the third drawer: earrings, bracelets, small brooches, all typical of a woman's costume jewelry and noticed they were atop some type of small photo. That snapshot was face down. He reached, pulled out the print and read the writing on the back of it. In Mariana's handwriting: "Why would Marcus have this snapshot of my brother Tully?" He turned the snapshot face up and was momentarily stunned.

"Ron," he yelled, "Come here quick. I've found something."

Ron raced from the den through the living room into the bedroom to see an incredulous Marcus standing in the middle of the room gasping for breath, all the while gazing at a little snapshot. Ron went up, looked over Marcus' shoulder and said, "That's just one of my shots of the guy with a part of his ear missing. One of the suspects of the 'C' scam team. Where did it come from?"

"Oh, God," moaned Marcus, "That snapshot is of Tully Lucas, Mariana's younger brother."

"The hell it is. I took that photo on the City of San Francisco on our trip east."

"Are you sure?"

"Positive."

Marcus turned the snapshot over. Ron read the question written on the reverse side. "Who wrote that?" he asked, then reaching, took the little revelation, studying it carefully.

"Mariana," was Marcus' sorrow-filled reply. He was silent, then brought his hands to his face to hide his horror. Through them he moaned, "I must have dropped it during the afternoon I first reviewed Waddell's instructional file. I heard Mariana enter the apartment while I was in the den going over the suspect photos. In my hurry to close the file before she came in the room that snapshot must have fallen on the floor without my noticing it. I'm sure she found it later that evening just before we went to bed."

"You mean this is a snapshot of your wife's brother?"

"Exactly."

"Have you ever seen another picture of him? Have you met him?"

"The answer to both of those questions is no. He wasn't in any family photo I have seen, nor have I met him. I saw him on the train, just as you did. Mariana said he was never home. He didn't attend our wedding. She apparently had a genuine dislike of him, seldom talked about him and never described him. I've met her older brother. He's not too bad a guy, just spoiled."

Ron was quiet, thinking and so was Marcus. Finally Ron spoke, "So what? How in the hell would Tully know you?"

"I'm not sure, unless his father sent him a wedding picture of Mariana and me, like the one on the piano in the living room."

Ron left the bedroom, strode rapidly to the piano, took the wedding photo, and studied it. Then he spotted a phone on a side table in the living room, went to it, and called the office. "Estelle, let me speak with Waddy. It's urgent. This is Ron Evans."

"I'm sorry, he's in conference, Mr. Evans. Can I have him return your call later?"

"No, you can't. This is more important than any damned conference."

After a few seconds a querulous Waddell answered the call. "Ron, it better be important."

"Boss, it is probably more so than either of us can imagine at this time. Please drop what you are doing and come to Marcus's apartment now. Man, are you going to be surprised."

"Ron, I'm working with five chief operatives trying to get some inkling on what the hell has happened to our counterfeit surveillance."

"And I'm telling you, Marcus and I may have the first real clue—right here, that's why I'm calling."

"What is it?"

"You come over and find out. It's better you learn here than in the office, then the three of us can talk in private."

"I'm on my way but your finding had better be for real. This is an important meeting."

"Tell the other five to stay in town until you call them. I think you're going to need them, maybe more." Ron hung up the phone with just the hint of a smile.

Waddell, in his office, looked at the operatives around the table. "Boys, an emergency has arisen. I have to leave the office for a while. Sorry I can't continue the confab, but don't leave town. Tell Estelle at the front desk where I can reach each of you. I'll call as soon as I can." Then he rose, put on his suit coat, raincoat and left.

"Jeez, something really special must have come up," said Smithers.

"Knowing Waddy as we do, you can bet your sweet ass on that," replied senior operative Bill Whitehead. The team leaders left the office.

□

Waddell arrived at the Lucas apartment and knocked on the door. Evans let him in. "This better be for real," said Waddell to Evans. Waddell entered, saw Marcus sitting in a lounge chair near a sofa, saw the steely excited glint in his eyes and said, "Marcus, what the hell has gotten Ron so excited?"

"He'll show you," Marcus answered.

"Take a seat Waddy," Ron motioned to the sofa.

Waddy sat without removing his raincoat. "Now what?" he asked, a little agitated.

"This," responded Evans and he handed him the snapshot.

Waddell took the little photo, looked at it. "So what? It is one of the snapshots you took on the City of San Francisco, the guy with the jagged ear."

"Turn it over," said Ron.

His boss did and read the question, was quiet for a few seconds, then, with a bewildered look on his face turned to Ron, "Who's handwriting is on the back of this snapshot?" he asked.

"Mariana's," replied Marcus. "I found the photo in her locked jewelry case a little while ago when Ron and I started to inventory her belongings. That creep is Tully Lucas, Mariana's younger brother."

Waddell's eyes shifted back and forth between Marcus and Evans. They grew wider with each shift. He looked again at the picture then the handwriting. "Mother of Mary," he said softly, "You may have the key, but how did she get it?"

Marcus explained what he surmised had happened. Waddell nodded his head affirmatively several times during Marcus' discourse. When his young operative finished his explanation, Waddy looked querulously at Marcus. "Why didn't she tell you that she had found the snapshot?"

"I don't really know. All I can think of is that she was worried about what trouble her disclosure might bring to her family, particularly her father. Though Mariana disliked her brother, she just couldn't believe he is a criminal."

Waddy looked with compassion at Marcus. "You could be right, oh so right. She was such a lovely, tender person."

Ron was eyeing Marcus. "Stop it, Marcus. You've got to stop that remorseless self-guilt now!" he said sharply.

"Go to hell," was Marcus' reply as he swiftly rose, entered the bedroom and shut the door.

"That poor devil, he blames himself for all of it," said Ron.

"It could be partly my fault too," said Waddell as he once again studied the snapshot.

"Not you too," replied Ron. "What is this, self-flagellation time?"

"Better now than later," replied Waddy. "You're right, from this time forward we have real work to do. I'll handle Marcus."

He went to the door, didn't knock, entered and stood before Marcus who was slumped in a lounging chair.

"Marcus," he said, "There is much work to be done. In addition, you have to straighten out your affairs and your wife's estate. As soon as this mess is solved, I will personally see to it that your family and Mariana's family are fully informed. So help me, God, I will. I'm damned glad none of them knows what we are beginning to learn. They could be in real jeopardy and if they knew or even suspected, God only knows what might happen." He stopped, looked seriously at Marcus, then continued, "I didn't take you on as an operative to protect you. I employed you because you are strong, smart and resilient as well as having guts and noble feelings. The time is now if we're going to solve this case without more serious consequences."

Marcus looked up at his boss, now it was Waddell's time to feel a chill. Marcus eyes betrayed the quiet rage he, Waddell, had viewed once before. "There will be no more sorrow. I'm ready, let's get moving," said Marcus to Waddell. His young associate rose with steely composure and the body alertness of a stalking leopard.

They entered the living room. Evans was surprised at the regained composure of his college buddy. He couldn't grasp it.

270

The three sat and Waddell started the conversation. "First, I will call the Boston field office, have them assemble background material on the Lucas family, all of them. We have to find out how many of them are involved in this scam and to what extent. However, our main focus right now will be Tully Lucas and whatever other aliases he may use."

"Mariana told me he lives at the Cathedral Towers Apartments in Washington, D.C. also that he works for some kind of art gallery in the Georgetown area of D.C.," said Marcus.

"That really helps. I'll alert the D.C. office to start a search there. Ron, for the time being, you stick by Marcus like a shadow. Marcus, you should start probate proceedings as soon as you find your wife's will. Complete your inventory here as soon as possible. Then I want you to file a change of address card with the local post office. I'll give you your new address."

"Why?" asked Marcus.

"Because, my friend, for your protection you are temporarily going under cover with Evans. Your phone here will be monitored. We will give you the wire tape of each day's incoming calls, all of them. But, you have to make it available to us so that we may check those we desire."

"No problem," replied Marcus. "I've got no secrets except those in my heart."

Evans was quietly absorbing the scene.

Waddell, watching Marcus, continued, "When we are ready to start the true unraveling of this matter, you, Ron and I will be the lead team. I owe each of you that privilege."

"Thanks, boss," replied Evans.

Marcus was quiet for a few seconds. "I can hardly wait for that time to come," was his calm reply.

"Marcus, after you and Ron complete the inventory here and after you check your lock box for her will, pack all the gear you will need for at least a couple weeks. Ron, call me when you are ready to close the apartment. I'll send a car to the apartment garage. Marcus, you don't mind lending me your wife's garage sensor so we can get in, do you?"

"Hell no," was Marcus' reply.

"Someone from the office will meet the two of you here at the apartment. Then go by the inside fire escape steps to the garage, I'll meet both of you at the office. Oh, by the way, the windows of the car will be tinted. Just make sure no one sees you go down those steps."

"Isn't that a little overkill?" asked Marcus.

"Not if no one here knows when you left or where you've gone."

Marcus raised his eyebrows in surprise. "I guess you're right. Evans will call you as soon as the job is done."

"See you later, boys," said Waddell as Marcus handed him the garage door sensor.

After the inventory was completed, Marcus and Evans went to the Chase Manhattan branch that contained Marcus and Mariana's joint safety deposit box, a large one. Marcus withdrew Mariana's will. In addition, he found information concerning her investment account with Auchincloss Redpath and Parker. He whistled when he saw the value. "I just had no idea," he mumbled. There also was a New York Life Insurance policy in the sum of fifty thousand with her father as beneficiary. He took it to send to Brian. He stuck Mariana's will into his jacket pocket, locked the box, returned it to its slot, called the attendant to lock the box outer door and left.

Upon returning to Marcus' apartment, Evans arranged for the phone tap and filled out the Post Office change of address card. Marcus signed it. Eventually, all his mail would end up at the New York field office.

As Marcus entered his den in the apartment, he called out to Evans, "I'll be here for a while. I have to send an insurance policy to Brian Lucas and review Mariana's will." He shut the den door, looked around the room and his stomach churned at the thoughtfulness of his former mate, "For so short a time," he said quietly.

He opened Mariana's will, unfolded the note attached to the document and read:

> Marcus dear,
> We have had so little time to discuss mutual business matters. I did ask you not to change your will until we really could talk about our estates. And I agreed not to change mine. But, God forbid, if something should happen before that time, I have jumped the gun a little. I have added a short codicil to my will. I want you to have a place to live and write, regardless of the

future, so I have devised the apartment to you as well as all my personal tangible property, my engagement ring, in particular, should be yours. I have also asked that you serve as the executor of my estate. I will make more changes when we have further discussed the matter.

I hope to God it is never necessary to implement the accompanying codicil, but who knows?

I love you,

Mariana

By the will codicil, he had been appointed executor. In that document, she left him the apartment free and clear of any obligation except the association monthly charge, together with all furnishings, her personal belongings including her engagement ring and the Jaguar to keep or dispose of as he saw fit.

The will bequeathed, the Purple Canary Press to Katherine Rogers, her former college roommate and now her associate editor. Radcliffe College was the beneficiary of the rest of her estate for, according to her will, that institution had given her much in the way of life purpose and sense of values. In her will, she bluntly stated that her dad had been her true mentor but needed no financial aid and that her brothers, particularly Tully, were unworthy of any gift as they had ignored her from birth. Her mother was not mentioned.

Marcus went into the living room. After discussing with Evans the pros and cons of his serving as executor of Mariana's estate, he decided not to do so. There was too much animosity from her father. In addition, his future was so damned uncertain, he would, when he filed the will for probate, request the probate court to appoint a corporate administrator with will attached to handle Mariana's affairs. He would feel much more comfortable with such an arrangement. Then he went into the den and placed a call to Katherine Rogers, told her the contents of Mariana's will as it applied to her. She wept openly and said over the phone, "Oh, my God, I don't deserve it. I'm so sorry it happened this way." She stopped and there was an awkward silence. Finally she continued, "Slowly, I'm beginning to recognize that you and Mariana, besides being devoted husband and wife, knew something that should be kept hidden, at least for the time being. Knowing Mariana as I did, I'm sure whatever it is isn't bad. As long as you want to maintain your dual identity with the Purple Canary, I consent to such an arrangement and will keep it a secret. When the episode is over please tell me what's behind the intrigue. I'm sorry I've been acting like a bitch to you. She was my best friend and it took me a while to realize that what secrets you two had were none of my business, that each of you had good reasons not to reveal them."

Marcus sighed in relief then said, "Thanks, Katherine, someday I will explain," and he hung up the phone.

Marcus returned to the living room and told Ron, "As soon as we get back from probating Mariana's will and I have completed packing my gear, you can alert Waddy."

CHAPTER 25

In the late afternoon, a car, with tinted windows, pulled up to the front entrance of The Wellingham—a quiet, residential hotel in an entirely different area of Manhattan. Marcus and Evans got out. The driver helped put Marcus's gear near the entranceway.

"Where's yours?" Marcus asked Evans.

"It's already in the apartment. I moved in a couple of days ago but I have to tell you it's not like yours and Mariana's. However, the place will do until we can sort through the present mess."

Marcus gave a feeble smile. "I understand," he replied.

As they entered the elevator, Evans told the operator, "Seventh Floor, please." On arrival, Evans led the way to a door at the end of a corridor, unlocked it and walked in. Marcus followed. Once the apartment door was shut, Evans turned to his co-worker. "Come here a second." Marcus walked over to him. "Take a peek," and Evans pointed to a peep hole that was camouflaged on the outside of the door by the apartment number plate. Marcus looked through the peephole. The whole corridor jumped at him.

"Some view," he said.

"That's why we are here. This unit has more protection gadgets than you can imagine. The Service has for years shared this apartment with another national security organization. It's a little hideaway in time of need. Not pretty, but relatively safe and comfortable. You take the bedroom down the hall. I'll take the one next to the living/dining room."

"Okay," responded Marcus, and he lugged his gear to his assigned area. He had hardly put the suitcases in the room when he heard a phone ring, wherever it was, then Evans voice, "Sure, boss, we'll be there in twenty minutes." He hung up the phone. "Marcus," he yelled, "Waddy wants us at the office, now."

Marcus needed no further bidding. When they entered Waddell's office, his boss, with his blue-gray eyes sparkling, arose quickly and shut the door, motioned to a couple of chairs and said, with an undertone of excitement, "Take a seat. I know you two have hardly settled in, but we will leave by air for Washington, D.C. tomorrow morning. Things are beginning to move rapidly."

"What's up?" asked Marcus.

Waddell replied, "We've heard from the Boston office and from the D.C. office. First, Tully Lucas is one of the sons of Brian Lucas and he is Mariana's brother. He does live at the Cathedral Tower Apartments in D.C. Odd thing is, there are two adjacent apartments, one with the name of Tully Lucas, the other with the name of Michael Weaver. From our investigation, we believe that Tully Lucas and Michael Weaver are one and the same person. Just who he's trying to fool, I don't know."

"I do," said Marcus. "His old man and probably others at the gallery."

"Could be," replied Waddell and he looked approvingly at Marcus. "Both of you have your disguises?"

"We do," replied Evans.

"When you awaken tomorrow morning, put them on. Take enough clothes for a week. We will head for D.C. on the seven a.m. Eastern Airline shuttle. You and Marcus will be staying in adjoining rooms at the Hotel Washington right across Fifteenth Street from headquarters."

"Fine by me," said Evans, "But you haven't told us why."

Waddell grinned, "I know. I'm coming to that. Marcus, you were right, Tully Lucas is connected in some way with the International Etching and Art Gallery on M Street in D.C. We're going down to be the lead team to find out just what he does there. I smell rats, a whole nest of them."

Marcus was excited. He hoped he could hide the excitement that was surging through him. He coughed then stuck his hands in his pockets.

"Here are two street maps of the area, a red dot indicates the location of the art gallery on each map. Also, here are two of the finest small cameras with the best distance lens known to man." Waddell handed a map and camera to each of his associates. He continued, "There are thirty-six color snaps to a roll. Starting day after tomorrow in D.C. each of you will have a small panel truck and a driver. There will be view areas on the side panels of each truck. From those view areas, when each of you are on station across from the gallery, you will take a picture of every damned soul who goes in or comes out of the gallery street entrance. There will be plenty of film in each truck. Make sure your cameras are set for a date and time stamp on each shot. By walkie-talkie you will coordinate your shots so that most will be at the same time but from different angles. There will be reliefs for both of you from time to time. Necessities of life are provided in each vehicle. You will leave your posts at six p.m. and bring your takes to the D.C. office. There will even be night crews on location if I think it's necessary. You are to be in my office by seven a.m. each morning for a review of the photos or slides from the negatives of the previous day. We will discuss any change in strategy at those sessions. A couple of operatives acting as potential art purchasers will, from time to time, get views inside the building and the gallery. In addition, the gallery telephone lines will be tapped. The local FBI and D.C. homicide will cooperate because of the murders of Fosberg and Mariana. Keep a sharp eye. Any questions?" asked their boss.

Marcus and Evans looked at each other, then Waddell. "Not yet," said Evans, "But I'm sure the time will come."

"So am I," replied Waddell.

Marcus was truly surprised at the quickness and thoroughness with which Waddell had implemented a program following his initial information. But he was curious. "Where will you be?" asked Marcus.

"On the second floor of a small building that overlooks the rear parking area of the gallery. Whenever I think it necessary, I will communicate with each of you by radio. Radio conversations will be handled by your driver. See you tomorrow, boys.

"By the way, the next time you see me and from then on until this caper is solved, I'll be white-haired, with a goatee and slightly heavier. But you'll recognize me. I'll always have a pink carnation in the lapel buttonhole of my suit coat."

"You don't need to wear a carnation on my account," said Marcus, "I couldn't miss that pigeon-toed walk of yours." Evans laughed.

"It's not for you two, it's a symbol for those in the field who may not know me so well. See you tomorrow boys."

"How about us?" asked Marcus.

"Hell, your make-up pictures are already displayed on our permanent rogues gallery, you'll be recognized even by the elevator boys," responded Waddell as he walked out of the office.

Upon leaving the New York office, Marcus and Evans took a cab and had supper at Mama Leon's Restaurant. Later they returned to the apartment, packed their gear in order to be ready for the morning flight to D.C. They then turned in early.

□

The next day after Marcus and Ron had settled into their rooms at the Hotel Washington, they walked over to the Secret Service Headquarters. Evans went about his business. Waddell introduced Marcus to the office staff who would be their support group on the operation. Marcus was shown the office layout, including the interrogation rooms, communications headquarters, the indexing system on counterfeit bills and coins, the latest scanning devices to determine counterfeit bills. Around noon, Evans met with Marcus and Waddell. The trio strolled up the street to the corner of New York Avenue and Fifteenth Street, N.W. and had lunch in the S&W Cafeteria. Following lunch, Waddy took Marcus and Evans to the service garage, identified the small vans each would use, showed them the interiors where the film holders were located and taught them how to use the slide vent for camera viewing. While sitting in one of the vans, Waddell pulled out a camera similar to theirs and demonstrated the snapshot process, including lens focusing, date and time setting, film loading, setting exposure, ejecting filled cartridges and storage. He made each man go through the process until he was sure there would be a minimum of spoiled shots. Then the trio returned to headquarters.

Later when Marcus and Evans left the office, they took a cab to Hall's Seafood Restaurant on Seventh Street, S.W., one of the few places in town where blacks and whites could comfortably enjoy a libation and dinner together, particularly in the arbor covered outdoor eating area. As Marcus entered the restaurant and saw the nude mural over the bar, he remembered the mural over the bar in the Shanghai Lounge and Seafood Grill. His thoughts went back briefly to the first night he had met Samantha Kingsbury. How long ago that seemed.

Following supper, Marcus and Evans took a cab to the Howard Theater near the intersection of Fourteenth and U Streets, N.W. to see a movie and to hear Duke Ellington and his band entertain on stage, a delightful evening for both men.

After the show, though it was late and a long walk through a mostly black neighborhood, Marcus and Ron decided to walk back to the hotel. Neither man gave thought to trouble—racial trouble— ethnicism and segregation were not then violently polarized. There was no visible mutual antagonism and there was a semblance of mutual respect—in public at least.

During their walk, Marcus spoke, "You got a girlfriend? Have you ever thought of marriage? You're not a bad-looking guy."

Evans smiled at his friend. "The answers to those questions are no, no and thanks." He looked wistfully at his friend. "I've said most of it before. I'm overeducated and undercolored for most women of my race. And I'm overcolored and disturbingly educated for the women of your race. Just how in hell I'll ever find a loving mate, I have yet to figure."

As they crossed the intersection at Fourteenth and T Streets, N.W., a light chocolate-skinned hooker in her garb of the evening sidled up to Evans.

"Old daddy, you interested in a trick?" she asked.

Evans, in his elderly disguise, looked at her with disdain and said, "Thanks, no, and if you don't want to be fingered by the law in the next thirty seconds, leave." She knew the meaning and left immediately. After resuming their walk, Ron turned to Marcus, sighed and said, "That's about as good as it ever gets."

In silence, the two friends continued down Fourteenth Street.

For the next week Ron, Marcus and Waddell were at their posts taking reams of color snapshots. Early each morning at the office, those shots were reviewed by the trio, either on film slides or photos. At first no pattern could be observed. However, on the beginning of the ninth day of surveillance, in an early morning review, Marcus said, "Run that last frame again, will you?" Ron showed the frame on the screen. "You see that young lady going into the main entrance of the gallery, the one carrying a brief case?" and Marcus pointed.

"Sure," said Waddell.

"She is wearing flat heels, seems shorter, but I think I recognize the build. We've seen her before."

"When?" asked Waddell.

"Starting with yesterday's take, lets run the slides and photos going back day by day," said Marcus.

"Ron, put yesterday's rack on, but run it from closing time to early morning," said Waddell.

Ron followed his boss's bidding. The threesome observed closely. No match. He began to run the rack from two days before. They had viewed about ten colored film shots when Marcus said, "Stop! Look at that young lady," and he pointed. "She has on high heels and different attire, but I think that female has the same build as the one in the first slide we set aside."

"Lets compare them," said Waddell.

They reviewed both slides. "Possible," said Waddell, "Hold both of them out, lets back up further." They did and, over the next hour reviewing the past eight days they pulled out three more slides of the rear view of a female, apparently the same young lady always entering but never leaving the gallery.

"Why don't we ever see her come out?" asked Ron.

"I'll be damned," said Waddell. "Wait a minute." He left the room, soon returning with another circle of slides. "These are the ones I took from the second floor rear window of the building that is behind the gallery. I never thought to coordinate my shots with yours but each has a date on it. There are nowhere near the numbers you have. And the angle is poor because they are almost overhead shots but, let's review them."

"Run the same dates as the ones we have set aside," suggested Marcus.

"Good thinking," replied his boss. He started and was moving the viewer frame by frame.

Just as he was about to push the advance button again, Marcus said, "Hold it."

"Why?" asked Ron.

"Because, though we can't see her whole body view from the picture angle, isn't that the same color dress as the gal in the first frame we set aside?"

They compared the two shots. Ron walked to the screen and looked carefully then observed, "Shit, I think you're right. It has the same date. But who is the guy with her?"

"That's Tully Lucas," said Waddell. "That shot, as you can see, is about five hours after your morning shot."

"So that's why we never see a frontal shot of her leaving the main gallery entrance," said Marcus.

"You could be right," retorted Waddell. "Let me run the rest and see what we find."

Ron ran the rest of Waddell's slides. Sure enough, the gal, whoever she was, always left the premises with Tully Lucas by auto from the rear parking lot.

"Why doesn't Tully Lucas ever use the front entrance?" asked Ron.

"I'll bet he wants to be seen as little as possible using that door. He's no fool. In addition, I'm sure he doesn't want to be seen in public with his so-called girlfriend at least not going in and out the front door together," replied Marcus.

Marcus was excited, Waddell was energized. He picked up a phone on the conference table and made an in-office call. "Ted, I want you to call Blake at the District FBI office and Lieutenant Fulton at D.C. Homicide. I want a tail put on Tully Lucas day and night. I am sure that events will be moving faster." He hung up fumed to his junior operative, "You are one observant rascal, Marcus. I knew I did the right thing taking you aboard."

"Who is the female?" asked Ron.

"I'll lay you two to one odds, its the same dame that was on the City of San Francisco with Tully," replied Marcus.

"How in the hell can you tell?" asked Ron.

Marcus, with fire dancing in those hazel eyes of his, smiled and replied, "The casino taught me in a hurry how to recognize shapes, forms and attitudes. It's damned near as important as the card games. That's not all, she's most always carrying the same briefcase. I'll bet she is the courier, the bag lady of the operation."

Waddell was studying Marcus. "You could be right, so very right," he said quietly. "And, you know what? We don't have a clue as to who she really is, but we soon will."

Ron looked at Waddell. "I think I spotted that guy Leverbee in some of those slides."

His boss grinned. "I did a couple days ago. I didn't say anything to the two of you then. We already have a tail on him. By the way, I've determined that the gallery buys a large amount of stationary, almost but not quite matching the grade on which the original C notes are printed."

"I smell smoke," said Ron.

"Doesn't it smell invigorating?" replied a grinning Waddell.

To Marcus the increased pace of events was not only thrilling but for some reason he just knew it would be fulfilling.

"Boys, you can take the rest of the day off, check with the office around 6:00 p.m. I need to correlate some data before we make our next move," said Waddy.

Upon leaving the office, Marcus and Evans went their separate ways, Evans to meet a couple of friends, Marcus to take a walking tour of the area to see the White House and the State Department building. After that, he took a taxi and spent the rest of the day in the poetry section of the Library of Congress.

□

When Marcus returned to his room in the Washington Hotel at 5:45 p.m. he noticed the flashing red button on the wall evidencing a phone message. He lifted the receiver and inquired if he, Marcus Bosconovich, had a call.

"You have, indeed," was the operator's reply. "Your boss, Waddell, says you've been idle long enough. Something is about to happen, he'll meet you in front of the hotel at six twenty p.m."

"Thanks," said Marcus. He glanced at his watch, he only had thirty minutes to grab a bite to eat and he was hungry. From a note left under his room door he knew Evans had already left for supper.

Marcus was on time at the entrance, watched as the black, government-licensed car with Waddell in the back seat pulled to a stop. He got in beside his boss and asked, "What now?"

Waddell replied, "We have tapped the phones to the apartments of Tully Lucas and Michael Weaver. I just received word that Michael Weaver reserved a ticket for one Lorraine Driscoll on the nine p.m. nonstop train to New York. I know she is at his apartment. I want us to determine if she is the girl in the photos and may be the one who was with him on the City of San Francisco, the bag lady. You and I are going to follow her as she leaves his apartment to go to the station. We're going to watch her get on the train. I've already alerted the New York office to have her under surveillance from the moment she arrives in New York. I will call in a more detailed description of her after she entrains for New York."

"Fine by me," replied Marcus and his adrenalin started to pick up.

In the government vehicle, parked at a vantage point, the two Secret Service men watched Lorraine leave the apartment building, enter a cab and head for Union Station. Marcus was sure it was the girl he had seen with Weaver on the City of San Francisco. They discretely followed her cab to the station. The driver of Waddell's car pulled up in a "No Parking" area near the front of the station. There Marcus and Waddell watched Lorraine leave the cab and get a Redcap to take her luggage.

A D.C. policeman patrolling the area walked over to the surveillance car, stuck his head in the driver's window and admonished, "Buddy, can't you read? Move on, you can't park here."

"Not so fast, officer," said Waddell. He showed his Secret Service ID. "We have a surveillance in progress and this car stays right here. The fact is, my partner and I are going into the station for a while. When we return, we'll need it."

The policeman looked agitated. "Okay, as long as the driver stays with the car."

"No problem," replied Waddell as he and Marcus kept Lorraine Driscoll in view.

"Come on, Marcus I want to get a closer look at that young lady," said his superior.

The two men hurried to the station door through which the object of their surveillance had just entered. There was no heavy crowd. The lawmen moved to within a few steps behind her.

Marcus observed a glitter from her left hand, the one carrying the briefcase. The little flash was reflected as the result of an overhead light. Marcus increased his stride as he walked to within six feet of the young lady's left side. Waddell saw the startled, yet fierce look that his junior gave her, then, much to Waddell's consternation, Marcus ran around the back of the young lady, to her right side and eased close to her. He saw Marcus's right hand reach quickly to his holster and his service revolver hidden by his suit coat, was being poked in her side. She stopped dead in her tracks. As Waddell approached, he heard Marcus hiss, "If you so much as shiver, I'll splatter your guts all over this floor."

He was instantly at Marcus's side and asked quietly but firmly, "Have you lost your mind? What the hell has gone wrong with you?"

"Not a damned thing. But this bitch is wearing Mariana's engagement ring. Just turn around easy like, young lady, start walking for the door through which you entered."

"How do you know?" queried Waddell.

"Go around the other side, take a look. It's a European cut diamond in a Florentine mount. There are damned few like it in this country. I'd recognize it anywhere."

Lorraine Driscoll was in shock, unsteady on her feet and was having a hard time focusing on the bushy-browed brunet with fierce hazel eyes. Was he crazy?

"I've warned you, Miss Driscoll, don't you utter a peep or, regardless of your rights, I'll drill you right here."

She looked from one man to the other, "Who...who...are you?"

"The Secret Service," Marcus said softly.

Lorraine fainted on the spot.

"Shit," said Marcus, "This complicates matters, but not much."

Waddell, for the moment, was absolutely stumped.

A couple of Redcaps came running over. By the time they reached where Lorraine had fallen, Marcus had placed his pistol back in its holster. He was kneeling by her side. He looked up, saw the Redcaps and said, "My sister has suddenly been taken ill. She's not heavy. I'll carry her to our car. It's just outside." He looked at Waddell. "Uncle Waddy, will you take her briefcase and get her suitcase from the Redcap?"

With the greatest of ease, Marcus lifted Lorraine in his arms and strode to the station exit door. Waddell was quickly at his side carrying Miss Driscoll's briefcase and suitcase. He now was alert, with his adrenalin flowing and he was watching for any deterring movement. There was none.

"Holy Christ, Marcus, are you sure?" Waddy hissed as he matched his employee stride for stride.

"If I'm wrong, we're in for big trouble," was Marcus's short reply.

"You've got no idea how big. What do you propose we do with her?"

"Take her to the office and as soon as she revives, begin to get to the bottom of this whole damned affair. She didn't faint because the pistol was in her side, it was when she heard the words, 'Secret Service.'"

"Man, if you're right, you really have advanced our schedule."

As the trio entered the fresh air outside the station, Marcus heard Lorraine moan, felt her beginning to sir. "Stay right where you are, young lady and everything will be all right."

Lorraine opened her eyes, looked at the guy who was carrying her. "You friggin' bastard," she murmured.

"I'll accept that, you murderous bitch," he responded as they approached the auto.

The driver of the Secret Service auto saw his two approaching superiors, quickly stepped out of the vehicle and opened a rear passenger door. Marcus put Lorraine on the seat then entered the car. Waddell went around to the other rear passenger door and entered. As he did so, the same policeman walked up and said to Waddell as he entered the car, "Now, I believe you. Quite an attractive haul."

"You bet your sweet ass she is," was the senior operative's terse answer as he closed the door. He leaned over the back of the front seat and said, "Harry, take us to headquarters." The long, black sedan with the tinted windows drove rapidly towards the Treasury Building.

By now, Lorraine had recovered from her initial shock. "Are you really from the Secret Service?"

"We are, Miss Driscoll," replied Waddell.

"I never in my life killed nobody."

"Please ma'am," responded Waddy, "I suggest you keep quiet until we reach headquarters. You don't have to say a word to us."

"Damn it, I know I don't. I'm a lot of not-so-nice things, but I'm no killer."

"We'll talk about that and much more later," responded Waddell.

Lorraine began to shiver, then cry. "Oh, what in the hell will become of me?" she blubbered through her sobs. Marcus and Waddell could tell she was truly frightened and apparently not just because of them. As the car left the station, Waddell told the driver to radio the FBI, then the D.C. Homicide Bureau, tell them that he and Marcus were headed for Secret Service Headquarters with a suspect in the counterfeit scam.

The auto drove into a driveway alongside the Treasury Building and up to a door. A guard was there. He recognized the car and when the occupants got out, he exclaimed, "Mr. Waddell, what a surprise."

"And how," replied Waddell. "We're going to take a trip up to headquarters. Tell HQ we're on our way and to have Interrogation Room A ready."

"So late?"

"Yes, so late. We're in a hurry."

The trio entered the building. Shortly thereafter, an elevator reached their floor level and the door opened. "Good evening, Samuel," said Waddell.

"Apparently," quipped Samuel as he looked at Lorraine.

"Take us to headquarters level."

"Yes, sir," responded the wide-eyed, evening elevator operator.

□

Once in the little room, Interrogation Room A, Marcus and Waddell sat across the table from Lorraine. The track light shown down on her, revealing a slender woman of not bad proportions. Her facial features were delicate, almost too delicate. Marcus observed the little scars on her face, near each ear. He could tell that she had undergone at least one facelift. He wondered what she looked like before. Her eyes were chestnut brown and almost sorrowful. God only knows the true color of her blonde-tinted hair. However, there was a steeliness about her that belied her looks, a steeliness from years of apparently battling adversity and Marcus wondered about her background.

Waddell spoke, "Miss Driscoll, you have the right to remain silent, the right to a lawyer before you say a word. If you elect to talk to us without a lawyer, anything you say may be used against you in a court of law."

"I've heard that line since I was sixteen," she smirked.

"Do you want a lawyer?"

"Not right now. Maybe later."

"Maybe later, may be too late."

"I'll take my chances," she retorted, then added vehemently, "But, I'm no killer."

"Where did you get that ring?" asked Marcus.

"From my boyfriend," was the nervous reply.

"What's his name, Michael Weaver or Tully Lucas?"

"I don't know Tully Lucas. He's the guy that has the apartment next to my Michael. He's supposed to be employed at the gallery, but he's never at either place. Michael says he's our contact man on the road."

"Miss Driscoll, when did Michael Weaver give you that ring?" asked Marcus.

She looked down at the diamond, adjusted the ring with her other hand. "Shortly after he came back from his last trip to Florida."

"Are you sure it was Florida?"

"That's what he said."

"When was that?"

"About two weeks ago."

"Did he tell you where he got the ring?"

"Yes, he had been back about a day and when he came home in the evening, he gave it to me after supper. I asked him where he bought it. He said from the pawn shop in Rosslyn, Virginia, across the river."

"Does it fit?"

"Not exactly. I have a little piece of adhesive tape wound on the back part of the ring," she opened the palm of her hand, revealing the tape. "He has asked me to marry him. I told him I would think about it."

Marcus's hazel eyes were cold and he was seething inside. "Miss Driscoll," he said, "Have you ever looked on the inside of the ring to see if there is an inscription?"

"Hell no, never thought about doing so."

"I suggest that if you take off the tape and look, you will see, finely engraved, the initial 'A' and the word 'Cavozzi,' C-a-v-o-z-z-i."

Lorraine was flustered and became increasingly nervous. Looked first at the ring then at Marcus.

"Take if off, look," was his sharp demand.

Slowly Lorraine removed the ring, took the tape from the band and cleaned that area with a finger. Then raising the ring, tried to look, squinted. "There's something there, but I can't tell what it is without my glasses."

"Get your glasses, read it," was Marcus's command.

Waddell was watching almost breathless. The whole counterfeit surveillance hung on her answer. On the other side of the large mirror glass that could be viewed from the outer room FBI Agent Ross and Sergeant Bucknell from the D.C. Homicide squad, stood and watched, engrossed.

Lorraine nervously put on her glasses, brought the ring closer to her right eye. She looked one more time at Marcus, then at the ring. She said ever so softly, "A. Cavozzi." Again looked up at Marcus. "So what?" she asked.

"That ring was my deceased wife's engagement ring. I gave it to her when we became engaged. My mother's maiden name was Cavozzi. This was my mother's ring and then my wife's."

Now Lorraine saw the predatory look in Marcus's eyes, a look of wild anger. Though he was across the table from her and Waddell sat next to him, Lorraine felt fear for her life as she never had before. She looked in terror at the bushy-browed, powerfully built young man in front of her.

Marcus's words were measured and each hit her as if they were meant to kill, not to wound. "Mariana Lucas, my deceased wife, was the sister of Tully Lucas who also goes by the name of Michael Weaver. And he killed my wife, his sister." In a flash, Marcus ripped off his dark wig, pulled off the fake eyebrows and moustache, glared at her, then hissed. "Now do you know who I am?"

"My God, the sailor," moaned Lorraine. For the second time in the evening, she fainted.

A member of the Service standing in the observation room, looking through the one-way mirrored window, raced into the interrogation room and after administering smelling salts to Lorraine, gave her a glass of water with a touch of brandy in it. The horrified young lady again regained her presence of mind.

"Miss Driscoll, you still have the right to a lawyer," said Waddell calmly.

Lorraine blinked a couple of times and shook her head as if to remove the cobwebs. Then her steely demeanor returned.

"I don't need any lawyer. I knew it was too good to last. What do you want to know. I'll tell you, but I am no killer!"

"I'm convinced of that," said Waddell. "Tell us all you know about the counterfeit operation and I assure you the charges against you will be greatly reduced. I'll see to it. I promise." He motioned to the one-way window mirror. Immediately a stenographer entered the room with her stenotype machine. "This is Cathy Reilly," said Waddell, "She is going to take your statement."

"Okay," was Lorraine's feeble reply.

"Miss Driscoll, before we start our interrogation, would you mind opening your briefcase, showing me the contents?" asked Waddell.

"No, sir," she responded sweetly. Taking the key from her purse, she unlocked and opened it.

Waddell looked and whistled softly in surprise. Marcus also looked. Inside banded in bundles of five thousand dollars each were ten bundles of counterfeit C bills.

"We'll take the briefcase and contents then give you a receipt," said Waddell.

"I don't want no damned receipt," was her retort.

"Now, would you mind opening your suitcase?"

"I mind, but what good would that do. You're going to open it anyway."

She was so right. Waddell opened the suitcase and checked the contents. Beside her expensive clothing was a professional disguise, a make-up kit that would have put the average quick-change artist to shame.

For the next two hours, Lorraine Driscoll, skilled disguise artist and master bag woman for the operation spilled her guts, giving details of her life including the counterfeit and conning operation as she knew it. When she finished, she turned to Waddell, "Sir, my life is now not worth a dime. If you turn me loose, I'll be dead before the night is over."

Marcus's fury at Lorraine Driscoll had melted during the interrogation. He really felt sorry for the Georgia waif who had never had a real chance since her parents were killed in a train wreck when she was twelve years old. Thank God, it wasn't his decision to make.

Waddell spoke evenly, "Miss Driscoll, you will remain in protective custody while we gather evidence for whatever action the government will take on this matter. The final disposition of your case will depend on how this whole affair ends."

"Thank you very much, sir," was her meek reply.

She looked at Marcus, shoved the ring toward him. "I'm sorry, so sorry. Knowing that bastard, Michael as I do I really don't want the ring. It is so large I thought it was a fake anyway." She smiled a bitter, twisted smile at Marcus, rose and a female attendant led her away.

Waddell stood, came around the table, placed his hand on Marcus's shoulder. "Marcus," he said, "Now the end is really in sight. You, my friend, are worth your salt. When her confession is transcribed and signed, the final sting will be under way. You provided the key to unlock the whole scam. I thank you."

"Where's that bastard, Tully?" asked Marcus with steely coldness, as he took the ring from the table, wrapped it in his handkerchief and put it inside his suit coat breast pocket. Waddell thought, "I'll wait until he calms down a little before I ask him for it."

"We'll get him shortly. I'll let you know. Let's go to the office lounge and chat a bit before you go home. You need to calm down," said his boss.

The two men left the interrogating room, went to the lounge. Waddell poured coffee for both of them. He carried the conversation away from the episode just finished, trying to get his junior employee to unwind.

Just before Marcus left the lounge, Waddell said to him, "Make sure you ask for your mail at the hotel. I had headquarters deliver your rerouted mail there this evening."

Marcus looked at Waddell in surprise. "I hadn't even given a thought about mail," he replied.

"There are always bills to pay and letters to write," said Waddell. "Besides that, there is your wife's estate to administer."

"Not the last," said Marcus.

"Why not?"

"I want the least possible friction with Mariana's dad. So I have declined to act. Chase Manhattan has taken over."

"Oh," replied Waddell and he knew Marcus was right in doing so. He was quiet for a few seconds, then, "Marcus, about your wife's engagement ring, you shouldn't keep it on your person, not as fast as this case is moving. Something might happen to it. Besides, it's the first piece of hard evidence we have, as the scam begins to unwind. Let me put it in our secure vault. I'll get a photo of it in a few minutes and attach it to a dated receipt. You can have the ring back as soon as the case is over. I give you my word of honor, I'll personally return it. Please!"

Marcus looked solemnly at Waddell. He knew his boss' request was not only legally correct, but a sensible one. He took the ring from his pocket and his eyes teared as he looked at it. He kissed the ring, then handed it to Waddell. "I know you will. Thanks," said a sorrowful Marcus.

□

At eleven thirty p.m. that night Marcus picked up his mail from the hotel front desk, went to his room, flopped on his bed, turned on the bed reading light and started to sort through the pile. Among others there was a "welcome home alumni" letter from Cornell University thanking him for sending his alumni association dues and asking for more. There was a request from the Navy suggesting that he consider joining the active reserve, then there was an envelope with his mother's familiar handwriting. His heart picked up a beat as he looked forward to reading her first letter since Mariana's death. Neither his mother nor his dad had communicated with him since he had notified them of Mariana's murder. He needed to be in touch with them because he just knew they were really troubled that he had recklessly or thoughtlessly caused her demise. He opened the envelope and was bitterly disappointed. There was no letter. Enclosed was an unopened envelope addressed to him at his parents' address. He could tell by the return address that the letter was from Samantha. Not one word had his mother written on the enclosed envelope. Now he was upset and, for whatever reason, increasingly felt the implied guilt that from time to time swept over him—occasionally nauseated him. He was angry at his family, all except Bernie. Didn't they know him better? Didn't they really care?

In that state of mind, he opened Sam's letter, began to read:

June 11, 1946

Dear Marcus,

I know I have been derelict in answering your letter. However, I do treasure it and have reread it dozens of times. It is a constant source of help. As time weaves her encompassing mantle, I become more isolated from the everyday world and that isolation has kept me from writing more frequently. But—here goes.

I no longer work and am now a resident in the House of Eternity, was admitted last week. The days and nights drift so slowly. So do I. The medication I take no doubt contributes to that feeling, somehow it does help to relieve the pain. That's one reason why today I write this letter.

Enclosed you will find the seventy-five dollars you loaned me. I saved it from my last three paychecks. You can't imagine what those few dollars meant to me. I can never repay you for your thoughtfulness, including the three hundred bucks I found in my coat pocket. You and Alice-Lee made my life worthwhile. She has been my day-by-day bulwark. As tough as she appears to the rest of the world, her constant friendship, her calls, her visits and the kindness she brings on those trips, I never believed possible. You two have shown me a side of life I never knew before. Before I leave this world I must take you to the side I lived and hated.

Yes, you were correct when you suspected that my anger was not just because of my Christmas disease or my current problem. I have already told you of my dismay at my parents in birthing me, both of them knew before I was conceived that my mother was a carrier of my original flaw.

Now the rest. I have two older sisters Erica, five years older than I and Ida, three years. Erica bares a striking resemblance to my deceased mother. After my mother's death, Erica gradually assumed not only the role of mother of the family, but most, if not all, of her mannerisms, hairdo, makeup and yes, even her voice. She sat in my mother's chair at the dining table and as time went on, her position in the house became not only mother-like, but wife-like. My father seemed to dote on her, almost a husbandly affection. It bothered me, but for a long while I accepted the relationship as that of a loving sister filling a needed role in the family. Then, one day when I was a junior in engineering, a day student at the college where my father is still a professor and the chaplain I came home early after lunch to pick up a report for a late afternoon class. I had inadvertently left it in my room at home. When I entered, the house was quiet. I thought no one was home. In those days I wore rubber-soled, black and white saddle shoes. They hardly made a sound. I walked up the stairs to the second floor hall and headed toward my room. As I passed the closed door of my parents' room, I heard moans of passion and Erica's voice excitedly saying, "Now, now, my beloved, now," and my father replied. "Oh, Erica darling, this is heaven." I could tell by the bed sounds what was taking place. I quietly listened for a few more moments. After that, I raced to my room, grabbed my assignment. As fast and as quietly as I could I fled, I vomited all over the sidewalk in front of our house. Never, never in my life had I suspected the relationship between my older sister and my father. I have hated their guts from that moment on. My own father, who taught morals, ethics and the Bible at my college was having such an affair with my sister—the very essence of what he deplored and taught as a vicious sin.

Though I remained silent about what I learned, I vowed to leave the house the minute I graduated from college and I did. That's not all. I just know that Ida, who was living at home, a graduate nurse working in the college infirmary, knew what was taking place and was waiting for an appropriate moment to use it to her advantage. Marcus, maybe I have no right to dump on you as I have done before and in this letter, but someone besides the creator and Ida should know. I haven't even told Alice-Lee. I never will. However, shortly after you and I first met, some yet inexplicable voice within me demanded that I trust you implicitly. I always will. I just had to tell you, for my sake and maybe for yours.

Marcus, did you marry the girl in your wallet? I ask because what immediately led to this letter was a dream I had last night. In that dream I was at the opening of a strange, softly-lit tunnel. As I stood at the entrance, suddenly from the yellow mist that drifted through it, the girl in your wallet appeared in a long, white gown and she beckoned to me to join her. Then, there was a flash, I awakened with my heart racing and I was covered with perspiration.

Is anything wrong? Are you two happy?

I no longer fear death because I have nothing to look forward to in this life. So, being human and needing to look forward to something I am awaiting what comes next—I sincerely pray that something will be better than the life I have lived on this tiny, imperfect segment of God's creation.

I can hold my pen no longer, will see that this note is mailed in the morning.

Please write soon.

Still the swallow,

Samantha

Marcus was not only surprised by the letter but was in shock over Sam's tunnel dream. That dream had to have been shortly after Mariana's death. How weird! What a hell of a life Sam has experienced and is still doing so. Right now the experience he was living didn't seem real either. It was like a dream—no, a nightmare, made even more so by Sam's revelations in her letter. When would he awaken? Truly awaken.

Marcus realized that Sam had little time left in this life. He looked into the drawer of the night table by his bed, found hotel stationery and an envelope. He retrieved his current notebook from his suitcase, sat on the bedside and using the notebook as a lap table, he penned his response to Sam. He addressed an envelope to her, placed the letter in it. After obtaining a stamp at the front desk, he would drop the letter in the mailbox in the lobby.

When Marcus finished writing his letter to Sam, he was still excited about the events of earlier in the evening. Underneath that excitement he had an ever-deepening anger at Tully Lucas who he was sure was the murderer of Mariana. He whispered, "Oh, my God, I'm beginning to hurt and hate as does Samantha. He shivered slightly, then said softly, "I need a drink and a bite to eat before I try to sleep." He took the elevator to the lobby, mailed the letter to Samantha and headed to the Hotel Washington Tap Room off the lobby.

□

The next morning when Marcus awakened, his mouth tasted like he imagined the bottom of a sick parakeet's birdcage would taste. He shuddered, couldn't remember if or when he had supper and he had no idea when he went to bed, or how he had found the way to his room. He knew he was now ravenously hungry. "I've never done this before in my life," he mumbled, stood swaying, still feeling the results of his over consuming Haig and Haig. The room swam for a few seconds. He drew a deep breath, felt better, then walked toward the bathroom. As he did, he saw a piece of paper stuck under the entrance door of his hotel room. He reached down to pick it up and all but fell on his face. "Whew, I must have really tied one on," he murmured. He straightened up, unfolded the note:

Marcus:

I have been ordered out of town on an assignment by Waddy.

Call him by eleven a.m. at the office. See you soon.

Ron

Marcus instantly knew who had helped him to his room, but couldn't remember seeing Ron in the Tap Room. He looked at his watch and realized it was long after normal reporting in time. He remembered the note, 'Call him by eleven a.m.' He thought, "Waddy knew about his night too. Damn, they are keeping a sharp eye on me and they are really considerate." He felt more comfortable in his new work than ever before. Now he was hungry so he headed for the hotel dining room. After a full meal, he was energized and wondered, "Where in the hell had Ron gone so suddenly?"

At eleven Marcus called his boss. "Marcus, are you feeling better this morning?" asked Waddell.

"I surely am."

"Are you ready for another quick trip?"

"I am indeed, where to?"

"Pack your gear and meet me at the hotel entrance in an hour. You and I are leaving for Boston on the one p.m. Eastern flight."

Marcus hesitated, then asked, "Why Boston?"

"I'll have plenty of time to tell you during our flight. Just be patient, everything is rapidly falling into place." Waddell hung up.

Marcus's adrenalin was flowing at top speed. Boston! Something had to be going on involving the Lucas family. Just what could it be?

CHAPTER 26

Brian O'Flanagan Lucas was having another bad day in his office. The court proceedings he had filed in New York trying to deny that crook Bosconovich any interest in his daughter's estate had suddenly come to a screeching halt. Dennis Forsythe, his New York lawyer, had called earlier in the morning to say that Probate Judge Jeremy Wills had, the day before, suddenly continued all further hearings. According to his lawyer, the Judge had determined that the pleadings filed had never been properly served on Lucas' son-in-law and Marcus couldn't be found. "I would kill him with my bare hands if I could find that monster," mused the senior Lucas. Much to his dismay, he had also been advised earlier during the morning by a long-distance call from a confidant, that Karen, his wife, was traipsing around Mexico with some half-ass dilettante he had never met. According to Brian's source, the couple were having a close encounter. And that private eye, Paul Cavalier who he hired on the advice of his son Tully wasn't giving him straight information on Marcus or his whereabouts. He doubted the so-called private investigator knew any more than he did where Marcus was or what he was doing.

He remembered yesterday afternoon when Priscilla, his secretary, called him on his intercom and said, "Some guy named Clarence Waddell is calling and says it's urgent that he speak with you."

Brian asked, "Why does he need to speak with me?"

"He said it is a very personal matter."

"Never heard of him, but put him on."

Brian had asked, "Mr. Waddell, this is Brian Lucas. What's on your mind?"

"Mr. Lucas, I'm Clarence Waddell, a senior U.S. Secret Service Operative. My associate and I would like to meet with you some time tomorrow at the latest."

"Why?"

"On a matter of great personal importance to you."

"How do I know you are not some high-binding scam artist?"

"Well, I suggest you call your good friend, Congressman John McCormack. He's home campaigning for the next election. He knows me and is aware that I am endeavoring to meet with you but doesn't know the reason why."

Brian Lucas had been surprised and bothered and realized the operative was serious. He had looked at his appointment calendar and replied, "I've nothing on my calendar that can't be changed to later in the day. How about ten a.m. tomorrow?"

"That will be fine," responded Waddell.

So, there he, Brian, was waiting for Mr. Secret Service and it was now ten a.m. His intercom phone rang, Priscilla White announced, "Mr. Lucas, a Mr. Waddell and his associate are here for their appointment with you."

"Send them in," he responded.

Brian's secretary opened the door. Waddell and his associate entered.

Clarence Waddell walked toward Lucas' desk and extended his hand. Lucas arose from his desk chair, started to shake hands with the senior operative, glanced over the operative's shoulder and saw Marcus, his son-in-law. He recoiled as if withdrawing his hand from a striking viper. "What the hell is this?" he asked sternly then abruptly sat.

Clarence Waddell stepped up to Lucas' desk and displayed his ID. He beckoned to Marcus. The young operative came to the side of his boss and showed Lucas his ID. Brian Lucas was in absolute bewilderment.

"Calm down, Mr. Lucas. This is only the first of several surprises in store for you," said Waddell.

"I'm going to call the police," responded Brian Lucas. His face was losing its pallor and turning pink.

"You don't have to worry about doing that. Call your secretary," and Waddell pointed to the phone. "She'll tell you there are two Boston Police plainclothes detectives seated in the reception room. I introduced them to her."

"What in hell's name is taking place?" bellowed Lucas.

"Please quiet down, listen and I will tell you. I'm endeavoring to right several serious wrongs and put an end to an episode you, at first, may not want to believe."

"Try me." Lucas was almost rigid with rage, his fingers strumming the arms of his large desk chair.

"Mr. Lucas, I consider this to be the best and safest location for the story to end. In addition, with what I know of you, you would only accept what I am sure will unfold if you see it with your own eyes.

"Do you recognize this as a family picture?" Waddell handed him a copy of the photograph Marcus had made from the original family photo on Mariana's grand piano.

"Yes," said Brian, "That picture was taken about six years ago when we were all together except for Tully, my youngest son. Why?"

"Where was Tully?" asked Waddell.

"How in the hell should I know. He's seldom around," spat out Brian.

"Do you recognize anyone in this snapshot?" This time Waddell handed the senior Lucas one of the snapshots taken by Evans on the City of San Francisco run to Chicago.

Lucas began to be suspicious. He looked at the photo carefully. "Yes," he said, "I do. That's my son, Tully. I have no idea who the bimbo with him is. Where was it taken and when?"

"The shot was taken on the easterly run of the U.P. train, the City of San Francisco, on December 31, 1945, New Year's Eve." Waddell turned the snapshot over and showed him the imprinted date.

"So what?" inquired Lucas.

"Do you have any idea why he was on that train?"

"None whatsoever. I didn't know he made the trip, if he did."

"In what kind of business is your son involved? Could he be associated with the International Etching and Art Gallery in Washington, D.C.?"

"Not only could be, he is. I helped him finance it in the beginning."

"Do you have an interest in that business?"

"Absolutely not. I only made him a loan. He paid it off over two years ago. What are you driving at?"

Waddell was not the least perturbed. He calmly continued his questioning. "Mr. Lucas, I ask you to think carefully. Did Tully, at any time, suggest to you that Marcus was a crooked gambler, a con artist not the poet he is reputed to be?"

"Yes, he did, but it wasn't really necessary. I had Marcus' resumè even before he married my daughter. I was suspicious early on." Brian glared at his son-in-law. Then he looked at the college graduation photo of his deceased daughter on his desk and fought back tears.

"Did Tully ever suggest that you employ a private investigator to try to find out more about your son-in-law?"

"Yes, he did. He suggested that I hire a prominent D.C. private investigator who is an acquaintance of his."

"Did you?"

"Yes, I have been receiving reports from him ever since, as he tries to ferret out Marcus's activities."

"Were those reports verbal or written?"

"Written. I have them in a file in my desk." He patted the desk top.

"Do you mind my taking a quick peek at them, I just want to see the address he uses."

"Certainly not," responded Lucas and he pulled the file from his top drawer, handed it to Waddell, wondering what the senior Secret Service agent was trying to determine.

Waddell took a look at the correspondence then returned the file to Brian. "Have you ever met this Paul Cavalier?" asked Waddell.

"I have indeed. Not long ago while I was in Washington, D.C. working out an overseas grain shipment with the U.S. Department of Agriculture, I arranged to meet him at his office in the same building tenanted by the International Etching and Art Gallery. I also went by to see Tully, but as usual, he was out of town."

"So, you would recognize Cavalier in a photo?"

"Certainly," responded Brian Lucas.

"Do you recognize him in this picture?" and Waddell handed him a snapshot showing Tully, his girlfriend and Leverbee.

"I do indeed. He is the man standing between Tully and the bimbo in the first snapshot you showed me."

Clarence Waddell studied Brian intently for a few moments, took off his glasses, cleaned them with his handkerchief, replaced them, then said very calmly, "What I am about to tell you you may not want to believe, but for all of our sakes you better believe. Mr. Lucas, I was on that train, in the club car where those photos were taken. I was, and am, working with a surveillance team trying to uncover a nationwide counterfeit swindle and a series of controlled crooked card games. Your son-in-law was returning from overseas and got into the poker game in which I was already a player. I didn't know him at that time. I soon learned he was not only an outstanding card player, but was adept at recognizing a crooked game and how the cards were being manipulated.

"For reasons of his own, he determined to beat the crooked card player in the game. And did he ever. In doing so, he unknowingly placed his life in jeopardy. Our team recognized his plight and saved his life. How, there is no need to go into." Waddell then proceeded to reveal the basics of the scam to Brian Lucas.

Brian Lucas was keenly interested in Waddell's narration, but he was beginning to have a queasy feeling in his stomach. Something was omitted, at least until now.

Waddell continued, "We now know who controls, is the brains of, the counterfeit ring," He stopped, looked sympathetically at Brian. "Unfortunately, it is your son, Tully. His chief henchman is your so-called private eye. He frequently uses the name of Oren Leverbee. He is an ex-felon and a suspected killer."

"Oh, Mother of Mary," whispered Brian. "Tully never seemed to be able to stay out of trouble though I prayed he would. I thought his operation was on the up and up."

"That's not all," said Waddell sternly, "I was with Marcus when we found Mariana's body in her apartment. Upon returning from a surveillance trip to California, he had come by my office to report in before going home. The three of us, Marcus, Mariana and I were going to have dinner together. I was by his side when we entered the apartment and saw her lying on the floor in the living room. She was dead, had been shot shortly before we arrived and her engagement ring had been stolen. Later, her ring was recovered from Lorraine Driscoll, the so-called bimbo. She is the young lady in the two snapshots with your son, Tully. She is his girlfriend as well as the bag lady for his stinking operation."

Brian's eyes began to widen in horror and understanding. "Don't tell me more. I now know what you're going to say. Tully killed his sister and gave my daughter's engagement ring to that creature. Oh God, how could this happen?" Brian began to shake as if he had suddenly been stricken with Saint-Vitus dance. Fighting for control he looked pathetically at Marcus and asked, "How does he fit into all of this?"

"Marcus joined the Service just before he married your daughter. Mariana agreed that he should do so, also agreed with me that no mention of her husband's occupation would be divulged until I so consented. As it turns out, for her to have done so might have put you and the Bosconovich family in harms way. At that time, none of us knew who headed the counterfeiting ring or where its headquarters was located. We now do," and Waddell looked down at a completely distraught father.

"I hate to tell you, but I have to. Your son, Tully and Leverbee are in Boston. They are due here in the next ten minutes. In your name, I asked them to come to your office, saying that the meeting was most important because it involved Marcus. I know they will be here."

"Did you call them?" asked a bewildered Lucas.

"No, by telegram confirmed by delivery. I realize now that I should have made different plans," said Waddell as he looked at Brian.

Brian Lucas had calmed somewhat, heaved two big sighs, straightened his shoulders. His eyes bore into Waddell. "No," he said, "This is where the scene should end." He looked at Marcus, "I am so sorry, so very sorry, we both lost our real love and it is my fault, far more than yours."

At that moment, Lucas' intercom phone rang. Priscilla said to Brian, "Your son and your private detective are here. Shall I show them in?"

"Please do," responded Brian.

The door opened, Tully Lucas and Oren Leverbee entered. Leverbee saw Waddell then Marcus. His eyes narrowed and he was momentarily in shock. Very casually, he started to reach inside his jacket with his right hand.

"Not another inch," said a calm voice behind him. There stood Ron Evans in his elderly disguise and his revolver pointing at Leverbee. Marcus gasped in surprise. Evans seemed to have materialized out of thin air. The senior Lucas watched in absolute amazement. Slowly Leverbee withdrew his hand and dropped it to his side.

Brian's usually pale white face was a dark pink and his temple veins stood out in jagged relief, like frozen bolts of purple lightning. Before Waddell could speak, Brian asked sternly, "Tully, is this picture of you?" and handed him one of the snapshots now on his desk.

Tully's eyes were saucer round. "Yes," he said meekly.

"Where was it taken?"

Tully looked at the picture, then at Brian. "I guess on the City of San Francisco when I was returning from Frisco after a sale of some etchings. I have no idea who took the picture."

"Whose etchings?"

"You never heard of him."

"Try me and see."

"Tyler Jenkins."

Brian shook his head from side to side then asked his son, "Who is the bimbo standing beside you?"

"Just a girl I met on the train."

"You lying bastard," was Brian's seething response. Suddenly Tully felt real danger, almost frantic danger.

"Was anyone else with you?"

"No."

"Think twice."

"No one," said Tully defensively and positively.

"Well, when was this picture taken?" and Brian handed his son the snapshot of Tully, Lorraine and Leverbee standing in conversation. Obviously, it had been taken on the same train in the same car.

Tully was beginning to perspire profusely at the same time leaked into the pad he was wearing. He started to answer. "Shut up, you fool," snarled Leverbee. "Don't say another word until you get a lawyer."

"Why would he need a lawyer?" asked a seething Brian Lucas.

Marcus' fury was making him feel faint. His temples pounded and his vision was blurred. Never in his life had he felt this way before. Waddell was watching both Tully and Leverbee with searing concentration. During the father/son verbal exchange he had very cautiously drawn his revolver. It was now in his right hand, partially hidden by his trouser leg.

"And did you get off the train in Omaha, Nebraska?" queried Brian.

Tully appeared to be a vicious animal cornered and bewildered. Brian continued, "After I sent you the wedding picture of Mariana and Marcus, you showed it to Cavalier, Leverbee, whatever name he goes by. You both knew Marcus was the Navy enlisted man who had beaten Fosberg at his own game—your game—counterfeiting and crooked cards—on a grand scale. Your gallery is only a front I know now. Tully, Tully, why, with all the legitimate money you could have made from my contacts in Washington? You, for some reason, became afraid your sister or Marcus might have found out what you really were up to. Your sister! How could you?"

In the silence that followed, Brian, in cold anger, reached into his desk and calmly placed on the surface the old Colt 45 he kept for office protection. He had never used it. Waddell saw and instantly knew real trouble had arrived. Marcus couldn't control the increasing beat of his heart. It raced. He was literally blinded by the tidal wave of fury and bewilderment that swept over him.

Suddenly, Leverbee whirled like a cat and fired at Evans. Evans fell like a rock. Tully whipped out his pistol and fired two shots at Marcus. Marcus went down. The senior Lucas reached for his revolver on the desk but never made it. His eyes rolled back in his head and, as he gasped for breath, his head dropped forward, hit the desk and his arms hung limp outside the chair's arms. Waddell, with the exterior steeliness born of years of service and practice fired two shots. The first tore through the belly of Tully. The second left a gaping hole in the neck of Leverbee. Tully Lucas dropped his pistol, grabbed at this stomach with both hands and sank slowly to his knees, his eyes, with approaching death awareness gazed bewildered at unconscious Brian Lucas then collapsed like a punctured toy balloon. Leverbee staggered, fell over a chair, made a soft moan, rolled onto the floor, shivered briefly and was dead.

The door to the reception office burst open and the two Boston plainclothes detectives entered with revolvers at the ready. "No need," said Waddell. "It's over, really over. Right now teams are closing in on the gallery in D.C. and on the 'con' rooms around the country."

Brian Lucas' right cheek was on his desk. He moaned feebly.

"Call an ambulance, two of them," Waddell shouted at the two detectives. "Have them bring trauma and resuscitating teams. I am afraid that, in addition to injuries to others, the senior Lucas may have suffered a heart attack."

In the reception room of the office pandemonium reigned. At the sound of the shots, Priscilla White had fainted and fallen across the intercom switchboard on her desk. Intercom phones were ringing in every office and personnel from those offices were rushing to the reception area. Waddell saw through the open door and yelled to the detectives, "Clear all staff members, including the receptionist, from the area so emergency personnel will have access." Then he turned to Marcus, lying prone on the floor with a bleeding grazing wound on the left side of his head, and the brunet wig had been blown away. In addition, blood was darkly staining Marcus' left pants leg. Waddell whipped off his tie, took his pocket handkerchief and balling it up, he placed it on the bleeding wound. He gently lifted his young employee's head and wound the tie around Marcus' head to hold the white cloth in place. He quickly tied a square knot over the handkerchief. He took his pen knife from his pocket, slit open the darkening pants leg. When he saw the injury, he gulped once or twice, whipped off his belt, drew it around Marcus' leg above the mangled knee then, using his fountain pen as a pressure point stopper tightened the makeshift tourniquet with all his strength. The bullet had torn a horrible hole. Marcus' left knee had been all but destroyed, the knee cap hung loose like a dangling milk bottle cap. Marcus showed no signs of life when Waddell started his endeavors but when the senior operative tightened his belt, holding firm his fountain pen, shutting down the blood flow from the leg wound, he heard a soft moan, like a sigh of thanksgiving from Marcus.

Waddell knew Evans was dead, first glance before he started work on Marcus told him that. Leverbee was a skilled killer. The frontal portion of Evans head had been blown away.

Glancing through the reception room doorway as he was tightening the tourniquet on Marcus' leg, Waddell saw the first emergency crew arrive and he hollered, "In here, with a gurney and quickly."

In short order Marcus was being tended to, lifted to the stretcher and tied down. Waddell was almost maniacal in his shouting, "Not until the entire staff says he is gone, do you stop work on him, you hear me?"

One of the emergency attendants turned his head toward Waddell, "Sir, not only do we hear you, I'm sure the emergency room over at the hospital hears you also."

Waddy calmed instantly. With a slightly shamed but appreciative look, said to the attendant, "Thanks."

Brian Lucas, unconscious, was wheeled from the office and also rushed to a hospital.

Waddy instructed the next team to take the bodies of Tully Lucas and Leverbee for autopsy and from there to the morgue. Inwardly, he hoped to Christ they would be dropped in a sewer before they got to the cadaver refrigerator.

Then he knelt by the body of Ron Evans. The senior operative had slowed his pace. The full impact of the episode was becoming focused on him. He looked tenderly at his dead associate. Ronald Evans was, to him, not only the finest man under his command but his friend, his darker-skinned friend who, in Waddell's opinion, had overcome life-long adversity like no other man he had ever met. Waddell had helped him to become the first black operative in the Secret Service. He knelt by him, put his arms across the crumpled body, lowered his head on his arms then tearfully prayed for his departed deputy.

He rose, looked at a watching police team. "Tell the morgue I will call them after the autopsy. Make no arrangements to dispose of Evans' body. Though not by blood, he is in fact a part of my family. Come hell or high water, he will be buried in our family plot at Oakhill Cemetery in Washington, D.C."

Waddell then went into the reception room and sat in the empty receptionist chair. Priscilla had been resuscitated and sent home in a taxi. He waited, watched until all had left—emergency personnel, police and office workers. As the evening stillness closed in, he picked up the desk phone, called his wife and as dispassionately as possible told her what he thought she should know. She listened intently then said, "Darling, I'm sorry—so sorry—it happened this way. Are you all right?"

"Yes, Aimee—no, Aimee—I don't know what the hell I am right now."

"Clarence, please listen to me. Don't do what I think you are planning to do. Catch the next plane, come on home, please."

"You read me right, Aimee," was his choked reply. "I'll be home in three or four days, after I sober up. I can't face you right now. It's the only way I can survive in this dog-eat-dog game. If the chief finds out and wants to fire my...."

"Please don't," was his wife's lamenting request.

Clarence Waddell hung up the phone and shuffled, stoop-shouldered from the office as if old age had suddenly dropped like a huge monkey, onto his back.

☐

Marcus was taken to the Massachusetts General Hospital emergency room, to the trauma operating section and the staff worked feverishly to save his life. For two days he was unconscious. When he finally came to, he realized his head was swathed with a large bandage. His ears rung and he was having a hard time trying to focus his eyes. The left side of his head throbbed and he felt excruciating pain from his left leg, could tell it was immobilized. The rest of his body he knew was still his and functioning. He had no idea where he was, in some hospital he guessed and could have cared less. His life was over. He had no idea how the fracas ended. His beloved Mariana was gone. The perpetrator of her murder had been identified as her own flesh and blood, her youngest brother. Marcus hoped he was dead. His wife's father, if he was alive, now knew the truth, so what? How about Evans and Waddell? Had they survived the onslaught? He was too weak to talk or read or even try to listen to the bedside radio. He felt as if he was roasting on a spit. He was now in the purgatory he had created for himself. Why, oh why, had he entered the Service? Mariana had said yes. He knew in his heart of hearts she had hated the idea and what it might stand for. Her eyes had begged him not to, but he couldn't stop from doing it, really another self-aggrandizing thrill-seeking adventure, albeit with the stamp of social acceptance and political correctness. Now he understood Mariana's reasoning, such an endeavor as he had entered into could never bring to fruition the full creative imagination of his mind, to add to the science of math or the startling imagery that, upon occasion, flowed from his poetic pen and she was right. He had not solved the battle between his body and his mind. At present he lay a human remnant of what he feared most—a crippled man.

A few days after he had gained enough strength to attempt to read, he requested a newspaper reporting the tragic event. For the first time he learned that Ronald Evans, Tully Lucas and Leverbee had been killed. Brian Lucas had suffered a minor heart attack but was recovering rapidly. Clarence Waddell had apparently quietly disappeared.

For fear of reprisal from residual members of the mob, no one but Waddell knew where he, Marcus, was supposedly recovering. And no one seemed to give a shit. He was in a secluded area of the hospital, a tiny room with no phone. He was fed three times a day, meals that made him nauseated. His wounds were attended to. The catheter that flowed from his shriveled sensitive friend, seemed to drain what little life he held. His other necessaries were handled with all the delicateness of demons who constantly were holding some weird ritual dance of death around his bed.

He heard nothing from any member of his family. The fantasizing memories of them tormented him constantly. When he thought of Mariana there appeared to him the vivid picture of her slumped at his feet in the apartment living room, a gaping hole in her back and chest, her life's blood spreading wastefully over the surface of the gray carpet. Then that discolored rug area would break into flame. He would close his eyes, throw his hands to his face, in an endeavor to fight the heat from searing his eyeballs, his brain. When he could no longer stand the heat, he would race to the protection of the cool pool at the casino and dive into it fully clothed. Only then would the chill of the water drive away the pain and the images. He and his eagle companion would once again be soaring until the painkiller wore off.

After two weeks and when he was strong enough, he underwent surgery on his left knee. Immediately thereafter, he was in a cast from ankle to hip. The attendant orthopod advised him that if all went well and with the aid of a walker, he would soon be able to walk a little, though his left leg would always be stiff and weak. When he had really recovered, he would never be without the aid of a crutch or possibly a cane. Marcus was deeply depressed. The part that had really made him Marcus Bosconovich was gone. He vividly remembered his mother's remarks, "Thrill-seeking is not a life," and he remembered Mariana's blue eyes begging him to seek a life where he could contribute, not jut be a thrill-seeker. None of this might have happened if he hadn't wanted the thrill of beating Fosberg at his crooked game. He feared that his mother, when she learned the truth of the episode would be saddened forever. He knew his sisters and his father would have lost all their respect for him. He was in the midst of his own hell. Marcus remembered he was to keep his mouth shut, not reveal his true identity or try to contact anyone, even Waddell.

He remembered his notebooks, filled with events, thoughts, feeling through his marriage and first three months of duty with the Secret Service. One of them contained the first letter from Samantha. He hoped they had been sent to Mariana's apartment by Bernie. Before too long those pages might serve as rats nests in his deceased wife's apartment, or was it his apartment? However, the one thing he had to do was find paper and a pen and place his present thoughts in writing so that maybe some day in the future some poor soul reading the written results of those thoughts, might use them in a beneficial way.

One morning, while stumbling to the lounge, he saw a notebook on the floor of the corridor. He glanced up and down the hall then doing a balancing act with his walker, reached down, picked up the pad and hastily put it under his dressing gown. While in the lounge he saw a fountain pen chained to a rack on a table. When no one was looking, he proceeded to break the pen from the chain, hid it among the pages of the notebook, then headed back to his room. The first ten pages of the pad were crammed full of medical notes. The remaining pages were blank. He tore those first ten pages into shreds and flushed them down the toilet adjoining his room.

When the section nurse was making her room rounds that morning, she found an unshaven, gaunt Marcus in bed busily writing. She casually remarked, "Good, writing a letter to your girlfriend, I see. You're beginning to get better."

"No, you frigging busybody, I'm not writing a letter to a girlfriend and I am not getting better."

"You truly are a bastard aren't you?" she said and her black eyes were seething.

Marcus raised his head slowly, those fierce hazel eyes bore into her. "Whether I am or not, I don't believe is any of your damned business," and went about his writing.

The foul-mouthed, uncouth, dirty cripple on "secure" 3B West became a patient to avoid if possible. And that was quite possible. More and more he was self-isolated from the outside world. Marcus was becoming increasingly embittered toward his family, toward Waddell who now had visited him once or twice, the last time to tell him he would henceforth be drawing disability pay, and asked him where it should be deposited. Marcus told him the account number and the Chase Manhattan Bank branch in New York to which the checks should be sent. Waddell would let him know when he could try and communicate with his family. There was a sheet of iciness between the two men, first on Marcus' part for letting himself be drawn into a situation about which he knew little and Waddell because he had appealed to Marcus with the thrill of adventure not a commitment to service.

☐

Weeks later his cast was removed and a brace was put on his leg. His head wound had healed. Another three weeks in the rehab center at the hospital, his blonde hair was matted, and long dirty blond whiskers almost completely hid his facial features. Marcus had resisted any and all attempts to maintain his personal appearance. He had reclaimed his clothing, shoes, key chain, wallet and various other personal items including the garage sensor he had loaned Waddell. He checked his wallet, he was still Wesley Young and he checked his shoes, yes, his Secret Service ID was there and his wallet contained a couple hundred dollars. He also knew the service was supposed to be taking care of his medical expenses through his health insurance. If it didn't, to hell with it, the hospital would have to find him. So, on a cloudy August morning when no one was looking, he dressed, slipped what personal items he had into a pillow case he took from one of the bed pillows and with the aid of his crutch, left the hospital at an opportune time, unnoticed.

Marcus hailed a cab, decided he would return to New York to his apartment to see if it was still his. He knew how he would get in. He just had to have his Pandora's Box, his notes. He hoped fervently Bernie had complied with his request. He boarded a late afternoon train for the Big Apple.

He knew where he would go after he had the box, back to Wollaston. He needed Mariana now more than ever. He had to be near her, have her forgiveness if it took forever. He was sure that there were plenty of rooms to rent in that suburban area. "If I can't find a room, I'll just sleep on the ground near her grave. I'll be that much closer to her," he mumbled to himself, "And why won't the constantly shifting fog go away? It's so hard to see clearly."

He arrived at his apartment building by cab, after midnight. He had determined he should not try the front entrance. He had no desire to be greeted by Henry Dimond, the concierge, or any resident, so he, with the aid of his crutch, quietly limped around to the garage entrance, aimed the sensor and quickly entered through the open garage door, crossed the parking area to the red exit light that led from the corridor to the elevator. He had to take his chances. He sighed in relief when, unobserved, he rode the elevator to the third floor, crossed the hall and entered the apartment. He turned on the overhead living room lights. The sight made him sick, nauseous. Maybe she would be coming home in the next half hour. Only he knew that wasn't true. Walking through the apartment, he saw the unopened package that contained his Pandora's Box on the kitchen table. He breathed a sigh of relief. "Thank you, Bernie," he said. Quickly he went to his closet, grabbed a suitcase, transferred what gear he had in the pillow slip into that carrier, placed the box in it and added whatever clothing he could jam into the travel case. Cautiously, he picked up the phone. It was still connected, someone was paying the bill, but who? He could tell it was no longer tapped. He called for a taxi. For the last time he walked through each room. When he entered his den he wept. He shivered as he left the apartment and locked the door. He didn't want to see the place again—ever. He took the elevator to the basement, left through the exit door of the garage and limped to the front of the building. In short order the cab arrived and at his request, took him to a cheap second-rate hotel off Broadway. Marcus paid the fare, took his gear and spent the night in the flea bag.

The next morning, after a bagel and coffee at a corner drugstore, he limped the streets with his gear until he arrived at the branch of Chase Manhattan Bank where he had his major account. He walked into the bank to a standing counter to fill out a check from his checkbook he had retrieved from his desk in the den. The two bank guards on duty sternly eyed the gaunt, bearded cripple. Undaunted, Marcus wrote out the check, took it to a male teller on duty and slid the draft through the teller's window slot. The teller peered at him through steel-rimmed glasses and asked, "Have you got some kind of ID?" thinking all the while that the bum had found the check in some back alley trash can.

"Sure," said Marcus. He leaned down, pulled from his right shoe his Secret Service ID card. The teller's black eyes enlarged to the size of small English walnuts. He stared at Marcus. He took the name and a number from the card. "I'll be back in just a moment," he said and raced to the assistant manager's office. "Mr. White. There's the strangest looking creature at my window wanting to draw three thousand dollars from what he says is his account. Here's the check, he claims to be a Secret Service agent."

"Reggie, I'll call the New York Secret Service office and see whether or not we can accommodate the young man."

"He's no young man, he's a damned derelict."

"Takes all kinds," said White.

White called the New York office of the Secret Service.

"This is Agent Ignatius Pearsall speaking," a voice responded.

"Mr. Pearsall, do you have a member by the name of Marcus Bosconovich?" asked Mr. White, then gave Pearsall Marcus' ID number.

"Certainly do, didn't know he was ambulatory yet."

"Would you describe him for me?"

"Well, he has wavy blond hair, hazel eyes, has gone through serious leg injury and walks with a heavy limp, if he walks at all. Why do you ask?"

"He wants to draw three thousand dollars from his account. Is it okay to give him the money?"

"Does he have it in his account?"

"My God, his checking account looks like the federal reserve bank."

"Well, why ask me?"

"Is he non compos mentis?"

"You only wish you had half his smarts. He's been through hell, but yes, he's sane. Give it to him. If any problem arises, the Service will make it good. Ask him to wait for me before he leaves the bank. I'll be there in ten minutes."

"Okay," responded the assistant manager. He went back to the teller's window, looked soberly at Marcus, "How would you like it, Sir?"

"Twenties and fifties equally," replied Marcus.

"Wouldn't you rather have some 'C' bills?"

"If I came up to you and asked you to cash a 'C' bill, would you?" White hesitated.

"There's your answer. I'll take it in twenties and fifties," Marcus said in a bitter, sarcastic voice.

The assistant manager counted out the money, put it in an envelope and gave it to Marcus. Marcus began to count the bills, and as he was doing so, Mr. White said, "A Mr. Pearsall called and asked if you would mind waiting for him. He'll be here in the next ten minutes and would like a brief chat with you."

Marcus glared at the man and replied, "When he gets here, tell him I'm sorry but I have an important meeting to attend." Marcus cast a venomous look over his shoulder at the bank officer and left. He took the first cab that would stop. "Take me to Grand Central Station," he said to the cab driver. When he arrived at the station, he hurried as much as he could, to a ticket window.

"Give me a ticket to Boston, Massachusetts," he said to a station ticket agent and pulled from his wallet several bills. The agent looked, saw that they more than covered the train fare.

"When do you want to go?" asked the reluctant agent.

"On the very next train available," replied Marcus.

"The next train leaves in five minutes. There is space available. How about your luggage?"

"I travel light, just this one suitcase," responded Marcus.

The ticket agent started to make a comment, saw the belligerent stare of Marcus, closed his mouth and quietly delivered the ticket. "Gate twenty-three," he said as he looked with disgust at the grimy cripple in front of him. Marcus took the ticket and change from the ticket agent, turned and headed for gate twenty-three. "You would think he was doing me a favor to sell me this lousy ticket," Marcus said as he limped through the station concourse.

CHAPTER 27

One evening in late June 1946, Alice-Lee Taliaferro received a telephone call from the hospice advising that her friend, Samantha Kingsbury, had died the day before. The hospice staff would appreciate it if Ms. Taliaferro would come by tomorrow in order for the staff to implement the written instructions and dying requests of their deceased patient.

The next afternoon when Alice-Lee, upon invitation of a staff member, entered Sam's room at the hospice, the big picture window was open and the lovely scent of California spruce seemed to make the room a part of nature. There was no foul smell of death or even illness. Sam would want it that way, she thought. Then she saw on top of the small bureau the neatly wrapped package addressed to her. She also found Sam's last note on the little bedside table. She sat on her dead friend's bed and read the all but illegible scrawl:

> Dear Alice-Lee,
> My last remembrances to you are in the little package on top of my bureau. The front desk will have the urn with my ashes. On your return ferry ride please spread them on the bay between Sausalito and San Francisco.

Marcus was my dream come true, but you have been the one who constantly has both feet on the ground and who made each day worth any attempt at living. That worldly appearce, seemingly diffident demeanor of yours hides a most inquisitive mind and the best down-to-earth, good friend I ever had.

See you later—I hope,

Sam

"Not a chance, not in the hot region where I will be going," said Alice-Lee in a whisper. She picked up the package from the bureau, looked one more time around the room, "Godspeed," she said, left the room, closed the door and walked quickly to the front desk, all the time making one hell of an effort to hide her true feelings. She asked the sister in charge of the desk, "Do you have what's left of Samantha Kingsbury here, in a jar?"

"And who are you?" asked the sister.

"I'm Alice-Lee Taliaferro. She left what's left of her to me."

"Yes," the sister grimaced at the apparent bold demeanor of her interrogator. "We have her ashes in an urn and were instructed by Miss Kingsbury, prior to her death, to give them to Alice-Lee Taliaferro."

"I'm the one," said Alice-Lee and she showed her California driver's license to the desk attendant.

The sister reached beneath the service desktop and pulled out a small, polished brass urn with a screw-on lid, tightly sealed.

"My, what a lovely flower vase that will make," exclaimed Alice-Lee.

"Have you no feelings for the departed?"asked the sister.

"More than you will ever know," responded Alice-Lee. "Is there a phone handy I may use?"

"In the booth over there in the corner. It's a coin-operated phone," and the sister pointed, then glared at the tall, confident woman in front of her.

"That's just fine, thank you," responded Alice-Lee. With her friend's last gift package and the urn tucked under her arm, she strolled over to the phone booth, saw the phone book hanging on a chain on an outside booth wall. Placing the package and urn at her feet, she picked up the phone book, turned to "Churches" in the classified section. When she found what she wanted, she reached down, took a pen from her purse, wrote a street number and telephone number on the outside wrapping of Sam's last gift. She entered the booth, dropped a coin into the money slot and gave the operator a number. Soon a pleasant masculine voice answered.

"All Souls' Episcopal."

"Who are you?" asked Alice-Lee.

"I'm Rob West, Assistant Rector."

"Are you busy, going somewhere in the next hour?" she inquired.

"No. Who is this and why do you ask?"

"I'm Alice-Lee Taliaferro, reporter for the *Chronicle* and an Episcopalian."

"What can I do for you?" queried Rob West.

"You can hold a quick memorial service for my departed friend, also an Episcopalian," she lied. "I've got her with me in an urn."

"Oh, I'm afraid I can't do that on such short notice."

"Your church has a small chapel off the main chancel, doesn't it?"

"Yes."

"Well, is it going to be used in the next hour?"

"Ah, no."

"Would a hundred dollar contribution make it worthwhile for you to hold a brief memorial service in the chapel for my departed friend?"

There was a momentary silence, then, "Cash or pledge?" inquired Rob West and Alice-Lee detected just a mite of mirth in his inquiry.

"Cash on the barrelhead—scuse me, the altar," responded Alice-Lee.

"Is it Miss or Mrs. Taliaferro?"

"Just Alice-Lee."

"Well, Alice-Lee, be here in twenty minutes and I'll do the honors. But, if the old man walks in there might be hell to pay."

"I'd rather pay for that at a later date. I'm only ten minutes away. I'll be there."

□

She arrived at the church in short order. Alice-Lee had noticed the main building with the chapel attached as she, in the past, had driven by it on her way to and from the hospice. There was red-headed Rob West in his robe ready for the service. He saw the urn.

316

"Alice-Lee," he said, "I'll take it." He again looked at the urn. "From the House of Eternity Hospice?" he inquired.

"Yes," replied Alice-Lee. "She was my best friend."

"Didn't she have any family?"

"None to speak of but she was the most gutsy gal I ever knew."

"What was her name?"

"Samantha Allen Kingsbury."

"What a lovely name."

"Nowhere near as lovely as she was," commented Alice-Lee.

"Shall we get started?" asked Rob West.

"Please."

Rob West, Assistant Rector, placed the urn on the top step of the two steps leading to the altar. Alice-Lee sat in the first pew of the chapel, reached for a prayer book, kneeled and the service began in due solemnity.

The young priest looked up from his prayer book several times, watched Alice-Lee and noticed her concentration on the order of prayer. He was surprised. No longer was she the rather hard-boiled, domineering woman who had conversed with him on the phone and who he saw enter the chapel. To him, she almost appeared ashamed at the anguish and emotion that had crept to the surface. In those few moments, the depth of caring that was hidden under the polished veneer of feminine aggressiveness was unveiled. That caring was sincere and loving. Her whole body and appearance during one brief interval seemed to him to be transformed, alluring, almost angelic. Then, as quickly as the transformation appeared, it vanished, as if she had willed it away.

When the service ended, Rob West retrieved the urn, handed it to Alice-Lee. "What are you going to do with her ashes?" he asked.

"As Samantha had requested," was Alice-Lee's guarded answer. She placed the urn on the pew seat where she had been sitting, took her wallet from her shoulder bag, counted out one hundred and fifty dollars then handed the sum to Rob West.

He saw the amount and said, "It's only supposed to be one hundred dollars."

"Oh, the little extra is for the Assistant Rector's discretionary fund. My friend would have wanted it that way," replied Alice-Lee.

"Alice-Lee Taliaferro, the church thanks you, I thank you. Peace be with you."

"That's kinda' hard to come by right now. But, time will tell. Thank you very much." She held out her hand and shook Rob West's hand in a strong grip. With emotions churning deep inside her, she turned, picked up her gear and the urn and left the chapel. She just couldn't let that young priest see how she really felt. She seldom let anybody do that.

Watching her go, Rob West muttered, "My God, what a personality of contrasts. I read her pithy column regularly. On the surface she is a tough, female journalist however, hidden underneath is a tender, caring quality she seems ashamed to admit to."

□

Alice-Lee drove her car onto the ferry at Sausalito. Once the water auto carrier was headed across the bay to San Francisco, she left her car and with the urn under one arm, walked to the starboard rail where she could see the Golden Gate Bridge. The sun was beginning to set. She thought, "What a lovely time to spread Sam's remains." She removed the top and tilted the urn toward the bay surface. The first discharge of ashes blew back, primarily over a swarthy, burly man standing immediately to her left and looking toward the bridge.

"What the hell, Lady, you crazy or something?"

Alice-Lee in true surprise, realized that in musing about her friend she hadn't thought about which way the breeze was blowing. It was a gentle southwesterly zephyr blowing directly against where she and her rail guest were facing. "I'm so sorry," she said. "My mistake," and she reached over and tried to gently brush the ashes back into the urn.

"Sure to Christ was. Can't you empty your boss's dirty, smelly, old cigar ashes at the office instead of out here? What kind of nut are you?" And the guy brushed vigorously with both hands.

Alice-Lee had the desire to call him a grumpy, old male born out of wedlock, thought better of it, forced a feeble smile and said, "Those weren't dirty, smelly, old cigar ashes, they were parts of my best friend." Immediately she turned, walked briskly away from the stunned individual and he shuddered at that thought.

She walked to the other side of the ferry and there she was facing Alcatraz. She opened the lid and poured the contents into the wind. "If any of them reach the poor souls in there and they realize what it

318

is and get upset, at least they can't get to me out here," she mumbled.

Then continued, "Sam, you really have had rotten luck on this earth. Even your ashes get screwed up, thanks to that bumbling friend of yours—me." She watched as some of the ashes settled on the water and others seemed to swiftly rise from sight. It was over in a twinkling as the ferry churned across the bay. "Oh, Sam," she mumbled again, "Nobody knew or cared but me." Alice-Lee shivered slightly. She couldn't tell whether it was from a sense of fear of the unknown, loneliness, or pity for her departed diminutive friend. Maybe all three, she thought.

Alice-Lee drove from the ferry to her apartment. When she stopped at the front door, Bernardo, the doorman, came to the car, looked at her and said, "You look like you just lost your best friend. You really look tired, I'll park your car in the underground for you."

Alice-Lee wanted to say, "What god-damned business of yours is it how I look?" Instead, she smiled wanly and said, "How right you are." She left the car, walked, swung open one of the heavy apartment entrance doors with her free arm. With the empty urn and gift package under her other, went to her mail box in the row of mail boxes in the main corridor. Her heart picked up a beat. "Geez," she mumbled as she looked at the envelope and thought, "At least I've got a letter from my guy. That will be a nice way to end this day. I'll read it when I'm relaxed on the sofa with a light brew." She took the elevator to her floor, sauntered to her door, opened it, stood for a second or two just to enjoy the sight. "God, it's good to be alive and home," she said as she shut the apartment door, then walked to a corner cabinet, placed the urn on a shelf, rearranged a couple of plates, tilted her head, smiled and said, "It really looks lovely there."

She went to her small bar, poured herself a light bourbon and water. Carrying her drink carefully, she flopped onto her new sofa, placed her drink on the end table, turned up the reading light, kicked off her shoes, opened the letter, and read:

Dear Alice-Lee,

I just don't know how to write this letter, but I must try. Time and distance sometimes do odd things to a person. They have to me. I have met a young lady about your age. Her name is Gabrielle and, yes, she is French. She is the daughter of a French financier. She is educated and charming. We have so much in common, that by the time you receive this letter, we will have been married.

The ring? Well, I would like to have it back. I can get good money for it over here. But, I'm too far away to put on much pressure about it. Let your conscience be your guide.

Ever your friend,

Joe

"You shithead," bellowed Alice-Lee toward the fireplace. "You unmitigated bastard. This, and after I got you your first job at the *Chronicle*. Oh Jesus, what a day this has been." Then Alice-Lee wept copiously, something she seldom did. As she was weeping, she transferred the ring to a finger on her other hand thinking, "To hell with him, its mine, I earned it."

On her return home, Alice-Lee was hungry, despite her sad trip. Now that hunger was converted to anger, almost self-destructive anger. "Sam, oh, Sam, now I really need you," she moaned. Suddenly she had to get out of the apartment, go somewhere, anywhere, just to get away from the hellhole of memories. "Where can I go?" she mused, then it hit her, "the Shanghai Lounge and Seafood Grill. The place Sam introduced me to. No one knows me there. I can get stinking drunk if I feel like it. Not a soul will give a damn." Alice-Lee called down to the doorman and asked him to hail a cab for her. She would be down shortly.

She put on an uplift bra, a provocative peacock green dress, a matching pair of spike heels, applied new makeup, picked out a light tan shoulder bag and headed out, "Anything to get away from this stinking den of an artificial affair of the heart," she muttered.

□

Cherrie, queen of the evening, was on her throne as she watched the tall, green-draped society reporter enter. Cherrie thought, "This is the second time within six months that I've seen her in here. I wonder where her little sidekick is?" She watched as Alice-Lee found a vacant seat at the bar, observed her look at the voluptuous females in the mural above the bar mirror, and saw the reporter subconsciously adjust her uplift bra. "Don't even try, honey," she murmured, "You're just not built that way." Alice-Lee ordered her drink, downed the jigger of some kind of whiskey and chased it with a swig of water. Cherrie was becoming really interested as Alice-Lee ordered a second drink, downed it the same way.

She saw the heavily built guy on Alice-Lee's right watching her every move. He was, to Cherrie, a male wolf quietly stalking his unsuspecting prey. Her study of Alice-Lee became more intense. She observed a certain sag of the reporter's shoulders. "My God, she's in trouble. But, why come here? This isn't your place, you should be in a church or in your lover's arms." Then it hit her, "I'll bet she's just lost her lover and doesn't want her world to know about it."

Cherrie was so engrossed in watching Alice-Lee, she forgot why she was there. A middle-aged, semi-bald, short guy came up to her. "Hi, Babe, you interested?" he asked and waited. Cherrie paid no attention to him as she watched the bar. "You hear me, you broad?"

"Get the hell away from me, you little creep, before I call the cops," Cherrie tartly replied. And he did. Cherrie continued her concentration. She saw Alice-Lee order her third drink, hold the jigger up to the mural then downed its contents the same way she had the others. "She's got quite a capacity," thought Cherrie.

The burly guy seated next to Alice-Lee who had been watching her from the start had kept track of the drinks Alice-Lee had consumed in such short time. He noticed they were beginning to take effect. He leaned toward her, put an arm around her waist. "Wouldn't you like to take a little walk to get some fresh air to clear your head?" he asked and smiled a knowing smile. Alice-Lee looked at him in surprise then at his arm around her. Despite the fact that she couldn't see him clearly, seemed to fade in and out of focus she didn't want any man's arm around her even if he looked like Clark Gable. "All men stink," she thought, "this one in particular."

"No, I don't want to take a walk. Take your damn arm back where it belongs," with a shrug she reached out and freed his arm from her waist.

"Oh, come on, Baby, I didn't mean no harm. You and me could have an enjoyable evening together."

"In a pig's ass," replied Alice-Lee. "You stinking lecher, if you touch me again, I'll kick your nuts off."

The guy's face turned purple with rage. "No fuckin', bar-crawlin' female, praying mantis is going to talk to me that way." And he gave her a backhand slap across her face.

An infuriated Alice-Lee almost slipped from her stool, recovered quickly, picked up the chaser glass of water and threw it in the face of her would-be wooer. For the moment, he was absolutely stunned and that's how long it took Cherrie to cross the floor from her booth to the side of Alice-Lee. "Look, you no good son of a bitch, you make another pass at my sister and you will land your sweet ass in jail."

Alice-Lee, growing increasingly befuddled, looked at her defender, saw a vague auburn-haired creature with bosoms bigger than any on the murals above. "Half sister," she said in a slurred voice.

"All right, half sister," replied Cherrie. "Let's get the hell out of here before trouble really starts." By now two waiter/bouncers were standing between Alice-Lee and her would-be male escort.

"Billy," said Cherrie to one of the men, "I saw it all happen. My sister is getting over a rough time. That jerk tried to make out."

"I did no such damned thing," replied the guy.

"I'm taking her home," said Cherrie. "But that bastard shouldn't have the privilege of the bar," and Cherrie pointed to Alice-Lee's former bar companion.

"He won't," said Billy. "As soon as you and your sister leave, we'll see that he is escorted outside."

"Thanks, Billy. Come on Sis, you need some fresh air and rest," said Cherrie, as she put an arm around an increasingly inebriated Alice-Lee. The female duo swayed and strayed toward the brown entrance door. Once outside, Cherrie hailed a cab then with the aid of the cabbie, poured Alice-Lee into it. Cherrie went around to the other passenger door, entered and asked Alice-Lee, "Where do you live?"

"Huh?"

"Where in the shit do you live, Miss Society Reporter Taliaferro?"

"Oh, the Sealcrest Apartments. How do you know my name?" slurred Alice-Lee.

"I've seen your picture in that society column of yours."

The whole scene of what was happening was fuzzy to Alice-Lee but she understood what Cherrie had said and was puzzled. "Why do you read my column?" Alice-Lee asked.

"Because I have to keep up with some of my best-paying clientele," answered Cherrie. "Take us to the Sealcrest Apartments," she told the cabbie. And they were off.

Bernardo, the doorman, was still on duty when Alice-Lee and Cherrie arrived. Alice-Lee was potted, unsteady on her feet. Bernardo saw her condition and helped steady her as Cherrie paid and tipped the driver. She put her arm around Alice-Lee, looked at Bernardo. "I can handle her, lad, just open the front door, please," she said.

"My, it didn't take long to get here did it? Where are we?" questioned Alice-Lee as she staggered toward the door.

"At your apartment house. Gimme your key, Miss Taliaferro."

"The name's Alice-Lee."

"All right, Alice-Lee, gimme your key."

"Here, take the whole damned bag. I couldn't find that key right now if I tried." She slipped the bag off her shoulder and handed it to Cherrie.

"What floor do you live on?"

"I don't live on the floor, my apartment s located on the fifth floor."

They struggled to a waiting, open elevator. As it started to rise, Alice-Lee wailed, "Stop this thing, I think I'm gonna be sick."

"You just better hold it until you reach your apartment. You'll be the talk of the building if you vomit in the elevator or on the expensive carpet in the hallway."

"Who in the hell are you, a guardian angel or something?"

"No, I'm your half sister. Don't you remember?" queried Cherrie.

The elevator stopped at the fifth floor. The door opened and the duo got off. "Which way?" asked Cherrie.

"Which way to where?" responded Alice-Lee.

"To your apartment."

"Oh! Let's see," said Alice-Lee and she looked glaze-eyed from right to left. "The one that's got my name beneath the knocker. I think I'm going to be sick."

"For Christ's sake, not yet," responded Cherrie.

Alice-Lee looked at her auburn-haired guide. "I didn't know angels had red hair," she slurred.

"Which way?"

"Oh, it's down there somewhere," and Alice-Lee pointed down the corridor.

Cherrie, with her arm around Alice-Lee staggered with her down the corridor, saw the nameplate, unlocked and opened the door.

"Whew, that was a long trip wasn't it? Where are we?"

"Your apartment, I hope."

"It better had be," said Alice-Lee as she stumbled in the direction of her master bathroom and made it, barely. Holding on to the back of the toilet tank with both hands, she rid herself of the remnants of the alcohol and more. When she was through she flushed the toilet, grabbed the sink with one hand, turned on the cold water faucet with the other, began splashing her face with cold water. She stopped, turned to Cherrie and after a weak smile said, "Not sick now but still pretty tight."

"You're one tough broad. I'll go and make some hot tea."

"Put plenty of sugar in it. I hate unsweetened tea."

"Sister, I'm in charge, you'll take it straight and hot."

"Why?"

"Because you're dehydrated now, you need liquid not sugar. Sugar only adds to the alcohol sugar in your system and helps to prolong drunkenness."

"How do you know?"

"Because I'm as good in my profession as you are in yours."

Alice-Lee could now focus and for the first time truly saw the auburn-tinted, bosomy woman who really must have been a charmer in her youth. She dried her face and as Cherrie turned to find the kitchen, Alice-Lee called to her benefactor, "Hey, angel, what is your name?"

"Cherrie," she said.

"Cherrie what?" asked Alice-Lee.

"Just Cherrie," was the answer.

"Cherrie, the kitchen is down the hall on your left," said Alice-Lee and she followed her.

Cherrie found a light switch, turned on the overhead light.

"Please turn it off, use the one over the stove. That overhead light is blinding me." Alice-Lee, feeling weak, slumped into a kitchen chair.

Cherrie did as Alice-Lee asked. Cherrie exhibited all the traits of a gourmet cook. In no time she had the teapot boiling and Alice-Lee's most expensive green tea in a tea holder then into a cup. She took one for herself. After pouring the boiling water into the cups, she sat across the table from her rescued new acquaintance.

"Alice-Lee, what compelled you to come to the Shanghai tonight?"

"Nothing compelled me," said Alice-Lee.

"Crap," said Cherrie. "That joint isn't your nightly rendezvous like it is mine."

"Why should I tell you anything?"

"Well, Miss High and Mighty, for one thing, I saved your skinny ass from being raped or battered or whatever. Secondly, you're a decent girl but mighty upset and you need to talk to somebody might as well be me. I'm no blabbermouth like most of your set. I could tell you things that would make your paper sell like a London tabloid but I won't."

Alice-Lee looked at Cherrie with increasing respect and thought, "Gee, she's knowledgeable, and underneath that rough air is almost a hint of aristocracy much more than appears on the surface." She said soberly, "Cherrie, you're right. As for my problems, well earlier today I disposed of the remains of my best friend, one of the strongest-spirited women I ever knew. Though small in stature, she was a giant in guts and effort."

"Was that the little brunette with you at the Shanghai about six months ago?"

"My God, you remember? You saw us that night?"

"Sure did. You two were so out of place I couldn't help but remember Miss Mutt and Jeff of mid-America slumming."

"That was the night Sam told me she was dying of cancer. I really needed to unwind."

"That little thing, dying of cancer?"

"She's gone—died a couple days ago. Today, coming across from Sausalito, I spread her ashes on the bay as she requested. Then I got home to find a letter from Joe, my fiancé, who is now in France on a newspaper assignment. That son of a bitch wrote me a 'Dear John' letter. He's going to marry some French floozy and wants his ring back."

"Meet the real world, dearie," said Cherrie. "I understand your desire to let loose. But, why didn't you just get drunk here in your own apartment instead of pouring it down at the Shanghai?"

"That bastard, Joe, had lived with me here for a year, sleeping with me. After he went overseas and before his letter, Samantha lived here until she went to the hospice. Suddenly, I hated the place."

Cherrie took a swig of her tea then said, "I understand your sadness about your dead friend. As for your feelings about Joe, don't blame it on your apartment. The place only reminds you of your lifestyle. Put the blame where it belongs, on yourself, your wishful thinking. You knew better. I can tell. You can't wish love on someone and you knew Joe didn't love you."

"How do you know?"

"Because I've lived a lifetime, maybe more."

Alice-Lee looked at Cherrie, "There is something about her that is good, bad and pathetically knowledgeable," she thought.

"Cherrie," she asked, "Where do you live?"

"That all depends," answered Cherrie.

"On what?"

"On who I am. Right now I'm Cherrie and I live in a one-bedroom apartment on the edge of Chinatown. It's in a stinking, falling down building, a cesspool of iniquity, but I guess it suits me."

Alice-Lee's befuddled mind was clearing. The snoop was back. "Where else do you live?"

"'The Ridge,' occasionally."

"'The Ridge,' the mansion on the palisades?" Now Alice-Lee was incredulous and sobering fast.

"Yes, when I am Shirley Ridgeway, I live at 'The Ridge,' was raised there."

"You, you are the daughter of Theodore and Mary Ridgeway?"

"Unfortunately," answered Cherrie.

Alice-Lee was now really studying Cherrie and thought, "I'll be damned, she does look vaguely like the portrait of the chubby young girl that hangs above the mantel of the fireplace in the library of that palatial home, only that girl had lovely, long, brown hair."

"I know you've been there numerous times. I read your column as I've already told you. You needn't wonder any longer. I can read the question in your eyes. Yes, that portrait over the library fireplace is me when I was twelve. If you tell a living soul who I really am but don't want to be, I'll come back and do to you what that guy at the bar threatened to do." Cherrie's eyes blazed with a simmering fire.

"Oh Cherrie, I'll never mention it. After what you did for me tonight, I am truly in your debt."

"Ah, forget it, I was just doing it for a sister," smirked Cherrie.

Alice-Lee was now genuinely interested in her new friend. "How? Why did it happen to you?"

"Still the snoop aren't you?"

"No, only interested in a woman who is more genuine than she thinks she is. I didn't mean to sound journalistically curious. You don't have to say another word. I apologize."

Now it was Cherrie's turn to be revealing. For some strange reason she trusted the reporter. "Oh, Alice-Lee," she stopped, sighed, then continued, "You can't imagine the life I led growing up. From the time I was four, my three older brothers bedeviled me, unmercifully. My dad was seldom around. Because I was chubby, my mother thought I was disgusting. She was skinny, far skinnier than you are. She saw beauty only in slenderness and I just wasn't built to be slender. My mom almost starved me trying to make me thin. I was sneaking to the refrigerator at every chance I got. And the private, girls' day school was a nightmare. All they could think about was dresses and boys and making out even when they were thirteen or fourteen. Peckers didn't mean that much to me. I had seen three of them continually since I could remember. There was not much modesty in my family, particularly my brothers, especially Malcolm. He started to finger diddle me when I was fourteen and, oh my God, before I realized it, I was screwing my brother and then all three of them. They threatened to kill me if I told my family. I lived in panic that I would get pregnant. And I did. By which one I don't know. Fortunately, I had an early miscarriage. I'm sure that my mother knew what was going on and condoned it. I later learned she had convinced her gynecologist that I was a nymphomaniac and at the time of my miscarriage, she demanded him to tie my tubes. He did. They've been tied ever since. When I returned from the hospital, I told each of my brothers if they ever touched me again I would kill the culprit any way I could. In addition, I did tell my father. He believed me and raised holy hell with my brothers and my mother. She defended herself saying I was a pathological liar and all but disowned me, alleging I was a slut, constantly out playing around with uncouth boys on the sly—not my brothers. I was becoming emotionally ill."

"Jesus, I can understand why," retorted Alice-Lee.

"I was in and out of mental hospitals for years. My dad set up a trust fund for me. I have never touched it, not yet.

"And of all the dirty jokes, as I was beginning to recover, I was

327

about twenty when my brother Malcolm came to me. He was then in love with a wonderful girl. He admitted how wrong he had been, was truly ashamed and offered to help me in any way he could. Just his admission was a great emotional relief to me. I couldn't help but admire him. He was the only one to own up to his dastardly acts. Two months later, he was stricken with polio. Now, he's wheelchair-bound and he never married his sweetheart. He has no real life, lives on the third floor at home. I call and talk with him most every night. There are times when I just have to go home and see him. That's when I become Shirley. But, I can't stand it for long.

"Many years ago, I decided since I was untrained, unschooled and since my tubes are tied, the one way I could make a living was with my body. There was no reason for me to do it for free. With my background, I couldn't offer myself to a decent guy. That kind of love is beyond my capacity, I know it. So, most of the time, I am as you see me now, Cherrie, Queen of the Evening." She stopped, cocked her head, smiled at Alice-Lee, then asked, "And you think you've got troubles?"

Alice-Lee stared at her new friend in utter amazement, then said, "No, my sister, I don't really have troubles after hearing yours. Is there anything I can do to help you?"

"Yes," answered Cherrie with a wry smile.

"Name it. I'll do it," said Alice-Lee.

"Just occasionally put me in your prayers. You do pray sometimes, don't you?"

"More than you or any one else will ever know," responded Alice-Lee.

"Good! Call me a cab, I've got to get back to the Shanghai. You're on your own from now on."

"You're not going back there this time of night, it's past midnight?"

"A girl's gotta do what a girl's gotta do," responded Cherrie. She headed for the living room to pick up her faux fur jacket.

When she reached the apartment entrance door, she stopped and turned to Alice-Lee. "Do you really like writing about the so-called 'society life?'"

"No," replied Alice-Lee, "But I do love writing. It's the only job I could get."

Cherrie's eyes gleamed as they studied Alice-Lee. "Why don't you write a real piece about your little friend, how she lived, suffered and died unknown not in any kind of recognized society?"

Alice-Lee walked up to Cherrie, put her arms around her fulsome body, kissed her on the cheek, leaned back and said, "Sister, you are one smart apple for all of your problems. I may just try and do that."

"Don't come down," said Cherrie, "I know my way out. I left my card on your little table by the sofa. Call me if you need me." Cherrie smiled, closed the door and left.

□

The next morning Alice-Lee awakened early with no real hangover, was restless. And she knew why.

She called Pat Kramfeld, gave her the assignments for two days and told Pat she had the flu, but would be okay by the end of that time, and to please ghost her column. Pat was delighted to do so. Afterwards, Alice-Lee sat in her apartment and thought and thought. Finally she began to write in longhand. She had no typewriter at her home.

□

Alice-Lee was at her desk in the newspit of the *Chronicle*. She had been back for several days the first of them not very productive in her assigned writing arena. At the end of that day, she took the subway, went to a suburban post office, rented a box and mailed a large, letter-sized envelope. Now she was heartsick, homesick and plain-long sick of the whole human race. With her left elbow on her desk and her chin in her left hand, she stared down at the sheet of paper in her electric typewriter as the third finger of her right hand pressed down on the letter S. Line after line of S's marched across the paper. Her mind, God knows where it really was, seemed to be gazing from some high cliff down on a wriggling mass of humanity that appeared to her like voracious, blind earthworms eating each other and reproducing all at the same time with no apparent conscience, no order, no feeling, no control.

"That's not quite as good as Paul Stephen's essay on "The Flight from Pain: the Life and Death Struggles of Samantha Kingsbury." Ryan Mitchell, the day city editor and assistant managing editor, had his hand on her shoulder, was watching the S's march. She jerked her finger off the typewriter and looked up over her shoulder at the smiling monarch of her area. She was surprised for he never came near her desk, seldom even said hello. She thought he saw her immediate work space as a breeding ground for cockroaches, poisonous spiders and leeches. She knew he considered society reporting as a leech's job. She also knew what she hoped he did not. Among the reasons she kept the job was because Mrs. Nickols, the social-climbing wife of the publisher, enjoyed seeing her name in the paper at least three times a week. Alice-Lee was made aware of that fact the first day she came to work. Spike Adams, one of the sports reporters told her it was a must when he dropped by her desk and introduced himself.

He covered horse racing. Mrs. Nickols' name had to appear in his work at least once a week. She was a racing enthusiast as well as a social climber and she owned a couple of fillies. Spike had told her, "I have seen her spavined misfits run on occasion. I am sure that the swift Rita Nickols can run faster than her horses."

Alice-Lee caught on quickly. Her column titillated Mrs. Nickols and her entourage, much to the disgust of Ry Mitchell, her boss. He never proofed Alice-Lee's copy. "Let it go as it is. It's crap," he had said early on to the compo editor. "When you need to, just cut from the bottom to make it fit."

Ry had read several of her columns when Alice-Lee first came to the paper. "The reporting isn't bad. She knows how to use the language. Why doesn't she ask for another assignment? I might consider doing so if she had the guts to ask for it," he reflected. Over two years had passed since he had that reflection. Then last Thursday, Jim Ellis, the Sunday Section editor, brought to his attention the essay, "Flight from Pain" by a Paul Stephens. The writing was an outstanding story about an unknown young woman in the Frisco area who had doggedly fought pain all her life and that life ended in untold agony like so many other quiet tragedies; not even a death notice. The writing was a tribute to all the unknowns who lived, suffered and died quietly, unnoticed and unheralded.

"It's longer than the usual Sunday essay but it's good, it's really good," said Jim Ellis. "I think we should run it just like it is. I've tried to find out who Paul Stephens is, but the return address is to a suburban post office box."

330

Ry said, "Leave it here, I'll review it and let you know by tomorrow morning." When Jim Ellis left, Ry wasn't being pushed, so he picked up the essay, started to read it. There was something oddly familiar about the style. The piece was well-written, worth the freelance fee for such work. After reading the story a couple of times, he determined to use it and started to okay the draft. Just as he was about to sign off on the article, he looked again at page three of the double-spaced typing. "Son of a bitch," he said quietly, "I could just feel it now I'm sure of it."

He left his office and walked over to Alice-Lee Taliaferro's desk. She wasn't there. "All the better," he said. He reached into the paper drawer, pulled out a sheet of typing paper, turned on the electric typewriter, placed the sheet in and typed pretty Polly parrot. "Hot damn," he said, "Paul Stephens, you've got something after all, but why haven't you asked?" He pulled out the sheet, turned off the typewriter and returned to his desk. He scribbled a note and clipped it to the story essay. "Jim, the piece is a go for Sunday. Send the freelance fee to Paul Stephens at the Post Office box number. Set it up as top lead on page D1 in this Sunday's review section."

□

Now looking down at Alice-Lee, he said, "Make the next row capital Ps and you've got a deal."

"What?" asked an astonished Alice-Lee.

"You heard me, Miss Taliaferro, make the next row capital Ps and you've got a deal. Do as I say please."

Alice-Lee punched the letter P on her typewriter and Ps spewed across the line.

"That's enough," said Ry. "Samantha Kingsbury was your good friend wasn't she?"

Alice-Lee gaped at Ry. "How do you know?"

The day city editor reached down, cut off the typewriter and pulled out the page. "Come on, girl, we've got to talk in my office."

Alice-Lee, almost in a daze, followed Ryan Mitchell to his glass-enclosed office just off the pit. They entered. He motioned her to a chair across from his desk. Alice-Lee sat. Ry closed the door. The newsroom clatter died. To Alice-Lee the silence was unnerving-foreboding. She shifted in her seat. Ry sat in his desk swivel chair and for the first time Alice-Lee saw the family picture on his desk: his wife, kind of tall like her, broad grin and three stair-step kids, two girls and a boy. Ry took off his glasses, blew his breath on them, cleaned them with a tissue, replaced them, then asked, "Why haven't you asked for another assignment? You're good, you're just wasting your time on society crap."

Alice-Lee was not only surprised, but flabbergasted. She opened her mouth to speak, decided she better choose her words carefully, looked down, then up at her boss. "I'm an only child and spoiled rotten by both my parents. They almost smothered me. I had to get out of the nest."

"Then you're not spoiled rotten, just spoiled," said Ry. He grinned.

"This is my first real job away from home. I just couldn't stay around Richmond, Virginia, any longer. My father has too much influence there. I wanted to start on my own and if I progressed, I wanted that progress to be on my ability, not my family name or contacts."

"That's understandable," replied Ry.

"Do you know how I got this job?"

"Haven't the slightest."

"Because my father used to date Mrs. Nickols, long before she married your boss. They have remained friends. So, when I graduated in journalism from Hollins College in Virginia and after doing society reporting for the *Richmond News Leader*, I told my dad I had to have some fresh air. He contacted her and just like that I was accepted. I didn't want anyone here to know how I got the job, I was afraid everyone did, and if I asked for another assignment, I was afraid how I got my first job might influence any request I made."

"Now I know why Becky, the idiot, was canned. Well, it damned well wouldn't have influenced me and doesn't. Every now and then a blind pig finds a ripe acorn. That's what Mrs. Nickols did when she asked her husband to hire you. Do you really like society reporting?"

"It stinks," said Alice-Lee matter-of-factly.

Ry reached across the desk, took her hand and shook it vigorously. "That makes two of us with the same point of view. How would you like to do some real reporting, in-depth, investigative work closer to your home?"

"What in the world are you suggesting?"

"Well, your story essay shows a knack for personalized in-depth reporting. It's a fine piece of writing about social conscience. We need a backup for Jeff Hilton, our Washington, D.C. correspondent. Now that the war is over there'll be a lot going on in the D.C. area, politically, sociologically, economically, every way you can think of that affects the nation. We want some distinctive tidbits—in-depth studies, the result of investigative reporting of events and people, interesting people, probably not known outside the D.C. area, not necessarily the hot shots, but characters that are synonymous with a nationwide changing mood—a direction—a warning. Your recent Sunday piece demonstrates your ability. Would you like a crack at it?"

Alice-Lee looked around the room, at the ceiling then at the floor. "Where am I? I must be in heaven, did I just come through the pearly gates?" She pointed to the door. Then she pointed to her boss, "Are you Saint Peter?"

For the first time, Ry Mitchell laughed in her presence, a genuine, bellylaugh.

"They said you had a sense of humor, I told them, no way. Now I believe them."

"Who's them?"

"The newsroom."

"Yes, Mr. Mitchell, I would jump at the chance for such an assignment—even jump at you except for the fact of what that picture tells me." She pointed to the family photo on his desk.

Again Ry laughed. "You are somebody so different than I imagined, up until now. So, you're an only child, your family has money and your dad has clout. Forget it. You're on your own. You can do well." The smile left his face and he was serious. "Now that you're grown, let them be your backstop for a loose ball. That's what families are for. That and the best rooting section you'll ever know."

"You must have been a sports reporter at one time," said Alice-Lee.

"Was, baseball, still love it. Now to business. It'll take me a couple weeks to find your replacement, God help her. And it'll take a couple more for you to break her in. You should be able to leave by July first. I hope that's enough time."

"I know a replacement," said Alice-Lee. "She's a cub here but has ghosted for me several times. Tomorrow would be enough time for me."

"We'll have your salary and expense account ready for your review and comment in ten days. Better hadn't be much comment, except 'That's just fine, I'll take it.'" Ry arose. "Now, I've got a paper to put to bed. If you have any questions, see me later." He left the room.

Alice-Lee sat, still partially stunned by the swift, almost unbelievable, recent course of events, from stinking devastation to sublime. She stood, exhaled deeply, looked out the glass-enclosed office into the newsroom and said softly, "There is a God after all. Gee, what a wonderful break." Suddenly, "Hot damn!" she yelled. A couple reporters working at their desks near the office heard her exclamation through the glass walls of Ry's office, glanced from their typewriters and saw Alice-Lee with her hands above her head, spinning like a dervish. They had no idea what had happened between the day city editor and the rather reserved, caustic, yet witty society reporter, but knew it wasn't bad.

☐

That evening, Alice-Lee called her parents to let them know she was being transferred by *The Chronicle* to Washington, D.C. Her father answered the phone. When she told him of her new assignment, he answered, "I knew you could make it on your own and you will now be nearer home, I promise not to interfere. However, I'm still on the board of trustees for William and Mary College. If you would be interested in a beginning lecturing post on journalism, I'm sure I can swing it."

"Thanks, Father, but I am happy doing what I do."

"I won't insist, I've grown also, but, can't promise for your mother. Here she is."

Alice-Lee could tell that her mother was truly surprised and relieved that she was moving closer to home. "Thank, God," said Eva, her mother. "What a relief to know you will be working closer to home, even it if is across the Potomac River in no man's land where they are spending our tax money as if it grows on trees. Call us before you start your trip home, particularly if you're driving. And if you do drive, promise you will call each night when you stop."

Alice-Lee couldn't help but giggle then replied, "Don't worry, Mother, about federal finances, Senator Harry Flood Byrd still has his hand on the money throttle. And, yes I will call most every evening."

"That isn't funny, Alice-Lee. Now that the war is over, the government has gone crazy spending tons of money overseas trying to rebuild what they blew up. Where will it all end?"

"Mother, you really don't have to fret about it. That's Father's job."

"He doesn't worry about it. That's why I do. Honey, I am so very happy you will be nearer. Bye Dear."

□

Alice-Lee was able to quickly sublease her apartment at the Sealcrest and much to her pleasant surprise, *The Chronicle* had found and leased a two bedroom apartment for her in the Colonial Village garden apartment complex on Key Boulevard in Arlington County, Virginia. The rent was less than half of what she was paying in Frisco. She was advised by the accounting office of her paper that the housing project was new, suburban and only a short distance from *The Chronicle* office in D.C. She arranged for the shipment of her furniture then drove her car cross-country to her new job and habitat. For her, that trip was most enjoyable.

□

Ten days after she left Frisco she was busy arranging furniture in her new home. The apartment was quite different from her last one — no bay view she had in Frisco, no doorman, but she could park her car at the curb right in front of her garden apartment door, and most of the tenants in the area were young like herself. There was an air of vibrancy and neighborliness that she liked.

Her phone was connected the second day she was in her apartment. In the late afternoon, she called home. Dora, the maid, answered, "Taliaferro residence."

"Dora, its me, Alice-Lee."

"Miss Alice-Lee, is you arrived safe and sound?"

"Sure thing Dora, is mother there?"

"Yes, honey-chile, just a second."

Eva Taliaferro took the phone from Dora. "My, I'm relieved you've arrived at last. Your father and I have been worried sick when you didn't call during the last three days."

"I told you when I last called en route that my phone wouldn't be connected for a couple of days after I arrived."

"I know dear, but you could have gone to a nearby drugstore and called collect."

And Alice-Lee thought, "Maybe I'm too close to home, maybe I should have stayed in Frisco."

"Tell father I'm here and my apartment phone number is Chestnut 3-4167. I'll call you this weekend and let you know when I can make a trip home."

"I'll tell him and we will be so glad to see you. It's been a long time."

"Since Christmas," said Alice-Lee. "See you soon and I love you both."

Alice-Lee hung up her phone then thought, "I guess I'll always be fifteen to them." She felt a warm glow because she knew they really cared. Sam, her deceased friend, had initiated her as to what real caring meant.

CHAPTER 28

On a hot, humid, enervating, typical late August day in Washington, D.C., Alice-Lee was having lunch in the air-conditioned, rooftop dining room of the Hotel Washington with Si Mendelsohn of *The Boston Globe* and Henry Fitzwater of *The Richmond Times Dispatch*. The trio had just returned from a briefing in the State Department press room.

As they sipped their premeal cocktails, Si spoke, "While I was home last weekend, I had lunch with Henry Baker who covers courts and crime for our paper. He told me the damnedest story. Part of it has been printed but the balance has been hanging in the air because no one on the paper can find the end of it."

"How on earth did you ever become a newsman with such obtuse statements?" inquired Fitzwater. "What are you talking about? What are the facts?"

Alice-Lee was enjoying every minute of the dialogue between her two peers and friends, both in-depth, investigative reporters. Each liked to tease the other with nonfactual, inconclusive observations, goading the other to inquire about facts and details, facts of some little known story, representing some great moral or ideal, or the lack of it.

"Why should I be factual when I don't know all the facts and the facts I do know don't lead to a conclusion?"

"Tell me wise observer and let's see if I can draw a conclusion," chided Fitzwater.

"Hell," said Si, "You can't draw a straight line, much less a conclusion. I'll tell you anyway just to stir your imagination. Yours too," and he nodded to Alice-Lee.

"In late June of this year there was a wild shootout in the Boston offices of Finley & Finley, the oldest, most reputable produce broker on the Boston Harbor scene. The owner and CEO of that organization is one Brian Lucas, a native Bostonian living in the Wollaston, Massachusetts area.

"That carbon copy of a western saloon brawl involved three members of the Secret Service—the owner of the produce company, Brian Lucas, his son, Tully and one Owen Leverbee, Tully's henchman. Turns out that, unknown to Lucas until that morning, his son was the mastermind and leader of a major counterfeiting ring in the U.S. The counterfeiters headquarters including the printing press was located right here in D.C. One of the Secret Service operatives was killed and another was seriously wounded. Tully Lucas and his henchman were killed in the fray. Old man Lucas suffered a mild heart attack."

"I have never even heard of the story," said Alice-Lee.

"I guess it ran on UP while you were driving across country coming to D.C.," replied Si. "And it wasn't all that important. There have been a lot of shootings going on in the States since the war ended, kinda like carry-over."

"I remember that story," said Fitzwater. "We picked it up on UP."

Si continued, "That episode has more convoluted twists and kinks than a poorly coiled garden hose."

Alice-Lee was interested, "How so?" she asked.

"Well, for one thing, it turns out that the Secret Service agent who was severely wounded was Brian Lucas' son-in-law, the husband of his deceased daughter. Until that morning's shootout, Lucas thought his son-in-law was a crooked card player who had married his daughter for her money. Also, until just prior to the shootout, Lucas didn't know his son-in-law was a Secret Service agent. Old man Lucas found out just minutes before the brawl that his only daughter who had been murdered a couple months before had been shot and killed by her own brother, Tully who was trying to find and kill her husband, the Secret Service agent wounded in the melee. At the time of Brian's daughter's death, she was the owner of a small, succeeding press in New York City called the Purple Canary."

"The what?" asked Alice-Lee. That company name was like a bell ringing in the far distance. She could hear it but couldn't tell from which church belfry it rang.

"The Purple Canary Press. Why?" asked Si.

"At the moment, I don't know. What was the daughter's name?"

"Mariana. Why?" again asked Si.

"Damn it, I still don't know. But seems I've also heard that name before," said Alice-Lee.

"Go on," said Fitzwater.

"Well," said Si, "It turns out that Lucas' deceased daughter's injured husband is something else beside being a Secret Service agent."

"An orangutan?" chided Fitzwater.

"No, worse than that, he is also an up-and-coming poet if he's still alive," said Si.

"Why do you say, 'If he is still alive?'" inquired Alice-Lee. Now she was focused, a memory was emerging.

"Because about six weeks after his injuries in the brawl, the young Secret Service agent disappeared from Massachusetts General Hospital. No one, not even the Secret Service, has been able to find him. Old man Lucas now recovered, is trying to right a number of wrongs he had imposed on his son-in-law. He has thrown his wealth behind the Service in attempting to locate him."

Alice-Lee was quivering inside from excitement. She tried to look calm as she asked, "Si, what was Lucas' son-in-law's name if you know?"

"According to the paper, his Service name was Wesley Young but rumor has it his real name is some weird Russian name like Orsonovich."

"Could it have been Bosconovich?" Alice-Lee's eyes were flashing.

"Bosconovich? You could be right. Rumor also has it that his poetry is quite acceptable. I've never heard of him."

"I have," said Alice-Lee, "His full name is Marcus Arent Bosconovich. He was in the Navy and is a young, outstanding World War II poet."

The strange glowing, gleeful look on Alice-Lee's face was a giveaway and told both men that their colleague had some additional facts that could be tossed into the convoluted equation. But would she?

"What more do you know?" Si asked seriously.

"Well, I first read about the name in a poetry review reported over a year ago in *The Chronicle*. Then I heard the name from a friend of mine. She has since died."

"And what else?" asked Si.

"Nothing except according to my friend he is quite a guy."

"How did your friend meet him?" asked Fitzwater.

"Nosy, aren't you? How does a gal generally meet a guy? I guess in some dive, like I first met the two of you."

"So that's what you think of the White House press room?" inquired Si and he smiled.

"About the same level," replied Alice-Lee. She tittered then continued. "No kidding, my friend met Marcus Bosconovich one night in a bar. He was no rowdy. He was most kind to her. She didn't get to know him very well but she was thoroughly impressed by him."

Underneath her composed, outward appearance, Alice-Lee was excited and at the same time shamed, more so than anytime since her boss in California had sent her to Washington. She was excited about the subject matter of Si's conversation. Ashamed because it reminded her that following Sam's death and for several reasons, including the rush of leaving Frisco, moving to Washington, D.C. and getting settled in her new apartment, she had packed Sam's unopened gift package in one of the boxes she had sent to her new residence. "Where was that package?" she wondered. "What could be in that brown wrapping paper?" She surmised that it could be a lead to one of the most interesting, unended stories she had heard of since her arrival in the capitol city. Now she was challenged.

"Boys," she said as she looked at her watch, "I've got to finish lunch in a hurry. I just remembered I have a two o'clock appointment."

"Alice-Lee," said Si, "You are one of the loveliest southern ladies I have ever met and one of the poorest liars. Fitzwater and I can see your sniffing from where we sit. Just remember where you got your lead."

Alice-Lee giggled. "I will," she said and shortly thereafter she left.

When she had gone, Si turned to Fitzwater, "She'll soon learn. We've tried every avenue you can think of to get the whole story although we have run into one dead end after another."

Fitzwater grinned at Si, then said, "Who knows, maybe she will find a little path you never discovered."

□

While Alice-Lee was riding home in a taxi, she wondered, "Why didn't I open that gift before I left Frisco?" Yet, in her heart of hearts, she knew. First there was Joe—the bastard, then she had given Sam so little in life and Sam had given her so much—her future. Alice-Lee's story of Sam in *The Chronicle* had been her springboard into real news writing. She not only felt guilty, but also there was a depth of caring that when she admitted it all but tore her guts out. That's why she didn't knowingly think about her deceased friend more often and that's why she hadn't opened the package. She was afraid to. In the cab where no one could see her she wept and her whole body shook from her unrestrained grief. The cabbie heard her, looked into his rear-view mirror and inquired, "You alright, Miss?"

Alice-Lee responded, "Thanks for asking. I'll be okay in a few seconds. I'm a little tired."

"Sure," said the driver.

Upon entering her apartment she went straight to her sofa, sat and pondered, "Where in the world did I put that package?" Then she remembered it was with Sam's urn in one of the unpacked boxes in her basement storage bin. Until that moment, she hadn't the will to retrieve the urn and place it on the corner cupboard she had shipped from Frisco. She had the urn on that cupboard in Frisco before she wrote the piece on Sam. She had to take it down after that article was published. She hurt too much when she looked at it. Now she had to find Sam's last gift package. Alice-Lee rose, went to her desk to find the key to the lock on her storage bin.

Once in her storage area, she opened box after box, checked and closed them. Finally she got results. She saw the brown paper-wrapped package and the urn—last reminders of her dear, diminutive friend. With tenderness, she pulled them from the rumpled newspaper packing. She felt guilty at not being strong enough inside, until now, to accept the sorrows those objects brought to mind. "Jesus, what would my friends think of me if they saw me act this way," she said softly as she, hugging the two objects to her breast, walked tearfully up the steps into her new home.

Comfortably ensconced in the folds of her sofa, with the reading light beaming over her shoulder and as the strains of Ray Noble's theme song, "The Very Thought of You" wove from her radio and gently filled the room, Alice-Lee opened her dead friend's gift. On top of a well-used copy of *Poems by Three Pacific War Poets* were two envelopes, one smudged and much used, the other unopened. On top of those envelopes was a small sheet of paper with the feeble remnants of Sam's once distinctive handwriting, "So that you will know why. Sam."

Alice-Lee tore open the unopened envelope from Marcus to Sam, looked at the postmark on the unopened letter and realized it was mailed four days before Sam's death. It had apparently arrived the day before Sam died, but her friend was too feeble to open and read it. Alice-Lee read:

June 18, 1946

Dear Sam,

I hasten to reply to your recent letter. Your dream view of Mariana in the misty tunnel defies my comprehension. And your inquiry was so on point. Just a few days before your dream, my wife was murdered. By whom I do not yet know, but if I ever personally catch the bastard, I will tear him apart limb by limb and enjoy every minute of the process. I too, rale at a god who would let such an event transpire. But then, maybe that's the way the creator preserves the good souls, he wants to store them early without letting them being subjected to, and enduring a lifetime of earthly deterioration.

Sam, I know from your last letter the darkest secret you have kept. I can understand your deep anger and resentment at your sisters and father. I agree with your attitude. We are the products of our age and our so-called morals are the unwritten rules that a society in a given era exhorts its members to embrace, consistent with that society's order, security and growth. But, the mind and feelings of man are not locked in place. There was a time and location in recorded history when such behavior as recited in your last letter was the accepted norm. Besides the idiots and the malformed resulting from such conduct, it produced the single, longest line of brilliant rulers yet known to man. Let your anger be tempered by sorrow for your father and sisters. They, in the final analysis, can no more control their ultimate feelings than you and I. Primarily for society's sake, we have to try and to mask.

Sam, whatever else, there is beauty at the end of the tunnel.

Just,

Marcus

My God, thought Alice-Lee, what an unusual guy. After reading and rereading both of his letters, she turned to his poems, read all of them carefully, then read them again before she went to her kitchen to scrounge for supper.

Later, when she tried to think back, she had a hard time remembering what, if anything, she had eaten. She was perplexed and deeply troubled by the story Si had told her earlier in the day, particularly when that episode was mixed with what she had just read—her last gifts from Sam: Who is Marcus A. Bosconovich? Where is he? Why did he so suddenly disappear? She was beginning to be intrigued, felt a strange obligation to Sam to find the answers to those questions and she wanted the story.

Once again she was the snoop, the reporter. She reached over to the little table on which sat a phone and a steno pad. She jotted down the return address on each of Marcus' letters, one was his parents address, the other was the Washington Hotel in Washington, D.C. She remembered the shootout, the names of Finley & Finley, Brian Lucas, Tully Lucas, his deceased son and that there were three Secret Service operatives involved. She also made a note of that fact. The next day when she finished the White House press conference, she would start her search for Marcus, hoping he was still alive. He just had to be. She stopped short: What the heck does he look like? She realized Sam had never described him to her except that he was handsome. "So was Joe," she said softly. After pondering briefly she knew where she would first turn for some answers.

CHAPTER 29

The next morning, shortly after the White House press conference ended, Alice-Lee entered the reception room of the Secret Service headquarters in the Old Treasury Building. She approached the desk on which there was a nameplate: "Laura Oliphant," and placed her *San Francisco Chronicle* press card on the desk. The silver-haired receptionist looked at the card, then at Alice-Lee. "What can I do for you, Ms..... How do you pronounce it?" she asked politely.

"Toliver," answered Alice Lee and she grinned.

"If it is permissible, I would like to speak with someone who is familiar with the International Etching and Art Gallery caper."

"Heavens child, everyone here knows about that scam. In what part are you interested?"

"The episode, the shootout that took place in the office of Brian Lucas in Boston. I think it was in late June this year."

"Wait here for a minute or two, let me see what I can do." Mrs. Oliphant rose from her desk and disappeared through a doorway to her right. In a couple of minutes she returned followed by a solidly built, middle-aged man with sharp blue-gray eyes much like Alice-Lee's.

Mrs. Oliphant walked up to the reporter. "You're lucky, young lady, the operative in charge of that little episode happens to be here today. Ms. Toliver, I'd like to present Clarence Waddell."

Clarence Waddell met the firm grasp of Alice-Lee. She said, "It's a real pleasure, Sir. Could we find a spot to chat for a few minutes?" Clarence Waddell was carefully studying the tall, confident reporter.

"Sure," he replied. "Follow me," and he led the way to a small empty office. He took a seat behind the desk, motioned for her to be seated in a chair opposite him. "Miss Taliaferro, tell me what's on your mind?"

Alice-Lee, after identifying herself, recited her recent conversation with Henry Fitzwater and Si Mendelson. When she had finished, she gazed steadily at Waddell and asked, "Was the real name of Brian Lucas' son-in-law Marcus A. Bosconovich?"

Waddell raised his bushy brows and asked, "Why do you want to know?"

"Well, first I've read his poems which I really like but more importantly, sometime ago he befriended a good friend of mine who has since died."

"What was his name?"

"It wasn't a he but a she. Her name was Samantha Kingsbury."

"Where did all this take place?"

"In San Francisco, shortly after Marcus returned from the Pacific at the end of Word War II and before he went home to Chicago."

"I take it that Samantha Kingsbury and you were close friends?"

"One of the closest I'll ever have," she replied. Then Alice-Lee told Waddell the sad tale of her friend and as much as she knew of Marcus' relationship with her.

"He is one of the most unusual young men I have ever met. I wish to God we could find him."

"What happened?"

"One morning, about six weeks after the Boston episode, Marcus, still an invalid, left the hospital unnoticed. We know he went to New York to what is now his apartment. Exactly when, we don't know. We have been checking periodically on his apartment since he disappeared. We know his younger brother had sent him a box which we didn't open. Marcus took that box from the kitchen table, put some clothes in a suitcase and a day or so later cashed a rather large check on his account at a branch of Chase Manhattan Bank. He told the bank teller he was in a hurry to get to an important appointment. After that he disappeared into the blue. We have found absolutely no trace of him. His parents, when they learned from me the truth of his occupation, have been frantic with worry. So has his father-in-law. The senior Lucas, for misguided reasons, had filed suit against his son-in-law, endeavoring to keep Marcus from receiving his rightful inheritance from his wife. That is until the sad event took place in his office. Since then, he has dismissed his suit and spared no effort in trying to help us find Marcus."

"Why in the world did Marcus pull the disappearing act?"

"Because I'm convinced that he feels laden with guilt and self-pity not only because of his wife's murder and the death of his good friend, Ron Evans, but to be as badly crippled as he was and is after his injury. Before that occurrence, he was an outstanding athlete. All of the events put together were more than he could handle. And...." Waddell stopped talking, looked at his hands on the desk.

"What?"

"I have read and reread his poetry since he disappeared, I now realize he is a far more sensitive person than I first thought him to be. Your story of his relationship with Samantha Kingsbury only adds to that conclusion. I kept him under wraps for about six weeks while he was in the hospital because there were loose ends of the episode to tie up. That's long passed. I would love to find him."

Alice-Lee watched Waddell. She knew his feelings for Marcus were genuine. Later, she wondered why she said what she did, but it just came out. "So would I and I intend to," she replied.

"Is there any more information I can give you?" inquired Waddell.

Alice-Lee was silent for a few moments, then, "Yes, there is. I really would like you to tell me how you met him, the story of your relationship."

Clarence Waddell looked at Alice Lee, his eyes boring deep. He knew she was a reporter and curious. He could tell she was truly interested in learning about Marcus and she was a good listener. There was now no reason why he could not divulge all he knew. He launched forth on his story. As he finished, he smiled and said, "Now you have it all. Any more questions?"

"Just one request," she replied. "I would like his family's current address if you don't mind."

"I know of no reason not to give it to you," he said and wrote the address on the back of his business card and handed it to her.

"I gave my card to your receptionist should you have a reason to get in touch with me," said the tall, confident reporter.

"Please keep me advised if you find anything," responded Waddell. Alice-Lee left.

□

Three days later, Alice-Lee was ringing the front door bell of the Bosconovich family home in Chicago. Marla answered the door. "Can I help you, young lady?" was her query.

Alice-Lee looked at Marla and liked her immediately. "Mrs. Bosconovich, I really don't know. I'm Alice-Lee Taliaferro of the *San Francisco Chronicle*," and she handed her business card to Marcus' mother.

Marla, a little querulous, asked, "And your mission, the reason for your being here?"

"May I come in and chat with you for a few minutes?"

"About what?" asked Marla.

"Your son, Marcus."

Marla looked with interest at the tall, calm young lady. "Please come, make yourself comfortable." She indicated the living room sofa, then studied the young patrician-featured woman and sat opposite her in a lounge chair. "Just what do you want to know about Marcus?"

"Do you know where he is? Day before yesterday I was in the office of Secret Service Senior Operative Clarence Waddell who is trying to find him. He has no idea where your son is at the present time."

Marla's eyes clouded. "Regretfully, we don't either," she replied "Why do you want to get in touch with him?"

"For several reasons. I would like to talk with him about the counterfeit sting and his role in the operation. More importantly, I was a close friend of Samantha Kingsbury."

"Sam Kingsbury?"

"Did you know her?"

"Heavens, no. I thought she was a he. Tell me, just who was Sam Kingsbury?"

In a gracious manner, Alice-Lee told the story of her close friend who lived in pain most of her life and died in agony. She told the story of Sam's relationship with Marcus—as much as she knew and could tactfully address. She finished by saying, "Your son was as gallant with her as any man, stranger or not could possibly be. I have read his poems. I need to meet him for Sam's sake, maybe mine," she smiled at Marla.

"You know his wife, Mariana, was murdered?"

Alice-Lee looked sympathetically at her host. "Yes. Mr. Waddell told me as much as he knew. He said she was a loving, thoughtful woman who truly worshiped your son."

Marla looked down at her hands fumbling in her lap. She softly said, "We never knew until after he was severely injured that Marcus was a member of the Secret Service. Mariana gave no indication. She loved him with an honesty that was amazing. I worried because of Marcus's thrill-seeking tendency. When she died, I thought I would also. I blamed her death on Marcus, thinking he was again involved in gambling and that her death was caused by some thrill-seeking escapade of my elder son. The only one in the family who thought Marcus was on the up and up was Bernie, our younger son. Though he didn't really know what Marcus was doing for a living, he was absolutely positive that his brother was not engaged in any illegal activity." Marla sighed, looked helplessly at Alice-Lee. "He was so right."

"Have you received any word from Marcus since his injury and disappearance?"

"None. We later learned he was sworn to secrecy even after he was injured. Mr. Waddell did come here, revealed to us our son's occupation, his selfless service, how he was injured and said he would notify Marcus when all was clear and our son could communicate with us. Shortly after that Marcus disappeared. We have no idea where he is. His disappearance is slowly killing me. The rest of the family is extremely worried and upset."

"Would you have any idea why he left the hospital?" asked Alice-Lee.

"If he wasn't taken by some remnant of the crooked gang, I have to say yes."

"Would you mind telling me the reason for your 'yes?'"

"My dear child, you have given me an example of the reason in your chat about Samantha Kingsbury. As smart and as strong a man as he is, or was, he is an odd mixture of a dreamer, an idealist and a thrill-seeker. His wife knew it. He saw the world from a different point of view than most people. I am sure that when Mariana was murdered, he, for the first time, saw the harsh reality of life even though he had been overseas in World War II. When the shooting occurred in his father-in-law's office and Marcus was seriously wounded, no longer was he a blithe spirit with real physical prowess. He realized he was human, frail and felt everything that happened was his fault. If he is still alive, right or wrong, he is being torn to bits by a guilty conscience and self-pity."

Alice-Lee's heart ached for the lovely woman. "Mrs. Bosconovich, may I call you Marla?"

"Certainly," she replied then smiled wistfully.

"I think you are right, Marla. For many reasons, including how kindly he treated Samantha and how he loved Mariana, I am determined to find him if he is alive. His story is worth telling, I do want to meet him and hear what he has to say."

Marla wept then regained her composure. "I hope to God you do find him. If you do, convince him that his family still loves him dearly. I do so want to hear from him—to see him."

Alice-Lee leaned over and kissed Marla on the cheek. "I have more reasons than ever to find him. I will," she said. Then she rose to leave.

As Alice-Lee left the house, Marla took one of the reporter's hands, raised it to her lips, kissed it and said, "Thanks my dear. For the first time I have real hope."

"Marla, would you mind if I call you from time to time to fill me in on Marcus' background?"

"Please do, I'll do anything to help you find him."

The two women parted.

□

Another three days and Alice-Lee walked into Brian Lucas' reception room. Priscilla White noted the ease and grace of the woman.

"How may I help you?" she inquired.

Alice-Lee handed her card to Priscilla and said, "Is it possible that Mr. Lucas can spare me fifteen minutes?"

349

"For what, Ms. Taliaferro?"

"To chat with him about Marcus Bosconovich."

"Do you know where he is?" and she showed excitement.

"No, but I'm determined to find him."

"Why?"

"Because he helped a very close friend of mine when she was in need and from what else I have learned about him his story is worth telling."

Immediately Priscilla grew defensive. Alice-Lee noticed. "Don't worry," she said, "My friend died of cancer sometime ago. I want to find Marcus and thank him."

"Just a minute." Priscilla opened a door and went into her boss's office. "There's a young lady reporter from the *San Francisco Chronicle* who would like a brief chat with you about Marcus."

"Has she found him?" and Brian's heartbeat increased.

"No, but she has a reason to talk with you."

"Send her in," he responded.

Alice-Lee entered the room, saw the dignified but positive-demeanored, gray-haired gentleman, well-recovered from his heart attack. She also saw the framed wedding photo on his desk top, such a handsome couple. She knew the bridegroom was Marcus and the bride was Mariana. She gazed at them with unashamed curiosity. She thought Mariana was truly beautiful and Marcus was indeed handsome, so virile-looking. She carefully spoke of her mission, a reporter's endeavor to locate Marcus on behalf of her paper and for other reasons.

"Did you know him?" asked Brian.

"No, but as a result of the information I've been gathering, I would like to," she replied matter-of-factly.

"I wish I had known him better," responded Brian. "I misjudged him in the beginning, hated his guts until the day the world caved in, in my office. If only Mariana had told me he was with the Secret Service. Now, too late, I know why she didn't, God rest her lovely soul." Brian then told Alice-Lee in detail not only what had happened on the fateful day, but about his daughter, her youth, her drive, her accomplishments and as much as he knew of her relationship with Marcus. He had needed to tell it to somebody. When he was finished, he appeared drained and slumped back in his chair.

"May I call you from time to time if I have any questions?" asked the reporter.

"Certainly, I would be glad to fill you in on any details," responded Brian Lucas.

Alice-Lee looked at him with sympathy and concern, waited a couple minutes, then asked, "Is there anything else you can tell me about the episode? About Marcus and Mariana?"

Brian shook his head negatively. Then he held up his hand and after a bitter smile said, "Only one odd little afterpiece of information but of no relevance."

"What is that?"

"Whenever I have driven out to Mariana's grave, in addition to other flowers I take or that are in the container, there has always been one fresh, separate, white rose."

"Do you know who places it there?"

"No. I watched for a couple days. No one came while I was there."

Out of nowhere, Alice-Lee remembered one of Marcus' poems she had read, the one entitled "The White Rose." It was a poem about nobleness, virtue and purity. Now she was excited. She rose with as much composure as possible. "Thank you, Mr. Lucas, you have given me much interesting information."

Brian smiled a wistful, sad smile. "Thank you for listening, young lady. If you get any word on my son-in-law, please let me know. I have several humble apologies to make."

Alice-Lee looked at Brian Lucas. She liked his frankness. And she admired the way he handled his grief.

He escorted her from his office, shook her hand and said, "Here's to luck for both of us."

"By the way, would you mind telling me where your daughter is buried?" asked Alice-Lee.

"Not at all, Holly Hills Cemetery in Wollaston," replied Brian and he gave her one of the Boston metro area maps stashed in a stand in the reception room. He opened it and put an "x" on the cemetery location. "You wouldn't have any trouble finding it after you reach Wollaston. But why do you inquire about her grave?"

"After my conversations with Clarence Waddell, Marcus's mother and you, I wish to pay my respects to her. Thank you for seeing me," she said as she left the suite.

After she had left, Brian turned to Priscilla, "She is a reporter for a paper out west. I don't generally like reporters, but for some reason, I trust her. She's decent."

Alice-Lee took a cab to her hotel. Once there she made arrangements to lease an auto. First she would drive out to the cemetery in the daytime in order to get her bearings. Then, if her instincts where right, she would return at night, for as long as necessary, and maybe, just maybe, she would find out who was placing the white rose. "Could it be Marcus?" she wondered excitedly.

In the early afternoon, she drove to Holly Hills Cemetery, stopped at the office to inquire as to the location of the Lucas family graves sites, was indeed glad she had made her first trip in daylight for the cemetery was a large one, sectionalized: Protestant, Catholic, Jewish and Noah's Ark, a pet cemetery. Slowly she wound her way through the quiet resting area. At last, she found the Lucas family plot almost on the perimeter of the grounds.

She left her car and walked to the foot of Mariana's grave, a grave with new grass peeking above ground. There she saw the headstone:

Mariana Lucas Bosconovich
Wife of Marcus Arent Bosconovich
and
Daughter of Karen Finley Lucas
and Brian O'Flanagan Lucas
Born May 16, 1916 Died June 4, 1946

She looked from the grave outward, beyond the wrought iron fence and saw the growing, gently waving field of barley. Further out she saw the green hills topped with a stand of birch trees. For some unidentified reason there flashed in her mind the image of the underscored part of a passage from the *Book of Common Prayers* given to her by her mother on the Sunday she, Alice-Lee, was confirmed in Saint James Episcopal Church in her home city of Richmond, Virginia. The 121st Psalm was her mother's favorite. The first four underscored lines Alice-Lee remembered:

I will lift up mine eyes unto the hills;
From whence cometh my help?
My help cometh even from the Lord,
Who made heaven and earth.

"What a lovely spot for a grave," Alice-Lee murmured. As she continued looking at the hills, she thought, "Marcus Bosconovich, whoever he is, had touched the lives of two gallant women and their deaths were only few days apart. Each had loved him and apparently in such different ways. Yet, to each of them, there was one commonality. From what she had learned, and for all of Marcus' physical and mental prowess, his greatest natural instinct was gentleness. That was apparent in his letters to Samantha, in his poetry as well as in the conversations she had with Clarence Waddell, Brian Lucas and Marla Bosconovich." For her, that was odd. She had never known a guy like that. She was more than ever intrigued and resolved to find the end of the ongoing story. She looked back at the grave and the green cone-shaped flower holder spiked into the grave.

In that holder was a lovely single white rose, the outer petals of which were just beginning to be tinged with yellow. On observing the flower, Alice-Lee said softly, "It has been there for a couple days, at least. I wonder if tonight's the night." She felt a quiver of excitement.

She could hardly wait for darkness to fall. Back at the hotel and during supper, she pondered, "I wonder what time the delivery arrives?" Just before she left her hotel room, she noticed there was a chance of rain, so she threw her dark blue, hooded rain cape around her shoulders, drove through Boston traffic to Wollaston and headed for the cemetery. Never once did she consider her outing to be a foolhardy one, tinged with possible danger. Puritan witches had died hundreds of years ago.

It was dark when she entered the open gates of the cemetery. The cemetery office lights were still on. She drove to a spot not too far from the Lucas plot and parked her auto in a little dead-end driveway that was surrounded by mausoleums which helped shield her car from view of anyone except those who wandered into that little lane.

She started walking on the grass toward the Lucas burial area. Every now and then, she felt a sprinkle on her hand, no heavy shower, but it added to an air of foreboding silence that hung heavy over the cemetery. She raised the hood to keep her hair from getting wet. As she quietly approached her goal she realized she wasn't alone. Standing stooped by Mariana's grave was a figure. In the darkness, she couldn't make out whether it was a man or a woman. She approached closer. Suddenly, the figure, aided by a crutch, whirled toward her and she was looking into the muzzle of a revolver. "What are you, some kind of a witch? Don't take another step or I'll blow your brains from here to hell and gone," a harsh and frightened male voice rasped.

Alice-Lee stopped, rigid with fright.

"Please," pleaded Alice-Lee, "I'm no witch and I'm not armed."

"Well, what are you doing here this time of night? Who are you?" The bedraggled figure stepped closer. She could see his face was covered with shaggy blonde whiskers and moustache, his clothes were shabby and he was scrawny. He was leaning heavily on a crutch. There was the strong smell of alcohol that seemed to envelope him. "This can't possibly be the same guy in the photo on Brian Lucas' desk," she thought.

Alice-Lee took a chance. "I came to find you, Marcus Bosconovich," she said with calmness and sincerity. "And my name is Alice-Lee Taliaferro."

"Your name is what?"

"Alice-Lee Taliaferro. I was a close friend of Sam...."

"Oh, my God, now I know who you are. Why...?"

"Please, put that pistol way. It makes me very nervous. I am here to do you no harm and call me Alice-Lee."

Marcus was mystified. Standing before him, was a sharp-featured woman in a dark cape, exactly like a witch's. "Are you sure you're real, not something I'm imagining, not a witch?"

Alice-Lee laughed gently, then said, "Some people have called me a bitch, but never a witch. Maybe that's what they meant."

Marcus' tension eased, he replaced his revolver. Alice-Lee saw a large, raised, flat tombstone nearby. She flashed her little light on it, read the identification and said, "I don't believe Mary Higgins would object if we sat on her for a few minutes."

Marcus had to smile at the control of the self-possessed young woman. He hobbled with the aid of a crutch, painfully lowered himself onto the slab, sitting as far away from her as possible and wondered, "Why had this weird creature come out here and at this time?"

Alice-Lee spoke, "I know your first question. It is 'why did I come here and now?' The answer is convoluted I'll admit. First of all, I'm a reporter for the *San Francisco Chronicle*. At present, I am stationed in Washington, D.C. Your disappearance from Massachusetts General Hospital after the International Etching and Art Gallery caper has caused all kinds of worry and speculation. Second, you were the most caring friend that Samantha Kingsbury ever had in her short, tragic life. I want to thank you for the friendship and caring you gave her. Third, I've read your poems a number of times. When Brian Lucas, your father-in-law, told me yesterday of the constant white rose on Mariana's grave, I remembered your poem, "The White Rose." I figured it had to be you. I had no idea you would be here tonight. I just took a chance. Next, Clarence Waddell, your parents, your sisters and yes, even Brian Lucas, have been desperately trying to find you. Each wants to tell you how ashamed they are for misjudging you. And, last, me, I started out to find the end of a story, an incomplete story that has been in the newspapers from coast to coast. The more I learned, the less I really knew. I guess you can say I had to try and find you, not only as a reporter, but for reasons I don't clearly comprehend."

Marcus' eyes shown with a steely wonderment. "If you ever tell anyone I was here, I'll hunt you down wherever you are and kill you with no remorse. And if you write about any part of this meeting I'll find you and tear you limb from limb. That's not all, you have no right to invade my privacy, to write anything at all about me without my consent."

Alice-Lee looked at the disheveled creature seated to her left and calmly said, "Marcus, I solemnly swear," then she again beamed the light on the tombstone upon which they were seated, "On the grave of Mary Higgins, no one will know where you are or have your story unless and until you say so."

Marcus was surprised for he thought the reporter was aching to have a scoop. "How do I know?" asked Marcus.

In the dark, Alice-Lee opened her purse, took out a business card with both her office and home addresses. "This will help you find me should I fail my word." She handed the card to Marcus. He took it without comment but with bewilderment. He had no idea that this tall, slender woman with the calm southern drawl could be so composed and sure.

"Will you tell me where you live?" she asked.

"And why should I do that?"

"In case I learn some member of your family is ill and desperately needs you."

Marcus felt uncomfortable but his bravado hung strong. "There's no way I could be of use to anybody now or ever."

"Marcus, stop being so self-centered, so bent on self-destruction. There are people who care about you."

"How do you know?"

"Haven't you heard a word I've said? I have talked with your mother, Clarence Waddell, Brian Lucas and others. They care."

"Bullshit," he spat out and glared at her.

"I don't know what that word means to you, but to me it is an excuse for no answer, an evasion to face life," said Alice-Lee sternly.

If Alice-Lee, in the dark, could have seen the fire in those hazel eyes, she might have been frightened, but she didn't, and wasn't the least daunted. "It's probably true you will never again experience the same love you had for Mariana, or hers for you. But, you have no right to throw away your life or disregard the sacrifices others have made for you, including your deceased wife, your parents, your brother, Waddell, Evans and even Brian Lucas. You're no paragon nor are you a devil. And you've made mistakes like any human being but instead of learning from them you're engaged in self-flagellation, self-destruction. And you know what, you are evidently enjoying it. You aren't the ever optimistic, caring guy that Sam or Mariana or your mother knew. Hidden beneath the blond underbrush of yours is a fake, a wimp, with no guts, no real guts. No, I won't tell a soul I saw you, nor will I release any of your story to the public. It's not worth telling. It is, in your own language, 'bullshit.'"

Alice-Lee, upset, with conflicting emotions searing through her, rose from the flat, raised tombstone slab and started walking away. She traveled several feet, stopped, looked over her shoulder and said, "Have no fear, I'll not follow you. I have come to a dead end. But, if sometime you really want to talk, you have my card." With a strong stride and now seething with anger at him, at herself, she disappeared into the rainy night.

Marcus was livid. Crippled as he was, he had a hard time restraining his desire to do something physically violent, whether it was to her, himself or some inanimate object. Instead he sat and pondered the remarks of this strange young woman whose face he could not clearly see and who had appeared out of the night like some hidden, hellacious conscience. Then he wept. Finally, wet through from the steady drizzle, he, with the aid of his crutch, rose and limped toward the all-night bus station that wasn't too far away from the cemetery entrance.

☐

Two weeks after her initial meeting with Marcus, Alice-Lee was in her Colonial Village apartment in Arlington, Virginia, preparing to go to a Press Club supper. She would drive to D.C. and be at the table with her peers—Si Mendelsohn, Henry Fitzwater and their wives. She knew she couldn't, wouldn't tell any of them what she had uncovered. The weird episode she had recently experienced troubled her deeply and constantly. Maybe she should have been more considerate of that poor crippled Marcus Bosconovich. She had seriously thought of going back to that grave at night in hopes of having more conversations with the lost poet.

She had just finished dressing, was on her way to pick up her evening wrap from her coat closet when there came a knock on the front door of her apartment. She opened it then stepped back in bewilderment. There standing before her was a gaunt, clean-shaven blond, in clothes slightly too big, draped as if once upon a time, long ago, he had filled them. She noted that he was hatless and his blond hair, recently cut and washed, was as unmanageable as the curls on an airdale. The dark circles around his eyes appeared to dramatically enlarge two owl-like hazel eyes, only those eyes revealed tragic sorrow, not cold hunger. He was leaning heavily on a crutch under his left arm. She had no idea who he was until he spoke. His first, almost whispered, words were, "I need help. I need to talk."

Alice-Lee gasped, recognized the voice. She couldn't help but feel compassion for the wounded soul before her. "Come in, Marcus," she said. He entered, looked around the neat living room, wondering where to sit. "Marcus," said Alice-Lee, "Sit anywhere that's comfortable, I'll be back in just a minute, I was about to make a phone call."

She disappeared into another area of her apartment for a few minutes. Then reappeared. He was still standing, slouched on his crutch. He looked at her. "I don't mean to keep you from some evening engagement but I couldn't telephone before I came over, I just couldn't," he said as he looked at the floor.

"Marcus, my evening's engagement isn't that important, not at all."

"When I last saw you, you said, 'if I ever wanted to talk, that I had your card.' I still have it. Yes, I do want to talk but only with the understanding we agreed to before."

Alice-Lee looked at the tormented guy. She had the strangest feeling she couldn't define. "I gave you my word. It still goes," she said calmly. Marcus believed her.

Before he could open his mouth she said gently but positively, "You have given me your conditions concerning any conversation. For your sake, I give you my prerequisites before we talk and if you don't accept them you will please leave."

Marcus was stumped, had no idea what was to follow.

"There is a phone in my bedroom where you can talk in private. You have three phone calls to make, at my expense. Call your family, call Mr. Waddell and call Brian Lucas. Tell them, in effect, you are now recovering, that you appreciate their worry and that as soon as things settle down a little, you will be in touch with them. I can understand your not wanting to tell them more for a while. By the way, if you don't know their telephone numbers they are in the little black book by the phone, use it."

She looked steadily at Marcus and she could tell that his emotions were churning, about what she wasn't sure. He stood, at first defiant, glowering around the room, then started to slump. The expression in his eyes changed from belligerent glare to a sorrowful stare. There he stood and stood, much of that time his eyes stared down, how far down Alice-Lee shuddered to think. Finally, he straightened, adjusted his crutch under his left arm, gazed back and forth as if undecided which way to go, to the front door or down the corridor to her bedroom and the phone. Then he looked over to where she sat and those eyes betrayed a look she had never seen before from any man. "Thanks, Alice-Lee," he said in a whisper and slowly limped to her bedroom. Alice-Lee sat as if petrified, and for some unexplained reason she was.

Until he made that move, she had no real idea of the tension within her but when he started for her bedroom, she burst into quiet tears. While he was gone, she tried to regain control of her emotions, fidgeted, attempted to read the *Evening Star* but couldn't concentrate, all the time hoping to God she had done the right thing. Thirty minutes later as she was standing and for the umpteenth time was nervously rearranging the objects on her fake fireplace mantle, she heard his crutch clomping down the hall to the living room. When he entered, tears slowly streaked down his hollowed cheeks, his eyes were reddened and evaded hers. "Mission accomplished. I reached all of them." The words were hardly more than a murmur.

She sank weakly onto her sofa, heaved a sigh of genuine relief, sympathetically looked at him and said, "Now, I'm ready to talk with you."

Humped on his crutch, he looked at her and said, "I don't know where to start."

"Start wherever you can, the point that is least discomforting. But, before you do, have you a place to stay?"

"Yes," he said, "I've leased a furnished one-bedroom apartment at Arlington Village on Columbia Pike, here in Arlington, and I have enough funds to get by on." He looked, found and dragged a straight chair from the dining alcove into the living room, then with his left leg stiff and extended, he awkwardly lowered himself into the chair.

"Please go ahead, Marcus, I'm listening," Alice-Lee said gently.

The End

EPILOGUE

Dear Reader,

Frequently embellished truth seems contrived. Because this is the true story of Marcus Bosconovich, I will attempt to make the ending simple and unembellished.

Marcus' meetings with Alice-Lee at her apartment became increasingly frequent: he was purging his soul. He had to, in order to try to discover himself, to make a new beginning. He had told her so. Why he chose her or she chose him, she initially didn't understand.

For quite a while she kept her feelings hidden. From the very start however, Marcus' disclosures were gut-wrenching to Alice-Lee. In many ways his revelations mirrored her own feelings. From him she was learning, really learning about herself to accept and reach out at the same time; it was a new dimension in her growth.

As Marcus's physical and emotional health improved, Alice-Lee benefitted. For the first time in her life, she felt she was needed by someone, a man. Now she wanted to be needed, not to dominate but to share. That sharing wasn't fueled by sexual desire, but by a noble desire, an ache, to share a life with someone she now really knew. For all his admitted failings, she loved him with a depth she had never felt before. Would he believe her? In their earlier meetings she had been verbally rough with him, far rougher than he had been with her. He had suffered through the tortures of hell when he lost Mariana, almost self-destructed. Except for that night at Mariana's grave, he had exhibited to her the same gentleness revealed in his letters to Sam and in his poems to Mariana. Would he ever love again, love her, trust her? She was doubtful. But, she had to try.

One afternoon when they had finished discussing some notes in one of Marcus' notebooks, he turned to Alice-Lee and asked her, "Why in the name of God do you put up with me and my mouthings? Most of the time for the last six months I've treated you like I was on a couch in a psychiatrist's office and you were the doctor." Alice-Lee was jarred by the questions. She frowned at him then a smile lit her face.

"I originally agreed to our conversations because I wanted a story, a news story. As that story started to unfold, I agreed not to tell it to anyone until you agreed. Then I became a part of the story. I wouldn't think of telling it now without your genuine consent—because," and she hesitated.

"Because of what?" asked a bothered Marcus.

"Because for the first time in my life, I truly love someone. I wouldn't want to lose you, ever." Tears welled in her eyes.

Marcus came over, sat beside her on the sofa, took one of her hands and kissed the palm. "How on earth could you love me, knowing what you know?"

"It's because of what I know that I love you. Even if we seem worlds apart."

"Alice-Lee, I've come a long way towards recovery. I still have a long way to go."

"Please let me be there with you."

As his arms enfolded her, she felt the most comforting warmth of her adult life.

Marcus leaned back, gently kissed her forehead, then held her closer than before. Struggling to be reborn, Marcus knew he had dumped, not gently placed, all of his eggs in one basket. He did it on the night of his first visit to Alice-Lee. For him, that was one last, desperate chance to find someone who, for all of his many failings would understand him, trust him completely when he unlocked his soul in making one last attempt to see if he could find a life worth living. Now, he realized, "Oh my God, how selfish I have been in my search yet she says she loves me. Maybe I would have made a go of it if she had just been understanding of my attempt, but no, she has told me straight to my face that she loves me not only for trying to put my life back together, but because of my admitted failures, and she wants to share my life."

Marcus was swept with a humble comfort from his trusting her and by a strange, wonderful inner glow from the feeling of intimacy just sitting beside her. He knew he would live again, really live, like never before. His eyes teared just a mite as he remembered who had truly introduced him to the possible value of really trusting—Sam. Now it was his.

So began the joint endeavors of Alice-Lee and Marcus.

☐

Shortly after that conversation, Marcus decided to sell his co-op apartment in New York City and needed some legal advice. He looked under "Lawyers" in the classified section of the Arlington phone book. Much to his surprise, there was the name of Gregory T. Morgan, his former skipper. Greg's office was only about four blocks from Alice-Lee's apartment.

Later Greg told Alice-Lee he was surprised by the call from Marcus because he presumed all along that Marcus was dead. After the War, he made a tedious search to locate him. He called the Navy, talked to Marcus' mother, and from her he learned that Marcus and Mariana had married and were living in New York. He had called Marcus at their New York apartment to no avail. In July 1946, while Greg was in the Big Apple on business, he had gone to the apartment house and learned from the concierge that Marcus' wife was murdered there. Marcus had disappeared, may have been murdered too. Greg was greatly relieved by Marcus' recent call.

Greg was also delighted to be of legal help to Cooky B. As a result of those efforts, Marcus and Alice-Lee became close friends with the Morgan family: Greg, Caroline, his wife and their young son, J.R.

While Marcus was on the mend, he became a part-time instructor in math and poetry at George Washington University. The local colleges and universities were still expanding with returning World

War II veterans seeking higher education under the G.I. Bill. The need for more college instructors and professors was evident. Marcus was a "find" for the university. He still had his full disability pay from the Secret Service. That teaching opening brought joy to Alice-Lee; Marcus was really improving.

Shortly after Marcus obtained his teaching post, he and Alice-Lee were married by a justice of the peace in a little office fronting Courthouse Road across the street from the aging red brick Arlington County Courthouse. Caroline and Greg were the only witnesses. There was no honeymoon, both newlyweds were working, just took the day off to get married. After the ceremony, Greg and Caroline took the bride and groom to an early supper at the local country club.

While sitting on the club deck and while their respective spouses were in the club "fainting rooms," Greg turned to Alice-Lee and asked, "What's wrong with Marcus's left leg?"

Alice-Lee responded, "Oh, he has a little problem."

From the tone of her voice, Greg knew better than to dig further. To ease her apparent discomfort of avoiding the real answer, Greg told her of the various episodes involving Marcus while Greg was aboard the LSM 460.5. Alice Lee became so excited at what she was hearing, goosebumps just popped out all over her. None of those episodes Marcus ever related to her nor were they to be found in his notebooks.

☐

One Saturday not long after the newlyweds moved into their new North Arlington home, Alice-Lee joined Greg and Caroline for lunch on the club deck. Marcus couldn't make it as he had to attend a teaching seminar at the university. During the meal, Alice-Lee looked seriously at Greg. "Marcus has kept voluminous notes of his life since he returned stateside. They form the background for much of his poetry. He has let me read those notes. Over quite a period of time, they have been supplemented by our conversations concerning their content, really a part of his recovery therapy. As a result of the notes and our conversations, what I have learned about him and others plus my ever deepening love and respect for him, I have written my version of his life since his return from World War II maybe a little something added here and there, but only to underscore the man he truly is. However, Marcus has been constant in his request that I don't attempt to publish my story. Despite my selfish desire, I have respected that request. Also, he has completed a new book of poetry. His new poems have deeper, more encompassing meanings. To me, they are beautiful, but these too, he has refused to submit for publication. There are a couple of copies of both manuscripts."

Greg was listening, looking out over the golf course. Caroline watched him with a faint smile then winked at Alice-Lee. Caroline knew her husband and she was signaling Alice-Lee that his mental wheels were really turning.

Finally, Greg looked at Alice-Lee and said, "I have a plan, but knowing Marcus as I do, it might take him a little while to accept it. Please let me have a copy of both manuscripts as soon as possible."

The following Monday, while Marcus was at work, Alice-Lee grabbed a copy of the manuscripts, called Caroline to make sure she was home and took both writings to her for delivery to Greg. As she left their house, she told Caroline, "When Greg reads my story, he will learn the truth about Marcus' limp." For one reason or another, Marcus didn't miss the copy of his manuscript.

Five nights later, Alice-Lee and Marcus were having an after-dinner coffee on the deck of the Morgan's North Arlington home. Greg rose and entered the adjoining family room. He returned shortly thereafter. A soft light filtered through the open doorway, it seemed to center on Marcus. Greg relaxed in his deck chair as the lilting strains of "Twilight Time" by Arty Dunn and the Three Suns drifted from the record player in the family room through that doorway. The night was quiet, serenely moonlit, the music seemed to surround and enfold them. Alice-Lee saw Marcus stiffen slightly, listen intently. As the recording continued, he began to smile with a look of male bonding as he studied Greg. She had never seen that look before. His admiration for Greg seemed to soar.

"My God," said Marcus softly, "Dream time from way back when. I knew what that recording meant to you when Radioman Craig played his regular evening salute to the bridge. What you didn't know was that it was soon beamed to the crew's quarters as well as to you. It became the off-duty crew members focus time, to dream and plan for the future, a future each of us realized might never happen. It helped make you one of us. It was almost like crew prayer time."

"I knew," responded Greg.

Marcus continued, "I haven't heard that recording since I left the ship. It is lovely, lovelier than I ever before recalled."

"I agree," replied Greg. He hesitated for a few seconds, then said, "I am aware of two good dreams that can come true, should come true. Despite your prior objections to anyone reading your wife's manuscript and your new poems, Alice-Lee has let me read her almost completed writing, the story of your life since you returned. Marcus, it is really worth telling and your new poems are richer, better by far than your old ones. Please consider letting both writings be published. I know a publisher who would really be interested. Don't blame Alice-Lee for letting me read the two manuscripts. If you say no, I'll return them to each of you with apologies for invading your privacy. Just remember, Marcus, there was a time when I regularly read your writings, never apologized, and later was truly surprised by your creativity. I still am, but now I am amazed by the creativeness of both of you.

"I realize that you don't want the true identities of the characters in your wife's story revealed to the public. That's easy. She can use the names given certain characters in the novel, *The Sandscrapers*, where they apply, like Mariana, Caroline, you and me." He continued, "I know the author and I'm sure I can arrange it with him. Your wife can make up fictitious names for all the other characters in her book, new dates, and new locales for the critical events. I can tell she has the ability to do that with ease. Your new poems can also be by Marcus Bosconovich. No one but you, Alice-Lee, Caroline, yours truly and the author of *The Sandscrapers*, will really know the true identities of the characters, the author of your wife's book and your poems. Think about it, please. Both volumes should be published."

Marcus intently listened to Greg. Later Greg told Alice-Lee, "It was the same look and mischievous, whimsical smile I first witnessed years ago. I just knew the real Marcus was back."

"I'll think about it," said Alice-Lee's husband.

That night, after their visit, Marcus and Alice-Lee returned to their new home. Marcus turned off the bedside table lamp, turned Alice-Lee to him and said, "My beloved lanky rebel, because it's your story of me, prejudiced as it is, if you really want to try and have it published, I am humbled. How blind you are. Go ahead, see what

Greg can do with your writing, but, only if you make it conform to his suggestion that the true identities are hidden. I've caused enough sorrow and my new poems, the volume titled *Seasoning*, if you think they have reader value, let Greg see what he can do with them also." What immediately followed was mutually fulfilling for the couple.

□

The next morning Alice-Lee phoned the Morgans. Caroline answered. "Hi, Caroline," greeted Alice-Lee.

Caroline yelped with glee and replied, "I can tell by the tone of your voice, Marcus has agreed to let you publish your book, your story of him. How about his poems?"

"Those too," Alice-Lee answered and continued, "Caroline, knowing Greg as I now do, ask him if he will write the prologue to my book, what he knew about Marcus until Greg left the ship and headed home. Before I met Greg, I knew nothing of Marcus's life aboard the 460.5. Marcus has never said anything about his life at sea during the war. There is no mention of it in his notebooks either."

"You know darn well Greg would love to. There are times when the upbeat side of dreamers as well as their frailties, should be told. Those stories help us all," Caroline replied and added, "I know."

Alice-Lee invited, "How about you, Greg and J.R. coming over to our place and having a 6:00 p.m. supper with us two weeks from today? By then, we'll have both manuscripts ready."

"We'd love to, what a celebration that will be," Caroline replied, then hung up.

Alice-Lee, sitting in their living room, on the sofa she had brought from California, remembered more happenings that had occurred over the last two years, the cornerstone of her husband's new life. Six months after Marcus first appeared at her apartment in Arlington, Virginia, and after persuasion by Clarence Waddell, Marcus went to Georgetown University Hospital for reconstruction of his left knee. He was visited in the hospital by Bernie, his younger brother. The true healing process for Marcus began at that time. A couple months later, with a small cast on his left leg and still on crutches he visited his family in Chicago for two weeks.

When he returned, he was much more relaxed. Alice-Lee learned from him that neither he nor Bernie have told their mother how

Mariana's ring had been stolen or how Marcus got it back. They never will. He didn't offer it to Alice-Lee and she would not have taken it, not with what she knew about it. The one he gave her suited her to a tee. However, with his mother's knowledge and consent, he has sold the Cavozzi ring. The sale proceeds, with the help of a trust officer for Arlington Trust Company form the fund for Bernie's college education. He wants to go to Cornell.

Marcus's dad, Sergio, swelled with quiet pride when he learned of his older son's gift to his younger brother, but Sergio will never know the source of those funds.

During the last year, Alice-Lee talked to Cherrie a couple of times. In one of those conversations, she gave Alice-Lee the opening to Alice-Lee's story of Marcus.

During that time Alice-Lee had several fill-in conversations with Marla Bosconovich, Brian Lucas, Clarence Waddell and Bernie Bosconovich but the great revelation chat was with Lorraine Driscoll sometime before Lorraine was released from custody. Alice-Lee asked Waddell if she could visit and chat with Lorraine. He consented with the priviso that she, Alice-Lee, would not reveal the location of Lorraine's safe haven. She agreed, and Waddell drove her there. He let the two of them talk alone. Lorraine, in their conversation, filled in so many gaps in Alice-Lee's story. Lorraine had been living with Tully, without the benefit of marriage, for over five years. She felt a strange attachment to him for he had been genuinely kind to her. She knew of his bladder problem and that he wore protective pads. She knew a lot more. Tully talked in his sleep. She had been awakened by many of his conversations. He talked to a never-revealed confidant, almost like confession to a priest. He had revealed how he had Mariana's pet dog killed and the whole schmeer of his trip to New York in disguise and how he planned, killed his sister and stole her ring. Time and again he would reveal his misdoings and repeat them. Not once did Lorraine ask Tully about them. She was mortally afraid to do so, and any disclosure to the authorities might ruin her chance for an early release. Alice-Lee agreed not to write about the disclosure until Lorraine had been released and disappeared from sight. Besides, who knew if the revelations were fact?

The Bosconovich family, Marla, Sergio and Bernie including

Bianca and Vince, now married, and their infant daughter, young Marla, will be visiting the bride and groom later this summer. And so will the parents of Alice-Lee.

When Brian's wife, Karen, in Florida, learned how Tully died, she damned her husband for allowing Tully to be killed and informed Brian that though Sean was his son, Tully was hers by Alfredo Bosticas. She was with him at that time and intended to stay. She demanded that Tully's body be shipped to her. Brian acquiesced. Divorce proceedings followed promptly.

He has since married Marjorie Hempstead.

Sean, Brian's older son, has married Sue Framingham, his long-time girlfriend and he, after the killing episode in his father's office, has returned to his father's side and is throwing his considerable energies into becoming a produce marketer, much to his father's delight and relief.

Marcus and Clarence Waddell have resumed their friendship. They meet frequently to chat. Some of those conversations deal with matters that are none of Alice-Lee's business. As a result of one of those chats, Alice-Lee learned from Marcus that, after the trials involving the International Etching and Art Gallery scam had been completed, Lorraine Driscoll was released from protective custody and given a light, suspended sentence. With the aid of the federal government, she has vanished from sight.

Irma, Marcus' younger sister, is maturing into a renowned musician. There is a singular haunting wistfulness in the sounds that come from her cello. Her music has fascinated listeners and musicians alike. According to Marcus, she has never really recovered from her loss of Irving and he doubts that she will ever marry.

Alice-Lee stopped her reminiscing, looked with glowing pride around the newly decorated living room and relaxed. She was beginning to be content, very content, but something seemed missing, had always been.

□

Early the following morning, the couple was standing on the back porch of their little home, looking down the backyard hill. Much to Alice-Lee's surprise, Marcus had no cane. He put an arm around her and with the other pointed to a large pin oak near their back fence. To him and

Alice-Lee, the sun's first morning rays bouncing off the dew on the slim, dark green leaves made the tree appear as if covered with many-colored, sparkling jewels. "That is one of the most thrilling sights I have ever seen. That tree reminds me of Joyce Kilmer and Isham Jones," he said.

"Why Isham Jones?" she asked.

"Because he is a fine musician and band leader. Late at night while lying in bed at home I used to listen to his radio broadcasts on station WGN from the Aragon Ballroom on West Lawrence Street in Chicago. His band's signature song was the musical version of the poem "Trees" by Joyce Kilmer."

A warm wave of emotion swept over Alice-Lee. She couldn't see the lawn, she couldn't see the tree. Through her tears, she saw her husband's hazel eyes boring into hers. It was a look she had seen numerous times before. The first time was on Marcus's initial visit to her apartment in Arlington, when during that conversation, he had looked at her and said, "Thanks, Alice-Lee." That look made her uncomfortable, she didn't understand it then. How gentle and persistent he had been for that look has never wavered or changed.

Suddenly, as if a veil had lifted, she recognized she was seeing the future, a future she had wished for, dreamed of all her adult life and didn't really accept she had it until now. The meaning of that look had been there ever since the night in Arlington when Marcus walked into her life.

Now she knew the how and why she had been able to write this story of Marcus. She said ever so softly, "Thank you, Samantha, wherever you are, for I have truly reaped what you had sown."

Marcus, hearing her comment, smiled and nodded in agreement.

Sgd: Alice-Lee Bosconovich

Printed in the United States
71078LV00004B/43